The
Book
of
Summer

BOOKS BY JAMES F. DAVID

Footprints of Thunder
Fragments
Ship of the Damned
Before the Cradle Falls
Judgment Day
Thunder of Time
The Book of Summer

The
Book
of
Summer

JAMES F. DAVID

TOR®

A Tom Doherty Associates Book
New York

This is a work of fiction. All of the characters, organizations, and events portrayed in this novel are either products of the author's imagination or are used fictitiously.

THE BOOK OF SUMMER

Copyright © 2008 by James F. David

All rights reserved.

A Tor Book
Published by Tom Doherty Associates, LLC
175 Fifth Avenue
New York, NY 10010

www.tor-forge.com

Tor® is a registered trademark of Tom Doherty Associates, LLC.

ISBN-13: 978-0-7653-5147-0
ISBN-10: 0-7653-5147-1

First Edition: June 2008

Printed in the United States of America

0 9 8 7 6 5 4 3 2 1

Thanks again to my wife, Gale, for being my first reader, and to Abby, Drew, Katie, and Bethany for keeping life interesting and worthwhile. Like a good book, I look forward to the next chapter in our lives together.

AUTHOR'S NOTE

There is usually a point in writing a book where I have to fight off the urge to put the story aside and work on something else. Either because of writer's block or because a new and exciting idea for another story occurs to me, in the middle of one project I will want to begin another story. I did not experience this with *The Book of Summer*. This is the story that I wanted to tell ever since beginning the chronicles of the Light in the Darkness Fellowship. Where *Judgment Day* tells the story of Mark Shepherd, who is called by God to be the "Moses" of his generation, in *The Book of Summer* we meet an ordinary young woman who accomplishes the extraordinary by simply being the kind of decent person God calls us all to be.

The
Book
of
Summer

PROLOGUE

The roots of the events depicted in *The Book of Summer* reach all the way to Earth, and forty years into the past. Various versions of these events have been published, including the Continuing Testament of The Fellowship, Shepherd, Breitling, and 2 Exodus. The most popular version of these events is *Judgment Day,* which is believed to be a synthesis of the first books of the Continuing Testament. While generally considered accurate, nevertheless *Judgment Day* sensationalizes certain events, and presents perspectives that are not reported in any of the books of the Continuing Testament, raising questions about the author's sources.

As in other moments in history where God intervenes broadly, and directly, the story told in *Judgment Day* begins with visions. Ira Breitling receives both a vision of a distant planet that God promised to his people, and the technological breakthrough necessary to make it possible. Reverend Mark Shepherd is called to leadership with a vision of himself leading God's chosen to the distant world. George Proctor is given the most unusual gift: the ability to see in the dark, and to see spiritual signs and beings. Breitling and Shepherd are then brought together and form the Light in the Darkness Fellowship, and set about building the infrastructure necessary to recruit believers, and provide the resources to build spaceships to take them to God's promised world. At the same time, George Proctor slowly builds an army to protect the Fellowship.

Unknown to the Fellowship, Satan is moving in the world too, and recruits Manuel Crow to be his willing servant. To assist Crow, Satan sends a demon in the body of Rachel Waters. Together, they recruit men and women whose blind hatred of Christians makes them willing pawns. Through legal, and illegal, means Crow uses these men and women to attack the Fellowship.

Crow arranges two attacks on Fellowship anti-gravity lifting spheres. For the first attack Crow hires a mercenary (Reynolds Mann), who fires a missile at a sphere. The mercenary is captured by Proctor, and accepts an offer by Proctor to trade information for his freedom. Proctor fulfills his promise by arranging for the mercenary to be marooned on planet America. For the second attack, Crow uses a contact in NASA to arrange an accident, and the destruction of one of the Fellowship's lifting spheres, killing the two pilots.

Crow also manipulates others into filing false charges of sexual abuse against the Fellowship, and then to have many of the Fellowship children taken away. Mark Shepherd is arrested and charged with sexual abuse. Barely surviving a jailhouse attack, Shepherd is eventually acquitted when George Proctor locates exculpatory tapes revealing how the children were being manipulated into recalling false memories. Daniel is one of these children, and is returned home still believing his father had molested him.

When the Fellowship finds a habitable planet, which they name America, Crow strikes again. With the help of a splinter CIA group, run by Mr. Fry, Crow arranges for the release of a variant of Ebola virus. Claiming the plague is extraterrestrial, Crow then spreads rumors, blaming the plague on the Fellowship. Quarantined, and harassed, Shepherd is forced to make the move to the new world, despite doubts that it is the world in Breitling's vision. Purchasing obsolete submarines, the Fellowship builds huge ships, called Ark Class, and moves thousands of believers to the new world.

Not everyone in the Fellowship is pleased with the move, and especially Daniel Remple. The son of a prominent member of the Fellowship, Daniel triggers a crisis on planet America when he impregnates a teenage girl, Melody Crane, and then refuses to marry her. Banished from planet America, Daniel returns to Earth, planning never to see his family again. Humiliated and rejected by the boy she loved, Melody Crane has no choice but to accept a marriage proposal from Robert Evans. Evans has loved Melody since childhood, but knew such a pretty and popular girl was out of his reach. Her trouble is his opportunity.

Once the fledgling colony is established on America, Shepherd is introduced to Grandma Jones, an African-American woman, who has recruited a large group of inner-city men and women looking for a better life for their children. Impressed by her faith, and stung by criticism of the lack of diversity in the Fellowship, Shepherd agrees to transport them all to planet America.

Manuel Crow's boldest move, striking deep into the heart of the Fellowship, is to kidnap, and impregnate, Ruth Breitling. Rescued by George Proctor, Ruth returns to the Fellowship, and she and Ira flee to planet America. On the long space voyage, Ruth dies in childbirth, leaving Ira with a son, fathered by their chief enemy.

Rising in power to president of the United States, Manuel Crow finds himself increasingly frustrated by his inability to stop the Fellowship, and orders an attack on the Fellowship compound in Mexico and the Fellowship space station. Recovering the Fellowship sphere shot down by the mercenary Reynolds Mann, Crow recruits one of Ira Breitling's former colleagues to rebuild it. Blaming Breitling for the death of his graduate school girlfriend, Kent Thorpe manages to restore the sphere and they use it to lift a space shuttle full of troops to orbit and overrun the Fellowship space station. Daniel Remple's father is killed in the attack, and several ships are captured. Worst of all, Mark Shepherd is taken prisoner.

With their technology in the hands of their enemies, the leaders of the Fellowship set in motion a contingency plan, sending asteroids hurtling toward Earth. The Fellowship then moves its people from planet America to Promise—a newly discovered planet that fits Breitling's vision. At the request of Grandma Jones, she and her people stay behind on planet America. When Crow's invading force arrives at America in the captured Fellowship spaceships, the Fellowship springs a trap and destroys their ships in orbit and on the ground.

Grandma Jones and her people capture the surviving troops and enslave them.

With the Fellowship now beyond his reach, Crow takes advantage of the asteroid bombardment, declaring martial law, and himself president for life. His one prize is Mark Shepherd, whom he has imprisoned. As life in the United States of America deteriorates under Crow's leadership, George Proctor leads Alaska in revolt and secession, setting up an independent republic. By capturing Trident submarines and their nuclear arsenal, Proctor ensures the independence of the Alaska Republic, and his position as president.

Twenty years after his imprisonment, Shepherd is finally released in exchange for oil from Alaska, and returns to the original Fellowship church in California. Tipped off by Proctor, his friends from the Fellowship land on Christmas Eve to take Shepherd with them to planet Promise. When soldiers capture them, Daniel Remple, the rebellious teenager grown up to be a soldier himself, rescues them. Together, they all leave for the world that God first revealed to them in Ira Breitling's vision.

The Book of Summer tells the story of Grandma Jones's people, the enslaved soldiers, and their children. The central character in this story is a second-generation slave, Summer Lund, whose courage, gentleness, and unwavering faith in God change the lives of the people who encounter her. Summer Lund's story continues to inspire people to this day.

1

SUMMER LUND

Master Rice's Farm
First Continent
WINTER, PLANET AMERICA

The Saturday night knock on their cabin door was one of Summer's earliest memories. As slaves, Summer and her family were lucky to have a cabin to themselves, but the cabin came at a price. A price they had no choice but to pay on Saturday nights.

When she was little, the knock would not wake her, her mother would do that, and then with her blanket wrapped around her shoulders she would go next door to Lucy's cabin. Some Saturdays, Lucy's boys would come to their cabin. Those were the best Saturdays, since she didn't have to give up her bed and her mother wouldn't cry the next morning. As she got older, she would lie awake on Saturday nights, pretending to sleep, watching her mother. Her mother would work her loom, fingers and hands busy, but eyes flicking to the door at every sound. Summer was on her best behavior on Saturdays, knowing her mother would be quick-tempered. Summer would stay out of her way, taking care of her little brother, keeping him safe from scoldings and cuffs. On Saturdays, it was best for Summer and her brother, Rocky, to stay out of the way.

Tonight, the knock came later than usual. Her mother took a deep breath before she opened it. It was Master Rice. He was a big man, six feet two, and muscular with large hands that he used to hammer sassy slaves into submission. Summer's mother had felt those fists. Summer had not. Not yet.

"Good evening," Master Rice slurred.

All through Summer's childhood, she had known Master Rice as a drunken man, framed in the dark doorway. Summer did not wait to be told to leave. Shaking Rocky awake, she wrapped his blanket around his shoulders, and then took her little brother's hand.

"Not tonight," Summer heard her mother say. "I've been having morning sickness."

Her mother pressed her nightgown against her stomach, although it was too soon to show.

"Don't bother me none," Rice said, still grinning.

"I'm worried about the baby," her mother argued.

Master Rice lost his smile.

"I'm sorry," Summer's mother said quickly, lowering her eyes.

Summer pulled Rocky toward the door. Master Rice's hand fell on her shoulder as she tried to pass.

"Summer, you are starting to fill out some," he said.

His breath had the sour booze smell that Summer had come to hate—it was the smell of Saturday night. Whenever she smelled it, something bad happened. Master Rice pushed her bangs from her face.

"You got your mother's good looks," he said.

Summer kept her head down. Lately she had noticed the master watching her when she did her chores around the farm. Summer deepened her resolve to not eat, to keep herself skinny, and not become a woman.

"Better go now, honey," her mother said.

Master Rice shot her a hard look. Summer knew her mother would be crying come Sunday morning.

"You can go now," Master Rice said, gently squeezing her shoulder.

Summer hurried out with Rocky, her heart pounding. Slave or not, no one ever said no to Master Rice. No one ever contradicted Master Rice. And no one but Grandma Jones ever told Master Rice what to do. Even then, he often disobeyed.

When Lucy Mills opened her door to find Summer and

Rocky shivering on her doorstep, relief spread across her face. Then she pushed the door open wide.

"Go to sleep, boys," she said as Summer and Rocky came in.

Rocky walked straight to the mattress next to Passion's bed. Rocky and Passion were friends and always slept next to each other. Summer would share Lucy's bed. Passion stirred when Rocky climbed over him to his place, but the other boy slept sound. Some people laughed at Passion's name, and some at Dolby's, but Summer knew Lucy's secret. She had heard Lucy tell her mother that "Passion" was "Sampson spelled sideways, sort of." They had laughed themselves to tears at that. "And Dolby, well that's the best I could do with the letters from beloved." Then they had hugged and cried. Lucy had named the two boys for her secret husband.

"Would you like a cup of tea?" Lucy asked.

Summer liked Lucy. She treated Summer like a friend.

"Please," Summer said.

Lucy had a small fire going, a pot hanging over it. Using a rag, she lifted the pot off its hook, and then filled two ceramic mugs with water. Then she wrapped tea leaves in a strip of cloth and repeatedly dipped it in one cup, then the other. Then she handed a cup to Summer.

"Mama didn't want him to come tonight," Summer said.

Lucy froze, her cup almost to her lips.

"What do you mean, Summer?"

"She told him she had been throwing up."

Lucy started shaking her head.

"He'll hurt her, won't he?" Summer asked.

Lucy usually did not lie to Summer, but she did now.

"No. He won't want to hurt the baby."

Lucy sipped her tea to hide the lie. Summer knew Lucy had lost a baby after being beaten by Master Rice.

"Babies are worth something," Lucy continued. "At least when they get big enough to work. He could trade a strong boy for a dozen chickens or maybe even a goat."

"Is that what he got for Leo?" Summer asked.

Lucy frowned at Summer. "You are your mother's child," she said. "Is there anything you won't ask?"

Summer knew Lucy well enough to know she was not offended. Leo had been gone for two years now.

"He got that blue hound for Leo. You know the one he's so proud of?"

"Blue Belly. It hunted down Will when he ran off," Summer said.

"Yeah, that's the one."

"You ever hear from Leo?" Summer asked.

"I've heard of him, not from him. He's working the lumber mill down south."

Summer had heard people talk about the mill at Lumber Camp. It was dangerous work, manhandling giant logs into the saws, setting chains, minding the huge blades that cut the timber. Slaves had died doing the work. More had lost fingers and hands. The only jobs worse were in the mines.

"I miss Leo," Summer said. "He was funny."

Lucy smiled.

"My boy Leo made everyone laugh. I think that's probably why Rice got rid of him. He couldn't stand seeing us happy, even for a minute."

Summer had noticed that none of the adults called Master Rice "Master" when he was not around.

"Lucy, can I ask you something? It's kinda personal."

"It's not the first time," Lucy said, smiling.

"It's about me. Who's my father?"

Lucy gave her a sad smile.

"You want to know if Rice is your father?"

"I don't look like him. Rocky does, but I don't."

"You mean your skin color?" Lucy asked.

Summer nodded her head. Her skin was a deep tan, but not the dark brown of Master Rice.

"Color doesn't mean anything around here. Half the children on America are a mix, Summer. Look at mine."

Summer knew that Lucy and Patrick Sampson—a field slave—had been secretly married. She knew Patrick was the father of her last two boys, but Leo had been dark skinned.

"So, Master Rice is my father?"

"No. Casey was pregnant when Rice bought her. The man that owned her before Rice had to get rid of her when his wife found out what he had done. Rice's wife isn't as particular. She does a happy dance every time he leaves her bed."

Lucy put down her cup and did a little jig. Summer smiled. Lucy could be as funny as Leo.

"What's his name? My father?"

"Better talk to your mother about that. I want to stay friends with Casey."

Lucy nodded.

"Time for bed."

They had shared Lucy's bed many times. Summer crawled in and slid next to the wall. Lucy blew out the lantern, then they both wriggled around getting comfortable, pulling the quilt up to their chins. Summer's mom made the quilt from scraps and gave it to Lucy for Christmas two years ago.

"Lucy," Summer whispered.

"What, honey?"

"Do you ever think about running away?"

There was a long silence.

"All the time. But where would I go? It's not like back on Earth. There were cities every few miles. There were highways criss-crossing the whole continent. If you didn't want to live in Los Angeles, then you could up and move to Atlanta, or New York or Walla Walla. But here there's nothing much more on America than New Jerusalem, some farms, and a couple of mines. Other than that, it's nothing but wilderness. I wouldn't last a week."

"Some have tried."

"And died. Or been whipped, or maimed, when they were caught. Oh, I think about it, honey, and some days I think I would rather die than do the things I have to do."

Lucy was talking about Saturday nights.

"I can't leave my boys. I just can't."

Now Lucy was near tears. Summer tried to distract her.

"Was there really a town called Walla Walla?" Summer asked.

Lucy rolled onto her side, facing Summer.

"Yes. And Kalamazoo, and Wichita."

Summer giggled at the funny names.

"Yonkers," Lucy said. "Tulsa. Lubbock."

Summer was laughing hard now, but trying not to wake the boys. Her stomach hurt.

"Queens. Knoxville. Oklahoma."

"Stop," Summer managed, afraid she would wet her pants.

"That last one was a state," Lucy said.

"What's that?" Summer asked, controlling herself again.

"It doesn't matter," Lucy said. "Toledo."

Summer was laughing again.

"Scranton. Honolulu."

"You're making these up," Summer said, gasping for air.

"Cincinnati," Lucy said.

Holding her stomach, Summer controlled her laughter.

"No one would name a city after sin," Summer said.

"Really!" Lucy said. "Well, Miss Smarty Pants, there *was* a city named Cincinnati and if you think that name was bad—are you ready for this?—Helena."

Summer laughed until she cried. She knew Lucy was making the names up, but they were so silly she could not help but laugh. They settled down after that, and soon Lucy fell asleep. Snug in Lucy's bed, Summer worried about her mother, and then about herself. She fell asleep the same way she did every night, fantasizing about running away.

2

REYNOLDS MANN

Eastern Wilderness
First Continent
WINTER, PLANET AMERICA

The bow was drawn, the arrow aimed just behind the front shoulder where the striping began. The deer emerged slowly out of a patch of hollow, woody reeds poking through the snow. Rey Mann held the bowstring in two fingers. It was a homemade bow, the twelfth he had fashioned. This one was painstakingly carved from the heart of a tree he found growing along the coast, and easily the most powerful. The animal was not a deer, of course—deer lived on Earth—but it was good eating and he needed the meat.

King crept forward, the deer's head coming up at the movement.

"Stay, King," Rey whispered firmly.

Rey had raised King after killing his mother and the rest of the litter. King was doglike, but with longer, thinner legs, and a flat bulldog face. His eyes were like half marbles, bulging and always wet. He had no tail. King was the sixth "pet" Rey had taken in out of a desperate need for companionship. Two of his former pets had eventually tried to kill him. One wandered off and never came back. Rey killed the other two when they proved to be worthless. The largest of his pets were always named "King," the smaller ones, "Sport."

King took another step forward, whining. Whining was the only sound the carnivore could make, although he had a wide range of frequencies to whine in. Rey had heard King rumble like a tuba, and then range up like a violin and out of human hearing.

"Quiet!" Rey hissed.

The striped deer was nearly clear of the reeds, which were sturdy enough to deflect an arrow. Its belly dragged in the snow as it moved slowly. Another step or two and he would have fresh meat. Then King lunged, his excited whine quickly climbing out of hearing range. Startled, the deer cringed and then bolted. Rey tracked it, releasing the arrow. The arrow flew high, striking a tree with a loud *thunk*.

King's species did not run; instead they bounded, in high, long leaps. Their natural habitat was grasslands, and the unusual hopping gait in a small predator gave it both speed and a vantage point. King was bounding now, but the snow impeded his jumps, as he struggled for footing. His head appeared regularly over the reeds, as if he were racing after the striped deer on a pogo stick. Soon they were both gone, somewhere deep in the forest. King had no chance of catching the deer.

Cursing King, Rey searched for his arrow. It took him three days to make an arrow, so his policy was, "no arrow left behind." He found it stuck in a gum tree. Rey hated gum trees. The wood was hard and the tree secreted a gooey substance that coated the outside. Insects stuck to the goo and were slowly dissolved. Rey had never seen so much as a bird land in one of these trees.

The arrow was buried deep. The cold had hardened the goo, but it was still sticky. Looking at the penetration, Rey was pleased with the power of his new bow. Now he struggled to free the arrow, careful not to touch the gummy bark. The arrow snapped as he tried wiggling it free. He cursed his clumsiness. Losing the arrow was bad enough, but he'd lost the metal tip too. He threw the worthless shaft down the deer trail where King had disappeared. As if called, King came bounding back down the trail, knocking snow everywhere, tongue lolling.

"Where's the meat?" he snarled at King.

At the word "meat," King sat, expectantly.

Furious with King, Rey cocked his leg, ready to kick the

worthless beast into a snow bank. He stopped himself. King was the only "friend" he had on this godforsaken planet.

Frustrated and meatless, he turned toward the cabin. It was too late to continue the hunt. Dressed in tanned skins that he had fashioned into a parka and pants, he headed across the clearing. Sick for most of the fall, Rey had not been able to hunt and smoke enough meat to last until spring. That meant winter hunting and fishing. He had broken through the ice once already, and nearly frozen to death before he managed to scramble out of the hole and strip off his clothes. Hunting was just as dangerous. Once he had been several kilometers from the cabin when a blizzard struck. He spent two days under a fallen log, waiting that one out.

It was harder to find game now than when first marooned. Over the last twenty years, game animals had learned to give his cabin a wide berth. The few small game animals remaining were little better eating than rats and disappeared completely during winter, hibernating in burrows. Digging them out was not worth the little meat they provided.

Movement in the reeds ahead stopped him. An animal stepped out, paws crunching the snow. He knew the animal. It was dangerous and it never hunted alone. Slowly, Rey pulled an arrow from his quiver, nocked it, and slowly drew the string. This animal was a predator, feline in appearance, with muscular legs and a long snout, lined with fangs that protruded from its mouth even when closed. It had no tail. Its eyes bulged like ping-pong balls glued to its face. Primarily brown, it was just starting to get its white, winter coat. Rey called them "wolves" despite the feline appearance. One of his former "Kings" had been a wolf. Rey had killed that King in self-defense.

Slowly, Rey turned his head, trying to spot the predator's partner. King whined, head cocked, watching the snow bank to their left.

"Good King," Rey said, seeing a slight rustle in the reeds protruding from the snow.

Suddenly, King wheeled and bounded away, leaving him to face the wolves alone. Rey didn't bother to curse King. King's species were scavengers, not hunters. Rey, however, was descended from the top predator on Earth and he would not die without a fight.

He had seen wolves hunt so he knew how they attacked. He kept his bow aimed straight ahead, but with his attention on his peripheral vision. The attack came from the side. He was ready, and spun. The wolf headed straight for him, completely unfamiliar with the concept of a weapon. The second wolf attacked a couple of seconds later in a pincer move. Rey held the bowstring, bow flexed to the maximum. Years of hard work had made his body strong, and he was steady. The first wolf leapt. He released the string. The arrow plunged into its exposed chest, nearly to the feathering.

Rey stepped back as the body crashed at his feet, spraying snow into his face. The second wolf leaped before he could nock another arrow. He dropped the bow and tried to thrust the arrow into the beast's throat, but he didn't have time to get a grip. Bringing his left arm up protectively, the wolf took the bait, chomping down on his forearm. They went down together, Rey pushed deep into the snow. Ignoring the pain of having his arm shredded, Rey pulled his hunting knife, stabbing the wolf over and over, probing for something fatal. With every plunge the wolf's jaws tightened, threatening to snap his arm in two. He was still stabbing when he realized it was dead.

Lying under the carcass, he rested until the pain was too great to ignore. Wedging his knife in its mouth, he pried the jaws wide, extracting his arm. Then he wriggled out from under the carcass. Brushing off bloody snow, he found his sleeve was torn and soaked in blood, but he could move his hand and fingers. Using his knife, he cut his sleeve off, and then sliced off three long strips. Folding what was left into a bandage, he used his teeth to help tie the bandage over his wound. Getting to his knees, he waited—briefly the light faded from his eyes, but then came back. That was good—he did not pass out. Now he got to his feet, and stepped to the wolf he had killed with the arrow. Putting his foot against its chest, he used his good arm to extract the arrow. It came out hard, but wasn't broken and the tip was intact. He put it in his quiver, and then used his bow as a crutch to steady himself.

"King!" he shouted.

No answering whine. No bounding faithless companion. Holding his arm across his chest, bow in his right hand, he left the clearing. Soon the bandage was soaked through and drops of blood fell to mark his trail. It couldn't be helped. He had to make it to the cabin before dark. The nastier hunters came out at night, and this time of year they were all famished.

The second half of his hike took twice as long as the first. Weak, and still bleeding, he was easily confused, losing his way twice on animal trails he had walked a hundred times, now nearly invisible under the snow. He found his way to the right trail, took a wrong turn again, and then found his way back once more. The sun was half gone when he came to his clearing. King was lying by the front door, sleeping.

He woke King with a kick and the animal jumped up, snapping at Rey's leg.

"Get out of the way!" he snarled.

Now King bounded up and down, realizing his meal ticket was home. Rey unlatched the door, started through, and was knocked aside as King shoved in past him. Falling against the doorframe, Rey pinned his wounded arm. Blood spurted from the soaked bandage. He staggered in, exhausted and feverish. He'd had infections from wounds before but nothing that came on this fast. There was water in a pitcher on the kitchen table and he drank deep and long, letting some spill across his face. Now he cut a slice of smoked meat from the haunch that hung from his ceiling. There were more in the smokehouse outside but too few to last until spring. Sitting at his table, he ate half the meat, finding he had no appetite. King bounced excitedly next to him. He tossed the remainder to King.

A drop of sweat trickled down his forehead. He ignored it.

Now he cut away the bandage, tearing away the scabs that had already formed. Blood still seeped from the punctures but there were no gushers—he wouldn't bleed to death. There was no cloth to use for bandages, but he kept a basket of absorbent leaves he used instead. He took one now, pressed it in place, and tied it tight with the strips he had cut from his sleeve. Now he took another drink. He was getting hotter by the second. His Earth-evolved system had gone to war against whatever alien bug had gotten inside.

He stripped off his shirt and then splashed water on his chest. The drops were icy needles wherever they touched. Now groggy, he stood, swayed for a few seconds, and then stepped to his cot, sitting. The room floated left and right for a few seconds. When it stopped moving, he realized the door was still open. He tried to stand but was too dizzy. He sat again, eyes on the door. King pranced into view.

"Shut the door, will ya?" Rey said.

King ignored him, sniffing at a crack in the wood floor.

Rey fell back, legs still on the floor. He managed to shift sideways and pull his legs up before he blacked out. It was dark when violent shivers woke him. He managed to wriggle around, covering himself with the tanned hides he used for blankets. Then he was out again. It was a dreamless sleep, coma-like. There were moments when violent trembling brought him close to consciousness. Those moments were rare and the memories jumbled. Was it daylight? Night? He remembered both. Finally, the pain ebbed, the shivering subsided and he dreamed.

He was alone. He was always alone. He stood on a bluff looking out at a great forest that stretched to the horizon. At first he could make out nothing in the vast, variegated green sea. Slowly, he saw details. A river snaked diagonally, connecting small lakes here and there across its path. There was a sprinkle of small clearings. Now he could see hills and valleys. Then when he thought he had seen it all, there was something new. Barely distinguishable on the far horizon was a thin undulating shape. It was smoke. Not the smoke of a forest fire, but the controlled smoke of a chimney. Now anger boiled up in him. Then hate. Instinctively he knew who the smoke belonged to—the man who had marooned him. George Proctor had betrayed him with the help of Mark Shepherd. They had a deal. In exchange for the name of the man who had hired him to attack one of their spaceships he was to be set free. But they had tricked him, substituting the freedom of loneliness for the freedom of choice. Marooned on the opposite end of the continent from their settlement, he had lived with hope for years. Proctor had sworn on a Bible to set him free, not maroon him, and he expected him to keep that promise. Many times the wind in the trees had fooled him into rushing outside, expecting to see a shuttle in the sky, coming to take him home. He had never believed in God, but Proctor claimed to. Shepherd, too. But Rey had learned their professions of faith were as empty as their promises.

Now he strained to see the source of the smoke. Like an elusive memory, he could sense the source but not quite see it. He stepped forward, trying to see, forgetting he stood at the edge of a precipice. He fell. He was afraid, but not of dying. He was afraid he would die before he could take revenge for the lies they had told and what they had done to him. The rocky base of the cliff rushed up at him. Consciousness returned as he struck the ground.

He was back in his cabin, his head pounding. Strangely, his injured arm was numb. He willed it to move. It moved, weakly, trembling. Now he tried to sit up, but the weight of the hides was too much. He threw them off one at a time and now felt the chill of the room. The door was still open. It was snowing again, an inch of snow on the floor inside the cabin. How long had he been out? Looking around he could see the cabin had been ransacked—King!

Everything that had been on a shelf was on the floor. The plastic containers containing his corn flour and salt had been knocked over and opened, the floor dusted with both. The supply of meat that hung from the ceiling was gone, with nothing but gnawed bones left. He stood, wobbling. It was all he could do to stand. His lips were cracked, his tongue swollen. He was dehydrated and starved. King was sleeping in the corner, a furry contented ball. Ignoring King, he looked for the pitcher he kept filled with water. It was on the floor, empty. He bent, picking it up. When he stood he nearly blacked out. Carefully, he walked to the door. Hand on the doorframe, he bent down, then used the pitcher to scoop up snow. Sweeping the snow clear with his foot, he closed the door, and then walked to the fireplace. He didn't trust himself to bend, so he sat on a stool. There was nothing edible in his fire-making pouches and King had left them alone. He took a pinch of dried moss and covered it with a small pile of twigs. Then he used the flint and steel to ignite the moss. Dizzy from the pain in his head, he forced himself to feed the tiny flame carefully. Flames eagerly consumed the dry wood. He built the fire up until he could feel the warmth, and then put the pitcher of snow next to it. He tended the fire until the snow was melted. He drained the pitcher even after his stomach cramped from the cold. He managed to get up and get back to the door. The wind was howling now, the snow driven almost horizontally. It was already drifting. He filled the pitcher with snow again and closed the door. The small fire was already making a difference. The cabin was warming. He sat by the fire again. Its heat quickly melted the second batch. He drank half of the water. As his cells hydrated, other needs demanded his attention. He was starving, but there was nothing left in the cabin. King was an omnivore, although he preferred meat. As if on cue, King was at his side, pushing between Rey and the fire. Rey moved, letting King curl up by the fire.

Rey got up and shuffled around the cabin. The meat was gone. King would have eaten it first. The last of the purple berries were gone, the floor stained where King had finished those. His store of corn was nothing but gnawed cobs. Even the crunchy fruits he called "tarts" were gone. King hated those. There was more corn and fruit in the cellar next to the smokehouse. He went to the window, looking out. The wind was howling, the snow so thick he couldn't see the smokehouse. In his condition it was risky to go even that short distance.

He found his old parka and pulled it on. His left arm was still numb but functional. Then he took a hide from his bed and wrapped it around his shoulders. Even that small additional weight made his legs wobble. He opened the door but could not bring himself to step into the storm. There were already foot-high drifts against the cabin. Even if he made it to the smokehouse, he would have to dig out the door. Behind him King whined, complaining about the draft. Rey shut the door and dropped the hide from his shoulders.

The anger from his dream returned. He was alone because of the hypocrites he had trusted. Alone, he had no chance to survive, let alone thrive. He knew, in his condition, if he went out that door he would die in the storm. He also knew that if he did not eat soon, he would not have the strength to stand, let alone fight his way through drifts to his food. None of this would be a problem if he had neighbors. Community meant security. Proctor and Shepherd knew that and kept him from their community. Proctor and Shepherd wanted him to die. In that, they had failed. They had underestimated him. Rey resolved not to die from this infection; not from anything. Not until he had his revenge. They thought they were untouchable thousands of miles away, but they had underestimated him again.

Rey's axe was leaning against his woodpile. He took it now, summoned his remaining strength and swung, severing King's sleeping head. Then he squatted, butchering his former pet.

"I'm coming," he said out loud, thinking of Proctor and Shepherd, "and revenge is coming with me."

3

JEPHTHAH'S PROMISE

Eastern Wilderness
First Continent
WINTER, PLANET AMERICA

"Why couldn't you have marooned me in Tahiti?" Rey shouted at the sky.

He had broken through the icy crust on his way to the shed. On his knees, buried to his waist, he cursed George Proctor and Mark Shepherd.

"I will eat your hearts," he screamed.

Winter had come early this year, burying his cabin and anything else that held still. The first snow came when he was injured, and then the storms had rolled through regularly as if on a schedule. The last one had been a blizzard followed by a day warm enough to melt the surface snow. Plunging temperatures followed the lone warm day. The forest was now coated with a quarter inch of ice, making travel treacherous. Limbs as thick as his arm regularly broke off, shearing off smaller limbs and crashing to the icy surface below. He had spent the previous day chipping ice off his cabin, the smokehouse, and outhouse. The outhouse roof sagged dangerously under the weight and it started him worrying about the shed by the river. He had put half a winter into building a canoe in that shed and he wasn't going to lose his project now to an overloaded roof. The canoe would save him miles of walking, and weeks of time. After two decades of hoping for rescue, now every second that kept him from revenge mattered.

He managed to get to his feet, and then back up on the crust. It held, but now he walked gingerly, slipping and slid-

ing. When he got to the steep slope that led to the river's
shore, he sat and slid the rest of the way. He carried a hammer and used it like a pickaxe to slow his descent. Once he
was safe at the bottom he mentally added "ice treads" to the
list of supplies he would need to reach the west coast.
He had no idea how to fashion ice treads for his boots, but he
would have many long winter nights to work it out.

The shed was still standing, the roof intact but sagging.
He went to work immediately, chipping at the ice with the
hammer, sweeping off large chunks with his gloved hand.
The gloves were new, made from King's tanned hide. They
were surprisingly supple and water resistant. He had enough
of King's hide left over for another pair and made a mental
note to fashion another set. It took an hour to chip away
enough ice to satisfy him. Then he chipped ice from the
door, unbarred it, and went in.

There was no heat in the shed; his breath created great
white clouds. The shed had log walls, but the roof timbers
weren't much thicker than broomsticks. Built by the Fellowship explorers who had discovered the planet, whatever they
kept inside couldn't have been valuable or they would have
protected it better. The canoe he was building now dominated the large interior space. He had the frame done, and
had started covering it with a skin.

Finding something to cover the frame was proving difficult. He started by building a model canoe and experimenting with several kinds of tree bark. Some of these could be
peeled off in large swathes, and then glued to the frame. All
of these turned out to be too flimsy. He then tried laminat-
ing sheets of bark. While the skin was tougher with the lam-
inate, water softened the sap he used to glue the layers
together and they separated. Finally, he gave up and experimented with animal skins.

He started with the tanned hides he had in his cabin.
When stretched across the model frame, all quickly soaked
through. He then tried coating them with the sap he had been
using for glue. It was better, but still soaked through. He
wouldn't get a mile in his canoe before he was swamped. No

combination of hide and sap worked. Stumped for nearly a month, he then remembered the gum trees. The goo on the tree was as sticky as flypaper and impossible to work with. Even as the air temperature dropped, the exterior remained sticky. Finally, he tried heating the surface of the tree. When hot, the exterior gum became runny. Surprisingly, it wasn't flammable and he couldn't set it on fire even with a direct flame. Rey imagined even the worst forest fire wouldn't bring the gum trees down.

Keeping the gum warm, he painted it on different skins, discovering it left most of them sticky and useless. Then he tried it on the skin of a sloth-like creature that spent its days hanging upside down and eating leaves. Sloth meat was inedible and the skin difficult to tan, so he had killed only one. Now he discovered that whatever made their meat taste bad, reacted with the goo from the gum trees, making a shiny surface and toughening the skin. Best of all, it became waterproof. Sloths were easy targets and he could get as many skins as he needed, but not until spring. The sloths disappeared in winter. They were too slow to migrate, so he assumed they hibernated, but he had no idea where.

The half-built canoe was safe. Satisfied, he secured the shed again, and then studied the river. The shed had been built at a wide bend in the river. The river came from the north, then turned west where the shed had been constructed. The shore was sandy with easy access. One hot, dry summer after he first discovered the shed, the river had receded and he found fishing tackle on a snag. He lost the tackle again a month later. Several times he had walked the shore of the river in both directions. To the north, the river meandered through heavily wooded hills, winding steadily north. To the west the river narrowed and quickened as it passed through rocky terrain. After a few miles, the shore became steep with loose rock. He would need pitons and ropes to climb those cliffs—and a partner. He had neither. When scouting the river, he cut across country, trying to pick it up again, but the rocky terrain became a mountain range that drove him further and further south. He finally gave up.

Looking to the west now, the river looked forbidding with thick sheets of ice along its shores, and ice-encrusted trees along its banks. He wanted to leave now, to finish the canoe and launch it, risking the river and the ice floes that occasionally floated by. But the canoe wouldn't be ready until he could kill more sloths.

He left the river and began the treacherous hike back to the cabin. Along the way he checked his snares—nothing. Winter game was scarce, with most animals migrating or hibernating. With the little meat he had in the smokehouse he would be hungry by the time the herds returned. When he got back to the cabin he stoked the fire—wood he had plenty of—and then spread out the maps he had found in the cabin. They were really photographs taken from orbit. Some were heavily marked up, some torn, some rolled up and stacked in a corner. That first winter, Rey had almost used them for fire starters; instead he decorated the walls with them. Now he studied the photos, planning a route.

The river flowed past the shed and due west for thirty or forty miles before turning southwest, and then directly south, emptying into a large lake. Mileage was only an estimate since the photos didn't come with a scale. He had made his own, stepping off the distance from the cabin to the river. He used that distance to create scales for photos that took in more of the region. There were photos of most of the continent, although some were from so high in orbit they showed only gross physical features. The photo he prized most of all was of the west coast. There, in a valley about a hundred miles inland, someone had written in red pencil "#1 colony site; well watered; fertile; moderate climate."

There were five sites marked on the map. The site ranked #5 was on a bay in the southwest region. He was living at the site ranked #4. Another site, #3, was further south on the west coast and the one ranked #2 was on the shore of the large lake to the south. Rey had quickly fixated on the #1 site. They wouldn't have marooned him so close to the lake site—if by too close you meant five hundred miles—if they had settled there. If he was wrong about the colony being at the #1 site, he could continue on to the #3 site. That would leave only #5 to check, the least likely based on their rankings.

He kept his supplies list on the wall and now used a blackened stick to add, "ice treads." The list was two columns, both running floor to ceiling. Without a pack mule it would be impossible to bring it all. He knew that, but had months to decide what was essential.

Rey took a break, putting a pot of water over the fire, and then added a small amount of meat, corn, and starchy tubers that grew wild near the river. Soup stretched his meager supplies. The tubers took a while to soften, so he let the soup simmer. He lit a lantern and then reached for the only book they had left him—a Bible.

He had ripped out a handful of pages when he started his first fire, but when he realized there would be nothing else to read he had spared the rest of the book. Even then he had refused to read it for nearly a year. Eventually, that Bible became a symbol of hope as he convinced himself that the fact they had left him only one book meant they would come back for him. After all, he reasoned, if they intended to leave him for long, they would have left him more to read. After a year of loneliness he then convinced himself that the reason they hadn't come for him was because he had not yet read the Bible they had left. He examined the book carefully, looking for some kind of sensor that would tell them when he had read it. He found nothing. Then he was convinced there must be a camera hidden in the cabin and that they were watching him—he found no camera. Still, he clung to the hope that somehow they would know when he had read their Bible and come. So he read it. They did not come. He read it again. They did not come. He read it over and over and still they did not come.

He picked it up now. The well-thumbed book was limp, the pages dirty. Many times he had thrown the book across the room, furious at Proctor for his hypocrisy. He threw the book out the front door the day he read, in Colossians, Paul's admonition: "Do not lie to each other, since you have taken off your old self with its practices and have put on the new self. . . ." Proctor had lied to him. Proctor knew Rey never would have agreed to being marooned when he offered to give Rey his freedom in exchange for information. The Bible flew out the front door that evening and lay there until morning.

For a long time after that, Rey avoided the New Testament. He detested the weakness of Jesus. Any man following His teachings would become a perpetual victim. Rey preferred the Old Testament, where the strong ruled and the weak served. Now he thumbed to a favorite story in Judges—the story of Jephthah the Gileadite. He liked the story because it reminded him of his own life. Jephthah's mother was a prostitute. Rey's mother was little better. Jephthah was driven away by his own family. The Bible reports "Jephthah fled from his brothers and settled in the land of Tob, where a group of adventurers gathered around him and followed him." Rey admired Jephthah. Being despised did not weaken him, it strengthened him. Jephthah became a bandit and warrior and when the people who had driven him out were attacked, they came begging Jephthah to help them. He made them plead and then cut a deal before he agreed to help. Then he proceeded to destroy their enemies and more. The last part of Jephthah's story wasn't as happy. To guarantee victory over his enemies, Jephthah promised God that if God helped him he would sacrifice whoever came out of the front door of his house when he returned victorious. But when Jephthah came back after his victory, it was his only child, his daughter, who came out to meet him. True to his word, he made a burnt offering out of her. Rey admired a man with that kind of commitment.

Rey finished reading the passage again, stirred the soup and poked at the tubers—still too tough. Rey identified with Jephthah in many ways. He was a warrior, he thrived when others despised him, and was a man of his word. He was not like Proctor, who was a proven liar. Thinking ahead to when he found the Fellowship colony, he was realistic enough to know it would be impossible to kill them all. He would have to use stealth to kill as many as possible, but they could get lucky and kill him. Proctor had gotten lucky when he caught him shooting at a Fellowship sphere back on Earth. There was even a bigger problem. No one had ever walked across this continent, only flown over it. The terrain, the weather, and the unknown: these were his first enemy.

Thinking of the Bible passage, Rey made a promise—Jephthah's promise: "God, if you are up there—or out there—I'll make the same deal with you that Jephthah made. Get me safely across this continent to where my enemies live, and I'll kill the first person as a sacrifice to you."

Now he scooped meat and vegetables into a bowl, and then poured in broth. He added a pinch of sea salt. Salt was precious since he had to travel to the coast and extract it from seawater through the slow process of dehydration. It was essential to food preservation, so he used it sparingly.

He sipped his soup, enjoying the warm trickle down his throat. Then he fantasized about whom he would meet first and the pleasure he would take in watching them die.

4

ENCOUNTERS

Master Rice's Farm
First Continent
SPRING, PLANET AMERICA

Summer hated rain. The rain soaked the ground. Then the tramping animals, field hands, and servants churned the soil to mud. Then the mud was tracked into the big house where it was Summer's job to keep the floors clean. Between scouring dishes in the kitchen, assisting the cook, and answering the constant calls from the master's wife, Summer didn't need to get down on her knees every few minutes to wipe the mud from the master's wood floor. However, here she was again, on her knees, bucket beside her, rag in her hand. Wipe, rinse, crawl a few steps, wipe, rinse, crawl a few steps, endlessly. Slowly, she worked her way from the sitting room back toward the door.

Suddenly someone slapped her on her bottom. She squealed from shock and pain. It wasn't a playful swat, but rather a full, strong, blow. Red-faced, she turned to see the grinning face of Wash.

Washington Rice was Master Rice's oldest boy, and two years older than Summer. Summer's mom called him "mean as a snake," but Summer had never seen a snake. No one born on America had ever seen one. But Summer knew snakes were evil from the Book of Genesis. Wash was evil too. As far back as Summer could remember Wash had tormented her and the other slave kids. Nearly as tall as Master Rice now, lean and muscular, he liked to walk around with his shirt off. Vain as a chicken coop rooster, everything had to be about him. A few years ago, when he still played games with the slave kids, he always chose the sides, picking all the good players for himself. He set the rules and broke them when it suited him. However, if anyone else broke a rule he punished him or her with his fists.

Summer would never admit it to Wash, but he was good looking. All the girls talked about him—slave and free. Like Master Rice, Wash liked to shave his head on the sides, but unlike Master Rice, he let his curly black hair grow long on top. He kept it trimmed neat, making a flat-top that other boys tried to imitate.

"Couldn't help myself," Wash said grinning wide. "Not with a tempting target like that."

Summer was still smarting from the blow, tears welling. She wanted to rub the pain away but wouldn't touch her bottom with Wash watching. She remained on her knees, sitting on her legs. She ignored Wash, rinsing her rag over and over.

"What's a matter, Sum? It ain't like I used a whip on you or nothing."

She continued to ignore him, eyes on the muddy water.

"Not talking, huh? Well, then, get back to work, girl."

Summer continued to rinse her rag, waiting for Wash to leave.

"I said get to working! You better have them muddy prints off the floor before Mama sees them."

Summer could hear his anger building. Rinsing her rag one last time, she tried to wipe the floor without bending over but the floor was clean where she was sitting and she would have to lean forward to reach the next muddy print.

"Well, girl? Do I have to get a whip to get you to do your work?"

Knowing what was coming, Summer gritted her teeth, then leaned forward and wiped up the next print. The crack on her bottom was worse than the first and she gasped in pain. Wash howled with laughter.

"What you gonna do? Cry? Why, Summer, I barely touched you."

Summer was crying. Partly from pain. Mostly from humiliation.

"Now get back to work."

Summer wiped a tear but sat on her legs, her bottom still stinging.

"Oh, get on with it, girl, I'm not going to do it again."

Wash was lying. Summer knew it as sure as the rains came in the fall. She also knew he would not leave her alone until his fun was over. Vowing not to cry anymore, she leaned out, exposing her bottom. The slap came again, hard and quick, and right on top of the last. Summer bit her lip but held her position, trying to see the muddy floor through tears. Suddenly there were heavy footsteps—the sound of Master Rice's boots.

"Pa, I was just having some—"

The slap across Wash's face was as loud as a whip crack.

"She wasn't doing her work," Wash stammered.

Master Rice dragged Wash down the hall away from Summer. Master Rice's voice was loud and sharp and Summer's hearing was good.

"I wasn't doing—" Wash tried to say.

"I told you not to touch her," Master Rice said.

"I wasn't gonna—"

"I told you she was mine," Master Rice said.

"She's a scrawny thing. What do you want her for?"

"You listening to me?"

"You can have her," Wash said.

"She's mine already," Master Rice said. "Everything and everyone on this land is mine. Including you."

Wash didn't say anything. That was smart. Wash was not as strong as Master Rice. Not yet.

"If you touch her you'll get a taste of the whip. Not my belt this time. The slave whip."

Wash said nothing.

"You hear me, boy?"

Master Rice held Wash against the wall, his face inches from Wash's.

"I hear you," Wash said softly.

Summer wiped the floor. Master Rice came back down the hall, Wash fleeing in the opposite direction. Summer pitied the first slave he ran into.

"You okay, Summer?" Master Rice said in the silky voice he used on Saturday nights. "He didn't hurt you, did he?"

"He was just playing," Summer said.

"If he plays like that again, you tell me. You hear that?"

"Yes, Master Rice."

Summer would never voluntarily talk to Master Rice about anything.

"Good girl," Master Rice said, pushing a lock of hair out of her face and putting it behind her ear.

"You do good work, Summer," Master Rice said.

He watched her work for a minute, and then left. Summer sighed with relief. She was still more afraid of Master Rice than Wash, but just barely.

When she finished scrubbing the floor she turned to see new footprints at the other end. She gave up, returning to the kitchen where the cook put her to work peeling potatoes. She took the potatoes to the back porch. It was cold, but the cook liked to have the potato peels go right into the garbage. When Summer sat on a stool to peel, she winced. Her bottom was badly bruised. There would be purple handprints there by morning.

She was halfway through the stack of potatoes when someone galloped into the courtyard, mud flying everywhere.

"Master Rice? Where's Master Rice?"

The man on the horse was Rollie White, one of the sons of Carl White who owned the farm next to Rice's. White had only half the land and slaves of Rice but was still the second largest landowner on America. White was as cruel a master as Rice. Rice came around the corner, a light drizzle falling, his face shielded by a broad-rimmed hat.

"What is it, boy?" Rice demanded.

"We've got a runner, Master Rice," Rollie said excitedly. "My father says to bring your best dogs. We're gonna run him down in the morning."

Wash came to stand next to his father.

"We'll be there just after sunup," Rice said. "Now get yourself down and get something to eat."

"Thank you, sir," Rollie said, sliding off his horse.

A slave took charge of the horse, leading it off to be groomed. Playing the gracious host, Master Rice led Rollie to the kitchen through the back porch where Summer sat peeling potatoes. Rollie hesitated when he saw her, looking her over like she was for sale.

"Maybe you better get yourself inside," Master Rice said sharply, blocking Rollie's view.

"Yes sir," Rollie said quickly.

Summer did not feel protected. She felt threatened by Master Rice's possessiveness. She could not live like this, not like her mother and the other women that Master Rice owned. There had to be somewhere better—even dead would be better. She would rather explain to Jesus why she gave up God's greatest gift than live another day afraid.

Her after-supper chores took her until dark. Slaves were supposed to be in their cabins after dark, but she took a minute to divert to the old barn. It was still used for storage, but seldom visited now. When she was sure no one was looking, she slipped inside and then crept through the machinery, lumber, tools, and sacks of seed, to the back. A set of stairs led to the loft, and underneath the stairs were a couple of loose floorboards. Working the boards free, Summer revealed a small space she had discovered years before. In the space was a backpack she had rescued from the trash heap. She knew it came from Earth, because of the fabric. It was waterproof and slick. Summer could not imagine weaving something that dense. Nearly torn in half when she found it, Summer had stitched it back together. Now she pulled out the stolen paring knife and dropped it into the pack. It was only one of many items she needed. However, no matter how long it took, she would prepare, and when Master Rice's Saturday night knock was for her, she would not be there.

5

FIRST STEPS

Eastern Wilderness
First Continent
SPRING, PLANET AMERICA

Rey closed the cabin door, wedging two bars in place to make sure no animal would break in. Rey thought of burning the cabin, since he would rather die than live another year alone, but Rey reasoned that if the unexpected happened in the first weeks, he could return to the cabin and wait another season before he left again. So, he had stored his supplies of crop seeds, his extra clothing, blankets, skins, virtually all of his tools, and extra food. They would be there if he ever returned.

As he walked away, pack on his back, rifle in his hand, he didn't turn around. He never wanted to see the cabin again. He had wasted two decades of his life in that cabin and only the worst accident could ever make him return to it.

Pockets of snow still hid in the shadows, and the trail was nothing but a mushy path to the river. It was partly cloudy today, with little threat of rain. Occasionally, the weak spring sun peeked through, warming him as he walked. Early blooming plants greeted him here and there, but it would be a month before spring showed her full face.

At the river he dragged the canoe from the shed and then to the sandy shore, one end in the water. Then he retrieved two more packs of supplies from the shed. He secured the shed, and then lashed the packs into the canoe. Now he pushed the canoe into the water, stepping in and kneeling in the rear. He picked up his paddle and stroked away from the shore into the current. He looked back, seeing the shed sheltered in the trees. It was the last human structure he would see for a long time. A quick chill rippled through him. He wasn't leaving home behind—it had never been home—he was leaving familiarity behind. As soon as he entered the river canyon ahead, every step of the way would be unfamiliar. It was a price he would have to pay to get his revenge.

He let the river take him at its own pace, using his paddle as a rudder. Leafless trees lined the shore, a few flowering shrubs sprinkled among the trunks. A few early birds were back, flitting from tree to tree, soundlessly. Rey had never adjusted to planet America's birds. They were beakless creatures with bulging eyes. He had never considered one for a pet.

The river narrowed, the flow quickening. He concentrated, ignoring the scenery, watching for snags. Every spring thaw brought new logs and debris, creating unpredictable navigation hazards. The entrance to the canyon was coming up fast. Ahead on his left was the last point where he could beach the canoe and portage it back to the shed. He shot past it, angling to midstream. Now the trees thinned, the shores becoming steep rocky slopes. Large boulders sprinkled each shore, tops protruding from the river, stepping stones for giants. The canyon entrance pinched the river into rapids and Rey found himself moving faster than he had in twenty years. He shot the rapids, deftly stroking and dragging his paddle to keep the canoe in the middle of the stream.

Rey entered the canyon. There was no shore, now, just steep cliff walls. Ahead, the river split into two channels. Rey could see spray over both channels, but the rocky island in the middle blocked the view ahead. He took the channel with the least spray. Bearing right, he craned his neck to see ahead. Now the river was a bouncy choppy mess, and he was buffeted from side to side, his paddling almost useless.

The canoe suddenly dropped, diving deep into a wave. Momentum carried him through, but the canoe was half swamped, riding low now. He cursed himself for not thinking to bring something to bail with. There was no time anyway. He fought the river, maneuvering around the rocks he could see, colliding with submerged rocks he could not see. To his left across the island he saw the river drop away sharply into a ten-foot waterfall. The spray at the bottom told him the river was pouring onto rocks.

His channel was dropping rapidly too, but in a series of foot-high drops. He bounced down the ten-foot drop as if he were bumping down a set of stairs. The last drop was steeper, and the canoe dove deep again, then fought its way back up. The canoe was riding so low now he could hardly maneuver. Suddenly the river widened and slowed and he used his cupped hands to bail. He floated, concentrating on his bailing, letting the current take him into an eddy. Floating in a lazy circle, he reduced the water level from a worry to a bother.

Rey looked back up river, seeing the cascade he had just navigated. Rey shook his head in disbelief. If he had been able to scout the river before launching he would have been hiking across country. He'd had only a few seconds in which to decide—if he had picked the other channel he would surely have capsized, losing his supplies and probably drowning. At best, he would have found himself in a canyon with sheer walls. Instead, because he had relied on himself and his instincts he had beaten the first challenge of his journey. With renewed confidence, he paddled back into the river and aimed his canoe downstream.

6

CROSS COUNTRY

Eastern Wilderness
First Continent
SPRING, PLANET AMERICA

Many long days of paddling upstream had made Rey strong, and now he could paddle for hours without rest. He kept near shore, although the river, not much more than a creek now, allowed little room for maneuvering. Rey's skills with the canoe had become finely honed, especially compared with the first day of his journey, when he had successfully navigated the canyon. Now, four weeks later, he was running out of river to navigate.

The river by his cabin had taken him west for a long distance, and then began meandering south. Then he came to several large tributaries, forcing him to choose. He picked the most westerly. Frequently forced to portage around impassable stretches, he often considered abandoning the canoe. However, crossing unknown country without a map would be even more difficult, and dangerous. It would come to that soon, but until then, he stuck with the river.

The river eventually became a stream, and then narrowed until little more than a creek. In full bloom now, the forest overhung the narrow stream so completely that the sky was a kaleidoscope of blue and shades of green. Ahead he could see a break in the foliage. At the same time, the stream flow quickened, forcing him to paddle more quickly. After a hundred meters of furious paddling, he broke free of the current and the forest and emerged into the lake that formed the headwaters of this stream.

Rey took two strokes into the lake and then froze. He wasn't alone. To his right six huge animals stood, staring at him. The four-legged creatures were standing in the lake, most with their barrel chests out of the water. They had long necks that ended in huge heads that looked much too large for the giraffe-size necks. They were saddle colored with dark manes running down the back of their necks. The nearest was the largest, and it stared at Rey with bulging eyes in the same way Rey was staring at it. The animal had wet greens drooping from its fleshy lips. Rey untied his rifle, resting it across on his lap.

A slight breeze pushed the canoe toward the animals, so Rey carefully paddled away. The animals watched, fascinated. From the rear of the group, a small one splashed toward Rey. With its head barely out of the water, the little one had its curious eyes fixed on the canoe. Rey paddled faster. As the little one approached, an adult honked an order, and butted the calf. The calf squealed, reluctantly turning around. Squeaking protests like a petulant child, the calf waded back into the herd. Rey hurried away.

Rey guessed the animals were herbivores, but a curious animal big enough to step over an elephant could easily swamp him. When Rey felt safe, he stopped paddling and floated while he chewed on a piece of beef jerky. He had been lucky again. Traveling by river had kept him out of the reach of many predators, and so far he had not crossed paths with anything dangerous living in the rivers. The stream he had been following for the last two weeks had been too shallow for anything large to lurk in the depths, but even something the size of a badger could swamp him.

He pulled out the photomap he had been using and traced his route from the shed where he had built the canoe, down the big river, through the canyon where he had nearly been swamped, downstream to the tributary where he had turned northwest. A week later he had made a mistake, taking the wrong fork and wasting three days paddling upstream until he realized his error. He had returned downstream in a day, then picked the correct fork on his second try. Now he was at the lake that fed that fork. Rey held the photo close to his face, studying the shore. No significant tributaries fed the lake.

He gave up. After carefully stowing the map, Rey paddled the perimeter of the lake, eyes on the shore, looking for a feeder. He dared not complete the circle because of the animals feeding on the eastern shore, but he was sure any stream on that shore would lead him east, or south. He gave up and retraced his route, now looking for a place to beach. Rey spotted an opening in the trees where a snag stretched from the forest into the water. The shore was a clutter of low greens. Rifle in his lap, Rey paddled along the log and then coasted to shore. The canoe gently wedged against the bank. Rey waited. He watched. Now he stepped out into the water, dragging the canoe up on shore, and then knelt. He waited again. He watched. He listened. There were deep forest sounds of the wind in the trees, distant birdcalls, and the occasional skittering of small animals. Now Rey entered the forest, scouting one hundred meters deep and then arcing back first in one direction and then another—nothing.

Feeling safe, Rey unloaded his canoe and dragged it into the forest to the exposed roots of the fallen tree. He turned the canoe over, wedged it against the roots, and then tied it tight. Then he returned to his packs. He had started with three packs of supplies but only two were left. Soon Rey would be living off the land. He divided what he had left into two piles, packed his carry-pack, put it on, and walked into the forest fifty meters and then back. Then he took out a third of what he had packed and stuffed it into the other pack. Now he buried the extra pack at one end of the tethered canoe. He doubted he would ever see either again.

Now Rey looked at his rifle and his bow. One he would strap to his pack, the other he would carry at the ready. The gun relied on twenty-year-old ammunition that was precious to him. He would need it to maximize his killing effectiveness once he found the Fellowship. Still, the forest he faced was unexplored and untamed and if there were animals as big as those in the lake, there might also be predators big enough to bring them down. He decided to carry the rifle.

Paddling uncharted rivers and streams had been fraught with dangers of one kind, but the forest was much more dangerous. Putting the pack on, Rey entered the forest. The Fellowship had not seen fit to leave him a compass, so he navigated by landmarks and the sun. Deep in the forest, landmarks were useless. However, the sun was bright today, and Rey used it by estimating time of day and where it would be in passage. Keeping the sun on his left, he cut through the forest. The canopy was thick, so thoroughly filtering the sunlight that there was little undergrowth. Still, he carried the best tool the Fellowship had left him, a machete, and hacked at anything that annoyed him.

The ground sloped up, but the incline was gradual and he made good progress. He was confident he could find water, so he drank generously from one of the plastic bottles he used for a canteen. About mid-afternoon, the soft mushy ground dried up and then turned rocky. An hour later he broke out of the trees. To his left the ground dropped gradually, the forest continuing. To his right was a steep rocky hill topped by a bare knob, higher than the trees. There was no reason to climb to that knob except for the view. But without a map, that view could save him days of walking in the wrong direction. He climbed.

An hour later, the sun behind him now, he stood at the top looking out across the forest. The view shocked him—he had seen it before. It was the scene from the dream he had had after the wolves had attacked him and infected him. Just before he woke he had dreamed of standing on a bluff and looking out across a forest. This was that scene, complete with the silver river cutting diagonally across the forest and the many small clearings and occasional lakes. Now he studied the far horizon. It was there that he had seen the smoke of a chimney—nothing.

Now he sat, thinking, remembering all the times in the Bible that God had directed people with dreams. In fact, Rey's Bible began with Joseph interpreting dreams in prison—he had torn out everything before that. For a moment, he considered the possibility that there was a God and that that God was telling him something. At the same time a deeper part of his mind understood that if there was a God, that he had tried to murder men and women called into God's service. His sins against God were too great to bear and so his unconscious cobbled together another explanation, one that was guilt free. Now he understood the dream was the result of latent psychic powers that everyone carried inside them, but few developed. Yes, that was the explanation, Rey reasoned. Now warming to his rationalization, he added to it. It had to be the extreme isolation that he had suffered for twenty years that drew out his abilities, honing them, making him sensitive to his future. That explanation relieved him of guilt and freed him once again from God's control. It also gave him great hope. Maybe his dreams would show him the way to the Fellowship's settlement and to the first person he would kill to fulfill his promise to God.

Now he rose, feeling free from moral obligation and therefore powerful. There was no universal right or wrong when you set your own moral agenda. And for Rey, at that moment, in that place, what was right was revenge and what was wrong was failure. He would not fail.

With the strength of purpose, he hurried back down the hill, back into the forest. Recklessly, now, he hastened, less aware of the sounds and movements hidden in shadows. He felt invincible, marching confidently since he had seen his future and that future led to a cabin with a smoking chimney. He kept going until almost sunset, not so foolish as to risk walking in the dark. He searched for a safe campsite, finally settling on a semicircle of trees that grew so close together, only a small animal could squeeze between them. Rey leaned the rifle against the nearest tree and then gathered enough wood to keep a fire burning all night. Using his hatchet, he began chopping off thin slices for kindling. He chopped and chopped, lost in a fantasy about his newly discovered psychic powers. Then he buried the hatchet in a thick limb he had gathered, and took the smallest pieces and some dried moss to start his fire. He was imagining himself learning to control that power, to see the future on command, when something wrapped around his chest.

Reflexively he slapped at it—it was thick and ropelike, and tightened with dreadful strength. Now he was being lifted. He looked up to see another dangling tentacle reaching for him. Peering higher in the gloom, Rey spotted a brownish mass hanging from a limb fifteen feet above him. His fear intensified as he saw other shadowy creatures suspended on the nearby trunks. Just as his feet left the ground he grabbed the rifle—just in time—by its barrel. Now he was rising rapidly. He kicked the other tentacle away as his feet cleared the ground. Above him a head appeared in the brown mass. There was a furry face with large round eyes—flat, not bulbous. Now he could see two clawed hands, reaching for him.

Rey clutched the rifle, the trigger out of reach. With his arms partially pinned he had to work it up in short jerky motions, careful not to drop it. The face was right above him now—there was a mouth, with teeth. Rey felt the stock, worked the bolt to load a cartridge, then jammed the barrel into the center of the brown bulge and pulled the trigger. The recoil tore the rifle from his awkward grip.

The rifle report triggered squeals from the figures in the surrounding trees. Then as one, tentacles shot out, seizing branches, and the creatures swung, Tarzan-like, from limb to limb, trunk to trunk, disappearing into the forest gloom.

His arms still pinned, Rey wriggled, reaching for his belt knife. Something dripped on him—blood. The grip loosened, and then released. Rey fell, absorbing the shock with bent knees. He rolled, picking up the rifle as he did, getting ready to shoot again. The lumpish creature slowly separated from its branch, losing strength with each drop of blood.

From the ground, Rey could see it had four legs. The front pair were limp as if paralyzed, the back two still clamped to the limb. Slowly, the back legs lost their grip. One of its tentacles snaked around the limb just before the last two legs released. Using its tentacle, it fell slowly, almost gently setting down. Rey backed up, rifle on the animal. It moaned and rolled around, trying to get to its feet. Its tentacles extended and retracted randomly, slapping out, showing amazing elasticity. Rey picked up the hatchet, ready to chop one in half if it snagged him again. A few minutes later it died.

Rey scanned the trees, seeing nothing. He thought of moving, but it was too dark to risk it. The gunshot had cleared the trees as far as he could see, so he stayed. Quickly, he lit the fire, building it up. It took some time before he could relax. Keeping the rifle and hatchet next to him, he turned to the carcass.

"Make a dinner of me, will you?" Rey muttered, anxious for fresh meat. Now he rolled the mass over, studying the face. The large eyes were closed now. The eyes surprised him since they were unlike most animals on the planet. While not quite flat, they lacked the marble-like bulge. There were two half-moon shaped fuzzy ears, and a nose so flat he could hardly distinguish it. Two fleshy, brown lips marked the mouth. He did not bother to part the lips since he had already seen the sharp teeth—it was a carnivore. He dragged the carcass as far from the fire as he dared, then he felt in the fur and found a short neck below the head. He cut its throat clear to the spinal column to make sure it was dead. He then let the carcass drain.

Next he slit the animal from neck to groin. As he started to skin it, he saw movement by the head. Rey jumped back, reaching for the rifle. Looking at the half-butchered carcass, he knew it had to be dead. Rey crept close again, rifle ready. Leaning nearer, he saw two small eyes staring over a shoulder. Using his foot, he rolled the animal up onto its side. A small head protruded from the fur.

Knife in one hand, Rey felt along the back—there was a pouch. Rey ignored the baby, rolled the mother back over and gutted it, strange intestines spilling out. Cutting two rectangular patches of skin from the creature, he set them aside.

The fur was soft and the hide might tan well. Next he tried to cut one of the tentacles from where it attached just below the armpits—it would make a good rope. It was like cutting through an automobile tire. When he finished sawing it off, he left the other attached. It was too much work.

He buried the entrails, sliced off some meat, and then returned to his fire. He hung the two skin patches on the back of his pack, underside to the fire so they would dry quickly. Then he cooked the meat, finding it edible but not tasty. Then he built up the fire and wrapped himself in his blanket. Around midnight he heard the carcass being dragged away. He'd expected it. Hand around his rifle, he threw more wood on the fire, and waited until he was sure the scavengers would settle for the easy meal. Eventually, he pulled his blanket close and went back to sleep.

First thing in the morning he checked the trees to be sure the tree octopi—that's what he had named them—hadn't returned. He ate the rest of the cooked meat, stirred the fire, and then tied his blanket to the top of his pack. Putting the pack on, he picked up his rifle and continued his trek.

The encounter with the tree octopus had resensitized him to the dangers confronting him. It also weakened his confidence in his prophetic ability. Dreaming about dangerous animals would be more useful than dreaming about valleys and cabins.

The day promised to be hot, so he kept up a quick pace, planning to rest during the worst of the heat. After a couple of hours he came to a small stream. Brush and fallen logs protected the stream, but he worked his way through spongy greenery and over a rotting log. When he reached the bank multiple splashes erupted as small amphibians fled. He squatted on the bank, waiting until he could see straight to the green bottom. Cupping his hand, he drank the cool, clear water. When he brought a second handful to his lips something snaked around his neck.

Startled, Rey spun, looking behind him, swinging his rifle. There was nothing there. Then he felt something on his neck again—it was on his pack! Rifle in one hand, he pulled the strap off his left shoulder, transferred the rifle, and then dropped the pack onto the ground. Now he brought the rifle up. There, peeking out of his pack, was the baby tree octopus. The little animal's eyes were wide, large brown pupils fixed on the rifle barrel just inches from its face.

"You just scared six years of life out of me," Rey shouted.

The baby cringed, sinking deeper into the pack.

"Get out of there!" Rey ordered.

The baby tree octopus ignored him, almost disappearing inside. Rey pulled his knife.

"Get out of there or I'll eat you for lunch."

The big eyes stared at him from inside the pack. Rey tapped the back of the pack, where the pieces of its mother's hide hung.

"You want to join her?"

Rey realized its mother's smell might have attracted the baby to the pack when it fled the pouch.

"Get out of there or I'll rip you out!"

Risking his fingers, Rey reached inside and took the infant by the scruff of its neck like one would a kitten. He pulled, but the baby tree octopus had attached itself with its strong little legs. As Rey pulled, its tentacles wrapped around Rey's wrist, caressing him. He gave up, afraid the baby's claws would tear through the pack. Now he remembered how it had reached for his lips when he was drinking. Cupping his hand, he held the water above the pack. The baby's head slowly emerged, and then its tentacles arced up and into the cupped hand. Then alternating, the tentacles slurped up small amounts of water and squirted it in its mouth.

"Cute trick," Rey said, fascinated.

Rey got it another handful. It drank about half, and then settled back inside.

"You can't stay in there forever," Rey said. "When you come out, you're gone."

Rey decided there was less risk to the pack, and his fingers, by letting the thing stay inside for now. Putting the pack back on, he started off again. He soon forgot about the little creature. An hour later he pulled a piece of jerky from his pocket and started chewing. He felt movement then, the baby tree octopus climbing higher on the pack, and then onto his shoulder, gripping the strap of the pack and Rey's hair. He felt its fuzzy face press against his cheek. Then a tentacle probed at his lips.

"Hungry?"

Rey pulled a wad of half-chewed meat from his mouth. A tentacle snatched it. He heard the baby chewing next to his ear. Then the tentacle was back. He fed it again.

"All right, because I killed your mama, you can ride until tonight and that's it."

The tentacle tickled the corner of his mouth. He opened it and the baby reached inside, helping itself.

Rey chuckled, taking another bite of jerky.

"I'm still not carrying you all the way to the west coast," Rey said, his resolve all but gone.

7

REY AND OLLIE

Eastern Wilderness
First Continent
SUMMER, PLANET AMERICA

Ollie feared open spaces and let Rey know it every time they crossed a meadow by pulling Rey's hair and humming his worried hum. Rey winced with each tug, but let the tree octopus express himself. Examining the meadow in front of them, this time Rey shared Ollie's fear. It was wide and deep with a river along one edge and steep hills at the other. Going around would be difficult if not impossible. Still, it was not the open space that bothered Rey, it was what occupied it.

In the meadow were forty or fifty large animals. The animals were grazing—a good sign—but they were armed with thick, moose-like antlers. The animals themselves were smaller than moose, being proportioned more like cows. They had wide heads, a long snout, and long prehensile lips used to rip up the thick, leafy ground cover. The mini-moose had protruding eyeballs the size of a light bulb. The animals came in a variety of colors—white, rust, brown, tan, and black—in contrasting stripes. If there was a difference between the males and females Rey could not see it—maybe they were all male? All female?

Cautiously, Rey stepped into the meadow. When he did, every head snapped up and pointed at Rey and Ollie. Ollie tugged Rey's hair. One tentacle came around and pulled on Rey's beard.

"Easy, Ollie," Rey said. "We don't want to stampede them."

Rey walked deeper into the meadow. The herd was spread out and he would have to pass close to those near the river. As Rey moved nearer, he saw smaller animals in the center of the herd. These lacked antlers or sported miniature versions of the adult antlers. The juveniles were particularly interested in Rey, but made no move to get closer.

There was nothing between Rey and the bank now, except low shrubs. The color of sage, the shrubs were protected from grazing by thousands of tiny thorns. Ollie pulled Rey's hair again, a tentacle whipping out to point at the river. Rey followed the point and saw a ripple in the water. Rey stopped, studying it. The ripple came toward the shore as if it could see Rey. Deep in the murky water, Rey could make out a large tubular body. The snake-like creature stopped swimming, settling to the bottom. Now two stalks appeared from the water. Something was studying the meadow.

"Good eyes, Ollie," Rey said, pulling a bit of meat from his pocket, letting Ollie snatch it from his hand.

Rey kept moving, but rethought his escape plan. If the mini-moose attacked, he had planned to jump in the river.

"Keep your eyes open, Ollie," Rey said.

Ollie hummed a worried hum.

The mini-moose ahead began moving away, grazing as they went, one large eye always trained on Rey and Ollie.

"We've got them worried, boy," Rey said to Ollie.

Ollie clamped tighter to Rey's shoulder. The mini-moose continued to shy away, moving directly ahead and not to the side.

"Hey, Bullwinkle, go that way!" Rey shouted.

Shouting froze the mini-moose, heads up. Ollie's worried hum intensified. Rey stopped, seeing that the entire herd was heads up—except, they weren't looking at Rey. Suddenly, the ugliest animals Rey had seen on this planet burst from the forest ahead. They looked like long legged boars, with bristly snouts and long fangs. The mini-moose turned and bolted. Rey and Ollie found themselves facing a stampede. With Ollie tugging on his hair, Rey stood his ground and fired at the onrushing mini-moose. They came on anyway. Turning, Rey ran, Ollie clamped tight to his shoulders, head twisted, watching behind and slapping Rey with his tentacles to get him to go faster. With the bulk of the herd to his left, Rey was forced toward the river. When the trees were near enough Rey risked a cut through the thundering herd. He saw one of the predators pounce on a mini-moose, dragging it to the ground, jaws clamped on the neck. Hooves churned the earth as the powerful predator overwhelmed the mini-moose, and it whipped the mini-moose around, clipping Rey with the back hooves. Stumbling, Rey fell flat, his rifle knocked from his grip. Ollie leaped from Rey's back to the nearest tree, climbing rapidly—Rey could not blame the little guy for abandoning him. Everyone and every animal on this planet had abandoned Rey.

Hurting, Rey rolled toward the river to get out of the way of the stampede, his pack cutting painfully into his back. He came to a stop on his stomach, searching for his rifle. It was lying near the top of the bank. Rey lay still, listening to the sounds of mini-moose being torn to pieces. He wanted to be the forgotten prey, the one too small to bother with. He was not. One of the carnivorous pigs snuffed its way to the edge of the bank and then stopped by Rey's rifle, curious pink eyes locked on Rey. Rey still had his bow, but it was strapped to the back of the pack. He pulled his knife instead. Then something touched his shoulder—a tentacle. He looked up to see Ollie hanging from a branch by one tentacle, the little tree octopus trying to pull Rey up to safety with the other. Rey loved the little creature for that. Gently, Rey pulled the tentacle loose, and waved Ollie to get out of reach.

Rey remained still, knife in hand, knowing that the pig was confused. It had never seen anything like Rey before and seemed unsure if he was edible. Then with a snort, it charged. Rey started to rise to meet the charge but froze when he heard splashing behind him. Throwing himself flat, he covered his head with his arms. He was drenched as the creature from the river arced its long neck over Rey and snatched the pig in mid-charge. With a whip of its long neck, it threw the pig into the middle of the river and then lunged again, driving it under. While the creature thrashed in the water, Rey crawled to his rifle and then into the trees, away from the feeding pigs and the river snake.

When he was well away, Rey rested, leaning against a tree trunk. With a "plop," Ollie was back on his shoulder, tentacles caressing Rey's beard. Softly, Ollie hummed his happy hum.

"Same to you, buddy," Rey whispered, scratching Ollie under his chin. "Let's get out of here, Ollie."

Ollie crawled to his place between Rey's shoulders, locking his claws on pack straps and hair, head pressed against Rey's cheek. Both were quiet until they could no longer hear the pigs feeding. Then Rey whistled the theme song from a television show he had watched as a kid, and Ollie hummed along.

8

RUNNERS

Master Rice's Farm
First Continent
AUTUMN, PLANET AMERICA

Cook woke Summer early with three sharp raps on the door. Groggy, Summer crawled out of bed, trying not to wake her brother and mother. Outside, she went directly to the wood-pile, grabbed an armload of firewood, and carried it in to the kitchen stove. Then she fetched fresh eggs from the hen house. Cook had bacon frying when Summer brought the eggs. Cook broke the eggs in the bacon grease, then fried up leftover potatoes. Summer sliced a loaf of bread and set the table with plates, mugs, silverware, butter, and two kinds of jam. They worked without talking, a well-practiced team.

Master Rice and his four boys came in just as Summer finished setting the table. Wash gave her a hate-filled look. Montiel—the quiet Rice boy—avoided her eyes. Malcolm, who was twelve, made kissing sounds at her. Will, the youngest, just scrambled to his place. This would be his first slave hunt. Two of Master White's slaves had run the day before.

Summer hurried back to the kitchen and then helped carry the food. The boys waited until Master Rice filled his plate and then lunged for what was left. Master Rice and his boys never said grace unless the mistress was at the table. Even then, prayers did not come easily to the lips of Master Rice. Cook brought coffee, pouring it for Master Rice and Wash.

"Meaghan, don't you ever feed that girl?" Rice called as she and Cook turned to leave.

Meaghan Slater, or Cook as she was known, was one of the oldest slaves on the planet, with a back criss-crossed with scars, most earned by sassing Master Rice. Summer knew Cook had been important back on Earth and had not taken well to slave life. She had had half a dozen masters. Master Rice was the last stop for slaves like her. Rice either broke them or killed them.

"I can put the food in front of her, but I can't make her eat it," Cook said defensively.

"If I was a suspicious man I'd say you were eating her food too," Rice said.

The boys guffawed, food dropping from their mouths. Cook was a plump woman. She blushed with anger, but said nothing. Cook had a sharp tongue when she chose to use it.

"That right, Summer? You not eating? Something wrong with my food?"

"No, Master Rice," Summer said.

Rice's younger boys were still wolfing down breakfast but Wash was listening, watching.

"Then why are you so skinny?"

"I eat, Master Rice," Summer said.

"See that you do, Summer. I've got to take care of my property. I've got standing in the community. People look to me for leadership. How do you think it makes me look when you walk around with your skinny legs and arms? They might think I've been mistreating you. If one of my horses was as skinny as you, Grandma Jones would confiscate the poor thing. Do you want people thinking I'm a bad master?"

Summer said nothing.

"Well?" Master Rice asked sharply.

"No, Master Rice."

"Now you eat three meals a day like a woman's supposed to, or I may need to do a little attitude correcting."

"Attitude correcting" meant whipping.

"Yes, sir," Summer said, eyes on the floor.

Now she and Cook hurried out. Master Rice said something as they left and the boys erupted in laughter.

Back in the kitchen, Cook poured herself a cup of coffee—an expensive treat for slaves—and then fried up two thick slices of bacon and two eggs, and then slid them onto a plate in front of Summer. Summer picked at the eggs with a fork and then ate half of one piece of bacon.

"It won't work," Cook said.

"What?" Summer asked.

"You can't stay a little girl forever, Summer. You're sixteen. You can't hide from the woman you're becoming. You were always a beautiful child, Summer, and you'll be a beautiful woman. You can't hide that no matter what."

Summer broke the yolk of the egg, yellow fluid running across the plate.

"There's a name for the disease you have," Cook said.

"I'm not sick."

"It's not a disease of the body. It's a disease of the mind. It's called anorexia nervosa."

"I'm not sick."

"I admire you, Summer. You're strong willed. You've got more courage than ten girls your age. You have more courage than I ever had."

Summer had seen the stripes on the cook's back. She knew she wasn't as brave as Cook.

"But it's a dangerous game you're playing. You can die from anorexia, Summer."

"There are worse things than dying," Summer said. "In Matthew Jesus says if we are slaves in this life we will be first in heaven."

Cook didn't believe in God, heaven, or hell. Many of the original slaves were like her. Now she shook her head sadly, her short-cropped gray hair gently swaying.

"The only happiness you can count on is here in this life, Summer. Find what happiness you can. Live. Outlive Master Rice. That's the best revenge."

"Even when Master Rice dies there will still be Wash," Summer pointed out.

Cook frowned, and then ran her hand through her hair.

"Yes, well, we'll just have to outlive him too," she said.

Now Cook turned to the frying pans, scraping the grease into a can to save it.

"Cook, if you were to run away, where would you go?"

Cook froze. Then she spoke without turning around.

"If someone hears you talking like that, we'll both get a whipping."

"Sorry."

Cook scrubbed. Summer played with the runny yolk.

"Honeymoon Valley," Cook said softly.

Summer had never heard of the place but didn't ask Cook about it. It was dangerous talk. Instead, she tucked the name away in her memory.

The rain had stopped by the time the master and his sons rode off for the hunt. They took three dogs with them, the hounds yelping with excitement. Master Rice had the best tracking dogs on the planet. Whoever had run off would be caught by the time the day was out.

With Master Rice and the boys away, there was little threat from the whip. The mistress rarely left the house, and Rice's two daughters were still young enough to want to play with the slave kids, not torture them. There were six hired hands, but they were off chasing the runaways. That left Emeka Nkosi, the overseer, and considered a fair man compared with the master. Overseer Nkosi only whipped slaves on Rice's orders. Mostly, a simple "Do I hafta tell Master Rice about this?" was all it took to keep a slave in line. Nkosi spoke with an accent and had the blackest skin of anyone Summer had ever seen. His teeth were large and bright white, and when the right mood took him he would talk of his life back on Earth. Sometimes he spoke of living in New York and driving a taxicab—Summer thought she knew what that was. More often he talked of growing up in a desert country. Summer had never seen a desert and could not imagine going more than a couple of weeks without rain. When the mood touched him, Overseer Nkosi could entrance her with talk of strange foods, stranger animals, and the people he lived among, who had a different religion. That was the hardest for Summer to understand—what a different religion would be?

Summer grew up knowing there was only one God, who sent his only Son to die for everyone's sins. His Son was crucified in our place, so that we wouldn't have to be. Three days later he rose from the dead and proved that death wasn't the end. Everyone knew that Jesus paid the price of sin for all the people, and if you accepted Jesus into your heart, you could go to heaven and live with God forever. It was all written down in God's book, even the names of the people who witnessed Jesus' death and resurrection. To Summer, it was so complete, so hope-filled, that she could not imagine anyone not being a Christian. Certainly there weren't any other religions on America. There were a few who didn't believe anything—like Cook and some of the other slaves—and some who didn't act like the Jesus they claimed to follow—like Master Rice—but no other religions. Once she tried to get Nkosi to explain one of the religions from his birthland on Earth, but he refused. "That was a dead end then and it's a double dead end now," he said.

Harvest time was coming and soon the slaves would be shuttled from farm to farm to bring the crops in. It was also sourberry season. The purple berries grew in the valley where Master Rice's farm spread, nearly filling the eastern end of the valley. Sourberry was tasty as jam, canned well, and made a good pie that the master liked. Without the bosses around, Nkosi sensed little work would be done. Instead of spending the day shouting at lazy slaves, Nkosi sent most off to their work and then organized a berry-picking expedition.

Nkosi hitched a team to the big wagon, and then loaded it up with slave children to do the picking. Lucy went along to supervise the little ones so Nkosi would not have to. Nkosi pushed a fishing rod and tackle box under the seat with the lunch Cook had packed. Rocky and Passion were the first in the wagon. Summer was selected to go, as well as Nicole, Summer's best friend. They were the same age, but Nicole had filled out, getting unwanted attention from Wash. Master Rice didn't bother Nicole and her mother, Monica, like he did Summer and her mother and Lucy. Like her mother, Nicole was short, with large thighs and hips. Her face was small and round, and her nose nearly flat. No one called her pretty, but she was not self-conscious, and when children called her names she gave as good as she got—except to Wash. Nicole had a scar across her left cheek she earned from sassing Wash. Wash did things to Nicole Master Rice would never let happen to Summer.

The draft horses, Moses and Solomon, plodded at a lazy pace, so kids constantly hopped out of the wagon, ran alongside, picked flowers or chased weasels off the road and into the woods. Weasels were four-legged fur balls that were faster than any of Master Rice's dogs. They liked to run and would tease dogs or people by letting you get close to them before they took off. Nkosi said the weasels—not the kind on Earth—were nearly blind and waited until they could smell you before they ran. Summer didn't believe that. How could anything run that fast, dodge trees, and be almost blind?

After two days of rain, there was now a break in the weather. The horizons were clear of storm clouds, although to the west were thin bands of gray clouds.

"They won't get here before dark," Nkosi assured everyone.

As the sun warmed the air, the ground steamed. The track was muddy, but Moses and Solomon were strong and never slowed. Lucy rode on the seat with Overseer Nkosi. Summer and Nicole rode right behind on either side. Summer liked listening to the adults talk. Nkosi was in a good mood today, and he and Lucy were talking like friends, not like overseer and slave.

"I was a soldier," Lucy was saying. "Most of us slaves were. You know that, Nkosi."

"Was you born a soldier?"

"Yes. Army brat. I lived on seven bases by the time I left home. When I left it was to join the army."

"I was a soldier," Nkosi said.

This was new.

"I was thinking of making it a career," Lucy said. "Before I came here."

There was an uncomfortable silence. Summer knew that none of the adults had been born slaves. All of them had come from planet Earth and later were made slaves. Summer often wondered what it must have been like for her mother and Lucy and the others. Able to go where you wanted when you wanted.

"What about you, Nkosi? I take it that soldiering didn't agree with you."

"You can say that again," Nkosi said, chuckling nervously. "I didn't choose the soldier life. It chose me. Strangers came to our village in the middle of the night. They had guns. They took me and my brother far away, and there they marched us around in circles for three weeks. Then they gave us a uniform and a rifle and took us to another village. They told us the people of this village were the enemy. They told us the people in the village would kill our fathers and brothers and rape our mothers and sisters. We believed them. They weren't like us. They were Christians. So we killed them. We killed them all."

Lucy said nothing. In the back the children played. Two boys jumped out and raced around the wagon and team in opposite directions and then scrambled back in, laughing.

"But you're a Christian, Nkosi," Lucy said softly.

Nkosi did not seem to hear her.

"Then they marched us to another Christian village. On the way many were celebrating. Men were laughing and bragging about how many they had killed. I did too at first, but I could not keep it up. Every time I closed my eyes, I saw the faces of the people we had killed. Men, women, children. Even babies. My rifle got heavier with every step until I could hardly carry it. When they stopped to let us rest, I was too exhausted to eat. Yet, I could not sleep. At night the sky in my country was not gray like this. It was blue every day and black every night and the stars were like white-hot drips of molten metal. That night I lay looking up at the stars, too afraid to close my eyes. When I did I saw the faces of those I had killed. I knew I would never sleep again and if I had had the strength I would have lifted my gun and shot myself. Then a miracle happened. The stars began to move."

Lucy and Nicole leaned close. Nkosi's stories were always

interesting, but this was different. He was not just telling a story, he was baring his soul.

"The stars outlined a face in the sky and it spoke to me."

Then Nkosi stopped. Summer held her breath. Nicole bit her lip. Still Nkosi did not speak.

"What did it say?" Lucy asked softly.

Nkosi stared straight ahead as if in a trance. Just when Summer thought she would never hear the end of the story, Nkosi spoke.

"The voice said to me 'Why do you slaughter my sheep?' I had no answer because I did not know why. The Christians had done nothing to me. I played football with many of them when I was a boy."

Then Nkosi stopped his story again. Summer was sure he would never finish it and she could not hold herself back.

"It was Jesus, wasn't it? Jesus spoke to you!"

"Mind your place," Lucy said sharply.

On Master Rice's farm, children—especially slave children—were not welcome in adult conversations.

Nkosi chuckled. His laugh was deep and raspy.

"Yes, Summer. I believe it was Jesus who spoke to me. But I did not know it then. I knew nothing about Jesus other than he was a prophet. But that night I ran away from my brother soldiers and kept running until I got to America— the country back on Earth. Later, I learned they killed my brother to punish me for desertion."

Now no one said anything.

"God let your brother be killed and yet you still follow Jesus?" Lucy asked.

"God did not want my brother to die. God cried that day just like me. God didn't want those villagers to die either and He cried an ocean the day I helped kill them. God wants only good things for his children."

"He wants some of us to be slaves? To be bought and sold like animals," Lucy said, anger rising.

"There have always been slaves and masters," Nkosi said. "This was so in my old country back on Earth. It will always be so. Jesus did not come to free the slaves. Jesus came to open the doors for them to eternal life."

"Would Jesus tie a man to the whipping post and whip him to death?" Lucy asked, visibly upset.

"Jesus used a whip to clear the temple of money changers," Nkosi said. "Lucy, if you were not a slave where would you go? What would you do? There are men who must work for Master Rice, because they cannot manage themselves. Many people are like that. Each year there are fewer small farms and more big ones. Clyde Williams comes to work for Master Rice every day. If it were not for Master Rice, Clyde and his family would starve. Is he any less a slave than you?"

"He doesn't get whipped for working too slow!" Lucy said, "and Rice doesn't visit his wife at night."

"Doesn't he?" Nkosi said. "I do not know the full arrangement between Clyde and Master Rice."

"Clyde would never . . ." Lucy started, her voice trailing off.

"Desperate men do desperate things. Which is the greater burden, Lucy? Being a slave to Master Rice and having no choice, or being free and choosing Master Rice?"

Lucy said nothing. Summer wanted to speak up again but bit her lip. She knew her answer. She would take free. And she would never give in to Master Rice.

Only the children were having fun then, but after a few minutes of silence, the somber mood lifted.

"Nkosi, have you ever gone skiing?" Lucy asked.

"There was no snow where I grew up," Nkosi said. "After I moved to America I worked all the time."

"I loved skiing," Lucy said. "Especially cross-country skiing."

"What is skiing?" Summer asked.

Lucy turned, leaning over the back of the seat.

"It's a way of traveling over the snow," Lucy explained.

"Like snowshoes?" Summer asked.

Four pairs of snowshoes hung in the old barn. Summer had seen them used only twice, since the little bit of snow they got at Master Rice's farm was not usually deep, and did not last long.

"With snowshoes you walk on the snow, but with skis you glide. It's much faster and fun too."

"How can you do that?" Summer asked.

"Well, you see skis are long and skinny and curled up at the front. You attach your boots to the middle of the skis—just the front of your boot. Then you kind of glide-walk."

Summer tried to picture skiing, but could not imagine sliding on boards.

"I'll show you sometime," Lucy promised, and then turned around. "My friends and I would ski across country a long way away from the towns and highways. It was so quiet you could hear snow fall."

"I don't believe that," Nkosi said.

"Well, it's true," Lucy said. "Sometimes we would snow camp. I've never experienced peace and quiet like when we camped in the snow. Snow laden trees and ground muffled every sound. There were no birds singing, no insects buzzing—no sounds at all. Early in the morning I would sneak off by myself and ski a few miles from camp and be alone. Each of those memories is very special. I can tell you every detail about every one."

"Please don't. On this planet you can be alone by going a mile in any direction," Nkosi said, laughing derisively. "Here, to be alone is to die. To be together is to survive."

"Nkosi, there aren't any poets in your family, are there?"

"If there were, they froze to death sleeping in the snow."

Both Lucy and Nkosi laughed.

Summer smiled, enjoying the camaraderie, but soon she pictured herself gliding across the snow, alone, nothing but plains of white as far as she could see.

The sourberries grew thick around the north end of Whopper Lake. The size of fish that lived in the lake—all huge—gave the lake its name. No one had ever pulled a baby fish from the lake. "They must be born fully grown," Nkosi once said. They reached the lake, Moses and Solomon pulling the wagon across a mushy meadow that led to the shore. The far side of the lake was a steep and rocky slope that everyone called Mount Whopper, although it was really a hill. The sourberry bushes grew along the base of Mount Whopper, for a mile in either direction. Summer once asked her mother why they did not dig up some of the bushes and bring them back to plant at Master Rice's farm. "Because then there would be no more berry picking trips," her mother said. Summer never suggested it again.

They stopped at the north end of the meadow where the sourberry bushes began, the children scrambling out, grabbing picking baskets.

"Everyone fills their basket five times by lunch or you won't eat!" Lucy shouted as the children scattered. "Summer, Nicole, Nelson, unhitch Moses and Solomon. Rub them down and hobble them."

Nelson was fourteen, but big for his age. He often got assigned the work of older children, partly because of his size, but also because of his color. Nelson's skin was as white as most of the adult slaves. He moaned and complained now, while the other children were disappearing into the bushes for untold adventures. Normally, Nkosi would supervise treatment of the team, since they were worth more than ten slaves, but he already had his fishing pole and tackle box in hand and was heading south along the shore.

It took twenty minutes to unhitch the team and rub them down. Normally, they would take their time, since it was light work. But now they hurried and then led the horses out into the meadow and hobbled them. Both horses immediately ripped up big wads of the leafy ground cover. Nicole and Summer had brought aprons to protect their clothes from the berry juice. They put their aprons on, and then grabbed baskets. Nelson was already running after his friends. Nicole and Summer looked at Lucy, worried that she would want one or both of them to stay with her to collect the berries the children brought, packing them for the trip back.

"Well, what are you waiting for? The berries won't pick themselves," Lucy said.

Nicole cheered as they ran for the bushes. At this time of year the bushes were thick with berries and they could have stopped anywhere and picked, but what fun would that be? They ran through the bushes, playing hide and seek, chasing each other. Occasionally other children would pop out of bushes, or run by, their baskets holding a few berries.

"If you want to eat I better see some berries," Lucy called a few minutes later.

Now they settled down to pick. Sourberries ripened from spring to fall, but for most of the year, they were protected by two-inch thorns as thin and pointed as needles. But in fall, the needles became brittle, and fell away. They crunched under their feet now, leaving the berries unprotected. Summer set to work, her nimble fingers pulling berry after berry free, dropping them into her basket. The baskets were stained purple from previous years of use. Quickly, Summer filled her first basket, talking with Nicole as she did. Nicole had a crush on a slave boy called Melvin—from a farm to the north of Master Rice's farm—and talked about him, asking Summer if she thought he was cute. The farm where Melvin lived was poor, with only a dozen slaves to work the property. However, the master, Frank Ableman, was kind to his slaves, letting them marry and live together as families. Master Rice insisted, "Coddling his lazy good-for-nothing slaves is why his crops are so small." Summer thought it might also be because Master Rice had taken all the farmable land this side of the Big River Canyon.

"So, Summer, what do you think? Isn't Melvin cute—maybe a little?"

Summer didn't think so. Melvin was plump, with a large round head, and a big gap between his front teeth. But it didn't matter what she thought.

"I bet lots of girls think he's cute," Summer said.

"Do you think he likes me?" Nicole asked.

"Yes, silly," Summer said. "He's always staring at you in church."

Nicole giggled.

Summer's basket was overflowing, while Nicole's was only

half-full. Nicole ate one berry for every berry she put in her basket. Summer hadn't tasted a berry yet. She left Nicole, and carried her basket back to the wagon. Two other children were there, Lucy emptying their baskets into larger containers. Lucy emptied her basket and then handed it back.

"I'll need help with the lunch," she said. "When I call, you come."

Summer sighed, but nodded. It was still an hour to lunch. She filled her basket three times more before lunch. Only Nelson had picked as many as her. No one met Lucy's "five basket" quota by the time Lucy called Summer to help with lunch. No one needed to. The storage baskets were already over half-full with plump berries.

Cook had packed thick sandwiches filled with ham, a treat for the slave kids. There were cookies too—as big as saucers—one per child, and an apple. Apples weren't a treat since everyone had to eat at least three apples a week by Grandma's Rule. There was a jug of milk, and Summer's job was to pour a cupful for each child. Two cups of milk a day was another of Grandma's Rules. Most of the children took their food to the shore, sitting on rocks to eat. Summer and Nicole stayed with Lucy. Nicole ate voraciously, but Summer picked some of the ham out of her sandwich, and then started to hand it to Nicole. Lucy saw her and gave her a hard look. Instead, Summer tore off a piece, and kept the rest. When Lucy wasn't looking, she wrapped it in a napkin and tucked it in her apron pocket. Summer nibbled on the cookie, and then hid it away when Lucy's back was turned. Rocky would like the cookie. Summer ate the entire apple and drank all of her milk.

"Summer, take Overseer Nkosi his lunch," Lucy said, noticing she was done.

Summer was always done first. Summer put Nkosi's lunch in her basket, and then headed along the shore. She found Nkosi relaxing against a rock, his fishing pole propped up on a forked stick. A bobber floated a few yards out from shore. Two ropes were tied around Nkosi's leg. One went to the fishing pole and the other into the water.

Summer looked into the lake. Three huge fish were tied to the end of the rope.

"Overseer Nkosi," Summer said softly, and then repeated it louder.

Hat pulled over his eyes, Nkosi now lifted the hat, smiling when he saw the basket in Summer's hand.

"Good. I been ready for lunch a long time now."

"Sorry, Overseer, I brought it as soon as I could."

"You did fine, Summer," Nkosi said, taking the food from the basket.

Nkosi's lunch was like everyone else's, except there were two cookies and a bottle of root beer. Summer had tasted root beer once and thought it the most delicious thing she had ever tasted. The root beer was bottled by Master Lyon's slaves and available in the general store. Master Rice's children drank it every Sunday and on holidays. Nkosi was particularly fond of it and snuck a bottle whenever Master Rice was away. No slave would ever tell on him.

Now Summer took her basket and walked along the shore, past the children still finishing their lunches. She could see Nicole helping Lucy pack away the lunch, so she went back into the berry bushes, angling along the shore toward Mount Whopper. She randomly picked berries as she walked. She didn't want to get caught with an empty basket, but she was really exploring. She scared a weasel out from cover, the fur ball disappearing almost before she could see it.

"Blind?" she said to herself. "I don't believe it."

She reached the base of the hill. The bushes were thick here, well watered by the runoff down the mountainside. The bushes grew up the slope too, but quickly thinned, the ground too rocky for deep roots. Now she walked along the base, the berries so thick she didn't have to bend to pick. As she plucked at a cluster, she spotted someone hiding behind the bush.

"Come on out," Summer said. "I can see you. You can't scare me!"

Two people stood, both were white enough to be slaves. They were not part of the berry picking party and they did not belong to Master Rice. She recognized both of them from church. One was Kerry Little and the other Lonnie Zagjewski—people teased him about his name. They had to be the runaways.

"Please don't tell," Kerry said.

Kerry was a year older than Summer. He was lanky, already six feet tall, with brown eyes and brown curly hair that hung over his ears. Freckles covered his nose and cheeks. He had a quick mind and liked to tease, but in the fun way, not the mean way. His mother was a house slave for Master White and loved by the White's children, since she had just about raised them single-handedly. Sophia White was too busy gossiping to know what her children were up to.

Lonnie was shorter by a couple of inches and broad and strong. He had a huge head and thick neck. He had the "bowl" haircut common among slave children. Lonnie's skin color testified to a master's influence. When he was ten he won a steer-wrestling contest at the Gathering, beating slave children five years older. He had won it every year since. Master White often bragged on Lonnie's strength, saying he was not for sale at any price. Now he was a runaway and likely to be whipped to death.

"They're hunting you," Summer said. "You should go home. Beg Master White for forgiveness. Maybe he won't whip you."

"We're never going back," Lonnie said.

"No one's ever got away before," Summer said.

"That's cause they had no plan," Kerry said. "Me and Lonnie, we've got it all worked out."

Kerry held up a duffle bag.

"We've got food and supplies. Everything we need to survive on our own."

Summer thought of her own bag hidden back at Master Rice's. Did every slave have one?

"But where are you going to go?" Summer asked. "No, don't tell me!"

"We left a false trail," Kerry said confidently. "They're off on a wild goose chase."

Summer didn't know what a goose was.

"Then Lonnie and I waded up Whopper Creek so the dogs couldn't track us."

"That was my idea," Lonnie said with big childish grin on his face.

Summer tucked that trick away in her memory.

"We came this way because we knew the sourberries grew thick up here."

Summer was impressed with that detail too. The boys had gotten at least one meal off the land while they were on the run.

"Come with us, Summer," Kerry said suddenly.

Summer froze, terrified by her desire to run off with them.

"You want to," Lonnie coaxed. "You know you do."

Summer did want to run, but she needed more than the assurances of a cocky teenager and a half-filled duffle bag to convince her they could make it.

"I'd slow you down," she said, trying to convince herself not to go.

"Well, you are kind of skinny," Kerry said, looking her up and down. "But awfully pretty too."

Summer blushed. Digging in her apron pockets she handed over the rest of her lunch. Kerry tore the sandwich and cookie in half, sharing with Lonnie. They ate voraciously.

"Master Rice is hunting you, with his best dogs," Summer said as they ate.

"Has he got Blue Belly on our trail?" Lonnie asked nervously.

"Since this morning," Summer said.

"Won't make no difference," Kerry said. "Right now Blue Belly's got a nose full of buzzers."

Buzzers were tiny insects that swarmed when you crossed their path and liked to fly up noses, mouths, and ears. They made a faint buzzing sound that became a roar when they got down the ear canal.

"I laid a sweaty rag right on top of a hive," Kerry said.

Summer smiled, thinking of the surprise Blue Belly was going to get. Then she realized Master Rice would beat Sean Lonnigan, the slave that handled the dogs, for letting it happen.

"Well, you better go," Summer said. "And go that way. There are pickers all the way back through here. Overseer Nkosi is fishing over that way."

Both boys ducked behind bushes at the mention of Overseer Nkosi. Master White's overseer was quicker with the whip than Nkosi, but any overseer would drag them back to Master White.

"Thank you, Summer," Kerry said as the boys crept away through the bushes.

Kerry paused, looking up at her.

"I meant what I said," Kerry said.

"What?"

"You may be skinny, but you sure are pretty."

Summer couldn't help but smile. Satisfied with that smile, Kerry crept after Lonnie, the plump duffle bag over his shoulder. Summer resumed picking, watching for other children, ready to shoo them off so the boys could get away without being seen. When she was sure they were safely gone, she picked her way back to the wagon and emptied her basket. Summer and Nicole picked fast now, with only a couple of hours left before they would have to leave. The older children sensed the deadline and the baskets came back for emptying faster than in the morning. Soon Lucy shouted for everyone to "Fill them up and come on in!"

Summer and Nicole filled their baskets one last time. These berries would go home with them. Nkosi came back with six fish; almost too much for him to carry. Then he supervised the hitching of the team and soon they were off. Everyone was tired now, but a good mood settled in the wagon and soon they were singing hymns. Summer liked this part of the berry picking trips too but joined in half-heartedly. Part of her ached to be with Kerry and Lonnie, running for freedom. But the time wasn't right. Her mother was due soon, and she would need help with the new baby. Summer also needed more supplies and more knowledge. How would she feed herself if she ran? She could not live on sourberries forever. How would she outwit Blue Belly and the other dogs—and Master Rice? Looking down she saw the overseer's fishing pole and tackle box lying with the fish. She knew where Nkosi kept it and she knew it contained fishhooks and line. She tucked that away in her special memory and joined in the hymn singing enthusiastically.

9

KERRY LITTLE

Master Rice's Farm
First Continent
AUTUMN, PLANET AMERICA

The runaways weren't caught that day, or the next, or even the next week. So life at Master Rice's farm was miserable, and for a change the master did not just take it out on the slaves. Master Rice's family and hired hands were cursed and cuffed too. Sean Lonnigan, the slave who handled the master's dogs, took the worst of it. He came back from the first hunt with a black eye and a broken rib. It took nearly a week to get the last of the buzzers out of Blue Belly's nose and then the dog was skittish about tracking. Boomer took Blue Belly's place, leading the hunt. Summer heard tell that Master Rice made Sean Lonnigan run with the dogs even with his broken rib. She believed it.

Master Rice was gone for nearly a week at one stretch, but again came back empty-handed. Lonnigan came back with a loose tooth and a split lip that time. Summer kept out of the master's way, anxious for the puff tree harvest. Master Rice hardly ever beat his slaves under the watchful eye of Grandma Jones.

They caught Kerry and Lonnie at the end of the third week. Early one morning Master Rice paraded in through the front gate, with Kerry Little stumbling along behind. The master rode between the house and the barn, taking his time so the slaves could gather. The master's boys rode ahead, whooping and hollering. Master Rice sat tall and proud in the saddle, his broad-brimmed leather hat cocked sideways. He had a rope tied to the horn of his saddle, the other end tied around Kerry's wrists. Kerry was dirty, his clothes torn, both eyes black and swollen. Dried blood covered one side of his face. Pulled along by the horse, Kerry staggered, exhausted, but if he fell he would be dragged. Behind him walked Sean Lonnigan and two leashed hounds. Boomer was missing.

The mistress, Fancy Rice, made a rare appearance, curious about the commotion. The slaves gathered too, shirking their work without fear. Master Rice wanted them to see this. Summer went to stand by her mother, but her mother pushed her behind with a strong arm and a firm warning. Summer leaned out, well shielded by her mother's swollen belly.

Barely conscious, Kerry could not know where he was. His face told the story of what happened when they found him, but there would be more bruises and more blood hidden under his clothes. Now the mistress called from the porch of the big house.

"Whatcha bring him here for? He ain't our problem."

There was a slight slur to her voice. Master Rice pulled up and looked down on his wife. Kerry dropped to his hands and knees.

"He is now. I traded Boomer for him."

"You traded one of your best dogs for an ungrateful runaway? He'll be nothing but trouble. Better to whip him to death now and get it over with."

Master Rice smiled wide, pushing his broad-brimmed hat off of his head, letting it hang from his neck by the ties.

"He won't be no trouble," Master Rice said, dismounting. A slave ran forward and took the reins.

"All he needs is a little attitude adjusting."

Summer winced.

"Nkosi, tie him to the whipping post and get the field hands in."

Nkosi grabbed Kerry by the hair and lifted his head. Kerry's eyes were barely visible in the swollen flesh. Blood crusted around both nostrils and under one eye.

"Master Rice, better to wait a few days. He's not going to feel nothing. This boy don't even know where he is."

The gathered slaves held their collective breath. Nkosi was trying to save Kerry's life.

"He'll feel it," Master Rice said. "We hardly laid a hand on him. You can bet he's faking. He's not getting out of this that easily. Runaways taste the whip, and he's a runaway."

Shamed by his inability to find the two runaway slaves immediately, Master Rice would not put off his revenge. Proud of his dogs and his skill as a tracker, Master Rice couldn't stand knowing he had been outsmarted by two teenage slaves. No slave had been on the run for more than three days before Kerry and Lonnie, let alone three weeks. Kerry would pay with blood for humiliating the master.

"I'm just looking out for your best interests, Master Rice," Nkosi argued. "This isn't some old cripple eating you out of house and home. This boy could be digging stumps up by tomorrow—next day at the latest."

"If he can dig stumps tomorrow, he can take his whipping today," Master Rice said.

"I'm just saying—"

"Tie him to the post or you'll take his place," Master Rice snapped.

Master Rice had no right to whip a free man, but everyone knew Grandma's Rules didn't always apply on Master Rice's farm. Nkosi signaled another slave forward, and they dragged Kerry to the cross-shaped whipping post. Kerry's shirt was stripped off and his hands tied to the crosspieces. The field hands were arriving, some came walking, those from the farthest fields in horse-drawn wagons. Now Master Rice left, going into the big house for his whip, which hung in a prominent place in his study. With his shirt off, Summer could see the full extent of Kerry's beating now. Purplish bruises covered nearly every inch of his back and sides.

"Summer, you stay behind me," her mother ordered, again pulling her behind.

Summer obeyed, but couldn't help but look around at Kerry, worrying. Master Rice appeared, his whip in one hand, a small jug of whiskey in the other—violating another of Grandma's Rules: Beer and wine were tolerated, but hard liquor was not. Master Rice sipped from the jug. Wash went up on the porch, asking for a taste. In a rare act of generosity, Master Rice shared the jug. Wash took a large mouthful and then swallowed it like he had been drinking it all his life.

Finally, the rest of the field hands arrived and Master Rice came down off the porch, Wash and the other boys right behind. The mistress and the girls stayed on the porch. No one suggested they not watch the whipping. The slaves parted for Master Rice and the boys. Nkosi had the whip in hand, ready.

"Look at his back, Mister Rice, he's never tasted the whip before," Nkosi said. "Ten lashes will teach him a lesson he won't forget."

"He'll taste thirty," Master Rice said.

The gathered slaves gasped and murmured. Summer had seen what twenty lashes did to Lionel Winston's back two years ago. It was two weeks before he could even take on light duties again.

"The last ten will be mine," Master Rice said.

There were more gasps and Master Rice smiled cruelly. The slaves knew that Overseer Nkosi had a feel for what a slave could bear from the whip, and a knack for glancing blows and over-striking, where the tip of the whip would hit wood and not flesh. Master Rice laid the whip on full.

"This boy ran away from a good master. He stole property and time that didn't belong to him. He had been fed and clothed and given a dry place to sleep by Master White and he spit in his master's face. When are you all gonna learn your lesson? By rights I could hang this boy, or geld him, but I'm going to show him mercy. I bought him so that I could teach him his proper place. Why, if I had let Master White take him home he would have gotten fifty lashes."

That was a lie. No one loved the whip as much as Master Rice.

"I saved this boy's life by buying him, and I'm prepared to be even more merciful. This boy and the other runaway were gone for three weeks. They couldn't have done that without help. No one can hide from Blue Belly and Boomer for three weeks. You all know that. So, someone helped them and I have a right to know who."

Master Rice turned in a slow circle. One by one the slaves lowered their heads.

"Now I figure that those who helped them were mostly from Master White's farm, but maybe others helped them too. Maybe there was a conspiracy."

Summer inched behind her mother willingly now, pulling Rocky close. Master Rice was a smart man and saw things that others could not. Summer was afraid he already knew her small role in Kerry and Lonnie's escape.

"So here's my offer to this runaway. After Overseer Nkosi gives him the twenty, I'll give him a chance to come clean. For every name of a conspirator that he gives me I'll drop one lash. Hear how generous that is? He doesn't have to feel any of my lashes at all if only he tells the truth. Now isn't that fair?"

No one said anything.

"Isn't that fair?" he shouted.

"Yes, Master Rice," the slaves said in low voices.

"All right then, Overseer, you can begin," Master Rice said, handing him the whip.

Now Master Rice and his boys stepped to the side, giving Nkosi room to work. The whip was coiled in Nkosi's hand and now he dropped the coils, then shook the whip so that it laid out across the packed earth like a snake, ready to strike.

"You brought this on yourself," Nkosi said. "May God

forgive me for hurting another of His creations and may God give you strength."

Nkosi pulled back his arm and then snapped it forward. The whip struck Kerry's bare back at an angle, the tip striking the wooden crosspiece. Kerry moaned, his body stiffening. He gripped the crosspiece and pulled himself upright.

"I told you he was faking," Master Rice said, seeing the strength in the boy's arms.

"Maybe he should get another ten for lying," Wash said. "Faking is just the same as lying."

"Shut up, boy," Master Rice snapped. "He belongs to me, not you, and I already declared the punishment."

Now Nkosi delivered the lashes quickly, evenly spacing them. Half of these were glancing blows that got more post than back. Kerry screamed when the tenth blow tore open his flesh from the right shoulder to his left hip. He screamed again when the thirteenth wrapped around his waist, the tip coming all the way around to strike over his left kidney. He whimpered with each blow after that. By the twentieth lash, his back dripped blood from a dozen places.

"That's twenty," the overseer announced, coiling the whip.

"More like ten," Wash complained. "Half of those were love taps."

"Well then, I'll just have to show our overseer how to do it right," Master Rice said, holding out his hand for the whip.

"I just didn't want to cripple the boy," Overseer Nkosi said, handing over the whip. "He's no good to the master if he can't work."

"He's no good if he can't obey!" Master Rice said, uncoiling the whip.

"All right, boy, I know what you're thinking. You're thinking that you can take another ten lashes just because you took the first twenty. So you're thinking you won't have to tell me who helped you. I know that, and you know that, so I'm not even going to ask you to give me a name. Not yet. First you get a taste of the future."

Now Master Rice walked a few paces from Kerry, reared

back and stepped into the blow. The slap of the whip on Kerry's back was loud and sharp, and blood sprayed in every direction. Kerry screamed, wobbled at the knees, then slumped, hanging by his bonds.

"Look, Papa, he wet himself," one of the younger sons said.

The boys laughed. Master Rice smiled.

"He'll do more than that before we're done here," Master Rice said.

"Now, boy, do you want more of that, or are you going to give me a name? Who helped you escape?"

Kerry didn't answer.

"Maybe he's unconscious," Wash suggested.

Without another word, Master Rice struck Kerry another powerful blow. Kerry's body convulsed. Blood streamed down his back. Summer turned away, tears in her eyes. Rocky was crying so she picked him up, letting him bury his face in her shoulder.

"Guess I was wrong," Wash said. "He's conscious all right!"

Master Rice and the boys laughed.

"Give me a name!" Master Rice said.

"No one helped me," Kerry said in a whisper.

Another blow. Kerry's body convulsed again. Now he was crying audibly.

"Give me a name," Rice repeated.

"It was just me," Kerry managed to say.

"You and that other boy," Master Rice said. "Did you forget about him? He's getting the same as you right now."

Another lash. Kerry screamed, twisted, and then hung limp, crying loudly.

"A name?" Master Rice demanded.

No response. Another lash. And another. Kerry took every strike and never gave up a name. He passed out after Master Rice's seventh lash. Master Rice gave him the last three anyway.

"Cut him down, then chain him in the old barn."

Overseer Nkosi directed the slaves, who hurried to the

boy. Careful not to touch his back, they carried him to the old barn. Patrick, one of the field hands, hurried for his medical kit. Patrick had been a medic in the army before he was enslaved. Master Rice didn't like slaves showing off their education but tolerated Patrick's because he helped keep the slaves working.

Overseer Nkosi directed everyone back to work. Summer had kitchen duties, since the master would want a hot breakfast. She went to work, helping Cook, setting the table and serving food. On one trip to the table she saw Malcolm, who was twelve, with his arms stretched out, imitating Kerry flopping, jerking, and crying.

"Oooh, I peed my pants," Malcolm said.

They laughed hard at that, Master Rice slapping the table, tears running from his eyes. Before she hurried out, Summer noticed that Montiel—only a year younger than Wash— wasn't laughing. Montiel was cut from different cloth than his father and brothers.

That night Summer's mother went into labor and Lucy, Summer, and Patrick tended to her. She gave birth the next morning to a baby girl. The joy they all shared was short-lived. Lucy fell quiet as she wiped the baby clean with a damp cloth. When she finished, Patrick gently examined the baby, checking fingers, toes, ears and eyes. Summer realized the baby's skin was milk white and her eyes were blue.

"Casey, your baby's eyes are blue," Lucy said, worried.

"It's too soon to tell eye color," Patrick said. "They're not fully pigmented yet."

"Look at her skin—this baby's white," Lucy said.

"Let me hold her," Summer's mother whispered, reaching out.

Lucy wrapped the baby in a small blanket and then handed her to her mother.

Patrick and Lucy exchanged worried looks. Summer understood. Master Rice considered Cassandra Lund his personal property in every way. He expected her babies to be his too.

"There's no way to be sure, isn't that right, Patrick? Skins come in all colors. Eyes too."

"Yes, sure," Patrick said too quickly. "Master Rice doesn't pay any attention to slave babies anyway."

"She's such a pretty baby," Summer's mother cooed.

"What's her name, Casey?" Lucy asked.

"Hope."

Patrick and Lucy exchanged looks, clearly disapproving.

"It's a good name. Pretty," Summer said, going to look at her new baby sister.

She was red, wrinkled, and pot bellied, but quiet—the best kind of slave baby. The quiet children took less abuse. Hope was looking around now, studying the flickering lantern flame. Summer studied her eyes. They were so light she could not imagine them turning brown. Now she wondered who the father was. She thought of the blue-eyed slaves first, but knew even men with brown eyes could father blue-eyed babies if there are blue-eyed relatives in their family—there were none in Master Rice's family. The only man she could rule out for sure was Patrick, since he had secretly married Lucy. It did not matter, Summer would love her new sister until the day she ran away from Master Rice.

"How's Kerry?" Summer asked as Patrick finished cleaning up.

"He's in bad shape," Patrick said honestly.

He kept his voice low, letting Summer's mother dote on her new baby. Lucy and Summer moved close to get the whispered details.

"He was cut to the bone in places and not by Nkosi. Rice did most of the damage. But the worst might be what they did to him before they dragged him here. He's got blood in his urine and maybe some in his lungs. Back on Earth I could get an X-ray and see what had happened inside, but Master Rice would have to take him into New Jerusalem for tests, and you know he won't do that."

"Will he die?" Summer asked.

"Summer, I don't know," Patrick said.

"He never gave any names, did he?" Lucy asked hopefully.

"Not one," Patrick said.

Every day after that Summer asked about Kerry, but Overseer Nkosi would say nothing except "He's alive," and Patrick would talk only about how his wounds were healing. For three days Kerry ran a fever, but it turned out to be "pop fever," which was common on America but unknown on Earth. Some of the older slaves thought pop fever was good for healing—something about the high body temperature killing bacteria—but Patrick insisted any fever was a sign something was wrong. Summer did not know who was right, but once when Rocky was sick with something Patrick couldn't name, Rocky came down with pop fever and was almost as good as new three days later when the fever broke. Soon, Summer was so busy with the harvest, she didn't have time to worry about Kerry.

Harvest came in regular waves, with one crop washing over the next, keeping everyone busy. There were apples to pick, potatoes to dig, and peaches, cherries, and other fruit to harvest and can. Field hands were busy cutting and baling hay and other grasses and feed for livestock. Both barns were slowly filling. The barrels in the fruit cellars were filled one by one and then stacked systematically according to Cook's firm direction. Cook insisted on this and Summer agreed since she was usually the one who had to crawl around in the cold, musty cellars looking for misplaced pears or plums.

Soon Master Rice's slaves would be sent to work the neighbor's farms, helping with their harvests. Only Master Rice had enough slaves to harvest his own land. It was a point of pride with Master Rice, but Summer had heard talk that other farmers thought it arrogant or even foolish, since he was feeding and housing more slaves than he needed—except at harvest time.

Every morning Summer hoped to see Kerry out and about, and tucked part of her breakfast into a pocket. She knew that Master Rice would have Kerry on starvation rations. On each of those days she ended up throwing the food to the hogs. Finally, on the day they gleaned the orchards for hog feed, she arranged to see Kerry herself. Picking up bruised and rotting fruit was one of her least favorite jobs, but it gave her the chance to volunteer to put the picking bags away. Overseer Nkosi agreed, giving her a warning look as she hurried to the old barn.

Kerry was still chained to the wall and wore no shirt, despite the cool days and cold nights. He was sitting cross-legged, head slumped, as if in prayer, a blanket draped loosely over his shoulders. Now that she saw for herself that he was alive, she tiptoed to the picking bin and stuffed the bags inside, then closed the lid quietly. When she turned he was looking at her. When he recognized her he smiled.

"I thought those were your chicken legs, Summer."

Summer didn't mind the mild insult but now she had nothing to say—nothing intelligent.

"Hi, Kerry," she managed.

Now he straightened, showing more of his chest. He had no body fat and his ribs showed clearly. Only house slaves ever got fat, but Kerry was half-starved, even for a slave. She could see where the tip of the whip had wrapped around his chest, leaving purple stripes along his sides. One ugly line reached up his cheek nearly to his eye.

"I brought you something," Summer said, pulling an apple from her pocket and walking forward slowly.

"Thanks, Summer," Kerry said, taking the apple and eating voraciously. "Don't worry, I'll eat the core too so there won't be any evidence."

Up close the wounds on his chest and face looked deep and painful, and her expression showed her feelings.

"It doesn't hurt so bad anymore," Kerry said. "Patrick gives me something to drink that helps with the pain."

"Thank you for not telling on me," Summer said suddenly. "Master Rice would have stopped the whipping if you had told him what I had done."

Kerry stopped eating, and looked at her with an intensity that made her uncomfortable.

"Summer, I wouldn't give you up to a master, no matter what they did to me. Besides, you didn't do so much. Mostly it was me and Lonnie all by ourselves."

"You were gone so long I thought you had made it. I hoped I'd never see you again."

"Well, thanks," Kerry said, feigning hurt feelings.

"You know what I mean."

Kerry smiled.

"We could have made it, except for Lonnie. He likes to eat too much."

Kerry laughed, and Summer joined him although she only half understood.

"We found a cave no one had ever seen before. It was far enough away so no one would see smoke from a fire. The plan was to winter in the cave, and sneak back a couple of times to steal some seed. Then come spring we would find a better spot farther away. There are still abandoned cabins and ranches out there. If we could get a crop going, we wouldn't need to come back at all."

"It sounds like a grand idea," Summer said, enthralled by the lure of freedom.

"Except for Lonnie's stomach it might have worked. He ate our supplies faster than we could snare game. We weren't putting away any stores for winter, so we had no choice but to sneak back to steal more supplies. We got some too, from Master Winter's farm but he let his dogs loose on our trail and tracked us to a creek we used to ditch the dogs. The next day the masters all showed up and Master Rice brought Boomer. Guess old Blue Belly wasn't up to it."

Kerry laughed at the trick he had pulled on Blue Belly.

"That dog could track a snowflake in a blizzard and Boomer's nearly as good. Boomer picked up our trail and tracked us right to the cave. We heard them coming and took off, but they ran us down by nightfall."

"What happened to Lonnie?"

"Master White took him. He was gonna take me too, but then Master Rice offered him Boomer."

"You should be proud," Summer said.

"Proud?" Kerry asked, puzzled.

"Master Rice has never met a slave before he thought was worth as much as a good tracking dog."

Kerry smiled wide, wincing when his smile threatened to split the cut on his face.

"I need to go," Summer said, turning.

"Summer," Kerry said as she reached the door. "I meant what I said about not giving Master Rice any names. And it goes double for your name."

Summer smiled, and then left the barn, thinking those were the sweetest words she had ever heard.

10

GRANDMA'S RULE

Puff Tree Forest
First Continent
AUTUMN, PLANET AMERICA

The last crop of the season was the hardest to harvest and took the most slaves. The first settlers on America had brought many plants and animals with them to make life easier, but many of those crops only grew in warmer climates. When the Fellowship fled America, they took with them the only transportation system capable of reaching distant regions of the planet. Now, Grandma's people were cut off from vital resources. The crop they missed the most was cotton. Wool was good for winter clothes, but summer demanded lighter clothing. The answer to their need was a forest about as far distant from New Jerusalem and its surrounding farms as anyone dared to travel.

In this forest, the trees had a puffy bark that would slowly swell as fall advanced. Just before the first snow, the bark could be stripped away and the fiber underneath ripped from the tree. The washed and bleached fibers could then be dyed, spun, and woven, just like cotton, creating a soft fabric that was slightly elastic. Summer's mother preferred it to wool for weaving.

It drizzled the day they left for the puff tree harvest. The slaves were packed in open wagons, huddled under tarps to keep dry. A skeleton crew stayed behind to tend the farm. Even the young children came along, assigned to carrying water and picking up scraps. With a baby too young to travel, Summer's mother stayed home this year. Summer hugged her mother goodbye, and then kissed Hope's forehead. Since Hope's birth, Master Rice had not come on Saturday nights, inflicting himself on Lucy instead. It was a guilty respite for the Lund family. Master Rice had paid no attention to the baby so far, not even to ask whether it was a boy or girl. But as Summer kissed Hope goodbye she could see her eyes would always be blue.

They spent the night at the Wilson farm; slaves from all over the region already camped, waiting for the long trek out to the Puff Tree Forest. New Jerusalem was the hub for the farms, which surrounded the city in all directions. Master Rice's farm sat on the eastern side of New Jerusalem, its farthest boundary the marker between civilization and the rest of the unexplored continent. On the west the farms spread toward the coast, which was a hundred miles distant. Few had ever seen the coast, although Summer once heard that a couple of slaves tried to float on a raft down the Pax River all the way to the ocean. They had capsized at the first rapids, one drowning. No one had ever tried to escape that way again.

Lucy and the other slaves of her generation greeted western slaves warmly, knowing them from when they were soldiers. There were new children to be introduced, and older ones about whom to exclaim, "My, how that child's grown." Master Rice seldom took his slaves to church, let alone town, so they were the center of attention. The masters were preoccupied with their own socializing, and left the slaves alone, so there was a party mood and much laughing and joking. With the harvests in, and food plentiful, there was much to eat. They finished the day around a bonfire, singing.

In the morning, they caravaned out to the Puff Tree Forest. The trek was all uphill, since the trees only grew in the foothills of the mountains. The temperature seemed to drop with each step up the mountains. There were frequent stops for fallen trees to be cleared from the seldom-used road. By the end of the day, though, they were high in the hills where the puff trees grew. Summer had never seen puff trees except at harvest, so she had never experienced them in full bloom. Their upper limbs were bare now, just a mass of jumbled twigs. She had heard that in summer they were covered with clusters of green leaves that slowly turned gold as fall approached. Summer had seen the patches of gold on the distant hills.

They camped for the night, getting things ready for harvesting the next day. Then they went to bed early, tarps spread between trees to keep rain off, and the slaves huddled together under blankets. Fires were kept burning but did little to warm them.

At dawn the overseers woke the slaves, shouting orders. Breakfast was a cold sandwich, a glass of milk, and an apple. Then it was off to work. Trees invading the Puff Tree Forest were culled. When finished with this chore, these hands would start felling the evergreens on either side, making room for more puff trees. Over two decades they had tripled the acreage of puff trees.

Cutters went in first, using razor sharp, two-foot curved blades to slice through the tough bark at ground level and then again as high as they could reach. Then they would slice from the high cut to the low, making six-foot panels that another person would pull away. The panels were collected and carried back to camp. Puff boards could be soaked in water and then flattened, and were used to make furniture and cover walls. They were even laminated to make large wooden sheets.

After the panels were removed, the pullers came next—
Summer's job. Exposed fibers were ripped from the tree.
Pullers reached high, pulling down the length of the tree. The
longer the fibers, the more useful they were, so the pulls were
long and slow. This was the second year Summer worked as a
puller, and she remembered how she ached the first morning
after a day's work. It would be the same tomorrow.

The work soon warmed her and she got into a rhythm,
pulling, ripping, and stuffing the fiber into a bag held by one
of the older children. When that bag was full the slave child
dragged it back to the camp to be emptied. As they worked
their way further from camp, the work of the baggers got
harder and harder. At camp, combers were at work straight-
ening and then rolling the fiber, getting it ready for transport
to New Jerusalem where Grandma Jones would oversee the
dividing of the crop.

It drizzled for an hour just before lunch, an irritating cold
rain. Everyone was soaked at mealtime, complaining there
wasn't anything hot to drink and no fires to warm themselves by. The crack of a whip shut everyone up. Summer
shivered through lunch, anxious to get back to work so she
could get warm. As soon as she could, she hurried back,
looking for freshly cut trees. Cutters were already at work
and she watched them slice rings high and low on the trees,
and then cut the long strips. They made it look easy, but the
men were strong and the knives sharp. As one cutter worked
around the tree, cutting panels, she noticed the last cut was
close to the first, creating a six foot long board only a few
inches wide. Looking at it, she remembered Lucy's story
about skiing on boards.

When the cutter moved on to a new tree, Summer stepped
to the tree and worked her fingers into the slit and pulled on
the board, working it free, and dropping it on the ground.
Now she knelt and pulled away much of the white fiber stuck
to the underside of the board. Then she stood and put one
foot on it, trying to imagine how a board that thin could keep
her on top of the snow. It didn't make sense to her, but the

slaves from Earth seemed to know about things like this. Now Summer hurried from tree to tree, looking for a similar size board. Finding one, she pulled it free. The two boards were almost exactly the same length, probably cut by the same man.

The other slaves were trickling up the hill now, and Summer picked up her two boards and walked nonchalantly past them back to the wagons. She found one of Master Rice's wagons, and looked for a place to hide the boards. She was leaning over the edge when she heard Overseer Nkosi's voice.

"What you got there, Summer?"

Overseer Nkosi was coming, eyeing her suspiciously.

"They're scraps, Overseer. I wasn't stealing them."

Overseer Nkosi took one of the boards and looked it over.

"They're too narrow to be good for anything. What use are they to you?"

"I thought maybe I could make shelves," Summer said.

"This narrow? I can get you something better."

"For spools, Overseer," Summer said.

Nkosi thought for a moment.

"Well, throw them in the back then and get to work. If Master Rice's slaves don't make their quota even you will get a taste of the whip."

Summer hurried back to work and spent the afternoon in enthusiastic labor, dreaming of gliding across the snow to freedom.

They worked three more days in the Puff Tree Forest, and each morning Summer had to work out the muscle aches from the day before. By then the wagons were fully loaded, leaving room for only the smallest children. Intermittent rains accompanied them for the three-day walk to New Jerusalem. Everyone was tired, but excited, since it was time for the harvest party that marked the end of every season. Only the unlucky were still on the farms and would miss the celebration.

In the center of town, a large tent had been set up where the slaves would eat and worship. The huge new church—the largest building on the planet—was for the masters and their families. The slaves delivered the crop to the co-op warehouses, which soon were filled to bursting. Jim Wish, president of the co-op, directed the tally, assisted by an old slave named Kent Thorpe. Slaves distrusted Thorpe, since he worked so enthusiastically with the masters. Master Rice had purchased Thorpe five years ago, but let him live in New Jerusalem to keep watch over the master's interests. Summer had heard her mother say to Lucy that it was like asking a fox to watch the chickens. With a fringe of long gray locks and a pinched face, the slightly bent and crooked man made small children shy away. Standing on the loading platform, Thorpe's eyes were busy, scanning the wagons, estimating the harvest, and keeping a tally sheet that would be checked later against the official list. No other masters had slaves doing their own tally; however, masters could inspect the grain silos and warehouses anytime they wished. Few exercised that right.

When the harvest was unloaded, the slaves were herded down the main street of New Jerusalem—the only paved street on the planet. The boardwalks were crowded with well-dressed mistresses and their children, watching the slaves come in. Younger slave children waved to friends on the boardwalk. If the children of masters waved back, their mother, or the house slave who worked as a nanny, slapped their hands. Summer hated this part of the harvest tradition: being gawked at by the families of the masters.

The masters—who were all men—and their wives were already gathered in front of the old church, the oldest building on America. Grandma Jones sat in her rocker in the middle, rows of chairs on either side. Legend had it that this was the way Grandma Jones greeted the soldiers who had become the first slaves. Grandma Jones rocked slowly, watching the slaves herded forward to sit cross-legged at her feet. Grandma's short, white hair contrasted sharply with her dark skin. Grandma was rumored to be a hundred years old, but Summer's mother pooh-poohed such talk. Still, Summer guessed she was the oldest person on the planet.

Slaves filled the town square and spread into side streets.

The slave population was outgrowing its traditional bounds and there were rumors that the masters were worried about how many slaves there were getting to be.

The masters were all black, of course, and once the slaves had been all white, with a few Asians in the mix. The second generation of slaves came in a variety of hues. The third generation was even more racially varied, although much lighter than the masters and their families.

Summer sat between Nicole and Lucy, whose boys were somewhere on the periphery, probably getting into mischief. The slaves slowly settled down, exhausted from three days of harvesting puff trees fiber, followed by three days of walking. Smoke from the barbecue pits drifted above the church, the aroma of roasted meats, vegetables, and fruits filling the square. Now Grandma Jones stood and those gathered quickly quieted. In her right hand Grandma held an open Bible. Grandma Jones spoke in a clear, firm voice, despite her age.

"Your masters tell me you have been good and faithful servants," Grandma Jones said.

It was the ritual beginning of the harvest feast and the slaves responded as they had been trained, clapping and cheering.

"In Ephesians 6:5–8 we are told 'Slaves, obey your earthly masters with respect and fear, and with sincerity of heart, just as you would obey Christ. Obey them not only to win their favor when their eye is on you, but like slaves of Christ, doing the will of God from your heart. Serve wholeheartedly, as if you were serving the Lord, not men, because you know that the Lord will reward everyone for whatever good he does, whether he is slave or free.'"

Grandma Jones, ruler of planet America, recited the passage from memory, without looking at the worn Bible in her hand.

"God is good," Grandma Jones said.

"All the time," the slaves repeated in unison.

"All the time," Grandma Jones said.

"God is good," the slaves replied.

"But God doesn't just speak to the slave. God has a message for the master as well. In Ephesians 6:9, God clearly lays out the responsibility of the master too. 'And masters, treat your slaves in the same way. Do not threaten them, since you know that he who is both their Master and yours is in heaven, and there is no favoritism with him.' "

Again, she spoke from memory, having delivered the same talk every year for two decades. Now she spoke to the ruling families gathered to her right and left.

"God is good," Grandma Jones said.

"All the time," came the reply of the masters and spouses.

"All the time."

"God is good."

"Masters and slaves, your teamwork has brought us another bumper crop."

Both masters and slaves applauded.

"Our numbers have increased, our farmable land grown by seven percent, our livestock are healthy and numerous."

"Glory be to God," slaves and masters said.

Ever since Summer could remember, Grandma Jones had reported good news at the harvest, although she could remember at least one hungry winter.

"Master or slave, makes no difference in the eyes of the Lord. Each has his or her place in this life, but there will be no difference when we meet Jesus in the clouds. So we must, by commandment, do our work with enthusiasm, glorifying God through hard work and sacrifice. No slave should shirk his or her duty and no master should abuse a slave."

Summer squirmed, knowing what was coming.

"To that end, to honor the commandments that God has given us, I ask you slaves, has any master mistreated you? Speak now and do not fear retribution for I offer you my protection."

Summer squirmed again, struggling to control herself. She wanted to jump up and yell out what happened on Master Rice's farm on Saturday nights, to tell about a young runaway nearly whipped to death, to take Grandma Jones to Master Rice's farm and show her the blood on the whipping post. Most of all she wanted to scream out a question: "Just why do you think so many white slaves give birth to black babies?" She rocked sideways, wrestling with her conscience. Suddenly, Lucy's hand whipped out, gripping her thigh and holding her down.

"Don't even think about it," Lucy whispered.

"I wasn't going to," Summer said, unsure of whether she would have given in to her conscience.

"Glory be to God," Grandma Jones said a few seconds later.

"Amen," the slaves and masters said.

Now Grandma Jones sat and the service began. There was singing, then preaching followed by an altar call. A dozen slaves went forward, kneeling in the front, being prayed over by Pastor Wills and his deacons. They would be baptized in the morning, then sent back to their masters' farms, still slaves, but now Christian slaves. No masters or their families came forward—they would never humble themselves in front of slaves.

The service ended with more singing and then it was time to eat. The masters and their families went first, followed by hired hands, tradesmen, and other free people, and then the slaves. The Gathering was the one time during the year when the slaves and masters ate the same food. Slaves dished out slices of beef or pork, or the native honey birds that were popular eating. There were roasted potatoes, yellow root, ears of corn, thick sliced bread, and a slice of apple or sourberry pie for everyone. More was cooked than could be eaten, so there would be seconds—a rare treat for some slaves. Summer accepted slices of honey bird, a little bit of the yellow root, and a slice of sourberry pie. She put two slices of bread in her pocket. Rocky found her before she finished eating, and she scraped the pie off her plate and onto his.

That night there were two parties. One party was in the big church, for the free people, and the other was under the big tent, for the slaves. Three fiddlers and a couple of guitar players took turns playing while the slaves danced.

There was no caller, but the dances resembled square dancing, with most couples dancing in small groups. Summer danced too, although no boys asked her to partner with them. Instead, she gathered a few of the younger children, mostly girls, into a group and danced in a loose circle. Nicole abandoned her when Melvin came through the crowd, and with a gap-toothed sheepish grin, Melvin asked Nicole to dance. Eventually, Summer lost track of them. Lucy danced with Patrick, and then, like Nicole, disappeared. Summer was happy for them, but sad for herself, as the boys her age and older passed her by.

Only a few cooks were roused early the next morning, the masters and their families sleeping late as well. Breakfast was served buffet style, the trays replenished regularly through midmorning. Summer ignored the eggs, bacon, sausage, pancakes, and mush, and took an apple and a glass of berry juice and then hurried off to help Lucy with the trading. Tables were set up in rows through the town square. Lucy was already there, directing the setup of Master Rice's goods—all slave made or grown. Summer carefully unpacked a year of her mother's labor. There were yards of intricately woven fabrics, and tablecloths, and clothes cut and sewn from her mother's cloth. There were smaller goods too: shawls, napkins, and table runners, all made from ends and scraps. There was even some of Summer's work: crocheted dolls and knitted scarves. They weren't as intricate as her mother's, but children liked them. House slaves, and city slaves, were already scouting out the goods, ready to hurry back to report to their masters about the wares. Early bargainers would get the best selection, late arrivers the best bargains. Several were watching Lucy and Summer unpack their goods. Summer was proud that her mother's work was highly prized among the masters and their families.

In addition to woven goods, Master Rice offered fancy wrought iron weathervanes, lightning rods, doorknockers, nails, spikes, and hand tools, hammered out by the best blacksmith on the planet. There were stacks of canned fruit too, and a few hard-to-get vegetables—Cook directed

Nicole in setting up the display. Down at the stables, the master had livestock to trade or sell and at the storage barns, seed, grain, and feed. It had been a good season, so even after the community tithe there would be plenty to trade. By Grandma's Rule, Master Rice would have to accept money for goods, but like most farmers on America, he preferred to trade, not trusting Grandma's "funny money" as he called it. Since farmers grew enough to feed their families and slaves, they did not need money to buy food. Craftsmen and tradesmen in New Jerusalem relied on money, but even they would trade when possible. Rice had directed Lucy to charge a premium if someone insisted on using money.

Lucy and Cook handled the negotiation, speaking deferentially and apologetically to the free people who came to trade or buy, and arguing enthusiastically with slaves sent by their masters. Lucy and Cook were good traders, and Summer thought they got the best of every bargain, accumulating new flatware for the mistress, a desk chair for the master, shoes for each of the master's children—that meant hand-me-downs for the slave children—a promissory note for fifty cabbage starts in the spring, corn meal, baking soda, baking powder, bonnets for each of the master's girls, and new leather hats for each of the boys. Elsewhere, the master and the mistress were doing their own trading; occasionally sending slaves back for trade goods. There was a pile of money too, but not as much as most of those offering goods.

Lunch was brought to their tables so they would not have to take a break, the negotiating nonstop now. Occasionally a master or a tradesman would get angry. Lucy and Cook would become even more apologetic, secretly signaling one of the slave children who served as runners to go get Overseer Nkosi, who was never far away. As a free man himself, he could return curse for curse and stand toe to toe without fear of reprisal. Arguments were quickly settled when Nkosi took charge.

In late afternoon, Summer was released to do her own trading. She had a few dolls and scarves of her own to trade. By Grandma's Rule, any work done after nine at night belonged to the slaves. Slaves were forbidden to have money, so getting trades to come out even was difficult. Summer had Christmas gifts in mind for her family, trading for a new pair of scissors, and scented lotion for her mother's calloused hands, a stacking toy made out of polished box nut shells for Hope, and a slingshot for Rocky. Slaves weren't allowed to own weapons, but she found the slingshot on a table loaded with toys. She traded her last scarf for three fishhooks. As dusk approached, she lingered near a table of books for a long time, reading the titles, wishing she had more to read than just her Bible. She left when an overseer showed up, catching her staring at the books. Hurrying away, she reviewed the list of items she would take when she ran away, wondering if a book was a luxury she could afford.

11

GRANDMA JONES

New Jerusalem
First Continent
AUTUMN, PLANET AMERICA

Grandma Jones watched the slaves herded into the square for evening worship. There were so many, now, the second generation with children of their own. She could pick out the original slaves, and knew most of their names. They had come as soldiers, ready to take control of her town and her people. But Grandma would not live under the thumb of anyone again and had turned the tables on them. However, two decades later Grandma wrestled with her conscience, but if there was another way twenty years of sleepless nights had not revealed it to her.

Growing up in the most powerful country on Earth meant

little to a black woman from the inner city. Watching two generations of her family lose hope, and then dignity, nearly drained away her faith. Grandma Jones lost one son to a junkie's gun, and then watched a daughter sink into a cesspool of drugs. Seeing nothing but that same road in front of her granddaughter pushed Grandma to contact Reverend Shepherd, asking him to take her and her people away to a new life. Through God's mercy, Shepherd had agreed, and her people found their way to planet America. At first life was everything she expected; however, they were still dependent on the Fellowship for supplies and transportation, and some of the old feelings of inferiority persisted. So when the Fellowship fled planet America, she took the opportunity to keep the planet for her people. She prayed that Shepherd was wrong, and that soldiers from Earth would not come to steal the planet from them, but they did come. So, she had made the hardest decision of her life and made them slaves.

Now the slaves were healthy, hardy people, toned by hard work, and compliant, respectful workers. Greeting friends and family, the slaves smiled, shook hands, hugged, and joked. The community prospered, there was order and security, and the slaves were a happy people. Seeing three generations of slaves, smiling and laughing, relieved some of Grandma's guilt. Slavery had set her people back a century, and she would not have inflicted that on anyone if there had been a better choice. Now, two decades later, the annual Gatherings allowed her to check on the slaves, and to assuage her guilty conscience. As a whole, the slaves were well treated, although not all had good masters.

Scanning the slave children she could see many of mixed race. Love would account for some of those children, but the power difference between slave and master explained most. Looking over the masters seated on either side of her, she saw a wide range of complexions, telling a similar story for the African-Americans who had settled America. While the exploitation of female slaves pained her, there were other cruelties visited on slaves. Jesse Rice, seated to her right, was one of the worst offenders, each year lowering the bar for the treatment of slaves. It hurt Grandma to know there were far too many of her people willing to follow Jesse's lead. Jesse's personal magnetism accounted for some of his influence, but most came from the fact that he was Grandma Jones's son-in-law.

Jesse Rice married Francine Jones, but the Fancy who caught his eye was not the Fancy who left Earth. Addicted to drugs, Fancy was dragged onto the shuttle that took her to the spaceship *Crucifixion* for the trip to planet America. During the five-month voyage, she had kicked her habit, slowly and painfully. Gradually, the old Fancy emerged, the Fancy Grandma Jones remembered her little girl to be. Pretty, funny, warm, and curious. As a child, Fancy wanted to be an artist, and her teachers in school praised her abilities. One of her sixth grade drawings won an award at the school art show. With nothing more potent than cold medicine on the long voyage, Fancy's body cleansed itself of the poisons that imprisoned her. Slowly, Fancy broke free of her addiction. She became civil again, began to socialize, and took an interest in her personal appearance. With newly trimmed hair, and a little makeup, Fancy's self-confidence grew and she emerged from her compartment on *Crucifixion* as a new woman. Bright and personable, she quickly became popular. Her old interest in art came back and she began to draw again with other artists, and then to model for men who drew flattering portraits of her. She could have had any of those young artists, but they were too conventional, too tame. Always attracted to dangerous men, she had found Jesse Rice, an ex-con, who converted to Islam in prison, and then back to Christianity when released. Jesse's mother swore to Grandma Jones her boy was a Christian once and for all, but Grandma came to understand that Jesse used religion to get what he wanted, just like he used his connection to Grandma.

Fancy sat next to Jesse, watching the slaves. Grandma did not have to smell her breath to know she had been drinking. Her dull eyes, slurred speech, and clumsy walk spoke volumes. Liquor was forbidden, but Grandma knew that rule was routinely flaunted. Jesse and Fancy regularly imbibed, making enforcement of the rule nearly impossible. After all, the others reasoned, if it was okay for Grandma Jones's daughter and son-in-law, then it was okay for everyone else. The same reasoning led to the whipping and maiming of slaves.

Life for the slaves was tolerable now, but Grandma Jones feared for their future. Although younger than most people knew, Grandma Jones was feeling her years, and without the high-tech medicine of Earth, there would be no heart-bypass operation, kidney transplant, pacemaker, or gene therapy. The first serious illness she contracted would kill her, leaving a power vacuum that Jesse was ready to step into. Grandma had to prevent that, while she still had the power. Giving the Council of Masters more power was the first step, but she needed to do more, and do it soon.

"You're frowning, Selma," Teresa whispered in Grandma's ear.

A friend through thick and thin, Teresa White was the first person Grandma had told of her idea of moving to another planet. Teresa had laughed in her face, then listened, and then believed. She had been an ally and counselor ever since.

"When you frown, you scare everyone, especially the slaves," Teresa said.

Grandma forced a smile. After all, everyone enjoyed the annual Gathering. It was planet America's equivalent of a county fair. Earlier that day, walking among the trading stalls, Grandma had been pleased by the quality and variety of products. There had been several years of bounty now, but Grandma's spiritual gift seemed to be the ability to find a dark cloud to go with every silver lining. The years of bounty led her to worry that her people would take them for granted, and not plan for the years of want that would surely follow.

To Grandma's right, one of the original slaves appeared, whispering to Jesse. It was Kent Thorpe. Thorpe was an un-attractive man, ill-used by Father Time. With almost no neck, a bald pate, and a pinched face, Grandma could not picture Kent Thorpe as attractive, even as a young man. A fringe of long gray hair hung almost to his shoulders, the gray locks curling at the tips. Thorpe's hunched shoulders twisted a little, making him lean slightly to the right. Grandma had seen slaves misshapen like Thorpe, but from beatings. To Grandma's knowledge, Thorpe had avoided whippings, beatings, and even slaps. From the beginning of his enslavement, Thorpe had been obsequious and conniving, accumulating inordinate power. Years ago, ownership of Thorpe had transferred to Jesse, and now Thorpe worked behind the scenes of Jesse's enterprises.

Thorpe had been part of the leadership core of the invaders. Colonel Watson, who commanded the ill-fated mission, suffered a heart attack while logging, just two years after becoming a slave. The other officers had eventually settled into their new lives, when they understood the hopelessness of escape—there was nowhere to go. Another of the invaders, Meaghan Slater, formerly the leader of a feminist movement on Earth, had suffered mightily for her arrogance, passed from master to master, her spirit unbreakable. Then Jesse purchased her for next to nothing, taking great pleasure in whipping her into submission. The worst of the original slaves, however, was known only as Mr. Fry. A troublemaker from the start, he stirred up trouble including two revolts that ended in the public whipping of a dozen slaves. A year after the last revolt, Fry strangled a master's son, and fled on a stolen horse. Jesse Rice led the hunt for the runaway slave, tracking him down two days later and bringing him back alive—mostly alive. Jesse threw Fry at Grandma's feet, his first challenge to her authority. The community gathered, and many called for Fry's execution. Grandma ordered the slaves herded into the village square, the slaves huddled together, talking in whispers, afraid of the repercussions of a slave killing a master.

Bloodied, but not broken, Fry struggled to his feet. Jesse knocked him back to his knees. With the people and slaves gathered, Grandma Jones's leadership was tested. Grandma exercised complete authority, running her community as a benevolent autocrat. However, her power flowed from her vision of a new life, and God's help in fulfilling the promise of a new life. With her vision fulfilled, her power depended on maintaining a sense of justice. Unlike earthly kings and queens, she had no genetic claim to leadership, and she refused to declare a "divine right" to rule. Noting her hesitation, Jesse taunted her.

"The Bible says, 'life for life, eye for eye, tooth for tooth,' " Jesse said.

A hush fell over the town square, all eyes on Grandma, who rocked in her chair on the porch of the church.

Grandma bristled at Jesse's partial quotation from Deuteronomy. She wanted to retort with Jesus' revision, where he held his followers to a higher standard and asked them to love their enemies and turn the other cheek when offended. She kept these thoughts to herself. This was the first serious crime in their new community, and she could not allow the seed of murder to take root.

"Slave Fry, for the crimes of running away from a lawful master, horse theft, and murder, I sentence you to be hanged. You have one hour to make peace with God. You had best spend that time repenting your sins, begging God to forgive you, and asking Jesus into your heart. How you use your last hour of life will determine how you spend eternity."

Fry's cursing that day was so foul, Grandma had him gagged so the children would not learn words unused in the community. Fry was swinging from a stout limb an hour later. The hanging confirmed Grandma Jones's authority and power. The people accepted her authority and her decisions, as if she were one of the biblical judges of Israel. Like Israel, however, the system was fragile, depending on human vessels. When Grandma Jones died, someone else would take her place. Jesse had positioned himself for ascension to power, but Grandma Jones knew there was no love for Jesus in Jesse's heart, only the love of power and a penchant for cruelty. She could not let Jesse become the judge of this community.

"Are you going to go through with it?" Theresa asked, keeping her voice low.

"It has to be done."

"Jesse's not going to like it," Teresa whispered.

"It's because of Jesse I've got to do it."

With a pat on her shoulder, Teresa leaned back.

"This should be fun," Teresa said. "And I get to watch it all from the sidelines."

12

WORSHIP

New Jerusalem
First Continent
AUTUMN, PLANET AMERICA

The last evening of the Gathering, there was a final worship, followed by one more speech by Grandma Jones. Summer sat with Lucy, intensely curious. This was the time when Grandma announced any new rules that the people were to live by. Grandma's Rules could not be ignored by anyone, not even a master. Grandma Jones normally decided on new rules after listening to the Council of Masters discuss proposals. Whenever the masters met, rumors about abolishing slavery or banning whippings swept the slave community. This year Summer had heard no rumors.

They gathered as before, but this time the square was lit with torches and lanterns. Pastor Wills finished the service by asking God to bless their labors in the coming year and then it was time for Grandma's Rules.

"Sometimes we make rules and those rules help the community," Grandma began. "Many of the rules about sanitation do just that. Sometimes we make a rule and it ends up in ways we didn't intend."

Grandma Jones liked to use "we," but she had absolute authority. It was she who had enacted slavery in the first place.

"Years ago we made the rule that slaves could keep any product of their labor that they produced on their own time, and that rule worked well for a while."

There was worried murmuring among the slaves. The free time rule had allowed slaves to earn for themselves what their master would not give them. It sounded like she was about to take it away.

"Now we find that slaves aren't just using their after-nine time to produce goods, but Sundays too. Sunday is the Lord's Day and is to be used for rest and worship."

Sundays were still workdays for slaves, but only to do routine chores like tending the stock, and repairing tools and machines, not the hard labor of fieldwork.

"We also find that too many slaves and free people are working too many hours. The Lord has blessed us with bumper crops in the last few years, and we can now afford to make a new rule. From this day forward, each slave will have one half day a week free from labor."

Slaves erupted in cheers, but not Master Rice's slaves. Summer searched for his face. He was furious, his face the one slaves saw just before a broken jaw.

"Is it possible?" Summer asked.

"Maybe with other masters, but Master Rice will find a way to cheat us out of it, you can be sure of that," Lucy said.

Summer agreed, but could not help but imagine all the things she could do with her half day.

13

REFORMS

Worship had moved to the new church, but the old church was still used for primary school, weddings, funerals, and meetings. By lantern light, the Council of Masters had gathered in the old church, many of them angry over Grandma's declaration of another half day off for slaves. With Grandma seated in her rocker in front of the altar, and Theresa seated behind her for moral support, Grandma listened to their concerns. Jesse complained the loudest and longest.

"Slaves were meant to work," Jesse argued. "Honest, hard work keeps them out of trouble. If they are working too many hours it's because they are lazy and don't get their work done when they should. Giving them more time off just rewards them for laziness. When the horse doesn't pull the plow I don't unhitch it, I get out the whip."

Murmurs of assent rippled through the gathered masters.

"If you do this, you just watch productivity plummet," Carl White said, echoing Jesse's argument.

Carl White owned the farm next to Jesse's. A burly man, with thick lips and a broad, flat nose, cottony hair, and skin nearly black from long hours in the sun, White was a striking figure. Handsome as a young man, White's affluence showed in the folds under his chin and his bulging waist. As owner of the second largest farm, White should have been influential; however, he lived in Jesse's shadow and seemed content there. If he ever had a thought independent of Jesse, he never expressed it.

"I've announced the rule," Grandma said. "The slaves would revolt if I took it back now."

"Let them try," Jesse said, eyes gleaming, lusting for a fight.

"If productivity declines, or if there are discipline issues, then I'll reconsider the rule next year," Grandma said, making sure everyone knew the rule was final.

"A half day won't make any difference," Master Flagg said loudly, getting everyone's attention.

Master Flagg was a small man at five feet four, with closely cropped gray hair, and a gray mustache. It was Flagg who supplied the community with coffee nuts. Years ago, Flagg discovered nut trees growing in a deep valley east of New Jerusalem. When he discovered that the ground nuts could be used to produce a beverage tasting something like coffee, his fortune was made. Many masters had stolen nuts from his valley to grow their own coffee nuts and break his monopoly, but the trees refused to grow anywhere but his valley. Not one to abuse power, Flagg had a reputation for being a good master, and Grandma Jones had little concern for the slaves who worked his orchards. An intelligent and cautious man, Flagg seldom spoke, so when he did his words carried weight.

"Give them a whole day for all I care," Flagg said. "What I do care about is how this rule came about. I recognize your right to make the rules, but proposed rule changes have always been brought to the council for discussion before you declared them. This change was not brought to the council and that concerns me very much."

Flagg sat down to a round of applause and multiple pats on his back.

"We did discuss it," Grandma began, and then waited for the denials to die down. "Just yesterday we discussed my concerns with productivity. You all remember that?"

"There was no motion on the floor," Flagg said loudly.

Other masters agreed vehemently. Flagg often spoke as if they used *Robert's Rules of Order* to run their meetings. In reality, there were no formal rules.

"Besides," Jesse said, taking center stage again, "taking away half a work day reduces productivity."

"Wrong, Jesse," Grandma said, trying not to sound conde-scending. Jesse was easy to rile. "As you were trading today, did you notice the quality of the work the slaves had to trade?"

"That's because they hold back the best stuff," a master shouted from the back.

"Not from me," Jesse said.

"That quality comes from incentive. What they make on their free time is theirs to keep. They invest more time and creativity in their own goods, because it gets them some-thing they want. Give them a little more free time and they will produce more fine goods."

"They should be producing it for their masters," Jesse said.

Half the room agreed, the other half waited, wondering where Grandma was going.

"With more good quality trade goods, the slaves can ac-quire more for themselves," Grandma continued. "They will become a bigger part of our economy and add to our pro-ductivity."

"We're doing fine without slaves," Jesse said, rewarded with widespread applause.

Grandma nearly laughed at the ignorance of Jesse's comment—slaves did virtually every bit of the manual labor.

"With more productivity, we can afford to put resources into developing our community," Grandma said. "We need sewers, storm drains, paved roads and bridges. Every spring everyone east of the Pax is cut off because of the runoff. A bridge would prevent that, or a dam. With a dam we could generate electricity again."

Some in the room nodded agreement at the mention of electricity. The last remaining generator was used to power medical equipment that was also on its last legs. Most of the children had never seen electric lights.

Grandma went on. "We need more steel and refined met-als. We should be establishing other communities, connect-ing them with roads. If we had a reliable route to the coast we could build ships, and begin a fishing industry. This com-munity needs more than two doctors and a dentist. What about artists? A university? With the way you have been making babies, we need more teachers."

Nervous laughter spread through the room. There was no hiding the illegitimate babies.

"This is our planet so we need to send out explorers, to find out what is out there that we might be able to use. What kinds of riches and medicines might be just over the next hill? To support all of that, we need to be more productive. We need fewer laborers and more of everything else."

Grandma Jones did not mention that increased productivity would also be used to support the government she was designing to replace her.

"We're doing fine without all of that," Jesse said.

This time no one but Master White agreed.

"Even if we did want some of that, cutting back on work hours won't get it done," Jesse added quickly to cover the silence.

"I disagree," Grandma said, still rocking in her chair. "A rested worker is more productive. A worker who shares the fruits of her labors is more motivated."

"A whip motivates just as well, if not better," Jesse said.

Many voices agreed with Jesse, but still a minority.

"Even if they get more time for themselves," Jesse said, refusing to concede that Grandma's new rule would stand, "what would they possibly trade for?"

"We feed and house the slaves, they don't need more than that," Master White said.

"Then we need to give them something to work toward," Grandma Jones said.

"Like what?" Jesse asked.

"Their freedom," Grandma Jones said.

Now Grandma Jones rocked faster, watching as the men in the room came out of their seats, surprised, concerned, angry, and confused, all talking at once.

"Going like you planned?" Theresa whispered in Grandma's ear.

"Just like," Grandma said. "Just like."

14

CONFRONTATION

New Jerusalem
First Continent
AUTUMN, PLANET AMERICA

Grandma let the council argue late into the night, pleased with her progress. The half day off was long forgotten, the masters now arguing over the emancipation of slaves. The only free white people on America were a few remaining hermits, too much trouble for even Jesse Rice to track down. So the concept of slaves buying their freedom frightened the masters. They saw it as a threat to the economic stability of their farms, and to their way of life. Although unspoken, they also worried about free white people succeeding, maybe even being more successful than the masters had been. Part of Grandma shared that concern, but a few free slaves would not threaten the second and third generation masters. They had never known anything but a superior social position, and would not easily give up their self-confidence.

Using a cane, Grandma walked the well-worn path to her cabin. Built in a meadow between the town and a lake, her small cabin was one of the few perks she had acquired through her position. The meadow was essentially a park. The only structure marring the open expanse was Grandma's cabin. She had it built with a wide porch, where she could sit and watch the town and the children who played in the meadow. Back on Earth she had lived in a highrise and looked out at other concrete towers, or down on a courtyard where her son had been murdered when a drug deal went bad.

Simon Ash opened the cabin door, stepping out of the way, avoiding her eyes. Simon was one of the original slaves. Not a strong man, Simon was claustrophobic, and had had to be sedated when traveling in the Fellowship Ark Class spaceship that brought Simon to planet America with Grandma's people. Later, he was forced to return with the soldiers and had been enslaved. While never abused, Simon's mental health had deteriorated rapidly, until one morning he was found huddled in the corner of a slave pen, knees to his chest, sobbing. Nearly catatonic, Simon was excused from labor, creating resentment among the other slaves. Two days later some of the slaves beat him, sending him back to his corner, a sloppy emotional mess. A frail man, and useless for hard work, Grandma had assigned him to kitchen duties. In the early days, the slaves were worked as a group, and fed and housed communally. Later, when the slaves were distributed to the masters, Grandma kept Simon. Pitying the poor man, she assigned him to clean and maintain the church, and then later her cabin. Now he served as her only servant, cleaning, cooking, and washing for her.

Simon seldom spoke, but was attentive, anticipating Grandma's needs. Although it had been more than a decade since Grandma had rescued him from the slave pens, Simon lived as if he could be sent back at any moment. Taking the shawl from her shoulders, Simon hung it, and then hustled into the kitchen, putting a kettle on the stove. Grandma ignored Simon, knowing he would bring the tea and a couple of cookies in a few minutes. Before Grandma could sit down, there was a rap on the door. Expecting Theresa, Grandma waved Simon back into the kitchen, opening it herself. It was Jesse.

"Whatever it is, it can wait until tomorrow," Grandma said.

"I'm leaving first thing in the morning, and I've got a few things to say."

Jesse placed his hand on the door, making sure Grandma could not close it.

"On the porch," Grandma said, knowing he would not leave until he had his say.

Four rockers sat on the porch. Grandma took her favorite, Jesse taking one to her left.

"You ought to build a proper house," Jesse said. "You are the queen of this planet and you should live in something that reminds the people of your position. They expect it."

"There's no such thing as royalty on America," Grandma said.

"There's certainly a class system," Jesse said. "You created that when you instituted slavery."

Grandma bristled at the reminder that she had condemned a group of people to slavery based on the color of their skin.

"Something I intend to undo," Grandma said, regretting it immediately.

Jesse chuckled, pleased with his quick victory.

"So this isn't just about freeing a few slaves to get them to work harder. You mean to let them all go free."

"It's inevitable, Jesse. Even you can see that. No culture can thrive with an injustice like slavery at its core."

"Worked just fine where I came from for two hundred and fifty years," Jesse said. "I think we can give it that long, and maybe a bit more. You can't tell me that wouldn't be justice."

Simon came out then, with a shawl over his shoulder and a tray with two cups of tea and a plate of cookies. He trembled when he recognized Grandma's visitor, and kept his eyes averted while Jesse and Grandma took the tea and cookies. Covering Grandma's lap with the shawl, Simon quickly retreated inside.

"I won't repeat the mistakes of the past," Grandma said. "Slavery served its purpose here, and now for the good of our people we need to evolve to a new system."

"So now you're talking about a whole new system?"

Angry with herself for revealing too much of her plans, Grandma tried to pull back.

"It will be a slow transition," Grandma said. "A few slaves buying their freedom won't be a threat to you."

"A single free slave is a threat to everyone," Jesse said.

"Why do you hate them so, Jesse?"

Jesse was silent, nibbling on one of Simon's cookies. Simon made the lumpy cookies with native nuts and dried fruits. Grandma loved them.

"I don't hate nobody," Jesse said. "I just know what's best for us; something you've lost sight of. Don't you remember what life was like back home? In high school I sat on the bench so a white boy could play. My brother did five years in prison for selling crack. The college boy he sold it to spent a month in a spa they called a treatment center. At the warehouse where I worked my butt off, a white man with just a year of experience got the controller's job instead of me."

"It wasn't fair, was it?" Grandma said.

"You know it wasn't," Jesse said, fuming over the long-ago slights.

"It isn't any fairer here."

"It may not be fair, but it's the way it's going to stay," Jesse said.

"You don't have any say over this, Jesse," Grandma said.

"We'll see about that," Jesse said, standing to go.

The threat hung in the air and Grandma locked eyes with Jesse, who stared back defiantly. Movement in the window caught their eyes and they glimpsed Simon, shrinking back from the window where he had been listening.

"You think that's the future?" Jesse said derisively, jerking his head toward Simon. "We can do better than that."

Jesse left, Grandma watching his back as he followed the path back to the village. Sighing, Grandma took another of Simon's cookies, wondering how many of the masters thought like Jesse. If there were many, she would be in for a fight, a fight she could lose. She would have to move up her timeline while she still had the power.

15

KENT THORPE

New Jerusalem
First Continent
AUTUMN, PLANET AMERICA

Kent Thorpe lived in a shed built against the back wall of the farmer's co-op. He had a bed, a small table, two chairs, and a stove. A small bin of wood sat by the stove. If he needed to refill the bin, he chopped the wood himself. There was a shelf with toiletries, eating utensils, two pans, and the lantern he used to go to the outhouse after dark. Another lantern hung from a hook high on the wall, lighting the room. A pan sat in the corner, catching the drip from his leaking roof—it was raining again. There was no window, but a two by two section of wall could be removed in summer, letting air circulate. The screen used to cover the opening was rolled up in the corner. As sparse as it was, other slaves envied his shed, and his position.

Owned by Jesse Rice, Thorpe's public job was to monitor Jesse's shares of grain and livestock routed through the co-op. Thorpe's real job was twofold. First, he worked with Jim Wish, the president of the co-op, to skim commodities from Rice's and other's tithes, and from the community stores. Thorpe's other job was to spy for Master Rice. Both jobs were beneath Thorpe's abilities, but kept him out of the fields and mines. Resigned to his fate, Thorpe had made the most of his life as a slave, ingratiating himself with the most powerful master on planet America. No other slaves trusted him, but they did fear him, and that was as good as respect.

At a soft tapping on the door, barely heard above the patter of rain, Thorpe opened it to find a wet and nervous Simon

Ash. Thorpe motioned for Ash to come in. Pausing in the doorway, Ash looked in all directions, making sure no one saw him enter Thorpe's shed.

"No one cares if you visit me," Thorpe said, annoyed by Ash's paranoia. "No one even notices you. You could walk naked down Main Street and no one would comment."

"I have news," Ash said, closing the door and speaking in a whisper.

Slowly, a puddle formed around Ash's feet.

"Ash, no one lives within a block of here," Thorpe said. "How many times have I told you, you don't have to whisper?"

Thorpe spoke loudly to make his point, but it only made Ash cringe. Thorpe gave up and played along, speaking in a near whisper.

"And what do you want for this information?"

"The usual," Simon said in a barely audible voice.

"Ash, you haven't given me anything worth the *usual*, since your warning about the surprise inspection of the grain elevators."

"This is important. This is big."

When Ash's voice rose, Thorpe believed him. Something had Ash riled up enough to speak at a normal volume.

"Fine, the usual, if it's worth it."

"What will it be?" Ash asked.

Bargaining was a new behavior for Ash. Normally, he took what he could get and scurried back to his cot in the storeroom of the old church.

"Your choice," Thorpe said.

Now Ash nodded enthusiastically.

"They're going to let slaves use money," Ash said, excited.

Thorpe sighed.

"Why would I care about this? Slaves don't need money in what is essentially a barter economy. No one does."

"I know, I know," Ash said, strangely excited. "It's what you can buy with that money."

Thorpe waited while Ash grinned moronically, forcing Thorpe to ask.

"What can you buy with it?" Thorpe asked finally, his patience nearly exhausted.

"Your freedom," Ash said, watching for Thorpe's shocked expression.

He wasn't disappointed; Thorpe *was* shocked. Emancipation never seemed possible—not in Thorpe's lifetime.

"Where did you hear this?" Thorpe demanded.

"Grandma Jones and Theresa talked about it."

Ash heard a lot of useful information as Grandma Jones's servant.

"When? When will this happen?"

"Grandma's going to announce the change in the slave money policy first, and then the chance to buy freedom later. Theresa told Grandma that the masters would have to be fed baby-spoonfuls, or they would never swallow it. The half day off is part of their larger plan to emancipate the slaves."

Now Thorpe sat on his bed, wondering how to use the information. What Thorpe desperately wanted was a way off America and back to his life on Earth. He did not see how this got him any closer to that goal. At the same time, he was sick of being a slave. He deserved to be treated at least as an equal by people he knew were intellectually inferior. No one on America—free or slave—could match his intellectual abilities. Even on Earth, precious few were his equal. Thorpe had been the one to repair a Fellowship lifting sphere, getting it flying again. Then with Thorpe at the controls of the sphere, they had used it to maneuver a space shuttle full of marines to the Fellowship space station and capture it. Thorpe was a genius—no one could dispute that fact—but on America, it was dangerous to be smarter than your master.

Feeding Ash's information about potential emancipation to Jesse Rice might get Thorpe a short-term reward, but he had more to gain in the long run if Grandma moved ahead with her plan—his freedom.

"Well?" Ash said impatiently. "It's late. I need to get back."

"All right," Thorpe said.

Pulling a gunny sack from under his bed, Thorpe laid out a selection of books. Ash knelt, looking at the titles. After several minutes, Ash selected two, looking back and forth between them, unable to choose.

"Take them both," Thorpe said, impatient to get rid of Ash so he could think.

"I'll be very careful with them," Ash said, excited. Then, tucking them inside his shirt, he buttoned up his coat.

Ash hurried out, leaving Thorpe with his thoughts. Using the filter of self-interest, he soon decided not to tell Master Rice, at least not immediately. Then slowly, he began to see how he could use the information to his advantage.

16

RESPITE

Master Rice's Farm
First Continent
AUTUMN, PLANET AMERICA

The nearly daily rains came as they always did this time of year, the temperature slowly dropping as winter approached. The rain seldom came in a downpour, instead taking the form of a constant cold drizzle, the skies a gray mat that stretched from horizon to horizon. For the next five months, that gray mat would greet them every morning and watch them go to bed every night.

There was more free time now, since there was little field work, and that meant more hands for the rest of the work, so Grandma's Rule of a half day off made no difference. Tools were repaired, new ones built, and wagons, carts, and carriages were repaired or rebuilt. The forge ran nearly night and day, and there was constant weaving and sewing. When the last of the fall crops were preserved or stored, they turned their attention to the puff tree fibers. With Hope slung on her back, Summer's mother directed the combing, bleaching, and spinning. Master Rice had not only received his fair share, but he had traded for large portions of other's shares. There would be enough thread and yarn to keep her mother and the other weavers busy until the next harvest.

With everyone gathered together for the work, there was much gossip. Every whispered story heard at the Gathering, every secret that had been spoken under an "if you promise not to tell" seal, was eventually shared, the juiciest often coming out last. This was the best time of year. Later would come the cabin fever, the constant bickering, and the depression that came from long hours of dim light and little activity.

Who was secretly married to whom, who fathered which baby, which master was sleeping with which slave, were all discussed in great detail, with or without accurate information. Nicole and Melvin came up in the gossip one day when Nicole was not around, and soon everyone knew about how close they danced at the Gathering, and how they disappeared for a time when no one could find them. Summer enjoyed the gossip, but wondered what was said about her when she wasn't around.

Kerry recovered and was put to work splitting wood for fuel. He wore leg irons, shuffling from a bunkhouse, to his chores, and then back again in the evening. One day Summer overheard the overseer telling Master Rice that Kerry might have some skills as a furniture maker, since he had worked with one at Master White's farm. Master Rice cursed Overseer Nkosi for his stupidity, ordering the overseer to use Kerry as a field hand. However, with little fieldwork to be done, the overseer put him to work mending furniture. Kerry did indeed have skills and was particularly good with the lathe, expertly shaping chair legs that pleased the mistress. Soon he was at work on a new set of dining room chairs, which caused excitement among the slaves, since the old—perfectly good—chairs would probably be distributed to the slaves.

Summer and Kerry talked whenever they could, careful not to let Master Rice see them. Kerry sensed, or had been warned by other slaves, that Master Rice had a special interest in Summer, and kept his distance when the master was around. Kerry asked a lot of questions, about her mother's weaving, where her mother had been a slave before, what Summer's chores were, what she liked to eat, and any other question that came to mind. Summer liked his interest and answered his questions, rambling on, giving more than he asked for. He never complained. In turn, he told of his life at Master White's farm, which sounded far better than life at Master Rice's, confirming something Summer had suspected. No matter how good the life of a slave was, he or she would always want to be free.

Summer continued to sneak Kerry food, supplementing his meager rations. Master Rice seemed intent on keeping him half starved. Summer willingly shared her food, despite the constant nagging from Cook. Kerry always took the food, but only after a "are you sure you don't need it?"

After the Gathering there was a noticeable change in Master Rice's routine. The master spent more and more time away, and sometimes other masters came to visit, talking with Master Rice late into the night. On each of these occasions, all slaves were kept well away from the big house.

Lucy had taken nearly the full share of Saturday nights since Hope's birth, but then one Sunday evening Lucy came to visit. While Rocky, Passion, and Dolby played, Summer and Lucy sat with her mother while she nursed Hope, enjoying adult-talk.

"It's been four weeks, Casey," Lucy said.

"He's visiting someone," Summer's mother replied. "I know that man. Have you asked around?"

"It's the same story with everyone," Lucy assured her. "No one's gotten a visit, but Patrick told me that Rice has been riding off for a few days at a time all by himself."

"This time of year?" Summer's mother said.

Summer's mother and Lucy both nodded knowingly at

that, and said no more. Summer thought she understood what they did not want to say, and it was confirmed two weeks later when Master Rice and Overseer Nkosi left in a wagon with two field hands in the back, and returned four days later with a new slave. Her name was Winifred, or "Winnie," Coleman, and she was eighteen. Summer knew her only slightly, since she lived on a farm about as far distant from Master Rice's as you could get. Summer remembered her from worship at Gatherings because of her red hair—rare on America—and her high soprano voice. She was fair skinned, her cheeks and lips bright with natural color, her figure voluptuous, her facial features petite. Lucy called her "prissy" but Summer thought her a perfect beauty. She wore the nicest dress Summer had ever seen on a slave—blue checked with a solid blue apron. She wore a knee-length coat—cut from cloth Summer's mother had woven—that lacked the patches that marked slave clothing. But what Summer remembered most of all about Winnie's arrival was the way Kerry's eyes followed Winnie as the wagon rolled up in front of the big house.

Winnie was given Summer's kitchen duties, resulting in much grumbling from Cook. Shortly after that, Winnie was given a cabin of her own to live in. The three field hands who had lived there were forced into another, already crowded cabin. With Winnie's arrival, Maser Rice lost all interest in Lucy and Summer's mother, who had been his favorites, and in fact ignored all the other women slaves. Slave families were relieved of a horrible burden and the reduced tension made life easier. There was more joking, more hugs, and fewer sharp words. Summer had more opportunities to practice her reading and her mother began to sing again while she worked her loom. Even Rocky and Hope sensed the change, both becoming less irascible.

Winnie was quickly relegated to a status saved for snitches, trustys, and the willing lovers of masters. The slaves were polite to her, because to be otherwise was to risk the wrath of Master Rice, but shunned her socially. Worst of all, she was denied entrance into the gossip circles, although she was frequently the subject of gossip. Because of her color, Winnie would never be accepted by the masters or their families, so when she was not working, she was alone. The mistress particularly disliked Master Rice's new toy, and cursed and cuffed her whenever Master Rice was not around. Cook tolerated Winnie because she had to, but complained to all about how useless she was, making Summer feel good about the job she had done.

The slaves might have been more accepting of Winnie except that Winnie seemed to enjoy her new role and even exploited her status. When Master Rice was around she would smile, laugh at his jokes, flutter her long eyelashes, and otherwise fawn over him. She seemed to feel no outrage over the way she was being used, and Winnie never sported the bruises, blackened eyes, and swollen lips that Lucy, Summer's mother, and other women did. Winnie turned out to be the only person on the planet who genuinely liked Master Rice.

Winnie's arrival had another positive effect. The master liked to show off her singing voice, and that meant regular trips for worship at the village church, where she was frequently featured as a soloist. Even jammed in the back with the slaves, Summer loved church and the ability to join with others worshiping God. She had been a Christian since she had answered an altar call at age six, much to her mother's dismay. Most of the original slaves had been soldiers, who came to America to occupy the planet and dominate the people. Instead, they had been enslaved. Few had been Christian before they became slaves, but many had converted since, and most of the next generation of slaves had accepted Christ as savior. But not Summer's mother (Casey), and not Lucy. Summer never gave up hope and prayed every night that they would feel the pull of the Holy Spirit.

Summer found that she was jealous of Winnie—her beauty, her voice, her power over men. Repressing her jealousy, Summer enjoyed the master's new interest in church, despite Winnie's frequent solos. Summer knew worship with a community of believers would be what she missed the most when she ran away.

The puff tree planks Summer had picked up at harvest lay under a pile of wood in a shed behind the old barn. Summer stacked wood evenly along the length of the boards to flatten them. After a month the boards were flat and stiff. Summer knew they needed to curl up at the tips, but she wasn't sure how to do that. Even if she could bend the boards to the right shape without breaking them, they would spring back to their original shape. That was just one of many problems she had to solve. She also had to rig a strap to hold the skis to her feet and then learn how to use them.

Summer took to casually asking the older slaves if they had ever skied. Many had, and talked enthusiastically about it. Summer quickly learned that there were two kinds of skiing, and most of the slaves had done the kind where a machine pulls you up the hill and gravity pulls you down. She also learned she would need poles to go along with her skis. She tucked that away in her mind, with all of her other needs, knowing the best way to keep from getting discouraged was to solve the problems one at a time, bit by bit.

Summer found herself in a period of grace since the attentions of Master Rice were totally focused on his new toy, Winnie. Wash kept his distance, unsure of whether his father still extended his protection to Summer. Besides, Wash was as infatuated with Winnie as Master Rice.

"That boy wants whatever his father has," Cook explained one day. "It's an Oedipal conflict."

Summer didn't know what an "Oedipal conflict" was. Cook often assumed Summer understood more than she did.

It should have been a happy time for Summer, but she couldn't help but notice the way Kerry's eyes followed Winnie whenever she passed. Sometimes now, Summer could not sleep, and would lie awake imagining her and Kerry together. Sometimes she would imagine them picnicking in the meadow, or dancing at the Gathering. Sometimes she imagined Kerry holding her close and kissing her. But most nights her fantasies were ruined by images of Winnie and Kerry together.

Summer took up her mother's profession and learned to work the loom. She had been picking up skills gradually by watching her mother and experimenting, so she made rapid progress. Soon, she was good enough to solo, but not good enough to work on her mother's projects. Her mother's textiles were too valuable to Master Rice. Instead, Overseer Nkosi repaired an old loom and set it up in the old barn. It was cold in the barn, so she worked with a lantern at her side for warmth and light, and a blanket wrapped around her body. At first her mother would come by frequently to check on her progress, but after a couple of weeks came only to help solve problems or make suggestions.

Summer was called back to work in the kitchen for the Christmas feast, helping Cook and Winnie prepare food for the master's table. There would be twenty guests from nearby farms, and so the oven was kept fired day and night, Cook getting no rest.

Since coming to Master Rice's farm, Winnie had developed a reputation of being a bit slow and clumsy. Summer witnessed it first-hand, now, watching Winnie trip, stumble, and drop trays, pans, and plates. Winnie was not a bright woman either, and Cook was so used to having to repeat herself that she gave every direction twice, even to Summer.

She and Cook were making pies, using a yellowish gourd that the first settlers discovered growing wild, and now cultivated in gardens. Cook had scooped out the gourds and cooked up the mash into a liquid filling that would cool to the consistency of custard. The concoction was heavily spiced and sweetened with honey, and the smell tickled Summer's nose. Summer was rolling out dough and cutting out crusts for the pies.

Winnie came through, putting her coat and mittens on. She was pouting, lips pursed, her motions exaggerated. Now she went out onto the porch, putting her boots on. Summer noticed the boots looked almost new. Cook and Summer worked quietly, ignoring Winnie's antics. Finally, Winnie went out the back door.

"Summer, I miss you," Cook said when Winnie slammed the door behind her. "That girl is the worst thing that ever happened to women—all beauty and no brains."

"Is that so bad?" Summer asked, still jealous of the way Kerry looked at her.

"More than you can understand," Cook said. "Winnie is what every man wants—easy on the eyes and so slow she makes the dumbest man feel like a genius."

"Not every man," Summer tried to argue, thinking of Kerry.

"Every man. No exceptions."

Summer frowned and Cook misunderstood.

"You're just as pretty, Summer. Prettier. But you've got the figure of a ten-year-old. Even so, men notice you."

"No they don't," Summer protested, knowing it was true, but needing to hear it said.

"They follow you with their eyes when you're not looking."

"But I'm skinny. Not like Winnie."

"That's because she eats, and the way she eats she'll look like me in five years. You can take that to the bank."

Summer had heard Cook say "You can take that to the bank" before, and had no idea of what it meant.

"Maybe I don't want men to want me for the way I look," Summer said.

Cook stopped mixing, looking over at her with an expression of admiration.

"That's right, Summer. That's exactly right."

Now Cook looked thoughtful, eyes falling to the pot on the stove. She started stirring again.

"At least that would have been the right attitude back on Earth," Cook said. "Back there a woman didn't need a man, she could make her own way in the world. We'd made so much progress that even marriage was just about obsolete. Women were so empowered that they married other women and had babies without men. We'd thrown off the shackles of sexism and were building our own society free of men. We had businesses, homes, families, and even sports teams, all without men. We sailed ships, climbed mountains, flew airplanes, did it all. We were free."

Now Cook stopped stirring and looked at Summer.

"Now look at me. Look at us. We're back where we were before the war for liberation. So what I'm saying Summer, is that there aren't the same opportunities here that we had back on Earth. Here men need women and women need men."

The last part came out of Cook hard.

"Anyway, you need to use whatever gifts you have to make your way in the world."

Winnie came in carrying firewood, dropping it by the stove. Her red hair was wet, her natural curl now just a sad droop.

"Get two more loads," Cook ordered.

"Why can't Summer do it?" Winnie complained.

"Because she is making crusts. Now get the firewood and then get out the tablecloths and iron them."

Winnie rolled her eyes, and then stamped back out the door. Summer watched her turn and go, noting the swell of her breasts and the curve of her hips. Absent-mindedly, she picked up the dough trimmed from the pie plate and ate it, wondering if she really was as pretty as Winnie. Then she ate another piece.

17

FAULT LINE

Eastern Wilderness
First Continent
AUTUMN, PLANET AMERICA

There were a hundred of the tiny pronghorns grazing, unaware of Rey. Keeping downwind, Rey inched to the edge of the field, waiting for the herd to get in the right position. He had his bow in hand, arrow ready. He had hunted the little pronghorns before but never managed to kill one. When frightened, they were incredibly fast, fleeing randomly. The little deer-like creatures bounded like kangaroos, jumping and twisting at the same time. Shooting one was impossible. However, Rey had a new plan.

The herd moved south, forty of the pronghorns in a pocket of the meadow that cut deeper into the forest. When the pronghorns were in position, Rey jumped from hiding, screaming a battle cry, bow in hand. He waved his free arm, shouting at the top of his lungs. The pronghorns bolted in all directions, making fifteen-foot leaps, seeming to change direction in midair, yet still missing each other as they fled. Rey ran to cut off pronghorns in the meadow pocket and managed to trap a dozen of the small speedsters. As he hoped, they bolted into the forest, dodging trees. Suddenly, one went down, snagged by one of Ollie's tentacles. The pronghorn twisted and kicked with its free legs but Ollie held tight, anchored to the tree with his powerful, clawed feet.

Rey shot an arrow into its side, just behind the shoulder. It continued to kick for a few more seconds, and then twitched violently before dying.

"Let it go, Ollie," Rey said, touching the tentacle that still wrapped a back leg.

Ollie released the pronghorn, climbing higher into the tree and then out on a limb. Then Ollie lowered himself by a tentacle to watch Rey butcher the pronghorn.

"Keep watch," Rey said.

Ollie pulled himself higher, latching himself to the bottom of a limb, head hanging down, earflaps protruding, eyes wide. As Rey worked, he marveled at how intelligent Ollie was. The tree octopus had become an extension of Rey, seemingly knowing what to do before Rey asked. To set the trap, Rey simply pointed to the pronghorns and then to the tree where Rey wanted Ollie to wait. Ollie had hummed a happy hum, and then attached himself to the tree, head and tentacles retracted. Even up close Ollie looked like nothing more than a bulge in the tree bark. The only worry Rey had was whether the pronghorns were too big for Ollie to trip. He needn't have worried. Ollie not only tripped the pronghorn, but held it too.

Rey threw bits of intestines up to Ollie as he worked, and then skinned the animal and whistled Ollie down. With the carcass over Rey's shoulders, Ollie waddled next to Rey. Ollie hated being on the ground, but he could walk, and even run. Swinging from limb to limb like a monkey was natural, but he adapted as needed. The little guy was strong too, and could lift nearly five times its weight.

Rey and Ollie were camped, taking a couple of days' break from the trek west. Rey started a fire and then sliced off strips of meat and hung them over the fire on sticks. Next he dug out his pot, filled it with water, and put it on a circle of stones next to the fire. He shoved coals and fresh wood under his pot, letting it flame up. Then he added dried corn, tubers, a pinch of salt, and bits of meat. It had been a long time since he had taken time to make a real meal and his stomach growled in anticipation. Ollie was hidden in the pack, only his big brown eyes showing, watching Rey cook.

While he waited for the stew to heat, Rey pulled out his photo of the region. He had passed through the parts of the continent with the more detailed photos. The one he had to work with now was from much higher, maybe from orbit, and lacked detail. If Rey was right about his location, the forest should soon give way to a plain. Whether that plain was a desert or grasslands, he could not tell. But what puzzled him most was a line that ran north to south, from one edge of the photo to the other. He guessed it might be a river, but it was surprisingly straight for a river. To Rey it looked more like a canal, or something man-made.

Rey would know what it was soon enough. The trees and undergrowth were thinning, telling him he was coming to the edge of the forest. The rivers and streams were less frequent too, which meant faster travel, since he didn't have to ford rivers, but it also meant he had to be more cautious with his water supply. The aerial photo showed a large lake on the other side of the mystery line. The lake was oval, and several rivers radiated out from it. In the orbital photo, it looked like a human eye. That region seemed well watered, but there was a lot of dry land between Rey and Big Eye Lake. If they could make it to the lake, he and Ollie would have plenty to drink. But getting there could kill them.

They broke camp the next morning. It was autumn now, and like forests on Earth, many of the trees were reaching the end of the summer growth cycle, their leaves darkening and starting to drop. There were other species, however, that kept their leaves, like Earth's evergreens, although Rey had never seen one with needles. More typical were clusters of leaves shaped like the bulbs of tiny Christmas tree lights. They were filled with gas and Rey could pop them by crushing them between his palms. As summer turned to fall, the bulbs changed shape, losing the gas center and twisting so that the clusters of bulbs took on the appearance of clumps of hair. Green was the preferred leaf color on planet America as it was on Earth, but a number of trees specialized in yellow all year round.

Occasionally, Ollie would climb up high on Rey and lean out, stripping leaves, berries, or fruit from trees. Ollie was a generous creature, every other tentacle-full pushed into Rey's mouth. To Rey's surprise, he could eat some of Ollie's scavenged food. Ollie climbed high now, stripping a pod of white berries from a bush as Rey hacked a way through. As usual, Ollie tasted them first, judging them as edible. Next he offered them to Rey. They were sweet, but Rey was cautious, eating only one, then putting the rest in a pocket. If his bowels did not take to the berry, he would feed them to Ollie later. By the end of the day he had a pocket full of the berries. By morning, he decided they were good and had some for breakfast. By noon the next day they saw no more of the berry bushes.

Three days later Ollie was a nervous wreck, hiding in the pack, coming out only occasionally to scold Rey for where he was taking them. They had entered a semiarid plain. It wasn't a high desert, since the terrain had been generally flat, or downhill, since he found Ollie. The arid conditions had to be produced by the weather patterns, although Rey could not see any mountains to steal the rain.

"Relax, Ollie," Rey said, comforting his partner. "I promise to camp under a tree if I can find one."

Ollie hummed his scolding hum. There were scattered trees on the plain, but as Rey looked into the distance he saw fewer and fewer. He also thought he could see a band of clouds on the horizon. He didn't like that since the terrain they were entering was prone to flash floods. Rey stooped, examining what he would be walking through. It was grass of some sort, with a wide blade that came nearly to Rey's knees. While it was shaped like grass, the color was gray, not green or brown.

A half day later, Rey tied a strip of cloth over his mouth. Every few steps he would stir up a cloud of insects that buzzed around his head. Ollie enjoyed the insects when they first appeared, using them for target practice and knocking them out of the sky with a flick of his tentacles. However, even Ollie quickly tired of them. When Rey was bitten on the back of the neck several times, he wrapped his spare shirt around his neck. The insects continued to buzz his face, going for his eyes. Walking through the bright, hot sun, insects swarming him, Rey began obsessing about sunglasses.

There were many things that the Fellowship did not think to leave him, but right now a pair of sunglasses was what he wanted most. That night he thought mosquito netting was the most important thing, but by midmorning the next day he was once again sure it was sunglasses.

The next morning the cloud bank still hung on the horizon and that puzzled Rey, since the occasional cloud that passed over was moving east. By evening he realized he wasn't seeing a cloudbank. With mounting concern, he continued his march toward the gray wall ahead, waving away insects, trying not to worry Ollie. Two days later he was standing at the base of a towering cliff that ran in both directions as far as he could see. It was a fault line, where two mismatched continental plates came together, and based on the photo it appeared to run the width of the continent. He could go no further.

18

THREAT

New Jerusalem
First Continent
AUTUMN, PLANET AMERICA

The late night rap at Kent's door told him one of his customers was not happy.

"I'm coming," Kent said, irritated.

Kent opened the door to find Jesse Rice. The man's mass filled the doorframe. Master Rice was smiling. The smile meant nothing.

"I didn't know you were in town, sir," Kent stammered, backing up.

"You've been holding out on me," Master Rice said, coming into the light of the cabin, and closing the door behind him.

Kent was trapped in his own cabin, with the most dangerous man on the planet. A man he had been systematically cheating.

"I'm sure I don't know what you mean, Master Rice," Kent said.

Master Rice moved around the cabin, picking through Kent's meager belongings. A book lay on a box that Kent kept next to his bed. Master Rice picked up the book and held it out.

"Well, slave, explain this," Master Rice said.

Kent knew this was not about Kent's illegal possession of a book. Few masters cared enough about the rule to enforce it. In fact many depended on the education of their slaves to keep books and records, both of which involved reading. Master Rice was one of these.

"I'll return it to the warehouse tomorrow, Master Rice," Kent said. "I've been sick and confined to my cabin and I thought the book would help pass the time."

"We'll let it go this time," Master Rice said.

Kent kept quiet, waiting for Master Rice to reveal what he knew. Kent wasn't going to beg forgiveness for a crime Rice may not know he committed.

"I let you keep that job at the warehouse because I expect you to give me information. Any slave can keep the books."

That was a lie, but Kent kept quiet.

"Why didn't you warn me that that old woman was planning to free the slaves?"

"I didn't know," Kent said.

"I think you did know," Master Rice said. "That spineless slave that keeps house for Grandma Jones tells you everything. Isn't that right? That's what you told me to get this job and this cabin."

"He must not have known," Kent lied.

"That right?" Master Rice said, now leaning against the door—the only exit. "I could get him alone and ask him."

Kent had no hope that Simon would keep their secret. Kent bluffed.

"I can go get him if you like," Kent said.

Master Rice studied him, the meaningless smile still on his face.

"I think he did tell you, slave," Master Rice said. "But you didn't want me to know about it. You see, I think you got an idea in your head that you might like to be one of those who get free."

Master Rice stepped closer to Kent, losing his smile.

"I swear I did not know. Why would I hide something from you that Grandma Jones would announce publicly anyway?"

"Well now, I think we're getting to the meat of the matter," Master Rice said, stepping closer. "Do you know why I bought you? It's because I know what you are. I know you're a twisted man who doesn't care about anyone but himself. You've never had a friend and don't want one."

Kent flashed back to his early life on Earth and the one woman who had loved him. Growing up, other children ignored or spurned Kent. The only birthday party he had been invited to was a cousin's. He had never been to a sleepover, and never had a birthday party himself—his parents knew no children would come. In high school he asked several girls out, and all refused. Kent knew the reason why he was spurned—his genius. The other children were jealous of him. However, in graduate school he found a woman who was intelligent enough to appreciate his gifts, and who therefore loved him. Constance Wong gave Kent a taste of what life could be. With her he would have a companion, a marriage, and even children. Ira Breitling took all of that from him, however, when his incompetence led to Constance's death. So, Rice was right when he said Kent had never had a friend, but Kent did once have a lover.

"I know what you are, slave, and that's fine with me as long as you use that twisted little mind of yours in the way I want. What I won't tolerate is you using it against me. You figured out some advantage to knowing about Grandma's plan before me. That's why you held back."

Now Master Rice was inches from Kent's face.

"I do what you tell me."

Rice was close enough now that Kent could smell alcohol on his breath.

"Let me make one thing clear, slave. You will never be free. You will never have another master. You are mine or you are dead."

Kent understood. He knew too much about Master Rice to ever be free.

"Don't you be dreaming about getting yourself emancipated. It's never going to happen, not for you, not for any slave. Grandma Jones is done running this planet—I'm going to make sure of it."

Rice turned to go and Kent sighed with relief—he would live another day. Then Rice whipped around and struck him. Unprepared, the fist to Kent's head nearly knocked him unconscious. Kent landed on his bed, the left side of his face throbbing.

"Remember that, slave. If you hold out on me again, it's just a taste of what I'll give you."

Then Rice was gone, and Kent lay on the bed, his quick mind calculating, plotting. It took only a minute to realize there was only one course of action. Master Rice had to die.

19

OBSTACLE

Continental Fault Line
First Continent
AUTUMN, PLANET AMERICA

"Slow down, Ollie!" Rey called.

The tree octopus ignored him, using tentacles and clawed feet to climb from rock to rock. The tree dweller wasn't built for climbing rocks, but the same tools that made him a master of the trees adapted well to cracks, ledges, and outcroppings, and Ollie moved confidently over the rocky terrain at the base of the fault line that blocked their way west.

Ollie was waving tentacles now, urging Rey to hurry. With worn boots, and only two limbs to grip with, Rey followed his little friend cautiously. Finally, he climbed up onto the rock where Ollie stood, looking down the other side into a large crevice. A huge carcass filled it. It was wedged deep, but the blood looked fresh. Rey looked up the cliff face. There was a smear of blood on an outcropping thirty feet above. From this close it was impossible to see the top of the cliff, but that had to be where the animal had come from.

Ollie was still excited, tentacles waving restlessly.

"We don't even know what it tastes like," Rey said.

It made no difference. Ollie would eat just about anything.

Rey studied the crevice, mapping a way down. Then he worked his way around to the best footing, and started in. Ollie tried to climb on his shoulder when he did, but he lifted the tree octopus down and then dropped his pack.

"Wait here. No sense both of us risking our lives."

Ollie stayed, but leaned over the edge, tentacles stretching out, following.

Rey worked his way down until he was just above the carcass. He could see blood dribbling down one side. The animal was bigger than an adult elephant, with four thick legs. The back legs were larger than the front, however, and its color was a muted green and yellow in a camouflage pattern. The skin was hairless. The head was wedged deep and what little he could see of the face was crushed, but there was a three-foot piece of a broken tusk jammed between the head and the wall.

Looking up once more, Rey wondered how it came to fall. It was a huge creature, four-footed and probably sure-footed. It was more likely that the animal had been stampeded over the edge by a predator. Rey could not imagine a predator large enough to terrify an animal this size.

The animal so completely filled the crevice that Rey could not see the shape of the hole or how deep it was. He decided not to step on the animal, worrying that his extra weight might dislodge it and send them both plunging deeper. Instead, he worked down until he could reach it and sliced through the skin. It bled when he did.

"Fresh meat tonight, Ollie."

Ollie hummed a happy reply.

Rey had to cut through a thick layer of fat to reach meat. Ollie would eat the fat, but Rey preferred meat. As he cut out thick oily slabs, he wondered about the coming winter. The thick layer of insulation suggested that the animal was prepared for a hard winter. Now as Rey cut the meat, he worried about Ollie. He didn't know anything about Ollie's species. He had killed the first one he saw. Did they migrate to warmer climates for winter? Hibernate? Did they spin themselves a cocoon and turn into something else? Rey hadn't made any preparations for winter, instead working his way north along the fault line toward what looked to be a gap. They should be there soon, but the temperatures were dropping every day, and already some nights the temperature had fallen below freezing. Even if they reached the gap soon he wasn't sure they could make the run to the great lake.

As Rey sliced he heard a trickling sound. He paused, leaning lower until his ear almost touched the carcass. He could hear running water. Rey finished the butcher's work, then climbed up high enough to hand the meat to Ollie. Ollie stretched his tentacles to the max, pulling the meat up and letting Rey climb empty-handed.

Ollie already had the meat in the pack when he reached the top. Clearly, Ollie was ready to find a place to camp—and eat—but there was daylight left and Rey wanted to follow the sounds of the water. It was scarce on the plain.

With Ollie in his place on Rey's shoulder, Rey walked fifty yards north, and then stooped, listening. There was a faint trickling sound.

"Hear it, Ollie? Water."

Ollie said nothing, having settled in for a nap. They hiked north for two hours, pausing occasionally to check for the sound of water. Sometimes Rey could hear it beneath a jumbled pile of rocks. Sometimes he couldn't. The terrain never changed during that hike; arid plain to the east, sheer cliff to the west, its base strewn with rocks of every size, some as big as houses. But now there was something new. Shoots of green sprouted out of a crack. Another hour and most of the rocks were ringed with green. The sprouts were flat stalks that feathered on the top. There was no late fall dryness to the shoots. The sound of running water was clear now, although Rey could not see any amongst the rocks.

Rey and Ollie camped that night, cooking the fresh meat over a small fire. Firewood was scarce. They sheltered under rocks, the temperature sinking to near freezing. Ollie attached himself to the overhang, refusing Rey's offer to share the blanket. Rey let the fire burn out, saving the last of the wood to cook breakfast. It was pitch black when the snap of a tentacle woke him. Hanging from the rock, Ollie had snatched up something wriggly. It was three feet long, skinny like a snake, but with double rows of small appendages on the bottom. It had a long, reptilian snout and two bulging eyes. When Rey sat up it snapped at him with a set of incisors that would make a crocodile jealous.

"Hold him, Ollie," Rey said needlessly.

Ollie slapped another tentacle around the wiggling thing, snagging it just behind the head. It was nearly as flexible as a snake, and Ollie struggled to keep it from twisting around and chewing into the tentacle holding its tail. Rey skewered it with his knife, right through its skull. That didn't kill it, so Rey twisted the knife around, destroying more of its diffuse nervous system. Finally, it stopped struggling. Then Ollie sniffed it, judged it inedible, and threw it out of the enclosure. Shocked from sleep to find a vicious little predator at his feet, Rey was now wide awake. Ollie, on the other hand, retracted his tentacles and pulled his head into the mass of fur that was his body. Then, clamped tightly to the overhang, he fell asleep. Rey was awake for an hour, jumping at every imagined slithering sound. On nights like these, he missed Earth's large moon. The tiny moon circling America made a poor nightlight.

By noon the next day, the dry plain had become lush grass-land. The feather-topped grasses were thick and larger shrubs were numerous. When they encountered their first tree, Rey had to take a break while Ollie climbed every branch. Once Ollie's therapy was completed, they continued north. That night Ollie slept in a tree and Rey camped at its base with a proper fire.

The next day the scattered trees became a wood and then a forest. Ollie was elated, and spent most of the day above Rey, swinging from limb to limb. He never strayed far. They had never encountered any more of Ollie's kind since Rey had killed Ollie's mother. Rey was sad for Ollie, but happy for himself.

They first heard the roar midafternoon. The humidity had been increasing noticeably, and soon the air was thick. Rey stayed near the rubble between the cliff and the forest, often picking his way among the rocks rather than risk the un-knowns of the forest. Ollie occasionally whistled excitedly, urging Rey to come kill something he'd found to eat, but Rey resisted. Ollie thought of Rey as a mighty hunter and would call him to kill anything and everything from four-handed chipmunks to one of the behemoths they had found in the crevice.

The shadow of the cliff ran deep into the forest when Rey finally saw what he had expected—a waterfall. Whatever fed the waterfall from above was dumping copious amounts of water over a wide area. There was a large lake spread out at the base. The waterfall had eroded the cliff, cutting a deep crescent, most of the center obscured by spray. Ollie climbed up Rey's back to his right shoulder. The roar from the waterfall was so loud he could not hear Ollie's hum.

Rey worked his pack off and pulled out the regional photo. Sitting on a rock, he studied it. Rey could make out the thin line that was the meeting of the two continental plates. Tracing the line north from where he and Ollie had first encountered it, he found the smudge he had been searching for. When they had started their hike north, Rey thought the smudge might be a break in the cliff wall. It turned out to be a waterfall and lake. Now he looked west of the smudge and could see a spider's web of tiny lines—-a river system feeding the waterfall.

Frustrated, Rey studied the map, looking north and south. There was another, much smaller smudge in the line, about as far south of where they first encountered the wall as they had traveled north. They would be well into winter by the time they reached it and it meant traveling back across terrain that was barely hospitable even in fall. Rey looked at the well-worn soles of his boots, and the rips and tears in his trousers and jacket. His dried foods were exhausted, and his clothes and equipment needed to be replaced or repaired. There was wood here, water, and a variety of game would be drawn to the water. Even if he headed south to the other possible gap, there was no reason to believe it would be any more accessible than this one. The only way he was sure he could continue west, was to travel south all the way to the coast. That would be a walk of last resort.

"Ollie, it's a dead end," Rey said.

Ollie hummed agreement.

"We'll winter here and figure out what to do in the spring."

Ollie did not object, not with trees to climb.

Rey walked to the lakeshore. Ollie climbed down, crawling from rock to rock out into the lake, and then attached himself to one, lying flat, head stretched out. Rey sat, enjoying the little bit of warmth from the sun, thinking about their chances of getting to the Fellowship. The futile northern trek had wasted a month of travel time. In the spring it would take another month just to get back to where he made the wrong turn, and then a month to find the other potential gap. If he had to travel all the way to the southern coast to get around the fault line, it would take all of next year's travel season. While the weather might be better in the south, the warmer temperatures and higher humidity would increase the variety of vegetation, multiply the insects, and increase the population of predators and prey. The risks would increase exponentially.

Rey estimated it might be fifty degrees now, but cooling, and the temperature would surely drop below freezing tonight. He was about to gather a generous supply of firewood for the evening, when he saw movement in the mist. Staring hard he saw an animal emerging, moving slowly through the lake. It stood on four thick legs, was green and yellow, and had two long curving tusks. It stood fifteen feet high at the front shoulder but the back legs were longer, its haunches higher than the front. There was no tail. It had an overhanging brow and wide blunt snout that it repeatedly dipped in the water, its head under for long periods. Rey recognized the species as the one they had found in the crevice. Then another came out behind the first; smaller, but similar.

Excited by the possibilities, Rey studied the waterfall and realized it was recessed into the cliff, the spray distorting his depth perception. The lake was not only between Rey and the cliff, but filled the opening that led back to the waterfall. There was a gorge through the gap in the cliff wall, and somewhere in that space was a way up. Just then Ollie let out an excited squeal. Holding up a furry creature snatched from the depths, Ollie hummed proudly.

"Good work, Ollie," Rey shouted.

Rey got up to look for firewood. Things were going his way again. He only wished the Fellowship knew he was coming. He wanted them to lie awake, worrying and wondering who would be the first to die.

20

SNOW

Master Rice's Farm .
First Continent
WINTER, PLANET AMERICA

It was still dark, everyone but Cook and Winnie still snug in their beds. The master wouldn't be up for an hour, the mistress and the girls for two or three. Wash would sleep until noon, unless Master Rice took it in mind to roust him earlier just out of meanness. The other boys would wander down to the kitchen over the next few hours, the youngest getting up first, the oldest later. None of them would go out in the cold this early.

As quietly as she could, Summer uncovered her puff tree boards. They were still flat and stiff. Out of her pocket she pulled the leather straps she had been working on. She had talked to everyone she knew about skis and bindings, making sure she didn't talk to any one person too long.

The straps would hold her foot to the skis at the toe, but let the heel come up. Slaves had demonstrated the motion for her, but there was no way to really understand how it would work until she tried them. She was looking for a way to attach the straps when she realized there was someone behind her. Frightened, Summer turned. By the light of the tiny moon, Kerry smiled.

"Summer's got a secret," Kerry said.

Summer put the straps behind her back. She hated distrusting everyone.

"What are you doing here?" Summer asked, trying to sound calm.

"Without those leg irons, I'm a lot quieter."

Now there was an uncomfortable silence. Still smiling, Kerry looked at the planks.

"These yours?" Kerry asked, kneeling.

Summer didn't say anything.

Kerry picked up one of the boards and stood it on end. It came nearly to the top of his head.

"Well, it's not firewood. I suppose you could be planning to panel your cabin but you would need a lot more than just two for that. Oh, wait. Maybe you're making a pair of skis."

Summer gasped.

"How did you know? I never told anyone."

"I listen. I watch. I figure things out."

"You won't tell?" Summer asked.

"Tell? Summer, I'll help you."

"You can't. If you get caught the master will whip you to death."

"Then I just won't get caught," Kerry said, smiling.

Now Kerry put the board back by the first.

"The tips need to be pointed and curved up," Kerry said, tracing a line on the skis. "Let me see your straps."

Summer hesitated.

"The ones behind your back," Kerry said, holding out his hand.

Summer gave them to him and then squatted next to Kerry.

"These are pretty good," Kerry said. "They'll have to attach somewhere around here. Of course you can't just wrap them around the skis or you won't be able to slide on the snow."

"Can't I just nail them on?" Summer asked.

"It won't hold," Kerry said. "At least not for long. Screws would work better, but they're hard to get. Let me see what I can do."

"Kerry, you can't help," Summer said. "I don't want you to get in trouble."

"Like I said, I just won't get caught."

The master's whip had left a scar on Kerry's face, and when he smiled the stiff scar tissue on that side would not contract. It left Kerry with half a smile, but half a smile from Kerry was worth more than a whole smile from any other boy.

"Trust me," Kerry said.

Summer did trust Kerry, although every time she saw him flash his half-smile at Winnie, very un-Christian thoughts went through her head. Three weeks after Kerry had caught her with her puff tree planks, it snowed steady and hard for two days. When the storm ended there was more snow on Master Rice's farm than Summer could remember in her short life. Early the next morning, she hurried to her hiding spot but found her puff tree planks missing.

She looked for Kerry all that day but could not find him. Suspicious now, she worried that Kerry might have used her skis to make another run. She tried working at her loom, but every sound brought her hurrying to the door to see if Kerry had returned. At suppertime, she was leaving when a hand clamped on her shoulder. She gasped.

"Easy, Summer," Kerry said, laughing. "It's just me."

Summer punched him in the stomach.

"Oof," Kerry said, gasping.

"Don't scare me!" she said.

"Sorry, Summer," Kerry said. "You're stronger than you look. Of course you need to be strong if you plan on skiing."

Now Summer's anger evaporated.

"Skiing?"

"Meet me here an hour before dawn," Kerry said, and then hurried off.

Summer danced through the thick snow back to her cabin. Her mother noticed her bubbly mood but said nothing. After dinner, Summer wrestled with Rocky, bounced Hope on her knee, and joked and chatted with her mother and Lucy when Lucy came by for tea.

Summer rolled out of bed early, explaining she had promised to help Cook. Kerry was waiting by the barn. Kerry looked at her disapprovingly.

"You're going to ski in a dress?" he asked.

"It's all I have," she said defensively, at the same time

knowing she would have to have pants by the time she was ready to leave. "I can do it."

"Not many could, but I bet you can. Come on."

Kerry led her across the snow-covered fields to the woods. There, Kerry picked up a large branch and walked backwards, brushing away their tracks. It was slow going, but she appreciated the caution. They traveled deeper into the forest than Summer had ever been in that direction. There was danger of running into a leaper, or a pack of dingoes, but Summer was confident the master and his dogs had cleaned the leapers and dingoes out of the woods for miles.

Finally, Kerry led her to the remains of a tree struck by lightning. Half the tree had sheared off, breaking apart as it hit the ground. The remaining tree was split, but survived and was healing itself and sending up new branches. Summer knew this kind of tree was hard to kill. Even if you cut it down, the stump would sprout and even the fallen pieces would send down roots and send up shoots. Kerry stopped in front of the tree, pushing aside a long plume of moss and reaching into the hollow core of the trunk, pulling out a pair of skis.

Summer smiled, reached for them, hesitated, and then hugged Kerry instead. Her planks had been transformed from flat boards into what she imagined skis should look like. The tips were curved up and pointed and there were bindings attached at the center of the skis, ready to strap to her feet. Now Kerry pulled out two poles, each with a leather loop on top and a leather basket around the bottom.

"How did you do all this?" Summer asked.

"It's all made with scraps," Kerry said. "I curved the tips in a steam box. It took me all of one night, but they bent real easily once I had them hot enough. The poles are made out of the canes I used for the bedroom chair I made for the mistress."

Summer turned the skis over, examining the bottom. Nail heads were recessed into the bottom.

"I used rivets to attach the straps," Kerry said. "They're countersunk so they won't affect the gliding."

"They're perfect," Summer said.

"Try them on," Kerry said, putting the skis flat.

With Kerry helping her, she buckled the straps. Then, holding onto the poles, she tried moving her feet back and forth. The skis moved easily, sinking deeper into the snow.

"I waxed the bottoms," Kerry said, "but I wasn't sure which kind of wax to use."

"This feels good," Summer said. She didn't know that skis needed to be waxed.

"Time to solo," Kerry said.

Summer tried walking, scissoring her legs. She made it a short distance and then fell onto her side. Kerry helped her up and she tried it again, moving forward but mostly by pulling herself along with her arms. She was a distance from Kerry now, so she tried turning and managed to tangle her skis and fall again. Kerry laughed. Covered in snow, she struggled to her feet and started back.

"Bend your knees," Kerry encouraged. "You're not doing it right."

"How would you know?" Summer demanded, stopping back where she started.

Summer was disappointed. She had imagined herself gliding across the snow, not working twice as hard as walking to make half the distance.

"Here's how I know," Kerry said, reaching back into the tree and pulling out a second pair of skis.

"Kerry, you shouldn't have. I can take the blame for one pair, but how do I explain two?"

"I'm not going to let you have all the fun," Kerry said.

Kerry dropped the skis and buckled the straps with some familiarity. Taking a second pair of poles from the tree, he turned to Summer.

"Like this," he said.

Now Kerry leaned forward, bent his knees, and began to scissor his legs and arms in synchrony. He moved across the snow with some ease, although he wobbled a bit as he moved. Soon he had disappeared in the tree shadows. Then he was back, almost gliding.

"You've been practicing," Summer accused.

"A few hours," Kerry said.

"All right, you cheater, now teach me."

And Kerry did. By the time the sun made it too dangerous to practice anymore, Summer had learned to move with less effort, although she fell every time she tried to turn. They practiced every morning for the next two weeks until the rains returned and melted the snow. By then, they could move with some ease on the flat, and even manage to ski downhill without falling.

Without the snow, they could not practice, but after two weeks Summer was confident that even her marginal ability would give her an advantage if Master Rice pursued her in the snow. More importantly, she now dared hope that when she ran, she would not have to go alone.

21

MEDIUM OF EXCHANGE

New Jerusalem
First Continent
WINTER, PLANET AMERICA

Cathy knocked on Thorpe's door at the usual time on the usual night. Unlike Simon Ash, Cathy did not try to hide her visits. Cathy carried a small basket covered with a napkin. Thorpe could smell fresh baking.

"Apple muffins," Cathy said.

Thorpe's mouth watered. Cathy's masters ran the only bakery in New Jerusalem and she had learned every secret the man and his wife knew. Cathy held out the muffins. With effort, Thorpe held back.

"They're delicious," Cathy coaxed, puzzled by Thorpe's reticence.

"The price has changed," Thorpe said, the aroma weakening his resolve.

Cathy reddened. Cathy rarely got angry with Thorpe, but he remembered each occasion distinctly. Cathy was a large woman, as tall as Thorpe, and muscular. Her body was fit, and she ran with her mistress every morning; one of the few people on America who did not find enough exercise in daily living. She kept her hair cut short as if she was still in the military, giving her a slightly masculine appearance.

"Of course I'll accept these tonight," Thorpe added quickly, taking the basket.

Thorpe uncovered a selection of books spread out on his bed. Suspicious now, Cathy quickly selected a book while Thorpe unpacked the warm muffins from the basket and then handed it back. Cathy put the book in the basket and then covered it.

"A new price?" Cathy asked, suspiciously.

"Baked goods and a dollar," Thorpe said, unsure of how much to charge.

"Money?" Cathy repeated, surprised.

"A man can only eat so much," Thorpe said.

"I didn't think we'd found your limit," Cathy said, glancing at his bulging waistline.

Cathy's anger was subsiding as she wondered why Thorpe would want money. Cathy had access to money, since the bakery was one of the few businesses that welcomed money.

"A dollar is too much," Cathy said.

Thorpe was pleased. Cathy had accepted the new medium of exchange, and was negotiating. Pricing services was new territory to Thorpe. All currency on America was paper, with the smallest denomination being a tenth of a dollar. By Grandma's Rule, a bushel of wheat was one dollar—wheat came the most distance and was therefore the most expensive. Corn was the cheapest commodity, since it grew in abundance, and grew locally. All other prices sorted themselves out around the wheat peg. Thorpe was not sure how many loaves of bread could be made from one bushel of grain, but he guessed several. There were other ingredients of course, and the cost of fuel for the oven. The bakers owned four slaves—two of them Cathy's children—who would have to be fed and clothed. Those costs had to be recouped in the price of bread. Thorpe knew that a simple loaf of bread cost half a dollar. The more popular specialty breads cost more.

"A tenth of a dollar and no baked goods would be fair. Slaves can't keep money, so it's risky to use it. It's not against Grandma's Rules to carry around a basket of muffins."

"True," Thorpe said. "Of course, someone might ask where you got the ingredients?"

Cathy's eyes narrowed to slits and her anger started to rise again. Thorpe might have pushed her too far.

"You aren't the only one with books," Cathy said firmly.

"I'm the only one with access to the book warehouse. I have the best selection."

"Two tenths and no baked goods," Cathy said.

"Half a dollar and a basket of baked goods," Thorpe countered, trying to judge Cathy's mood.

They argued a bit more, settling on a half dollar and a half basket of baked goods, but for two books. Cathy left, sure to spread the word about the new price. Thorpe guessed he would lose some business at first, but most slaves had goods that could be turned into cash, and as long as slaves were banned from reading, he would remain the best source for new reading material.

A few dollars a week from the slaves would hardly be enough, Thorpe knew, but he had other ideas for accumulating cash. He waited until everyone was in bed, and then took a lantern and headed to the co-op. The door was not locked; of course, no doors were ever locked on America. Thorpe did not try to hide his light since he frequently came and went from the co-op at all hours. Thorpe pulled out some tally sheets and spread them on the counter to cover himself in case anyone happened to come in. Next he went to the cabinet that held the co-op account ledgers. Jesse Rice had given

him a key to the cabinet lock shortly after he arranged for
Thorpe to work at the co-op. Thorpe found the ledger he was
looking for and removed several pages. Then he returned the
ledger, and took several blank sheets of ledger paper. Just
before closing the cabinet, Thorpe looked in the cash box. It
was full of loose bills.

Back in his shed, Thorpe pulled his own records from
their hiding place under the floor. He compared the official
sheets with his parallel books, working out a scheme for
stealing from Master Rice some of what he had helped Master Rice steal from the community stores. It would require a
third set of books, but nothing challenged Thorpe's keen
mind on America, except deception and manipulation. With
a Ph.D. in physical chemistry from a premiere university,
Thorpe was the most educated person on the planet, yet even
Thorpe was not free to use his abilities, and even if he were,
there were no technical challenges worthy of him. Embez-
zlement was beneath him too, but it was that or hoe vegetable gardens all day long.

Mentally mapping his manipulations, Thorpe estimated
how much he could safely divert without raising Rice's suspicions. Settling on a comfortable amount, Thorpe went to
work altering the books, cutting himself in for a share of the
spoils.

22

OASIS

Continental Fault Line
First Continent
WINTER, PLANET AMERICA

The oasis proved to be a cornucopia for both Ollie and Rey. There were four kinds of edible fruit, a tuber that boiled up like a potato, a nocturnal rabbit-sized rodent that had never seen a predator like Ollie, the amphibious mammals that Ollie liked to fish out of the lake, and on occasion, a herd of the yellowish monsters from the high plain would wander out of the waterfall. There were some Ollie-only specialties too, like the yellow fungus growing high in the trees that looked like dried cottage cheese, and six-legged beetles that lived in nests hanging from low limbs. Rey refused to try the beetles, and spit out the tiny piece of cottage cheese he'd tried when it triggered a gag reflex.

Rey's favorite food was a crunchy fruit with the consistency of an apple, but with a taste closer to plum. The fruit was coated with spines, but they broke off easily. Rey and Ollie had picked as many as they could find, scraped off the spines, wrapped them in a hide, and stored them in a shallow hole under the tent. Rey munched on one of the fruit now, studying the rocks around the edge of the waterfall. He had made three tries at finding a way into the crescent-shaped gorge and past the waterfall, but the only clear path was straight down the middle and he had no boat. With the temperatures barely climbing above freezing during the day, Rey would freeze to death if he tried to swim it. There was also a strong current, with the water flowing away from the waterfall. Where all the water was going was another puzzle.

Rey had followed the sounds of deep water to the waterfall, but where the lake was draining was still a mystery. There was no river, stream, or even a creek leaving the lake.

Rey took his time eating the pear shaped fruit. He could not afford waste, and he ate every bit down to the core, which was made up of tiny gray seeds. As he nibbled, he walked along the shore, looking into the water. The waterfall constantly churned the water, the ripples obscuring the bottom. How Ollie spotted the little mammals that swam in the depths, Rey did not know. Rey crunched into something hard, and looked at the fruit. He had taken a bite of the core and could feel seeds in his mouth. He spit out the biggest mass, pushed the few remaining seeds around in his mouth, and then swallowed them. Then he threw the core into the lake. As soon as it hit, something shot from the depths and swallowed it, disappearing as fast as it appeared.

"There's another reason not to go swimming in this lake," Rey said out loud.

Ollie was in a tree back by the campsite, sleeping, but Rey talked to him anyway.

"Still, Ollie, our business is up there," Rey said pointing up at the top of the cliff, which was invisible in the mist.

Rey untied his coat, letting it hang open. The day was warmer than he had thought, despite the ominous gray clouds. Now he looked down into the water again.

"And just where is all this water going?" Rey asked loudly. "At the rate it's coming over those falls we should be drowning in the stuff!"

The more Rey thought about it, the more curious he got. That lake was keeping a secret and Rey felt he had a right to know what it was. Where was the water going and just how deep was the lake? Maybe only the center was deep and he could walk in the shallows along the side. Or maybe, there were stepping stones somewhere just below the surface and he could walk across, looking like Jesus. Rey was sweating now and took off his coat.

The more he thought about it the more he realized how timid he had been. His mind raced through the last couple of weeks. He and Ollie had been camped at the falls and had done almost no exploring. It was all so clear now to Rey. He had wasted valuable time playing "hunter gatherer." He was better than that. He had a mission. He had a promise to fulfill. He had people to kill.

He pulled his shirt over his head, then took off his pants. It started to snow but he didn't care. The flakes helped cool his body. More confident than he could ever remember being, Rey stepped into the water, barely feeling the cold. He waded out until the water came to his knees.

"This isn't so bad, Ollie," Rey said, even though his companion was back at camp. "I can feel a little current."

Rey walked a little deeper, the water reaching his crotch now.

"Whoa, that's refreshing," he said, giggling.

Now he splashed himself with water, and then laughing, he used the palm of his hand to send sprays of water at imagined targets. The current on his feet was strong now and he walked around, trying to map the flow pattern. With his feet he found large flat rocks on the bottom, making walking difficult. Now Rey knelt, reaching down, feeling along one edge of a rock.

"I can feel it, Ollie. The current. The water is going under this rock."

Now Rey squatted, taking hold of the rock with one hand and pulling. It moved, but only slightly. When it moved he felt his foot being sucked toward the rock. Excited by his discovery, Rey squatted again and used both hands. Feeling like he could lift a mountain, Rey lifted with his legs. The rock gave way, moving to the side. As he lifted it with strength he did not know he had, the suction increased. Suddenly, Rey's feet slid, and he fell, dropping the rock. Twisting as he came down, his buttocks hit the edge of the rock he had moved and then he was sucked to the bottom, his head submerging. Now his backside was wedged in the hole he had uncovered and held firm by intense suction.

Holding his breath, submerged in cold water, and stuck to the bottom, Rey felt no fear. To Rey it seemed funny and he snorted bubbles out of his nose. Then he tried to stand and could not, suction holding him fast. Rey tried again by pushing with his arms. He still could not budge. With a growing urge to breathe, the situation was not as funny. Still supremely confident, Rey tried again and failed. Now he was desperate to breathe, the pressure in his lungs intense. Rey scooted his feet back, trying to get them underneath. When he tried to stand, his feet slipped on loose gravel and he fell back, wedging deeper in the hole.

Rey's body felt like it was on fire, even in the cold water. The urge to breathe was intense, yet only now did he feel even the slightest fear. Once again he drew his feet back, put one hand on the rock he had moved, and pushed with his legs. Inch by inch, Rey pulled away from the powerful suction, and then with a *whoosh* he was free, his head breaking above water. He blew out carbon dioxide and sucked in oxygen.

"Ollie," he shouted. "I know where the water goes!"

As if it were the most important thing in the world, Rey ran back to camp naked, snow coating his upper body.

"Ollie, I figured it out. The lake bottom is porous. It's like a giant strainer!"

Hanging from a limb, Ollie put his head out, large eyes taking in the sight of naked, wet Rey standing in a snowstorm. Rey often thought he could see emotion in his little friend's face, and he saw it now. Ollie was concerned. Then a chill went up Rey's spine and he realized he was cold—but he felt great. He felt strong. He felt confident. Everything was so clear. Every one of his senses was finely tuned. He could hear more, see farther, think faster.

Still too warm to worry about clothes, Rey set about fixing up the camp. He had not gotten around to digging a latrine but with the snow coming he knew he would want one. He dug furiously. In the tree above, Ollie watched. The sun went down and still Rey dug in the frozen ground, making good progress. Suddenly he realized he would need more firewood and he took his hatchet and began searching for wood. Somewhere in the middle of that search he decided he was hungry and came back to cook up some meat. He just about had the fire started when he remembered his clothes and hiked barefoot through two inches of snow back to the pond. When he got back he noticed an unrepaired rip in his trousers and crawled into the tent to get his sewing kit. Halfway through the repair, he felt sleepy and decided to take a quick nap.

Rey woke the next morning shivering. The tent flap had not been secured and there was a breeze coming in. He had covered himself with a blanket, but it was too cold to sleep naked and he was shaking violently. He pulled a hide over himself, and curled up into a ball. He shivered himself back to sleep. When he woke it was midday. Ollie was tugging at his hair.

"Okay, okay, I'm awake."

Rey sat up slowly, his head pounding. He started shivering again when the cold air flowed under his covers. Quickly, he curled underneath again. Rey thought back to his bizarre behavior the night before. He had almost died by wading around in the lake, getting sucked under, and then had hurried from activity to activity, confident he could accomplish anything. It was clearly manic behavior but what had triggered it? Rey thought back, remembering the fruit he had eaten. He had eaten it before—but not the seeds. Rey dug another of the fruit out, then cut it in half. The center was thick with tiny gray seeds. Rey cut off a quarter of a seed and ate it. A few minutes later he felt a surge of energy.

"It's an amphetamine," Rey said to Ollie, who was reaching for the fruit.

Rey cut out the core, and then gave the pulp to Ollie. Now he took the core and began separating the seeds.

"You never know when you might need a little pick-me-up," Rey said.

23

SUMMER AND KERRY

Master Rice's Farm
First Continent
SPRING, PLANET AMERICA

Kerry kissed Summer on a warm spring evening. It was a
perfect moment, as precious and indestructible as a diamond.
She enjoyed the intimacy all the more, since Master Rice
seemed to have forgotten about her. Master Rice's infatua-
tion with Winnie continued unabated, and the relief among
the women slaves translated into patience, kind words, humming, laughter, and contentment. Even the weather contributed
to the general well-being, sending sun when they planted, and
rain when the seeds were in the ground.

The spring planting went well, and the unusually cold
winter killed off many of the insects, so there would be another bumper crop. That added to Master Rice's good mood.
Wash continued to bully the slave children, but he came by
his meanness naturally, so there was no point in complaining
and no one to complain to. Even Wash's crude comments,
gropes, and slaps on the bottom could not diminish Summer's happiness. She sang God's praises that spring, and
now questioned her decision to run away. If life could be like
this, was being a slave so bad? However, seasons change and
spring became summer, and her life became a nightmare.

Master Rice forgot about his insistence that Kerry work
the fields, so Overseer Nkosi ordered a lean-to built on one
side of the new barn, and then rounded up saws, planes,
hammers, chisels, clamps, sawhorses, and all the glues,
screws, and nails that a furniture maker needs. Kerry had a
talent and Overseer Nkosi nurtured it.

One night there was a post-curfew knock. Summer's mom cringed at the soft rap. Master Rice had not called since before Hope was born and she had come to believe he never would again. Heart pounding, Summer was ready to rouse Rocky and scoop up Hope for the trip to Lucy's. To everyone's surprise, it was Kerry.

"Sorry it's so late," Kerry said.

"It's after curfew, Kerry," Casey said.

"I know. I brought a gift for Summer."

Summer came to the door, trying not to smile and failing. His hands behind his back, now Kerry brought out a wooden box. The inlaid top had an intricate flower pattern, made from lighter colored woods. The glossy surface reflected candlelight, highlighting the fine grain of the dark wood.

"Don't stand in the doorway," Casey said.

Kerry stepped in, now uncomfortable and unsure of himself.

"For me?" Summer said, hopeful and surprised at the same time.

"If you want it."

Summer sucked in her lips, trying not to cry. Summer's mother discreetly retired to the stove, ostensibly to fix tea.

Summer took the box and set it on the table. There were two drawers in the bottom, and the top opened to reveal a tray that lifted out.

"This was my first try," Kerry said. "I'm going to make them to trade at the Gathering."

"It's beautiful," Summer said. "If the mistress finds out I have this—"

"She's getting one next week," Kerry said. "Don't worry. Hers will be bigger."

Now Kerry looked over his shoulder at Summer's mother, who was still finding things to do around the stove.

"Except, hers isn't like yours."

Kerry slid both drawers out.

"Now push here," Kerry said, reaching in the bottom slot.

Now the edge of another small drawer appeared and Kerry pulled it out.

"The top slot has one too," Kerry said. "A good place to hide the little things."

Kerry pushed the hidden drawer back in and then replaced the drawers, hiding the process from Summer's mother.

"I love it," Summer said.

Two nights later, just before curfew, Kerry took Summer walking. When they got behind the barn, he put his hands on her shoulders, looked in her eyes until she lost her embarrassed smile, and kissed her.

When Summer was the kitchen helper, Cook often warned Summer that "Men only want one thing from a woman." Summer guessed that was true with some men, but even the master found something in Winnie that was more than just lust, and Kerry was not anything like the master. Kerry's kiss was not just an exciting touch on the lips, it was a promise—not a bond—that would never be broken. With the heat of that brief kiss, their hearts melded, never to be separated again. Now Summer understood the marriage vow "Till death us do part." No other force in the universe could separate their hearts.

Summer never spoke these thoughts to Kerry and he never to her. Nevertheless, she knew they were true because her heart was never the same again.

Summer continued to gain weight, filling out, and everyone said she would give Winnie some competition if she did not work so hard to hide her new body. Summer's mother understood, however, and helped make her clothes shapeless shifts.

Summer and Kerry pretended they were just friends, but everyone knew the truth, and everyone helped keep their secret. Master Rice was hot-tempered and selfish, and he would not share anything with anyone, even something he no longer wanted. On Master Rice's farm, no slave loved any other slave, at least not in the open.

A field hand named Wilson showed Summer how to set snares. She practiced, setting them in the evening and then checking them in the morning. Every day she improved at selecting spots, baiting, and hiding her snares. Soon she snared something almost every day. She released most of the animals, killing only those too injured to release. She did not want anyone to know about her new skill. A weaver was not a hunter.

Kerry made two slings out of leather scraps, and they found something else they could do together. Setting up wooden targets, they took turns knocking them over. Like the skiing, it took a couple of weeks of practice but eventually they could pick off the targets in order, with hardly a miss.

"David might have killed Goliath with one of these," Kerry said one day, holding up his sling. "But I think God gave him a lot of help."

Summer agreed. A sling might discourage a half-hearted predator, but it would be a pinprick to a leaper. After a month of practice, Summer decided if she ever faced a dingo or a leaper, she would rather have a spear in her hand than a strip of leather and a few rocks.

Grandma Jones visited three times that summer, giving Master Rice more attention than any other farmer. Partly, it was to see her grandchildren, but mostly it was to keep an eye on Jesse. Just before each visit, as if Jesse knew she would be coming, the slaves received a half day off. There was no time off the week after. When Grandma visited, Master Rice showed her around the farm himself, barely able to speak civilly to her. Grandma Jones spoke kindly to each slave, asking him or her how they were treated, and if they needed anything. All said they were content. All lied.

Grandma Jones marveled over the weavings, praising her mother's work and Summer's too. Summer thanked her politely, wishing she could tell her the truth about life at Master Rice's.

Grandma Jones's one disapproving comment came when she found out that Winnie had a cabin all to herself. Looking at the fine furnishings in the cabin, and the red-headed beauty that occupied it, Grandma Jones clucked her tongue, and then looked Master Rice in the eyes and said, "May God forgive you." Master Rice shook with rage, but said nothing.

When Grandma Jones visited Kerry's wood shop, she fancied one of his rockers so much that she traded sugar for it. Kerry thought Master Rice had demanded too much for the chair and as Grandma Jones was leaving, Kerry gave her one of his wooden boxes to balance the deal. Later, Master Rice smashed two of Kerry's boxes in a fit of rage. When Summer bemoaned the loss of hours of labor, Lucy said, "It was better than smashing Kerry's head."

At the end of her third visit, Grandma Jones spent an hour with Master Rice in his study, their loud voices heard through the walls. When Grandma emerged, she ordered that all the slaves be gathered, even the field hands. Then, standing on the porch of the big house, with Master Rice fuming behind her, she made a puzzling announcement.

"I am pleased to announce that I am rescinding the rule against slaves having money. From now on you are free to sell your goods or services for money. I urge you to save your money. In the near future we will even allow you to open a bank account."

No one cheered this announcement, because they could not see how it would make their lives better. Even if they could acquire money, it would get them nothing they could not trade for. However, given the way Master Rice looked, Summer welcomed the new rule since the master was against it.

"What do you think it means?" Summer asked Kerry that night.

"It means nothing," Kerry said. "Money's only good for two things. One is for evening out trades, since it's hard to get equal trades sometimes. The other is to save it up to buy something that would take too many barter goods to buy— like a combine. It would take a barn full of goods to get a new one."

"She said we should save," Summer said. "Save for what?"

"It's clear to me what she's doing," Kerry said. "If we take money instead of goods, there are more goods for the masters. If Grandma makes a rule you can be sure it helps the masters more than it does the slaves. I can tell you I won't ever take money instead of goods."

Summer was not at all sure that Kerry was right about Grandma's motives. Thinking about the new money rule, she tried to see how it could help them escape but could not imagine how it would make a difference.

Summer and Kerry had accumulated quite a store of supplies, all carefully hidden. They hid most of the hoard as far into the woods as they dared walk. Kerry remarked that they were better prepared and better supplied than he and Lonnie had been when they made their run. Summer hoped so. One way or another, it would be Kerry's last run.

Plump and happy, Hope was a bright spot in a happy spring. Patrick came around often, checking up on Casey and Hope. Some nights, Patrick and Lucy would come over and they would play cards. Bridge was their favorite. Summer and Casey usually partnered, playing Patrick and Lucy. The cards were so worn and creased, that hiding your cards was as much a part of the game as strategy and luck. Casey and Summer cheated but not as much as Patrick and Lucy, who had a system of foot taps worked out and played footsie under the table. No one cared. No one complained. Everyone laughed a lot. Sometimes Kerry would come too, and then they played other games, sang, or just talked. Kerry said his mother claimed he was born talking and never stopped. Summer could believe that, since Kerry had something to say about everything. Summer liked that about him. She was just the opposite, especially in groups, and seldom spoke unless spoken to. She never volunteered anything to the master or anyone in his family.

One night Kerry came over on the day the Bible had rotated to their cabin. Kerry was excited to learn that Summer could read and listened for an hour as she read selections. Psalms were her favorite, and Kerry listened patiently as she read them all. Afterward, Kerry wanted to pray, and thanked God for Summer's gift of reading. Still an agnostic, Summer's mother declined to pray with them, but later told Summer she was happy that Summer had found someone who believed the same things she did.

Kerry's arrival at Master Rice's farm was a milestone, a

marker that signified the beginning of months of happiness for everyone, not just Summer. Summer wished it could last forever, but it was not to be. A scream in the night marked the end of that wonderful, amazing spring.

Half the village woke, some hurrying from cabin to cabin, checking, praying for the victim. There were no more screams. The next morning Winnie reported to Cook with a cut and swollen cheek and a black eye.

Winnie had no friends, and no one to confide in. Cook asked her what happened, but Winnie only mumbled "I fell down." Winnie was fodder for gossip every day, but now she was the only topic around kitchen tables, among workers hoeing vegetable patches, and in every shop on the farm. As a weaver, Summer worked long solitary hours at her loom in the old barn. Kerry usually found reasons to drop by a couple of times a day, and others wandered through occasionally, stopping to talk as long as they dared. Today Winnie came in, looking for picking bags.

Winnie nodded to Summer but did not speak. The swelling was down, her cheek still an angry purple. Summer spoke to her, moved by compassion, not curiosity.

"How are you doing?" Summer asked.

Winnie turned, surprised.

"Fine."

Now there was awkward silence.

"I'm looking for picking bags," Winnie said.

"You're in the right spot. I think they're under the baskets."

More silence as Winnie moved the wicker baskets and found what she was looking for. Scooping up an armload, Winnie started for the door.

"Don't you have an apron?" Summer asked.

Winnie stopped, confused.

"I was just supposed to get the bags."

"Your dress is so pretty, it's a shame to press those dirty bags up against it."

Winnie dropped the bags, brushing the front of her dress.

"I have an apron in the kitchen but Cook won't let me take it home."

Summer knew Cook established that rule after the tenth time Winnie had shown up without her apron.

"Take mine," Summer said, standing and untying it.

"Why? What do you want?"

"I don't want anything, Winnie. I have other aprons and I'm just weaving today. I don't need one."

Winnie came forward, her eyes filling with tears.

"Thank you. The master gets mad if I get dirty or mussed."

Winnie lifted the apron over her head and then turned while Summer tied it.

"I'll make you a couple in different colors," Summer said. "We've got lots of scraps. Then Master Rice won't have any reason to get mad at you."

"He's got lots of reasons," Winnie said morosely.

"I don't believe that. You're Master Rice's favorite. He loves to show you off. He gives you the best clothes and you have your own cabin. I guess that's why some of us are kind of jealous."

"Jealous of me?" Winnie asked, turning to see if Summer was teasing.

"Sure. You're the prettiest girl on the farm. Probably on the planet."

Winnie smiled, then reached out and pulled Summer's shift tight around her waist.

"I'm not as pretty as you, but I don't hide it."

Summer blushed, and then pushed Winnie's hands away, letting her shift fall straight, her body once again formless. Embarrassed, Summer quickly changed the focus back to Winnie.

"Well, he never hit you before," Summer said.

Winnie did not deny the master struck her.

"I never said 'no' before," Winnie said, and then turned, scooped up her bags, and left.

Summer prayed for Winnie for a half hour before she went back to work. That night she made two new aprons for Winnie, her mother and Lucy watching, puzzled. It took Summer most of the evening to decide to share what she knew. In the end, she decided Winnie would be better off if everyone knew. So she told.

By evening the next day, Winnie's life was better—people spoke to her. It was not her marked cheek that paid the entry price into the community of slaves, it was how she earned it. True, she had only her foot in the community door, but before it had been closed and locked. Winnie accepted the aprons gratefully, returning Summer's. Wanting to give Summer something in return, she whispered, "I think Kerry likes you."

"I think so too," Summer said, blushing, remembering Kerry's latest kiss.

Winnie never wore another bruise, so everyone assumed she never said no again, but now the slaves did not blame her. While a blow to the face improved Winnie's life, everyone else's life drifted back to what it was before. For some, life got worse.

Master Rice's eyes wandered again, as they had before the Winnie era. Wearing loose clothes, hidden away in the old barn, Summer was safer than she had been working in the master's house. Kerry became more attentive, finding reasons to visit Summer in the old barn and her home at night. Summer enjoyed it, but worried about what would happen if Master Rice caught them together. In the end, it was Wash who set things in motion.

One afternoon, Wash came to the old barn, looking for something. He soon forgot about it when he saw Summer at her loom, bright sunlight cutting through gaps in the siding. A shaft of light fell on Summer, lighting her face and hair like a spotlight. Wash's look told her all she needed to know. Leaning over the loom, she tried to get out of the light.

"I hear you're nearly as good as your mama with your weaving."

Summer sent the shuttlecock through, caught it, and pushed the pedal, tightening the yarn.

Wash ran his hand over the finished cloth, his dirty fingers leaving brown smears. Summer bit her tongue.

"Pretty, very pretty. Course, it's not as pretty as you."

Summer ignored him. Wash came closer.

"This is for the mistress, and I'm way behind on it," Summer lied.

"Don't let me bother you none," Wash said, now running his fingers through her hair.

"Look, you made me make a mistake," Summer lied, acting flustered and changing shuttlecocks.

"What, me touching your hair like this? I think maybe you got feelings for me, Summer."

"Leave me alone, Wash. If I don't get this done the mistress will have me caned."

Now Wash slid his hand down her back. Summer jumped up, backing away.

"Don't do that, Wash. I don't like it."

"You're lying, Summer. If you didn't like it why are you so bothered?"

Summer started for the door, but Wash grabbed her around the waist, lifting her from the ground and then turning her around. Summer pushed on his chest, trying to break the bear hug.

"Let me go. The master won't like it."

"He's got someone better'n you, Summer. Course you're number one in my book."

Now Wash waltzed her back and forth, half dancing, half dragging her toward a pile of hay.

"I'll scream, Wash. I'll scream for help and the master will beat you for this."

Angry now, Wash slapped a hand over her mouth, holding her tight with his other arm.

"You won't say nothing to no one, or I'll be doing the beating."

Summer could not make a sound, so she could not stop what happened next. She saw the flash of light and the figure framed in the doorway. Wash was too intent on controlling her to notice, until Kerry's hand clamped on his shoulder. Summer saw the fear in Wash's eyes, assuming his father had caught him. However, when he saw the white hand on his shoulder his confidence returned and he swelled with righteous rage. No slave could lay a hand on a master.

Kerry spun Wash around. Abruptly released from Wash's grip, Summer fell back. There was no time to beg Kerry to stop. Confident in his social dominance, Wash did not expect the fist that broke his nose. Wash collapsed to his knees, wavered, then went down on all fours. Blood flowed from his nostrils. Summer caught Kerry's cocked arm before he could strike again.

"Don't you ever touch her," Kerry hissed.

Collecting himself, Wash rocked back, sitting on his heels.

"I can hang you for that," Wash said, his eyes filled with malice. "But that would be too kind."

Wash staggered to his feet, still groggy from the blow. Then he walked carefully out the door.

"You've got to run," Summer said, pushing Kerry to the door.

"Not without you," Kerry said.

Summer hesitated. She was not ready. They needed more supplies. They needed to know where they would run. Taking off impulsively would be foolish. However, it was Kerry's only hope.

"All right. I'll go with you. Let me get my pack."

"No time," Kerry said, taking her by the hand. "We'll have to use what we've got stashed."

He was right. They hurried to the door. As they stepped through, Wash clubbed Kerry with a board, sending him to the ground. Summer threw herself on top of Kerry, taking the next couple of hits across her back.

"Get off of him, Summer!" Wash roared.

Kerry was not moving, the back of his head bleeding. Summer continued to protect him. Now Wash grabbed her by the hair, trying to drag her off. Summer kicked Wash in the shins, getting him to release her. She turned back quickly, covering Kerry. Now Wash hit her hard, bruising her ribs, knocking the wind out of her. She held onto Kerry, gasping for breath.

Frustrated, Wash began striking her randomly, trying to

force her to move, but his heart was not in it. He was holding back and she knew she would survive. Now there was shouting and voices coming closer and soon she could see a circle of legs. Wash stopped, looking around at the ring of slaves.

"He did this to me!" Wash shouted, afraid. "I don't care about her."

"He didn't mean it," Summer said. "He was protecting me."

"Liar!"

Wash hit her across the shoulder blades again and again. The crowd of slaves murmured, then their collective voice grew angry. Summer's mother tried to break through, Patrick and Lucy holding her back.

"Stop it," came a tentative slave voice—a woman.

"Yeah, stop hitting her!" said another.

Wash hesitated and then smacked Summer on the bottom. It was a light blow and barely hurt.

"Stop it, or we'll stop you!" said another slave—a man this time.

Wash paused, board raised to strike again.

"You won't do nothing!" Wash said, voice wavering.

"You hit her again and find out!" a man shouted.

Wash hesitated, desperate to reassert his authority, afraid of the mob. A gunshot broke the deadlock. The slaves parted, eyes on the ground, letting Master Rice through. His rifle on his hip, Master Rice dared any slave to look him in the eye. None did. Summer remained on Kerry, protecting the man who owned part of her heart.

"What's this about?" Master Rice demanded.

"Look at me, Pa," Wash said. "He did it and Summer's trying to keep him from being punished."

"Get up, Summer," Master Rice said.

Summer obeyed, speaking as she did.

"Wash attacked me in the barn. Kerry was only protecting me. Punish me if you want to punish someone."

"Get up, Kerry," Master Rice said, kicking Kerry in the side.

Kerry did not move.

"I said, get up, boy!" Master Rice said.

"Master Rice?" Patrick said, coming through the crowd. "Let me look at him."

"Go ahead but be quick."

Patrick checked Kerry's pulse and breathing, and then felt his neck. Then Patrick rolled Kerry up on his side and opened an eyelid. Then he gently rolled him flat again and examined the head wound.

"He's unconscious. He may have a concussion; maybe a cracked skull."

"Well, get him out of here then," Master Rice groused.

Patrick signaled men forward, and they gently turned Kerry onto a picking sack before carrying him away.

"Someone find Overseer Nkosi and tell him to chain that boy up!"

Now Master Rice looked around and one by one the slaves peeled off, going back to their work. When everyone was out of earshot, Master Rice turned on Wash.

"You touch her?" he demanded.

"I was just fooling around. I didn't hurt her."

Master Rice slapped Wash, restarting the flow of blood from his nose.

"I told you to keep your hands off. She's mine."

Summer wanted to hide, ashamed of being discussed like a piece of furniture.

"Everyone's yours. Where's mine? Huh?"

"All this is mine because of my sweat and blood," Master Rice said, sweeping his arm around. "I have all this because I knew what I wanted and I went out and got it."

"This farm was here before you came," Wash said, risking a beating.

"A few shacks and some cleared ground—you call that a farm? I built this farm, cleared more land, and bought the farms all around me when they couldn't make a go of it. Everything on this farm is here because of me, including the slaves."

It was an argument Summer should not have been hearing.

"You've got the redhead and every other slave worth having," Wash shot back. "When do I get mine?"

"When you earn it," Master Rice said.

"Or when I can take it," Wash said.

Master Rice used his fist this time, knocking Wash to the ground. Now the blood poured, covering Wash's nose and cheeks. Fist still balled, rifle in his other hand, Master Rice towered over his son, daring him to fight back. Wash stayed down, wiping away blood. Finally, Master Rice remembered Summer.

"Are you hurt? Did he break anything?"

Summer hurt from head to toe but would not give Wash any satisfaction.

"I'm okay."

"You have Patrick check you out anyway," Master Rice said.

"Yes, sir," Summer said, and then hurried away.

Kerry was in Summer's cabin. Patrick had shaved the scalp around the wound on the back of his head, and then sewed up the gash. Nothing else could be done. Master Rice would not take a slave to town for treatment—especially one he hated. Kerry refused to die, although the longer he was unconscious the more concerned Patrick became. Twice a day, Patrick forced water down his throat, but not food, fearing internal injuries. After a week, Patrick was ready to begin force feeding, but then changed his mind—for at last Kerry slowly rejoined the living. After a restless night of twisting, turning, and talking, Kerry woke to find he was blind.

"He's faking," Master Rice declared when told.

Storming into the bunkhouse where Kerry lay in a cot, Master Rice thrust a candle in his face, burning Kerry's nose before he flinched. Summer was there, moving away from the bed when Master Rice glared at her.

"He wasn't hit in the face!" Master Rice said to Patrick. "There's nothing wrong with his eyes."

"The eyes just receive the images," Patrick explained. "Making sense of it all takes place back here in the occipital lobes," Patrick said, touching the back of his own head.

"That's just where Kerry got hit. I think the concussion caused some bleeding or nerve damage. If you would let me take him to town for an X-ray I could find out."

"Then what would you do? That won't give him his eyesight back."

"If it's a blood clot Dr. Hanson might be able to operate—"

"He doesn't do brain surgery. No one does. If he's blind, he's blind for good."

Lying in the bed, Kerry heard all of this but did not react.

"What a waste," Master Rice said, walking to the door where he paused, talking to the overseer.

"Find something he can do or he doesn't eat," Master Rice said, then stormed out.

Only after the master was gone did Kerry's tears flow.

Summer prayed that Kerry would get his eyesight back, even knowing God had already spared his life. That should have been enough, but Summer wanted it all. She and Kerry were going to run away together. Now that could not happen. Summer spent the next week wondering whether her desire for freedom was greater than her love for Kerry. About the same time, Kerry's attitude toward Summer changed. He would claim he was tired when she came to visit, and even when he would let her stay, he mumbled short answers and never volunteered any thoughts or feelings. He was shutting Summer out of his life. She knew why, and loved him for it. He was giving her the freedom to run. She rejected the gift, committing herself to staying with him. Kerry had given up his sight for Summer. Summer would give up her dream for him. A week later Kerry's gift was for naught.

Winnie's one-time "no," and Wash's move on Summer, shook the master out of his contentment. Wash was the oldest son, but there were others to come. The master needed to reassert his rights.

Saturday night the week after Kerry woke, there was a rap on their cabin door. Summer's mother blanched. Both she and Summer were in nightgowns, ready for bed. Wrapping herself in a blanket, Casey answered the door. Master Rice smiled, liquor on his breath, a jug in his hand.

Tears dripped from her mother's eyes as Summer wrapped herself in a blanket, and then roused Rocky. As Rocky went out the door, Summer gently scooped up Hope. The master blocked the door.

"You stay, Summer. Casey, take the baby and get out."

Instantly furious, Casey's tears dried.

"No. You can't! I won't let you!"

Even drunk, Master Rice was quick and powerful. Casey took the fist on the side of her head, collapsing in a heap. Master Rice moved in, kicking her in the side. Quickly, Summer dropped Hope back in her crib, the baby waking but not crying. Master Rice kicked her mother again before Summer could cover her with her body. Now the master stopped the attack. A few seconds later, Master Rice laughed.

"Summer, if you don't take the prize I don't know who does. Now get off her before I kick you off."

"Get up, Summer," her mother said. "I'd rather die than let you take my place."

"You can't stop him," Summer said. "Nothing you do will stop him."

"Summer," her mother started, then broke down in tears.

"I'm in God's hands now, Mother. He can't touch my soul."

"I can't live with this."

"You can, for Hope's sake," Summer whispered.

Now Summer rolled off, remaining on the floor. Crying, her mother kept her eyes down, took Hope, and went out the door. Master Rice slammed the door behind her, startling the baby. Now all three of the Lund women were crying.

24

THE GORGE

Continental Fault Line
First Continent
SPRING, PLANET AMERICA

Rey checked the lean-to one last time. He and Ollie, and a variety of insects and small mammals, had wintered together in the little log structure. Now he was leaving it for good. Nothing left was worth taking. Rey had kept busy through the winter repairing tools, tanning hides, making new clothes and boots, and drying meat and fruits.

With Ollie waddling at his side, Rey carried his rifle and pack to the raft at the lake's edge. He secured them both and then checked his ropes to be sure they were handy and ready. He had spent many long winter hours in the lean-to, weaving the ropes out of stringy vines that infested some of the larger trees. About as thick as a shoelace, the vines were nearly strong enough to hold Rey's weight. When woven together they were as strong as any nylon rope.

Now Rey surveyed the lake, and the ropes he had pre-positioned. Rey had scouted the lake from every conceivable angle and had even ventured out into the lake on logs, and then on the raft, to prepare for this effort. Even in winter the waterfall never stopped and the lake never completely froze. However, freezing weather reduced the flow enough for Rey to see more of the entrance to the gorge. Although he tried every vantage point, Rey could not see any way out of the gorge, and yet large animals regularly appeared from the gorge and then disappeared inside again.

The lake was spotted with protruding boulders and Rey had lassoed many of these. The loose ends of these ropes were anchored with buoyant chunks of wood. He would use these ropes to pull the raft against the current. Once he got to the neck of the gorge, he would reach his last pre-positioned rope. After that, he would make it up as he went along.

Ollie protested, refusing to get on the raft. The tree octopus was arboreal and limited his lake excursions to fishing. Using a bit of dried meat, Rey lured Ollie on. There was no need to strap Ollie down. As soon as Rey pushed off, Ollie clamped down tight, tucked his head in and did his imitation of a furry rock.

Rey paused long enough to take a small pouch from his pocket and remove one of the plum-apple seeds. He swallowed the gray seed, and then used a long pole to push himself into the lake. He was immediately fighting the current. Poling furiously, Rey made it to the first rope. He dropped the pole on the raft and quickly grabbed the rope, flipped it around a corner post, and rested. The seed was taking effect now and he felt strong. Pulling the raft forward, he reached the rock it was tied to and then worked the raft around to the other side, letting the current hold the raft against the rock. The next rope was dangling just out of reach. Rey used the pole to pull the float in and then pulled the raft to the next rock. The current was much stronger now.

Another rope floated out of reach of the pole. Choosing one of his ropes tipped with a hook-shaped piece of wood, Rey twirled it around his head and then threw it. He missed. High on a prickly fruit seed, he was confident he could do it on the next try—and he did. Now he pulled the rope to the raft, and hauled himself to the next rock. Repeating the procedure, he pulled himself into the mist on the south side of the gorge entrance. He was soon soaked and the log raft slippery. Ollie seemed oblivious, his head snugly tucked inside folds of his furry skin.

Rey had made it this far before and there should have been one more rope. He could not see it and the rock he thought it was attached to was almost invisible in the mist. Rey regretted eating the seed since now he could not trust his judgment. He was getting all kinds of crazy ideas about how to move forward. The craziest was to dive in the water and swim to the rock and attach a rope. Rey fought the overconfidence and instead took one of his coiled ropes and tried lassoing the rock. He missed. He missed again. What had been a light mist when he had explored this far in winter was now a downpour from the spring runoff. Whenever he tossed the rope, the heavy spray beat it into the lake.

Rey tried again and again but could not make the throw. Finally, he knew there were only two choices—give up and go back to shore, or swim for it. Even knowing his judgment was impaired, Rey took off his clothes and balanced on the edge of the raft. With a moment of clarity he hesitated. Then the moment was gone. He dove in.

The water was liquid snow, barely above freezing. In Rey's drug-fogged mind, the intense cold was distant, his immediate sensation that of inner warmth. Keeping as high out of the water as he could, Rey kicked and stroked furiously. The mist became indistinguishable from a waterfall and he was pounded. He made slow progress. Inching through the water, the rock gradually loomed out of the mist. With drug-induced energy, he burned body fuel like a marathon runner. Minutes passed, yet he kept up the pace. He was barely aware of pain—muscles, joints, and tendons—all begging for relief.

Then he was there, hand slapping painfully against the rock. He lost ground as he reached for it. Ten more strokes and he had it again. He hugged the rock, pulling himself from the water, sitting on top.

Too exhausted to crow, he beamed with pride. He had beaten the current. Breathing hard, heart pounding, barely aware of the cold, he felt like he had conquered the world. Then he realized he had forgotten to bring a rope with him. Suddenly, it all seemed so funny. Rey laughed at the absurdity of it. It was like getting a hole in one with no one around to see it, or like climbing Mount Everest but forgetting a camera.

Rey had burned off enough of the drug to understand he could not simply swim back, get a rope, and swim to the

rock again. He had to think of something. Remembering the
first rope he had thrown over the rock, he looked for it. He
could not see it but reasoned it could not have worked itself
off of the rock.

Slipping into the lake on the upstream side, Rey blew the
air out of his lungs, sinking. He felt along the rock. The rope
was three feet under the water, having loosened and settled
lower. Rey took hold, surfaced, and then worked his way
around the rock. Now the current carried him toward his raft
and he used the rope to slow himself, gently contacting the
raft. Rey tied the rope to a corner post and then climbed
aboard. The effect of the drug was about gone and he was
feeling the extreme cold. Wiping himself down, Rey dressed
again. Ollie exposed one eye, watching the spectacle.

"You could help!" Rey suggested, irritated.

Ollie closed the eye.

"Fine with me," Rey said, disgusted.

Shivering, Rey ate another seed. Ollie was watching again.

"That's the last one for today," Rey promised his friend.

Rey took hold of the rope and pulled the raft through the
mist to anchor at the rock he had swum to. Now Rey could
see more of the gorge. He had imagined the gorge as crescent shaped, but now saw that it was shaped like the Greek
letter Omega. The gorge went deeper than he thought and
curved back out of view in both directions. The waterfall
filled the space between where the gorge curved out of sight.
If there was a way out of the gorge, it had to be down one of
the canyons on either side.

Closest to the south wing of the gorge, Rey made his decision. Recovering his rope, he looked for a rock within reach
and lassoed it on his fifth try. Once he had pulled himself to
the rock, he found it was shallow enough to pole again.
Keeping away from the waterfall, Rey poled into the south
canyon. The mist was thick and he moved carefully as the
canyon curved gently to the east. The roar of the waterfall
diminished quickly as he lost sight of his winter home.

The sun was high now, penetrating the narrow canyon.
There was almost no current now, the canyon filled with

backwash from the waterfall. Rey fought the urge to hurry, poling carefully, looking for hidden objects. Now Ollie detached and reattached at the edge of the raft, leaning out and looking in the water. It was calm enough that even Rey could see fish and other swimming things occasionally shoot past.

Rounding the last of the curve, Rey knew he had been right. The canyon ended at a slope so long and shallow Rey could not see where it reached the top.

"I knew it, Ollie. That's the way out. We're on our way, Ollie. Nothing can stop us now."

Even knowing it was the drug, Rey could not help but imagine putting the sights of his rifle right between Proctor's eyes—or anyone else's. Someone was going to pay for what they had done to him.

Beaching the raft, he tied it up and then laughed at himself as he walked away. Ollie scrambled to his shoulder, anxious to be away from the water. Rey easily found the animal trail since the giants that frequented it had pounded it as flat as a highway. Even with his drug-induced energy, Rey soon found he was breathing hard. The slope was not as gradual as it appeared from the lake level. Carrying the pack was hard enough, but Ollie was three times the size of the little fur ball he had found in his mother's pouch.

"Ollie, you're getting too big for this," Rey complained.

Ollie ignored him, humming softly in his ear.

Anxious to get out of the canyon before dark and unwilling to make his friend walk, Rey ate another of the seeds. Ollie hummed disapprovingly in his ear.

"That's the last one for today," Rey said.

Then he picked up the pace.

25

PLOT

Kent Thorpe watched Grandma Jones from behind the church. With a shawl around her shoulders, she waddled into town. Despite her age, the woman was spry, and in good health. Kent had hated that woman since the day she ordered him bound and enslaved. Even now he was conflicted. Many times he had wanted to kill her himself, but now he found himself trying to keep her alive.

At Grandma's cabin, Simon paled when he saw Kent. Simon started to turn away, but Kent had seen him peeking through the curtains. He opened the door a crack.

"What are you doing here?" Simon asked, nervous. "Someone might see you."

"There's something important we need to talk about," Kent said, as kindly as he could manage.

"What?" Simon asked, suspicious.

Kent pushed the door open.

"Let me in. Someone might see us."

Simon looked around nervously.

"Grandma will be back soon," Simon said, near panic.

"This is about Grandma," Kent said.

"What about her?" Simon asked.

"You like working for her, don't you?" Kent asked.

"She is a good master," Simon said.

Kent did not have to be a psychologist to recognize the Stockholm syndrome in Simon. The claustrophobic Simon Ash had suffered through a long space voyage only to be tied up and have his freedom ripped from him. Then the early abuse the slaves suffered pushed Simon to the brink of insanity. When Grandma Jones threw him a life preserver, he grasped it with both hands. Devoting himself to the source of his misery reduced his anxiety, thus reinforcing his devotion. Ironically, any threat to Simon's relationship with Grandma terrified him.

"I have some bad news about Grandma," Kent said.

"She isn't sick, is she? I would know and she isn't sick. Is she?"

"No, Simon. You would know about Grandma's health. This is something else. It's Jesse Rice."

Simon trembled.

"He said he would never let Grandma go through with her plan to let the slaves buy their freedom."

"He said that?"

"You know how much he hates slaves. He won't stand for a single one getting free."

"He wouldn't stand for it, would he?" Simon said, realizing. "But what could he do? They can't outvote her. She makes the law."

"He told me he was going to kill Grandma," Kent said.

"He wouldn't!" Simon gasped. "I have to warn her."

"It won't matter," Kent said. "He would just deny it."

"He would, wouldn't he," Simon said, eyes darting back and forth, thinking.

"Sure, he would deny it and then he would bide his time, pretending to be loyal. Some day, maybe not in a week, or even a month, but eventually, he would do it. You should have seen the look in his eyes, Simon."

"I've seen that look," Simon said.

"He's a killer, you know that, Simon. If he says he'll do it, he will."

"I know," Simon said, trembling with the fear of living without Grandma's protection. "We have to do something."

"Not we, Simon, you. You can save Grandma."

"Not me. What could I do?"

"Master Rice is Grandma's son-in-law. He comes here regularly. You could put this in one of his drinks."

Kent held out a packet containing a small amount of clear crystals.

"What is it?" Simon asked, afraid to touch the packet.

"It will make him go to sleep, and he'll never wake up. It's better than he deserves."

"I couldn't," Simon said.

"You would let Grandma die?"

Simon easily accepted Kent's assignment of responsibility. Kent had known Simon before on Earth, when he had been an effective administrator for the Manuel Crow Foundation. Little of that man was left now. Anxiety had eaten him hollow.

"Take it, Simon," Kent said forcefully.

With jerky motions, Simon took the packet.

"Save Grandma Jones," Kent said, and then left Simon to do his dirty work.

26

CAPTURE

Central Wilderness
First Continent
SPRING, PLANET AMERICA

Rey squatted in the grass, his head barely clearing the tops of the deep green stalks. Ollie sat on his shoulder, neck stretched, trying to see. Rey surveyed the grazing animals from downwind. There were a dozen of the dinosaur-size yellow and green beasts that had led him out of Omega Gorge, but most of the animals were much smaller. There were a number of bipedal animals—something Rey had not seen before. They had heavy haunches like kangaroos, and smaller forearms, but lacked the heavy tail for balance. Instead, when they moved, they stood almost vertical. With mule-like ears, and a short, wide muzzle, they were the strangest looking animals Rey had yet met. They looked slow and vulnerable and that made Rey cautious. Nothing could be as defenseless as that species looked and survive.

Rey's attention was on a different animal. There were three different species of quadruped grazing in the mixed herd. One of these looked a lot like a cross between a llama and a horse, with long thin legs and long fur. The neck was shorter and thicker than a llama's, and the head was crowned with a small set of horns—both males and females had them. The animals sported a long tail that was hairless except for a large tuft at the end. The tails were constantly busy, brushing away insects that buzzed in great black clouds. Their backs were nearly flat, like a horse's, but sloped gently from thick shoulders to slightly narrower hips. The animals had a thin snout and black nose. They varied little in color; most were tawny with white chests. A few black and white animals were mixed in. As a whole, the animals looked sleek and powerful. About the size of a small horse, they were just what Rey was looking for.

Rey had picked out one particular pair—a doe and her fawn. After a winter of growth, Ollie was now too heavy to carry. Ollie could walk, and even run short distances, but he hated it and constantly climbed back to his perch on Rey's shoulder. Ollie needed to be weaned from riding Rey, but Rey didn't want to be slowed down by an animal that waddled along at about the pace of a hedgehog. Rey's plan was to get Ollie a ride and himself a pack animal.

Now Rey lifted Ollie down, the tree octopus instantly nervous, uncomfortable on the ground. Rey signaled Ollie to stay. Ollie responded by clamping himself to the turf and tucking his head and tentacles in. Rey dropped his pack next to Ollie, and then took off his coat and covered Ollie with it. Then he put one arrow in his belt, and nocked another.

Rey had learned to be a patient hunter. Creeping forward

one step at a time, he waited long periods between steps. His legs tired of being in a squat and he caught himself slipping a seed into his mouth. Rey spit it into his hand and dropped it in his pocket. He could use the anesthetic effect of the seeds, but it would also make him impatient.

Rey took nearly an hour to creep within range; the doe and fawn cooperated by grazing parallel to Rey. Occasionally, one or both would raise a head and sniff the air, black nose wrinkling with the effort. If they smelled Rey, they didn't recognize him as a hunter. Rey was well into the meadow now where the grass had been trimmed shorter by the herd and he was visible. Keeping still, the doe continued to graze, one bulging eye on Rey at all times. When the doe began to change direction, away from Rey, he knew it was time.

Drawing the bow he stood, aimed, and released the arrow. Rey was as good with the bow as he was with the rifle. The arrow struck the doe dead center. The mixed herd froze when Rey suddenly stood up, but the silence of the attack befuddled them. Even the doe seemed unaware that she had been injured. She started walking away, the fawn at her side. Then she staggered, caught her balance, and stopped. Rey shot her again. Now she squealed, staggered again, and then fell onto her side. The herd bolted.

Rey dropped into hiding again, letting the herd flee. The fawn started after the retreating herd but then hesitated, slowing to a stop a hundred yards from its dying mother. Rey guessed it wouldn't leave its mother. Now Rey crawled back through the grass and got his rope. On his return he grew bolder, getting within throwing range, then settling in to wait.

The fawn came back slowly, hesitating every few steps. Its mother was still breathing, the arrows marking the rhythm like the hand of a metronome. Finally, the fawn sniffed its mother and the blood surrounding the wounds. Rey stood and threw the rope, the loop dropping over the fawn's head.

It tried to flee, the rope tightening around its neck. The rope was nearly ripped from Rey's hands. Rey had been right about how powerful the animals were. The fawn bucked and kicked. Rey wrapped the rope around his waist, and then dug the seed from his pocket and ate it. Soon he felt up to the task of controlling the fawn. Rey slowly pulled the fawn away from its mother, letting it bolt here and there, shortening the rope whenever he had the chance. Soon, he had it on a short leash. Its large bulging eyes were wide with terror. Rey didn't try to touch it, or stroke it like it was a pet. It was still a wild thing. It needed to be tamed. He could do that with a stick or he could do it with patience. The seed in him wanted to use the stick, to break the animal here and now, but another part of him argued for patience. He would get a better pack animal if he stole its freedom bit by bit.

Ollie thought Rey had brought fresh meat when he saw the fawn and slapped out a tentacle to hold it so that Rey could butcher it. That triggered bucking and kicking, and Rey had to dance around, holding the rope to stay out of the way of hooves. Finally, the fawn settled down again, exhausted.

"Don't do that again, Ollie," Rey said softly but firmly. "This isn't lunch."

Ollie did not understand and a few minutes later hobbled the fawn again, setting off another round of bucking. Holding the rope, jockeying out of danger, Rey wondered if it was worth it.

"Maybe I should just let you walk," Rey said, angry with his friend.

Ollie hummed a puzzled sound.

"Just leave it alone," Rey said.

Ollie cocked his head sideways, hummed a sound Rey didn't recognize, and then whipped out his tentacles and snagged two of the fawn's legs.

Holding on for dear life, Rey took turns cursing the fawn and Ollie.

27

LOST DREAMS

Master Rice's Farm
First Continent
SUMMER, PLANET AMERICA

Master Rice ordered Summer to move in with Winnie. Humiliated, Summer expected ostracism from the slave community, but received only sympathy and kindness. With Winnie and Summer absorbing all the master's attention, the other women slaves shared guilt over their sense of relief. The community was open to her still, but Summer refused almost all offers of fellowship. Every other Saturday night she went home, where Lucy and her mother would be waiting, ready to talk, play cards, or just sit. No matter what they did, Summer would burst into tears at some point, not for herself, but for Winnie.

Winnie was a poor housekeeper, but modeled Summer's habits and soon helped with the dishes, washing, and cleaning. Using Summer's weaving scraps, they made new curtains, tablecloths, a patchwork bedspread, and chair cushions. While Winnie had no innate creativity, she did appreciate pretty things and loved Summer's decorating ideas. Winnie was vain, emotionally shallow, and intellectually limited, but she wasn't deliberately mean and was desperate for someone to talk to besides Master Rice. Rather than being jealous of having to share the master, she was overjoyed at having a friend.

Keeping Kerry busy was more work for the slaves than doing the chores themselves, but they found as much for him to do as they could. When there were potatoes or gourds to peel, Kerry reported to the kitchen, walking across the compound swinging a stick. When something needed sanding, Kerry sat in his former furniture shed and hand sanded. Some days he worked with Casey, holding skeins of string or yarn as she wound bobbins. When there were no chores to do, he sat in the sun, face to the sky, thinking. He never shared those thoughts.

Wash and his brothers discovered the fun of torturing a blind man. One afternoon, as Kerry headed to the kitchen to wash the lunch dishes, Wash grabbed a rake and set it in his path. Summer saw and called out a warning, but it only confused Kerry and he stepped on the head of the rake, the handle snapping up and striking him in the face. Kerry gasped, a hand pressed over his right eye.

"That's dangerous, Wash," Nkosi said, when he saw Kerry's black and swollen eye.

"It's not like he's using his eyes anyway," Wash said, he and his brothers erupting in laughter.

Tripping Kerry became daily sport. The Rice boys created endless variations on the game, putting everything in Kerry's path from manure to buckets of water. It got so bad, that Kerry was often late to his chores since he would get halfway there and then have to go back and change his clothes. Summer's heart ached for Kerry, but whenever she sat with him, he would not talk about it. He was still pushing her away, but she would not leave him no matter how hard he pushed.

Eventually, Kerry understood he could not drive her away, and some of the old Kerry returned. He was still reserved, holding the best of himself back, but it was enough to rekindle hope in Summer. Now she began to work on a new plan; one where a woman and a blind man could escape.

Master Rice stopped taking the slaves to the village church, although occasionally he would take Winnie in the back of the wagon when he and the mistress went. Nkosi explained that since there was so much work in the summer, that the master wanted them to rest all day Sunday. By Grandma's Rule, only household chores were to be done on the Lord's day. Most slaves used part of Sunday to work on their own trade goods for the Gathering; however, whenever he could, the master found Sunday chores that just had to be done. As for the half day off, Master Rice only remembered it when he heard Grandma Jones was out making visits.

Summer threw up the morning of one of Grandma Jones's visits. She was nauseated most mornings now. Summer had known for two months that she was pregnant, but did not have the courage to tell her mother, and not the heart to tell Kerry. Grandma Jones's first visit was to Winnie and Summer's cabin, as if she had heard the gossip. Grandma looked inside, praised the girls for how they had fixed it up, and then marched to the furniture shed where Kerry was sanding table legs. Grandma Jones gently asked what had happened, and when Kerry responded that it was an accident, she prayed for him, and then stormed off to the big house.

No one was sure how old Grandma Jones was. She had always looked ancient to Summer. Some said she was at least a hundred years old. However, the woman who stomped across the compound and then threw open the front door had the energy and power of a twenty-year-old. The subsequent shouting match could be heard in the compound, although only a few words could be distinguished. Slaves dawdled in the courtyard, listening. Even Grandma's driver, Simon, who normally visited with Cook, remained, pretending to tend the horse. When Grandma Jones stormed out as hot as she had gone in, the slaves heard one clear line.

"I'll put an end to this at the next Gathering!" Grandma said.

Stunned, but hopeful, Summer quickly hurried toward her loom, avoiding the master's eyes. It did not matter, the master was fixated on Grandma Jones's carriage, as Simon drove her back to town. Later she shared what had happened with Kerry, wondering out loud what it meant.

"Changes are happening, Kerry," Summer said, daring to let herself hope. "More time off, the right to have money—something has Master Rice upset like I've never seen him. Things are changing, Kerry, I'm sure of it."

"Maybe so, maybe so," Kerry said, searching for her face with blind eyes. "One thing is for sure, if Master Rice is against it, I'm for it."

Then Kerry smiled, and for a moment the old Kerry was back. Touching Kerry's face, Summer kissed him. She decided not to ruin the moment by telling him about the baby. Instead, she nestled against his side and described the sunset for him as best she could.

A few days later Wash and his brothers went hunting and came back with something squirming in a gunnysack. Slave children gathered, watching as the laughing boys dumped out the contents—a redback. The ten-legged lizards were a foot long, slender, with a triangle-shaped head and a long tail. A red stripe running from nose to tip of the tail gave the lizard its name. Redbacks were poisonous, injecting victims through two sharp fangs. The slave children squealed but did not run. They had seen this game before. As the lizard scrambled away, Wash picked it up by the tail, holding it out at arm's length and then yelling "Catch!" Then Wash threw it to Montiel, who caught it by the tail, jaws snapping at his arm. When Montiel threw it, Malcolm missed the tail, and then had to dance out of reach of the snapping jaws. The redbacks were runners, not fighters, and the lizard made another run. Slave children scattered, letting the redback through. Wash caught it just as Kerry came into the courtyard, swinging his stick, headed to the kitchen.

"Hey, blind boy," Wash called. "Catch this."

"No!" Montiel shouted.

Kerry froze, head up, knowing that something was coming. The redback struck his chest. Instinctively, Kerry pinned it with his free arm. The redback bit deep into his arm. Kerry screamed, trying to drop the lizard. Hanging by its fangs for a second, the redback then let go, and scuttled away as Wash and the boys erupted in laughter. Slapping a hand on the wound, Kerry turned back toward his shed.

"Kerry's hurt!" Rocky called, bursting into the old barn. "He got bit by a redback."

Summer found Patrick with Kerry, examining the wound.

Kerry was sitting and breathing like he could not catch his breath.

"Shouldn't you put a tourniquet on it?" Summer asked. "It would stop the poison from spreading."

"It's better to let it dilute," Patrick said. "Besides, it's too late."

Feeling his wrist, Patrick took Kerry's pulse.

"His heart is beating like a hummingbird."

Summer didn't know that bird, but she had heard the expression many times and knew what it meant.

Kerry was delirious for two days and nights. Sweating and wetting himself, his bedding needed to be changed four times a day. Knowing it would embarrass Kerry if Summer helped, she let Lucy and her mother nurse him. They knew how important he was to her and would take the best care of him.

Deadly to dogs and children, redback bites rarely killed healthy adults. After two days Patrick announced that Kerry would live. Relief spread through the slave community. In the fields, around kitchen tables, among workers, there was talk of getting revenge on Wash. It was just talk.

When Summer told her mother about her condition, her mother cried, saying she had guessed but hoped it wasn't true. They held each other, crying together until Rocky complained there wasn't any dinner. Lucy came that night and turned the tragedy into joy, saying, "Babies are such a miracle, it almost makes me believe in God." Lucy's children came over then, and they ate together, the boys playing until late, the women planning for a midwinter birth.

A month before the puff tree harvest and the Gathering, Wash and a couple of his brothers cornered Kerry in the courtyard. Forming a circle, they took his stick and then pushed him back and forth like a toy. Then Wash pulled a knife and cut Kerry's suspenders. One of the other boys yanked his pants down. When Kerry reached for his pants, he was kicked from behind, making him fall on his face. The boys pulled his pants all the way off now, taunting him, calling for him to come get them. Embarrassed and angry,

Kerry swung wildly, trying to find a face or body to punish. When he accidentally caught Malcolm in the side, the boys went wild, punching and kicking Kerry, and then stripping him naked.

Naked and bleeding, his back veined with scars, Kerry got to his feet, held his hands out, and started forward. Lost until he ran into something he could use to orient, other slaves called out directions. Kerry turned toward the sound of a friendly voice. Wash tripped him. Wash and the boys laughed.

Summoned by Rocky, Summer could see what was happening and hurried to her cabin, grabbing a blanket and then running back to the yard. Nkosi was there now, scolding the boys, careful not to cross the invisible line of class differences. Summer pushed through, wrapping the blanket around Kerry. He took the blanket gratefully, and accepted her help until she spoke. Thoroughly humiliated, Kerry thanked her, and then gently pushed her hand away.

Nkosi led him safely away and back to his shed. Summer visited him after supper, sitting with him. She talked and he listened. Near curfew, she stood to go.

"Summer, I would have married you."

"You still can," Summer blurted, forgetting that Kerry didn't know about the pregnancy.

"If the boys found out, they would do to you what they did to me. Of course it wouldn't matter, since Master Rice would kill us both."

"We could keep it secret."

Kerry did not respond. He just looked sad and far away. Impulsively, Summer kissed him lightly on the lips. Kerry smiled.

"Summer, never give up your dream of running away," Kerry said.

Summer paused in the doorway.

"I'm working on a plan for both of us," Summer said.

"Sure, Summer. That's great."

Kerry had that faraway look again. Summer left him like that, planning to check on him first thing in the morning.

Kerry was late to kitchen duties the next morning, so Cook sent Winnie to find him. Winnie came screaming out of the furniture shed. By the time Summer got to the shed, slaves were lifting Kerry down from the rafter where he dangled from a rope. He had balanced on a chair he had built himself, put his head in a noose, and tilted the chair over.

Summer collapsed next to his body, sobbing and crying. The heart melded with Kerry's heart by a spring kiss was broken.

28

INFESTATION

Central Wilderness
First Continent
SUMMER, PLANET AMERICA

A week after they captured Fawn, she was carrying a blanket and small load on her back. Ollie still rode on Rey's shoulders, although he had to spread across both now. Rey had fashioned a bridle, and Fawn accepted it, getting a slice of plum-apple for a reward. Rey was careful to make sure there were no seeds in Fawn's slices. The beast was trouble enough.

Ollie and Fawn ignored each other now, Ollie having finally given up on having Fawn for dinner. Fawn was easy to care for, since she fed herself and usually followed along behind Rey and Ollie. Fawn's tail was busy brushing away insects. Rey kept up a steady Minnesota salute as well. Occasionally, Fawn would get it in her head to go after a particularly attractive morsel off their path, and Rey would have to wrestle her back in line, but it happened less frequently with each day.

They were crossing the high plain, which was as dry as Rey had feared. The great river that fed Omega Falls came from the north, emptying over the fault line; not a single drop went south. It was spring, however, and every few days rainstorms could be seen in the distance, crossing the plain, creating short furious downpours and then moving on. Lightning was common, the resulting thunder reverberating across the vast, empty plain. Rey avoided low routes whenever possible, wary of flash floods.

Rey and his little family weathered two of the vagabond storms, sheltering as best they could in the lee of a hillock. They found water regularly enough to keep them hydrated, but that would end as spring turned to summer. Rey knew he would eventually need to fashion a way to carry additional water since Fawn drank more than he and Ollie combined. The grasses were the green of early spring, teasing the fauna with a lushness that could not last. By midsummer the plain would be tinder dry. He had to get across before then.

He was angling south for Big Eye Lake, the only clearly distinguishable feature in the photo he was using for a map. Rivers fed and drained the lake and he would follow one west. Without mountains, hills, or even an occasional tree to navigate with, Rey used early morning and evening stars to correct his track. It was crude at best, but the size of the lake gave him a reasonable shot at hitting it. If he missed it to the west he would hit one of the major rivers feeding it. If he missed it to the east he might walk all the way to the southern coast.

Occasionally they passed large herds, most made up of a variety of species. Usually, the mix included a few of the large beasts that he had seen in Omega Gorge. Rey called them yellow tusks, although the camouflage pattern on their skin was dominated by sage green, not yellow. Rey couldn't understand why Mother Nature had bothered to camouflage them since they were too large to hide. There was some of Fawn's kind, too. Fortunately, she ignored them. Most of the herds also included the two-legged mule-eared creatures that would make a Puritan laugh.

Even when they didn't see the herds, there were unmistakable signs—vegetation mowed in mile-wide strips, and piles of manure. Rey experimented with these, finding some that burned like buffalo chips. Now he collected them during the day to burn at night.

Ollie shifted position and Rey felt a mild irritation on his skin. It felt like sunburn, but Rey hadn't had his shirt off recently. Rey ate another seed, his treatment for all his ailments. By evening the irritation in Rey's shoulder had become an itch. The itch was nearly constant the next day, Rey's attempts to scratch it usually frustrated by Ollie's prostrate body. Instead, he treated his growing irritation with another seed or two.

By the next evening Rey knew it wasn't an ordinary itch. It was spreading. That night by firelight, Rey took off his shirt and twisted his neck around as best he could, examining his right shoulder. There were several red bumps with white heads. They looked like pimples.

"I'm too old for zits!" Rey said out loud.

Ollie poked his head out of the pack where he was hiding, looked around, and then pulled back inside. Fawn, whose only goal in life was to eat every bit of grass on the planet, briefly looked up from her grazing, and then dropped her head and went back to work.

Rey scratched the bump hard. The itching subsided, replaced by burning. He stopped. Just as quickly, the itch came back. Now Rey ate a seed, and then waited for it to take effect. When he could scratch the bumps and not care about the burning sensation, he picked at one of the white spots. The head of the pimple tore off, white pus oozing out, followed by clear liquid. Rey squeezed the bump and something white and wriggling protruded from the hole—a worm.

Disgusted, Rey tried to pull the worm out. The slippery thing managed to wriggle back inside and no amount of squeezing would bring it out again. Sickened by the thought of something living in his body, Rey pulled his knife and scraped the bump. He managed to tear more of the skin away, but he couldn't dig the worm out with the flat blade. Finally, he gave up, feeling along his back and shoulders. There were bumps from his right shoulder to his neck.

Rey tried again, cutting into another bump, and again the worm wriggled deeper. Now he had two bloody holes in his shoulder. Even with the seeds in him it hurt. Staring into the fire, he worried. Parasites weren't the kind of predator he was used to dealing with. He could kill wolves, and maybe even a pig, but the predator that might ultimately get the best of him was a worm. Rey shuddered at the thought of the worms in his body. Rey prided himself on being fearless and with a high pain tolerance. He had sewn up his own wounds, killed men in hand-to-hand combat, and murdered men he had only seen through the scope of a sniper's rifle. He hadn't given those men or their families a second thought, but now he obsessed about parasites in his body. He had to get them out!

The fire crackled, glowing embers escaping toward the sky like short-lived fireflies. The embers gave him an idea. He picked up a brand, letting it burn out, leaving a glowing tip. Taking a deep breath, he touched the red-hot end to one of the open sores. Even under the influence of the seeds, the pain ran deep and wide, and he could only hold it a few seconds.

Tears in his eyes kept him from seeing for a minute. When he could see again he found a blackened spot on his shoulder. He had no idea whether the worm was dead or not. Even if it was dead, there were worms behind his neck. He would never reach them. There had to be a better way.

The next morning his right shoulder throbbed when he put the pack on. Not only couldn't he carry the pack, he couldn't carry Ollie either. Instead, he strapped a blanket and a hide to Fawn's back, and then waited while the nervous beast settled down. Now he picked up Ollie to set him on Fawn's back. Neither animal liked the idea, and Rey found himself wrestling with Ollie and getting kicked by Fawn. With no other option, Rey tried over and over, getting the same result. An hour later he was bruised from shin to waist and his neck was lined with purple bruises from Ollie's twisting tentacles.

He gave up and compromised. Fawn was exhausted enough to accept the pack, instead of Ollie, and Rey shifted Ollie's perch to his left shoulder. Ollie still wrapped tentacles around Rey's neck, irritating the blisters there, but it was preferable to being choked and kicked.

Using dead reckoning, Rey started off again, trying not to think about his worm infested back, but every few steps he needed to scratch. By midday there was a bump growing where he had tried to burn the worm out.

29

SMOKE

Central Wilderness
First Continent
SUMMER, PLANET AMERICA

Three days later the worm bumps had spread across his neck to his left shoulder. Carrying Ollie was impossible now, and it took only half a day of walking for Ollie to accept a ride on Fawn. Since Fawn was used to the weight of the pack, Rey created a saddle using ropes and a hide stuffed with his spare shirt and pants. Fawn accepted this, and then nuzzled Rey for fruit. Next Rey blindfolded the colt, and then lifted Ollie onto Fawn's back. With Ollie perched on her back, Fawn couldn't see the tree octopus, and all went well until Rey made the mistake of snacking on a piece of jerky. When Ollie shot out a tentacle for a share, Fawn spotted it and realized where Ollie had gone. Fawn bucked, kicked, and twisted violently enough to make a rodeo bronco proud, but nothing but explosives could shake loose a tree octopus once it set its hook shaped claws. Ollie rode it out and that settled it. After that, Fawn accepted Ollie as she had the pack.

Once a day, Rey pawed through Ollie's thick fur, looking for infestation but never finding any. Fawn was free of the worms too, despite her much shorter fur. Fawn's coat was dense, however, like a plush carpet. Rey had no idea where he had picked up the parasites, but guessed they might be a larval form of one of the hundreds of insects that constantly buzzed around them. His long shaggy hair and beard protected most of his head and face, and he wore long sleeves, trousers, and boots. Occasionally, he was bitten on the back of his hands and his cheeks, but there were no worms there. The shirt and trousers he wore were made out of a soft, tanned hide. The shirt had no collar, so something could have landed on his neck and crawled inside, but when? How? He did not remember any bite on his shoulder.

Rey was nauseous the next morning and threw up his breakfast. He managed to keep a light lunch down and then took a long siesta. Rey's sleep was unusually deep and dreamless. He woke reluctantly, Ollie shaking him to consciousness. When his eyes focused, he saw Ollie holding up one of the long-tailed rodents that occasionally crossed their paths. Ollie had killed it himself and was very proud.

"Good boy, Ollie. Today you're a man."

Ollie stared back blankly, expecting more.

"All right, since you're a man now, I'll give you a man's name. You are now Oliver T. Tree Octopus. But I'm still going to call you by your nickname."

Ollie continued to stare.

"Okay, give it to me. I'll clean it for you. We'll eat it for supper."

That afternoon they came to the first tree they had seen since leaving Omega Gorge. It was a midget, only seven feet tall, but Ollie climbed every inch of that stubby tree. The tree had a thin layer of gray bark that covered a wood as hard as mahogany. Rey tried chopping off a limb but soon gave up. It wasn't worth the work. The branches were covered with clover shaped leaves that attached to the limbs with no stem. The sage-colored leaves were thick and hard to pluck. When Rey ripped one off, a few drops of clear liquid dribbled out.

Rey offered the leaf to Ollie, but he turned up his nose and refused to taste it.

"Let's camp here, boys and girls," Rey said, feeling weak.

It was too early for Rey to be this tired. With a few hours of daylight left, normally Rey would use all of it. America's day was three hours longer than Earth's. When Rey was wasting his life in the cabin, waiting for rescue, the length of day made no difference, but now the extra daylight would help him reach the Fellowship before winter. Rey managed to stay awake long enough to cook up Ollie's prize over a mound of flaming dung, but fell asleep before it was completely dark.

The next day the terrain changed subtly, rolling so gently that it was barely noticeable. They passed three trees this day and spent the night under a fourth. It was another short day. Rey threw up his dinner this time. That night, lying under the tiny tree, looking through the sparse leaves at the stars, his hand kept coming to his back and neck, scratching, constantly scratching.

"I need an ointment? Is there a Walgreen's around here somewhere?" Rey suddenly shouted.

Fawn jumped and Ollie looked down from his perch, checking for danger. Then Ollie went back to sleep and Fawn's head drooped again. Then Rey remembered the liquid that dripped from the leaf when he tore it off. Getting up he scratched the head off of one of the blisters, and then he tore off a leaf and let the liquid dribble into the open sore. He had no idea of whether he had just dripped poison into his body, so he stopped with one sore.

The next morning there was no change in the wound. Still, he repeated the treatment three times that day. The midget trees were now becoming more numerous, although not larger.

Rey gave up trying to eat whole meals, since he was leaving valuable resources along their path in half digested puddles. Instead, he ate small amounts regularly through the day. This helped alleviate the nausea, but he wasn't consuming as many calories as he was expending. If he kept this up he would starve to death with a pack full of food.

Mid-afternoon he spotted dark shapes in the sky ahead. They were circling, diving, then climbing again. He had seen them before—vultures. On America, virtually every ecological niche was occupied, just like on Earth. The birds circling in the sky would be part of nature's recycling crew. Rey had seen America's vultures descend from the top of the cliff when they were camped at the base of Omega Falls. The creatures would appear in the sky above Rey's kill, waiting while he skinned it and took what meat he could carry. Then they glided down with hardly a wing flap, folding their wings and dropping the last few feet. In the sky they looked like birds, but up close they resembled flying mammals, with four legs, plump, muscular hairless bodies that were white on the bottom and brown on top. Their broad wings were colored similarly, and folded in two places, so they tucked up neatly against their bodies when they landed. They were ugly things, with the face of a pug dog, and the teeth of a vampire. Occasionally, they would hiss and snap at each other as they fought over a bit of meat, or a juicy internal organ.

The terrain didn't give Rey many choices, since the hills were getting steeper and he didn't have the energy to climb any more than absolutely necessary. Rey continued, knowing the vultures were scavengers, not hunters. An hour later they came within sight of what they were feeding on. It was a yellow tusk. The terrain was rocky here, the grasses sparse. The yellow tusk has died in the middle of the only easy way through the valley. Rey's military training set off warning bells. This valley was barely wide enough for him to pass the yellow tusk's carcass, with high rocky sides. It was perfect for an ambush. Even knowing there were no humans for a thousand miles, Rey hesitated, studying the hillsides. Even animals used ambushes. Finally, satisfied, Rey started through, doubling his pace.

The vultures watched Rey come, bulging eye bulbs glistening in the sun. Then one by one, they screeched angrily, and then took to the skies. These flying mammals could not simply flap their wings and get airborne like a bird. Rather, they had to get a running start, unfolding their wings as they ran, and then jumping high enough into the air to allow their wings a full stroke under their bodies. Once airborne, their legs were pulled up and they looked like flying boxes.

With the vultures circling overhead, screeching angrily, Rey tried to hurry past the carcass. Ollie stood high on Fawn's back, thinking with his stomach. Rey studied the fallen yellow tusk as he passed. He couldn't see any signs of attack. The neck was intact, the intestines not torn open. The vulture had torn strips from the body, but there was enough meat here to feed a thousand vultures, not the dozen that were feeding. Rey was about past when he noticed marks on the yellow tusk's neck. Stopping, Rey looked closer. All along the neck were blisters with white heads, just like those on Rey. Now Rey thought back to the first yellow tusk, the one Ollie had found at the base of the fault line. Rey guessed a predator had chased it off the cliff. Now he wished he had examined the carcass more closely.

By midafternoon the next day Rey was staggering and made camp early under a small stand of the midget trees. There was enough dried dung around for a good fire, and he made soup. He kept the first small helping down, but made the mistake of taking seconds. He lost all of it as soon as the last spoonful was down.

The evening was cool, maybe sixty degrees, but Rey was hot, and not from the seeds. The worms were poisoning his body. Rey was tired enough to sleep, but lay awake thinking about what the worms were doing to his body. Just before sunset he noticed something unusual in the distance. There was smoke rising from behind a distant hill. Was this the chimney smoke of his dream? He watched the smoke until it was too dark to see it anymore.

The next morning he was up early, looking for the smoke. It was gone. Disappointed, he lay back down. Above him, Ollie stirred, confused about whether it was time to get up or not. Fawn was busy denuding the prairie. Finally, Rey forced himself up again. He fed Ollie, but did not bother to try and eat breakfast, since he would only say goodbye to it later. As he lifted Ollie to Fawn's back, he noticed the smoke was there again.

Now he took two of the seeds from his medicine pouch and swallowed them. It was a race now. The worms were killing him but there was a chance he could keep Jephthah's promise before he died. Then they were off, Rey's body burning from a combination of fever and adrenaline.

30

MEETING

Near New Jerusalem
First Continent
SUMMER, PLANET AMERICA

When the Fellowship left America, they abandoned more homes and villages than Grandma's People could use. So, Grandma moved her people into the most developed town, and occupied the surrounding farms. Even so, there were many unused structures, most of which had been cannibalized, their windows, doors, and hardware stripped. Many of these old buildings were little more than wooden frames now. Others, like the barn they were meeting in, were used for storage. This particular barn was located on the fringe of Carter Jackson's farm. Jesse had long had his eye on Jackson's pitiful little operation. That acquisition would have to wait, however, since he needed Jackson. In the unjust system created by Grandma Jones, each master's vote counted the same, no matter how big or small the operation.

A dozen masters were gathered in Jackson's little-used barn, sitting on bales of hay, sipping smooth corn liquor.

A still sat in one corner of the barn—one of the reasons Jackson repeatedly refused Jesse's offers to buy his land.

"I say she won't go through with it," Wilson said.

Wilson was another of the reasons they had gathered. Jesse needed Wilson and Jackson on his side when he moved against Grandma Jones. Both men were important, and both were conservatives and reluctant to change the status quo; Wilson as an influential farmer and Jackson as an entrepreneur, who made up for his small acreage with side business. In addition to Jackson's bootlegging business, he also sold a variety of popular spices, and imported sea salt from his salt works that one of his sons operated every summer along the coast. He was also the most successful scavenger on the planet, combing abandoned Fellowship sites for anything useful, including nails, screws, fasteners, hooks, needles, pins, hinges, pipe, wire, and wood trim. Jackson was the man to go to for the hard-to-get parts.

Jesse sighed theatrically, giving Wilson a pitying look.

"Did you ever think she would give slaves a half day off? What about own money? Reggie, how much more evidence do you need?"

Reggie Wilson was an obese man, with gray hair and beard. A tall, big-boned man, Wilson spread his weight over a massive frame. However, his thighs were now so fat that he no longer could sit a horse and came and went in a fancy buggy. It was widely known that Wilson's oldest daughter ran his farm now, his only legitimate son a peculiar boy who sat for hours staring at bugs or chasing dust motes. Still, it was Wilson who voted on the council.

"Letting them buy their freedom is a different animal," Wilson argued.

"Not to Grandma Jones," Jesse countered. "They are all stops on the same road, and that road leads to emancipation."

"Anything to what Grandma says about free slaves helping to improve our economy?" Jackson asked.

Small in stature, but with broad shoulders and thick legs, Jackson looked like a compact body builder. Jackson was a quiet man by nature, and not a debater. When he spoke, it was in the form of pointed questions.

"She talks like this is Earth," Jesse said to Jackson. "What do words like 'economy' mean here? What do we need money for when we can just trade for what we need? Money creates greed, and we don't need that here. Yet, she is forcing money on us."

There were murmurs of agreement, as if greed could not exist without money.

"Isn't slavery wrong?" Jackson asked in his laconic way, and then sipped his liquor, the room now deathly quiet.

"Leave it to you, Carter, to cut to the heart of the matter," Jesse said.

Nervous laughter spread around the circle of men.

Jesse knew emancipation was much more complex than just whether slavery was a fair institution, but it suited Jesse's purposes to oversimplify the issue.

"That's what it comes down to for me too," Jesse said. "I've thought and prayed about this since Grandma first mentioned her intention to free the slaves. You know the Bible doesn't prohibit slavery."

Heads shook up and down all around the barn.

"Jesus Himself never speaks against slavery. So, if the slaves are to be freed, it's because we feel it's what is best for them and for us. We all know the slaves will be freed someday, so we can put that question aside. The real question is whether it's best for them to be freed now, or a few years from now."

Jesse paused, letting the anticipation build. All gathered knew he was against freeing the slaves, but what they were looking for was a rationale that would give them the strength to join Jesse and block Grandma Jones.

"To answer that question I had to ask myself why Grandma enslaved the whites in the first place. Many people think it was because most of them were soldiers, and dangerous. But I know that wasn't the real reason. She enslaved them for the same reason she turned down the chance to leave with the Fellowship. Why? Because white people expected to look down on black people, and worse, black people expected to be looked down on. Grandma Jones wanted us to see that we didn't need white people to survive and that we could build a successful community without the help of white people. She wanted our children to learn that they could do anything they set their minds to and could do it without affirmative action, welfare, and handouts."

Heads were nodding enthusiastically now.

"Our children have been learning that lesson," Jesse said. "And, yes, Grandma Jones might be right that we need to be doing more like exploring and building roads and such. But just when we're ready to move to the next level of community, she wants us to turn to the white people to help us? That flies in the face of the reason she enslaved them in the first place!"

Now there were murmurs of assent.

"The slaves will be freed on planet America, make no mistake about that. The question is when? Well, I say the time isn't right yet, not when we're about to build up our community. Seems like exactly the wrong time. I say we talk about freeing the slaves when the first generation is gone—at least the first generation. When the slaves have lost that connection to the racist Earth culture, that's the time to talk about freeing them."

"Exactly right," Master White said.

"Makes sense," said another master.

"It's too soon," said another.

Jesse watched Wilson and Jackson. Both were nodding in agreement. Hiding a smile, Jesse celebrated inwardly. He now had a clear majority of the council on his side. Grandma Jones was now vulnerable.

31

MUD POTS

Nothing came easy now, not thoughts, not motion, not living. With his body awash in seed juice and worm excretions, Rey only just managed to keep moving. If not for the seeds— those wonderful seeds—he knew he would be lying on the prairie with vultures feeding on his body. The seeds gave him a chance to live long enough to fulfill his promise. God? What God?

The smoke was an unreliable guide, intermittent and strangely transient. Back at his cabin the smoke from his own fires would linger in the air, and more than once he had used the smoke from his own chimney to guide himself home from miles away. This smoke teased him, coming and going, quickly dissipating.

The midget trees were common now, although not a forest, and there were small birds that rested in the tops, taking flight when Rey passed. Ollie would occasionally shoot out a tentacle, trying to snag one, but the birds were wary and quick. Now there was a great plume of smoke ahead of Rey, and he staggered on, burning muscle now, every bit of fat burned from his body. Watching the smoke ahead dissipate, Rey struggled to understand. Something was wrong. Smoke did not act like this. Too confused to figure it out, he climbed another hill, noticing that the grasses were sparse now. Reaching the top, Rey's eyes were on his feet as he started down the far side. Then an alarm went off in his head and he froze, looking ahead.

Rey was looking down into a crater shaped valley. Midget trees were evenly spaced around the rim, as if planted every ten feet. The valley floor was a mix of blue pools of water and bubbling mud pots. Two dozen animals sprinkled the valley floor. Some wallowed in mud, others waded in the clear water. Steam floated over the valley floor. Just over the far rim, Rey saw a plume of steam shoot into the air—his smoke.

Rey sat, emitting a deranged laugh. He had wasted what might be his last day of life chasing a steam cloud. Ollie tugged at his hair. Fawn was ripping up what little grass grew in the bowl.

"Go climb a tree," Rey said to Ollie.

Ollie did, leaving Rey reclining, watching the animals. There were not any of Fawn's species in Mud Pot Valley, or the walking mules. Most of the animals looked like hairless wildebeests, the males sporting long curving horns. Both males and females were brown with sand colored vertical striping. There were a number of the tiny pronghorns too. Curiously, the animals engaged in a routine. First they would splash in the pools of water, and then lie on the bank near the mud pots. While there, birds would descend from their perches in the midget trees and hop about on the resting animals. Then the animals would get up and wallow in the mud pots, shake off the excess, and then wander up and out of the valley. A steady stream of animals came over the rim to replace those that were finished.

"It's a Doctor Doolittle spa!" Rey said to Ollie, even though his friend was hanging in a tree behind him.

Rey studied the birds that landed on the resting animals. No effort was made to shoo the birds away as they hopped from place to place, occasionally dropping their heads. Birds on America did not have beaks, so it looked as if the birds were kissing the animals. Then Rey thought of Earth's rhinos and the birds that rode their backs.

Rey hobbled Fawn and took the pack and saddle off. Then Rey took off his boots, and stripped off his shirt and pants, walking naked to the nearest pool of water. The animals watched him come, wary, shying away but not running. Rey put his toe in the pool. It was warm, but not hot. He waded in, the water getting hotter with each step. When it was as hot as he could bear, Rey sat slowly, letting his body adapt to the temperature. Finally, he sank his shoulders under the water, the itch from his blisters intensifying and then hurting. He stayed under despite the pain, and a minute later dipped his head, rubbing his hair and beard. When he surfaced the water around him was cloudy.

The heat of the water was sapping what little strength Rey had left, making him dangerously drowsy. He also worried about raising his body temperature even more than the worms and seeds already had. Forcing himself to get up, he walked from the pool to an empty place in the grass near an unused mud pot. A yellow tusk nearby watched him with a huge bulging eye until Rey flopped on the grass, and then the yellow tusk ignored him. The slight breeze cooled Rey's wet body, bringing his temperature down. Soon Rey was drifting into sleep. Rey knew how vulnerable he was—naked, his rifle and bow tied to the pack—he was just too tired to care.

Rey dozed. Suddenly Rey was awakened by a light touch on his back—a bird. Rey tensed but did not move. His head sideways, Rey opened an eye. The bird had brown feathers, a white belly, and little bulging eyes. Its legs were feathered all the way down and tickled Rey's skin when it moved. Its lips were set in a permanent pucker. The bird hopped along Rey's back, cocking its head back and forth, studying the terrain. Then it stopped, and dipped its head, its lips engulfing one of the blisters. Rey felt a pinprick and then mild pain as something probed into the blister. Then the bird pulled its lips back, the tail of the extracted worm slipping between its lips.

Another bird landed on Rey, but the first drove it off, Rey's body too small to share. The bird worked diligently and systematically. Rey fell asleep during the process, losing track of the bird's work. When he woke the bird was gone. A few minutes later another bird landed, hopped around on Rey's back, then flew off. Guessing he was clean, Rey sat up, letting his blood pressure equalize. Then he walked to the mud pots. Rey stayed in the shallows, afraid he would not have the strength to extricate himself from thick mud. After rolling in the muck he returned to where Fawn grazed, stretching out in the grass, letting the warm spring sun dry the mud to a powder. Rey fell asleep again.

When he woke, Rey dusted off but did not wash his body. Retrieving Ollie, Rey circled the crater's rim, camping in a stand of trees. He cooked soup again that night, eating a small amount. It stayed down. After supper, Rey took off his shirt and felt along his shoulders. Small scabs dotted his back. Rey slept deeply that night, and in the morning, as he drifted up toward consciousness, he dreamed again of the cabin and the smoke from the chimney. Sleeping late, he woke ravenous and ate a full breakfast. Then he returned to the crater rim. The spa was just as busy today. Ollie climbed the midget tree next to Rey.

"This isn't the place, Ollie, but it's like this," Rey said, remembering his dream. "It's a lot like this."

Turning to Ollie he scratched behind his fuzzy ears.

"Let's stay here a couple of days, Ollie. If that's all right with you?"

Ollie hummed agreement.

32

BIG EYE LAKE

Central Wilderness
First Continent
SUMMER, PLANET AMERICA

"Another thing I miss," Rey said loudly, "are sunglasses."

Riding on Fawn's back, Ollie ignored Rey.

"Are you listening?" Rey demanded.

Ollie opened one eye long enough to satisfy Rey.

"I said I miss sunglasses. You wear them on your face to keep the sun out of your eyes. They have dark lenses. I look good in sunglasses, Ollie. Really! Of course, everyone looks good in sunglasses. You'd look good in sunglasses, but that's not the point. The point is that when Proctor marooned me here he should have taken care of all my needs, and I mean all of them! How could anyone forget sunglasses? And chocolate? There wasn't so much as a single chocolate chip in the supplies."

Rey cocked his head, glancing at the sky—not a cloud on any horizon.

"A hat!" he said suddenly. "Not that coonskin cap I wore in the winters. I need something with a broad rim."

Since leaving Mud Pot Valley, Rey had regained his energy and his appetite. Much to Ollie's annoyance, Rey seemed to need to make up for the days of silence when he plodded along, stopping early and sleeping late.

"I wore a baseball cap a lot when I was a kid," Rey said, his mind drifting from thought to thought. "I got into a fight over it once. I was a freshman and a big guy—I think he was a grade older than me—yanked it off my head. His friends thought it was pretty funny, but they stopped laughing when Mitch hit the floor. When I got back from suspension Mitch and his friends got out of my way when I came down the hall. No one ever took my hat again."

If Ollie was impressed he hid it well.

The land was still primarily open plain, but there were enough midget trees to satisfy Ollie's need to climb and soon a new species of tree mixed in. Rey named them "pole trees." These trees were mostly trunk with a few stubby branches. From a distance they looked like telephone poles. Clumps of green pulp hung from the branches, like ugly Christmas tree ornaments. The balls were spongy, and if you squeezed them hard, a small amount of liquid oozed out.

"And toilet paper. Do you know they didn't leave me a single roll?"

Ollie did know about the toilet paper, and the chocolate,

and the sunglasses, since Rey complained about them incessantly.

They topped a rise, the plain spread out before them. The slope down was manageable, and in the distance Rey could see the forest thickened noticeably. Then to his right he saw the glint of water in the trees.

"How about fish for dinner, Ollie?"

Ollie hummed agreeably at the word "fish."

Rey led Fawn down the slope, more concerned about his own footing than that of his sure-footed colt. The pole trees increased in number as he worked toward the water and new species appeared. From a distance, one of the new trees looked like a slender trunk topped by a golden ball of leaves. Up close, Rey could see the oval leaves were similar in texture to many he had seen on Earth, although the color was a fall color, not spring. The other unfamiliar tree was green, like the ones Rey knew on Earth, and the leaves hanging on long stems were shaped like oak leaves. For some reason these trees were popular with birds, the branches filled with pairs of blue feathered, squeaking birds. Seemingly every possible forking branch held ball shaped nests, the nesting birds coming and going through a small hole in the sides of the nests.

The undergrowth increased too, and soon Rey pulled the machete from the pack. He hadn't used it since leaving Omega Gorge. Rey hacked a path big enough for Fawn to get through. As soon as they came close to one of the golden trees, Ollie pulled himself up the trunk and was gone. Rey continued through a thick mass of vines and came upon a path. It was well worn and wide enough for Fawn. Rey put the machete away and took the rifle in hand.

Cautiously, Rey led Fawn along the path, alert for any movement. Ollie swung above them, the trees close enough for him to do his Tarzan thing. The path ended at a sandy bank that sloped down to a river. Hoof prints and dung were everywhere. It was a watering hole and probably busy at dawn and dusk. Rey walked to the water's edge, looking up- and downstream. Trees and thick undergrowth lined both sides, the river curving out of sight in both directions. Leading Fawn back up the bank, he let her strip leaves while he looked at his photomap.

Big Eye Lake was easy to find in the photo, and he could trace several rivers feeding it. Now Rey found Omega Gorge and traced his finger toward Big Eye Lake. Rey had only crossed a few small streams since leaving Omega Gorge, and they were too small to be seen in the orbital photograph. Now Rey found the speck on the photo that he thought might be Mud Pot Valley and traced it back to Omega Gorge and then to the nearest river. Rey had not been walking a straight line—if this was the river he thought it was. He was also close to Big Eye Lake.

Now Rey took out his water, drinking deep, and thinking. He was sure he knew which river he was sitting by, and it came from the northwest. He could follow it for weeks before having to cross and turn west again. Rey knew that was the smart move, but Rey was also only a day or two away from Big Eye Lake. It was irrational, he knew, but it was the one landmark that he wanted to see. Back in the cabin, when he used the photos for wallpaper, Big Eye Lake had stared back at him night and day for twenty years. He just had to see it for himself.

Taking Fawn's lead and whistling for Ollie, Rey turned southeast. Killing the people who did this to him could wait a few days.

"Jell-O, Ollie," Rey continued as if the conversation had never stopped. "Red Jell-O, green Jell-O, yellow Jell-O, any color of Jell-O. I really miss Jell-O."

Rey left the animal trail late in the afternoon when an armadillo shaped creature as big as a boar waddled past. He was soon cutting his way through a bewildering variety of creepers, shrubs, and saplings. Little creatures skittered out of his path, birds took flight, and small creatures scolded him from hidden places. Keeping the river on his right, Rey cut a new path, Fawn happy behind, eating most of what he cut, Ollie swinging through the trees above. Rey was about ready to give it up for the night when he heard the sounds of waves lapping a shore. Cutting furiously, Rey chopped his way toward the sound, breaking free of the forest and finding himself on the shore of Big Eye Lake.

To call it a lake was to do it disservice, for Big Eye Lake was an inland sea. The deep blue lake spread out in all directions clear to the horizon. Ocean size waves rolled over each other, washing up a sandy shore. Huge sea birds with the wingspan of a Cessna cruised by in formation. Smaller birds ran along the shore in great flocks. To his right the sun was setting into the forest, giving a small island a reddish hue, as if it was on fire. Rey was spellbound.

"Look at that island," Rey said to Ollie, wherever he was.

There was no reply. There was never a reply. Rey collapsed onto the sand, suddenly depressed. He had seen many amazing sights on his journey, but had no one with whom to share the experience. He wanted someone to confirm the awe he felt, or argue with him, dismissing it. He would give everything he owned for someone to argue with over whether this body of water was a lake or a sea. What was the point of seeing all this if there was no one to share it with? He could not even take pictures.

"A camera! That's another thing they forgot," Rey shouted, sending seabirds into the skies.

Now his depression turned to anger. He had a life back on Earth and they had ripped him out of it and dumped him here. At least in Proctor's dungeon there had been fellow prisoners to ignore but also to listen to. His resolve renewed, he whistled for Ollie.

"We've got an hour of daylight, let's use it," Rey said, turning northwest.

33

TOP PREDATOR

Central Wilderness
First Continent
SUMMER, PLANET AMERICA

Spending day and night together, Rey had not noticed how much Fawn had grown until he fitted her with the water skins. These water skins were literally skins, made from amphibious animals Rey killed with bow and arrow. He knew water would be a problem as soon as they crossed the Silver River. The photomap showed no rivers large enough to resolve from orbit and the terrain was featureless. He had no way of knowing if there would be water before they reached the western mountains.

As he lifted the water skins into place, Fawn gave only a slight shudder. Even with Ollie in his place, Fawn carried the load easily. Fawn was growing rapidly, her horns coming in, and she frequently rubbed her head against rocks, mounds, and even Rey. Like a teething infant, Fawn was irritable unless her head was rubbed.

Looking ahead, Rey saw a field of stiff green shoots resembling reeds. Hoping they were edible for Fawn's sake, Rey started into the reeds. As soon as he did, half of them suddenly retracted into the ground.

"On second thought," Rey said to Ollie and Fawn, "let's go this way." Leading Fawn along the bank of the river, Rey skirted the field with the disappearing reeds.

Summer was waning, the verdant spring a distant memory. The trees were far behind and Rey was back to burning dung. With no trees to climb, Ollie was restless during the day and hid in the pack at night. Mixed herds roamed this side of the Silver River, but Rey had not crossed paths with one for a few days. Gathering dung for his evening fire, he paused, studying the dried manure. Rey had developed some expertise with dung, and had not seen this kind before. He broke up the pile and moved the pieces around. He found a piece of bone.

"Something around here eats bones," Rey said to Ollie.

Ollie hummed a worried hum from Fawn's back, poking his head out and surveying the horizon.

The days were long now, longer than on Earth, and Rey set an easy pace. Getting there was more important than getting there quickly. There was no sightseeing on that plain, since the only variation was in the length and type of vegetation, most of which Rey had trouble telling apart. Fawn was more discriminating, passing over seemingly juicy morsels for drier fare. Ollie found food to eat, Rey turning down most of his offers to share. Ollie's favorite, and the one thing Rey could eat, was small round fruits growing along thick stalks. The fruit had the consistency of figs and a nutty taste, although Rey limited the number he ate since they tended to loosen his bowels.

Water continued to be Rey's biggest challenge, but luck had been on his side. From time to time he would cross the path of a herd, and on two occasions he managed to follow them to watering holes. He was upstream of one now. The trickle of water that fed the tiny pool was completely overgrown with vines, virtually hiding the water source. The hidden trench also served to trap large animals unlucky enough to stumble into it. Rey had passed the remains of one such animal as he worked upstream and away from the watering hole. Several large lizards were tearing away remaining bits of flesh. The lizards disappeared under the cover vines, splashing into hidden tunnels. Rey was careful when he hacked his way down to the water source. The lizards remained hidden, preferring lunch to be already dead.

Rey followed the hidden stream north, the stream dividing like an artery into many small capillaries. With care, Rey managed to get Fawn across without foundering and then struck out west again. He had only a vague idea of where he was.

A half day's walk west, he saw the dust of a herd. The dust spread across the horizon like a low hanging fog. The herd was a long way off, but the size of the dust cloud testified to its numbers. Rey moved slowly, plotting a course that would let the herd pass to the south. Rey was especially cautious, since predators might be tracking the herd, hoping for stragglers.

Rey caught up with the herd at dusk. This was not a mixed herd of yellow tusk, walking mule, and pronghorn; this herd was of one kind, and like nothing he had seen on this planet. The biggest animals were two feet taller than Rey, the smallest adults about his size. Covered in various shades of brown fur, with white faces resembling a horse's, they ripped up clumps of grass with fleshy, hanging lips. They carried their weight on their back legs; the haunches lower than the front shoulders. What made them different from other herd animals were the front legs, which were longer and thinner than the back legs, with long curved claws. The claws made it impossible to walk with the palms flat, so they walked on their knuckles with a gorilla gait.

Ollie hummed a worried hum and then pulled his head in and retracted his tentacles, leaving a brown furry lump on the saddle.

"Coward," Rey said.

The horse-faced animals shuffled slowly, occasionally pausing to tear up the turf, digging out white lumps in cupped hands and then slurping up the lumps with prehensile lips. An occasional infant wandered close. Like the young of every species, they were frisky, playful, and jumped and ran about. Pairs backhanded each other with powerful slaps. Sometimes they rolled around like playful puppies, struggling for the dominant top position. At the back of the pack were some of the largest of the animals, but also the oldest. With shabby coats, bare patches, and gray faces, they struggled to keep pace.

"That's the geriatric ward," Rey said to the lump on Fawn's back.

Suddenly, the heads of the herd snapped up, several standing on back haunches, heads high, looking behind them. Then there was a screech, and a nightmarish creature came up out of the grass, charging into the herd. Ten feet tall, it ran on two legs, and was feathered from head to toe. Like a giant flightless bird, it had a long curving beak and thin legs ending in three-toed feet, tipped with long claws. With its head low, it attacked.

Fawn reared and tried to bolt. Rey held the rein, speaking softly to the frightened colt. Holding tight, Rey slowly reeled the colt in, rubbing her head and scratching around her horns. Fawn quieted, although she shook with fear. Rey understood.

The giant bird was drab colored, but its underbelly was flame red. It had stubby wings, which when spread showed more red. With camouflage colors on top, the bird would be virtually invisible squatting in the grass.

Breaking into a gorilla-like gallop, the herd stampeded. The chase was short. One of the old ones went down when a huge beak snapped a front leg. As he crumpled to the ground, the old horse-face knocked the attacking bird away with a powerful blow from its good foreleg. The carnivorous bird stumbled back, screeching its rage. Then it lunged again, getting a grip on the horse-face's neck. Rey did not wait to see the inevitable outcome. His experience with pigs told him to get as far away as possible, as quickly as possible.

Hurrying into shoulder high grass, Rey pulled the rifle from the saddle as he angled away from the fight, which ended quickly. Soon even the sound of the stampeding herd faded into the distance. When they climbed a small rise, Rey looked back across the sea of grass seeing nothing but a receding dust cloud. To the west was nothing but endless grass.

"That bird must be the bone eater," Rey said, shaking his head slowly. "Ollie, I've got to be honest with you. The odds of us making it to the mountains just changed, and not in our favor."

Ollie poked enough head out to show his wide eyes.

"I'm sorry I got you into this, Ollie, but we don't have much choice now. It's got to be farther back than we've got left to go."

Ollie stared but did not hum.

"Let's go find you a tree to climb," Rey said, pulling Fawn west.

Ollie hummed happy agreement.

34

POISON

New Jerusalem
First Continent
SUMMER, PLANET AMERICA

Jesse looked forward to this meeting with Grandma Jones. The old woman's incompetent reign would be over soon and this would be the first step. From a porch rocker, she watched him come across the meadow. He was uninvited and unexpected, and he had planned it that way.

"Jesse, things must be going well on your farm since you spend so little time there now," Grandma said.

Jesse settled into the rocker next to her, wondering about her comment. Did she know about his efforts to undermine her?

"Bring tea, Simon," Grandma said.

Jesse heard the window curtain behind them rustle, the ever-attentive Simon hurrying to do Grandma's bidding.

"You are wasting your time," Grandma said. "I won't rescind my rule."

"Maybe I'm not here about that," Jesse said.

"Then you're here about my plan to free some of the

slaves. You're easy to read, Jesse, you wear your thoughts on your face."

"I came to talk some sense into you. You don't seem to understand how you're splitting this community. People aren't ready for what you plan to do. I came to ask you to delay setting the slaves free."

"I'm not letting any free, Jesse, I'm offering them the chance to earn their freedom. It will take a decade for a man or a woman to earn their freedom. How is that a threat to you? No, I'm not delaying the announcement. In fact, I've been thinking of just the opposite. I've been thinking I'm moving too slow. This community needs a shot in the arm and this is the way God is telling me to do it."

"I've been talking to people—" Jesse began.

"You've been talking to masters," Grandma cut in.

"The masters speak for their families," Jesse argued.

"Those families don't always agree with the masters," Grandma said. "That's another mistake I aim to rectify. Instead of one vote per family, we need one person, one vote."

"Including drunks, landless, and hermits?"

"Everyone."

"Slaves too?"

"If I have my way the slaves will earn their way to voting status."

Every one of Grandma's words convinced Jesse that he had to act, and act soon before Grandma destroyed their community.

"Selma," Jesse said, using her first name deliberately. "Grandma" had become an honorific in the community. "I've been talking to the members of the Council of Masters and they're concerned about your leadership. Maybe it's poor decision making, maybe it's senility, but you've lost touch with the people."

"Senility?" Grandma snapped. "Since when is doing the right thing—"

Simon came out carrying a tray, cutting Grandma off. Simon put the tray on a small table that sat between the rockers.

There were two cups of tea, sugar and milk. When Simon started to hand them cups, Grandma dismissed him.

"That's fine, Simon, leave us alone now."

Simon withdrew reluctantly, watching them all the way to the door. Grandma took her cup, spooning in sugar and then adding a drop of milk.

"Do you ever miss skim milk?" Grandma asked suddenly.

"What?" Jesse said, caught by surprise.

"Skim milk, two percent, ultrapasteurized cans of whipping cream? What about oranges? Strawberries in winter? I never knew how much a treat they were until I couldn't have them anymore. And those are just the icing on the cake, Jesse. We need more willing workers to build a society that produces such wonders, not to mention medicines, inoculations, and antibiotics. Do you know we lost three premature babies in the last few years that would have been saved on Earth?"

"You're going to turn trained murderers loose on your own people just so you can get strawberries in winter?"

"You're deliberately missing my point," Grandma said.

"If this isn't senility, then I don't know what is," Jesse said.

"Babies are dying, Jesse."

"And freeing the slaves won't help that," Jesse shot back. Grandma sighed, and sipped her tea. Feeling victory, Jesse reached for his cup.

"Selma, it's too much too soon. I've talked to almost all of the masters, and a majority will back me. I plan to call a council meeting and put the issue to them. If you don't back down, I'll move to have you removed as leader."

Jesse turned his cup, looping his finger through the small handle.

"There isn't any constitution, Jesse, I don't rule by secular law. I rule by divine law."

Jesse froze. Grandma was pulling the spiritual card.

"Are you claiming divine right to rule? If so, Fancy is next in line."

"No, I'm only saying I ended up as leader because God

worked through me to get here. Are you saying God is through with me?"

"Maybe I am," Jesse said boldly. "Every leader in the Bible had to give way to the next generation."

"You?"

"Why not, I've got a clearer vision of what this community needs than you."

Jesse spun the cup nervously.

"You're forgetting something, Jesse. If you call a council meeting you're not the only one who can make proposals."

Jesse stopped spinning the cup. Now across the meadow he could see Teresa coming. Jesse did not want that busybody to hear.

"It won't matter if you don't have the votes," Jesse said. "And your days of being a dictator are numbered."

Teresa would be in earshot soon. Jesse put his tea down and stood.

"It depends on what I propose," Grandma said.

Jesse's mind raced, but he couldn't imagine a proposal that would threaten his plans.

"Propose away, Selma. I have the votes."

Teresa reached the porch just as Jesse stepped off.

"Don't leave on my account," Teresa said, knowing Jesse disliked her.

Ignoring her, Jesse turned, watching her settle into his rocker.

"It's not too late to get on the right side of this," Jesse said.

"I'll stay on God's side," Grandma said.

Teresa snickered, and as Jesse turned to stomp through the meadow, picked up Jesse's untasted cup of tea.

35

BONE EATER

Central Wilderness
First Continent
SUMMER, PLANET AMERICA

The horse-face herds took to moving at night to avoid the heat. By midmorning, they would settle into the grass, resting, adults taking turns walking picket duty around the perimeter. Just before sunset the herd would get moving again, walking through the night. Rey learned to rest during the worst of the heat, but travel after dark was difficult. America's tiny moon was bright and the night sky thick with stars, but the light was barely enough to travel by.

Rey rationed the water now, stretching their reserves between watering holes. Herd trails sometimes led to water, but the horse-faces used water more efficiently than humans, tree octopi, or pronghorns and Rey had to abandon many trails after fruitless miles in search of water.

The sun was setting ahead of them, making Rey wish for sunglasses again.

"Ollie, have I mentioned how much I miss sunglasses?"

Ollie ignored him. Fawn suddenly put her head up, sniffing and snorting. Rey stopped, and slid the rifle out of the pack. His bow hung ready along the side. Ollie sensed something too, his head emerging, tentacles wrapping around Fawn's horns. Rey saw and heard nothing. Now Fawn moved, pulling Rey. Rey let her lead, his eyes busy, his rifle ready.

"Easy, Fawn," Rey cautioned, the colt threatening to break into a run.

Stumbling along behind his aroused colt, Rey was about

to take control again when the tall grasses thinned, replaced by lower, greener vegetation. He immediately recognized it as the vines that covered many of the streams on the plains. Reining Fawn in, he gave her and Ollie water from the skin to calm them, and then pulled out his machete and went to work, chopping away the cover.

There was a depression underneath but no stream. Frustrated, Rey buried the tip of the machete in the ground and sat. He had been too generous with the water. The last skin was nearly empty. There was still some water in the bottles, but that would not go far between the three of them. Sitting in the sun, sweating from the effort, Rey knew he was only making his situation worse. They needed to bed down and let the heat pass.

Rey stood, pulling the machete out of the ground—the tip was dirty. Wiping the dirt away, Rey realized it was moist. Finding his shovel, Rey dug up a shovelful. Moist dirt stuck to the tip. Digging aggressively, Rey created a small, deep, basin. A small amount of dirty water puddled at the bottom. Rey dipped his finger and tasted it. It tasted like dirt.

"If either of you complain, you'll get no dessert tonight," Rey said.

An hour later, Rey had a deep hole with a few inches of water at the bottom. He let Fawn drink her fill first, and then Ollie, and then finished the water in the skin while he waited for the water to clear. Once particles had settled to the bottom, he could scoop off small amounts of clear water, transferring it to a skin. It would take all night to fill both skins if he didn't exhaust the water supply.

Rey took the pack and saddle off Fawn and then hobbled her, letting her browse lazily around the watering hole where the juiciest foliage grew. Then he built a little shelter, using the pack and his blanket. Ollie crawled into the shade, pulled his head in, and went to sleep. Rey was about to go to work at filling his water containers when he noticed the horizon. Heat distorted the air, distant images shimmering. Shading his eyes, Rey could see the horizon had a purplish serrated edge.

"Mountains!" Rey shouted. "Ollie, Fawn, I can see mountains!"

Fawn looked up, making sure there was no danger, then went back to eating. Familiar with his friend's occasional ranting, Ollie paid little attention. Rey danced for joy, hopping and bopping to music he had not heard for twenty years. Then he was angry again.

"A CD player! That's another thing they should have left." Then realizing he had no electricity and that any batteries left behind would have been expended long ago, he said, "Well at least a harmonica!"

Dripping with sweat, Rey lay on his stomach at the edge of the pool and scooped up water, pouring it over his head. Then he filled his smallest water bottle and transferred its contents to the skin. Rey still lacked a proper hat, instead wearing his spare shirt on his head, protecting his scalp from the worst of the sun. Eventually, the hot sun baked all of the energy out of him and he fell asleep.

The screech of a bone eater shocked Rey awake. Groggy, relying on instinct, Rey moved. There was a streak of red, Fawn reared, and then tried to bolt. Ollie emerged from the tent, head extended, eyes wide. Then the leaping bone eater, with its huge beak open wide, clamped on Fawn's neck.

Rey scrambled for the rifle, finding it in the grass. Bucking and kicking, Fawn struggled to break free. Ollie's tentacles whipped out, snaring one of the bird's legs, but with nothing but turf to grip Ollie was jerked free when the bird moved. The bone eater and Fawn danced in a circle. Rey took aim, unafraid of hitting Fawn. It was her only chance.

Even wrestling with Fawn, the huge bird was hard to miss and Rey put a bullet into its side. Releasing Fawn, it spun to face its attacker. Confused, the bone eater looked past Rey, then at Ollie, still wrapped around a leg, and then finally at Rey. Rey shot it again. This time the bird staggered but still no blood had seeped through the feathers. It plunged forward and at nearly twice Rey's height, the massive bird towered over him. Rey fed another cartridge into the chamber and pulled the trigger—misfire. The bone eater hesitated and then lunged. Rey rolled into the waterhole, curling into a ball. The bone eater collapsed on top of him, shoving him deep into the mud. Now the giant bird convulsed, and then died. Rey could feel the warm drip of its blood.

The bone eater was too massive to move, so Rey dug at the edges of the hole, making a space large enough to wriggle through. As soon as his head appeared Ollie wrapped tentacles around it, nearly pulling Rey's head off.

"Easy, Ollie. I'm going to need that."

Once out, Rey hurried to Fawn who was limping away, using a hopping motion with her hobbled front legs. Rey caught hold of her rein, pulling her to a stop. The colt quivered as Rey examined the wound. The bone eater had cut deep into Fawn's neck. The spurting blood told Rey all he needed to know. Rey put a new cartridge into the chamber, then pointed it at Fawn's head. She turned toward him when he did, looking at him through her large bulging eyes. One of Ollie's tentacles snaked around Rey's right arm, pulling the rifle away.

"She's dying, Ollie. This will stop the suffering."

Ollie moaned; a sound Rey had never heard.

As if to prove him right, Fawn's front legs collapsed, the colt falling to her knees. Her back legs buckled immediately. Now Fawn looked up at Rey, begging with her eyes. Ollie let go of Rey's arm, then snaked his tentacles around Fawn's head, pulling on the colt. Rey let Ollie try. He soon gave up, retracting his tentacles.

"It's for the best, Ollie," Rey said.

Then Rey shot Fawn in the head.

36

INVESTIGATION

New Jerusalem
First Continent
SUMMER, PLANET AMERICA

Grandma Jones was the last to walk away from Teresa's grave. Teresa's children had left a minute earlier, arms around each other, their spouses and children comforting as best they could. They had lost a mother and grandmother. Grandma Jones had lost her counselor, advisor, and friend. The community would grieve too, missing Teresa's booming voice, sharp tongue, and bawdy sense of humor. Grandma would miss her wise counsel and patient ear.

Simon held an umbrella over Grandma, shielding her from a light drizzle. Surveying the cemetery, Grandma sighed, knowing she too would end up there someday, but it was too soon for Teresa; especially for a woman who had never been sick.

Grandma thought back to the last night she had spoken to Teresa. Normally Teresa and Grandma would sit on the porch, talking, until late into the night. That night was different. Shortly after she arrived, she got sleepy and excused herself early. Her house slave found her the next morning, still in bed, clothes on, dead. On Earth, an autopsy could give them a cause of death, but here, the doctors could only guess. "Probably an aneurism," they concluded. They were guessing, but Grandma could guess too.

"Simon, we're going into town," Grandma said.

Faithful Simon walked a half step behind Grandma, down the gravel path from the cemetery and into town. Grandma walked the boardwalk, others stepping out of her way, respecting her mourning. Just past the bakery, Grandma turned into the pharmacy.

The "pharmacy" had once held their supply of painkillers, antibiotics, and blood pressure medications they brought from Earth. Exhausted years ago, they had slowly been replaced by local cures ranging from leaves to insect excrement. The pharmacy had a peculiar smell, not unpleasant, just a heavy stew of aromas. The walls were lined with shelves, holding bottles stacked three deep. The windows admitted bright light, yet no amount of light could chase all the shadows from the musty corners.

Milt and Sally Lowe ran the pharmacy, and had a knack for distilling the active ingredients from the original natural substances. Their one slave had been a chemistry major in college, and proved herself invaluable. Melissa's eyes widened as she saw Grandma.

"I'll get them, Ma'am," Melissa said, the slave hurrying into the back. Milt and Sally came out, wiping their hands on their aprons, smiling, issuing deprecating greetings. Milt and Sally looked as much alike as people of different genders could. Both were plump, both had broad, toothy smiles, and both wore their hair short and curly. In their aprons, they were as interchangeable as Tweedle Dee and Tweedle Dum.

"I've been having trouble sleeping," Grandma said. "Do you have anything that might help?"

"Yes, certainly," they said together, and then bumped into each other as they moved in opposite directions. Sally took a large jar of pink leaves from a shelf just under the counter, placing it in front of Grandma.

"Pink tea is very popular with insomniacs," Sally said. "I've used it myself and I slept like a baby."

"Do you have anything stronger?" Grandma asked. "I've tried the tea before and I don't think it will do the job this time."

Now Milt turned to the shelf behind them, pushing jars out of the way, finding the one he was looking for.

The jar contained dried snails.

"Many of our older—I mean senior—customers prefer

this. You can eat them, or if you prefer, I can grind them into a powder for you. No one's ever complained that they didn't work."

"How much would I have to take?"

"A half dozen should do it," Milt said, after a quick look to Sally for confirmation.

"Is there a danger of overdose?" Grandma asked.

"No, not really," Milt said. "You would have to eat fifty or sixty before there was much danger. Of course you would get a pretty bad headache if you ate more than a dozen."

Grandma knew it was not possible that Teresa could have eaten that many snails. First, she had never seen Teresa eat anything resembling snails, and second, Teresa was certainly planet-wise, and would not eat something she was unfamiliar with.

"That might be what I'm looking for, but I don't like the idea of eating that many snails. Do you have something more powerful?"

Milt and Sally exchanged looks and then Milt climbed a ladder to a high shelf, coming down with a sealed jar, wrapped in brown paper.

"We don't usually recommend this," Sally said. "We don't even like to talk about it."

Milt opened the jar and poured out a few crystals. Then he looked in the jar, seeming puzzled. Sally looked in the jar, and then at the crystals on the counter. Milt and Sally locked eyes, but did not share their concern. Milt turned to Grandma.

"You might remember the sleeping sickness from ten years ago or so," Milt said.

"It was mostly children," Sally added. "No one died, but some of the children slept for three days."

Grandma was embarrassed that she could not remember the incident, but there had been so many illnesses, accidents, and deaths.

"It was traced to hat fruit," Sally said.

"I remember banning the fruit," Grandma said. "But we eat the fruit now."

"We discovered that it wasn't the fruit that created the sleeping sickness," Milt said.

"It was a secretion found on the underside of the leaves," Sally said, proud of their discovery.

"However, even then it takes special conditions to turn the secretion into a sedative," Milt said.

"An early, hot spring does the trick," Sally said.

The way the Lowes split up their story, cutting each other off, and finishing each other's thoughts, annoyed Grandma.

"As long as you wash the fruit to get off any crystals, it's safe. The crystals make a very powerful sedative."

Milt indicated the crystals in the jar.

"What does it taste like?" Grandma asked.

"Slightly bitter, but you won't notice it," Sally said.

"We recommend the snails," Milt said. "But if you just can't eat that much, then a crystal of this will do."

"Just one crystal?" Grandma asked, looking at the tiny grains.

"Never any more," Sally said. "I recommend powdering it and taking only half the first night."

"A third," Milt corrected.

"Is it fast acting?"

"Almost right away," Sally said. "I would get ready for bed before I took it."

"Perhaps I'll try the tea one more time," Grandma said.

"We'll set some aside for you," Sally said. "We had another customer interested in the crystals too."

"Who?" Grandma asked.

"Jesse Rice," Sally said. "His wife's had trouble sleeping."

Grandma knew Fancy drank herself to sleep most nights, and slept half the day.

As she left the pharmacy, she noticed their slave, Melissa, watching from the back room. She ducked around the corner when she realized Grandma had seen her. When Grandma reached for the door handle, Simon ran into her, his eyes somewhere else.

"I'm sorry. I'm so sorry."

"Just get the door, Simon," Grandma said.

Walking out, Grandma noticed Simon linger, glancing nervously toward the back room of the pharmacy. Filled with suspicions, Grandma didn't know what to think, or who to trust. It was times like these that she needed Teresa most, and now she had been taken from her. Confident that God was still on her side, Grandma vowed to finish the journey, alone if necessary.

37

MOUNTAINS

Central Wilderness
First Continent
SUMMER, PLANET AMERICA

Ollie was flat on the ground, his head exposed, and his tentacles splayed out carelessly like spaghetti. The tree octopus was just too tired to retract them. With a dry mouth, cracked lips, and eyes so dry it hurt to blink, Rey studied the photo of this region. He knew he was on the border between the high-orbit photo of the central region and the low-orbit close-ups of the western region, but where exactly? The mountains he had been marching toward for months were relentlessly symmetrical, as if all were cut from the same template, making it hard to know which part of the range he was approaching. The photograph showed that the mountain range angled southeast, and was only a third of the length of the range that protected the coast. However, what Rey sought lay between the two ranges in one of several valleys. That spot was marked.

Rey's immediate problem was that he was lost. Tracing the mountains with a finger, Rey reasoned that if he followed the mountains south he would eventually come to where the valley west of the mountains in front of them emptied into the plain. He could then work his way up the valley to where site #1 rested. But how far south was the valley entrance? It was still blistering hot on the plain, but it was late summer and once he got into the mountains, his progress would slow. He did not want winter to catch up with him while he was in the high country.

Ollie was another problem. Built for the well-watered eastern forest, Rey's little friend was poor at water retention. He drank almost as much as Rey but traveled at half the speed. Rey stood tall now, looking ahead, estimating his chances. Then Rey felt the water skin. Now he made a decision that would either save them or kill them. They were dying anyway.

The distant sound of thunder turned Rey around. On the horizon he could see a gray band of clouds. Storm clouds like these were getting more frequent as they approached the mountains. If they produced any rain, it all evaporated before reaching Rey.

Opening the water skin, he lifted one of Ollie's tentacles and dipped it in the remaining water. Ollie sucked up a small amount and then squirted it in his mouth. Rey let Ollie repeat the process until there was only a little left. Rey did not drink any. Now Rey picked up Ollie and put him on his shoulders, most of Ollie's body resting on the pack. Then he started walking.

Ollie doubled the weight of the pack; the only compensation was that there was no water weight to carry. Rey was dehydrated, and his head and muscles ached. Carrying Ollie in the heat soon had him sweating away precious water he could not afford to lose. Rey's vision was blurry, forcing him to watch where he placed his feet. Even so, he stumbled so often that soon he could see nothing but the next spot where he would step. If Rey had enough water, the short, dry grasses he was marching through would be easy walking, but now each clump was a stumbling block. Intent on the ground, careful with each step, Rey nearly walked past his destination. Fortunately, Rey caught sight of the tree with his peripheral vision.

Ollie perked up when he saw the tree. It was another new species, but much taller than the midget trees. The anemic looking tree had a thin trunk coated with gray scales, and a thick mass of branches so dense it looked almost solid. It was as if the tree was standing on its head with its root ball at the top. There were a few leaves in that tangle of branches, but small gray ovals, and so few Rey wondered how they could feed the tree? Rey helped Ollie into the tree, steadying him as he crawled up, and then out along the bottom of the lowest branch. For safety, Rey wished Ollie would perch on top of a branch but there was no arguing with instinct. Rey did have confidence in the strength of Ollie's claws. Nothing but death would detach Ollie from that branch.

Rey fed the rest of the water to Ollie and then stroked his head a couple of times.

"I've got to leave you, Ollie," Rey said.

Ollie was too weak to hum so Rey could not read his mood. Rey took two of the gray seeds from his pouch and ate them. How many had he had today? He could not remember. It did not matter.

"We'll both die if I take you with me," Rey said, justifying what he was about to do.

Still no hum. As Rey turned to go, a tentacle wrapped weakly around his neck. Rey turned back and gently pulled the tentacle free.

"I can't carry you any further and you can't walk another step," Rey said.

Now Ollie seemed to understand, and retracted his tentacles, but kept his head out. Rey wanted to run, to get away from his pain, but forced himself to walk. He did not want to panic Ollie into following him. Rey looked back only once and saw Ollie hanging under the branch, head exposed, watching Rey walk away.

38

DESPERATION

The sun slid below the mountains and still Rey walked, stumbling nearly every step. The moon was little more than a fingernail in the sky, but under a cloudless sky, with a pollution-free atmosphere, the starlight was enough to avoid major obstacles. Still, the little ones tripped him with increasing frequency.

Rey tried not to think of Ollie hanging by himself, all alone. Rey had killed his mother and taken him from his tribe. Rey—and Fawn for a time—had been Ollie's family. Now Ollie was alone for the first time in his life. Rey forced the memory into a dark recess in his mind. Dwelling on Ollie was pointless.

Rey nearly walked into a tree. Cursing his stupidity, he reflexively looked for Ollie, worried he had wandered in a circle. Nothing hung from the lower branches. Now Rey took his knife from his belt and cut a mark into the trunk. The gray scales cut easily enough, leaving a bright white scar. As Rey cut away the scales, he noticed the underside of the scales were damp. Wondering if he had found a source of water, Rey touched the bark to his tongue. Quickly, Rey tried to spit out the bitter taste. Then he stumbled on into the dark.

The trees came more frequently now and the grasses were longer. He marked each tree that he passed with slashes, coding them so he could tell the order. By dawn the trees were so numerous he had to choose which to mark and then he finally gave up his system, marking occasional trees with a single slash. While the increasing vegetation meant water, there were no streams, rivers, springs, or pools. Rey forced himself to walk through the night, eventually forgetting to mark his path. Gradually, the cool of the night gave way to the heat of another long day.

The terrain became rockier, the ground uneven with patches of loose shale. There were different trees now, shrubs, and green grasses. These trees were thick with golden leaves giving welcome shade. In those tree shadows there were tall bushes, growing nearly to Rey's waist. Covered in clumps of clover shaped, green leaves, the shrubs reminded Rey of one of Ollie's favorite snacks in the eastern forest. Rey started to pick a handful for his friend when he realized what he was doing.

Stay focused, Rey, he reminded himself.

Dropping to his knees, Rey dug between two of the bushes. The ground was rockier than he expected, and dry. Rey followed the root of one bush deep, soon contacting a larger root. Probing with his knife, Rey realized the roots of the bush attached to the tap root of the tree. The floral equivalent of a leech, the bushes were sucking water from the tree that shaded them.

Rey took off his pack, cursing himself for not abandoning it sooner. Without the tools inside, he knew he could not survive, but he was dying anyway. Taking the rifle, a water skin, jerky, his seed pouch, and the machete, Rey continued toward the closest mountain.

Without the pack, Rey had new energy, which he quickly expended. Soon he was back to watching his footing and at the same time pushing his way through increasingly thick vegetation. Branches clutched his buckskins, his beard, and his hair. Soon he was hacking his way through brush, sometimes missing his target, the blade slicing dangerously close to his leg. Reckless from desperation, Rey pushed on. Then he crossed a path—an animal trail. Lined with gold crown trees, the trail ran parallel to the mountains. Rey looked in both directions but could see nothing to entice him one way or the other. Squatting, Rey studied the well-trampled trail.

The prints were similar enough to others he had seen to tell which way the animals had been walking. The freshest tracks were heading south. Rey turned north, reasoning animals returning from their morning visit to the watering hole created the tracks.

Drawing on the last of his reserves, Rey followed the path, heedless of the dangers. Mumbling to himself, stumbling over even the smallest obstacles, Rey drove himself longer and further than he would have thought possible. The forest thickened, the gold crown trees numerous, the parasitic shrubs gathered underneath like chicks under a hen's wings during a storm. Then the path sloped down and began to switchback down a steep hill. The forest opened up, the ground too rocky for many trees. Then Rey turned a bend and saw the watering hole. It was a large pool of water fed by a stream tumbling down a rocky slope on the far side. In turn, the pool emptied via a stream that ran west through a small gorge.

An automaton now, Rey ignored the little creatures that scuttled for cover. Dropping his machete, water skin, food and seed pouch, and rifle at the water's edge, Rey plunged into the pool. Drinking deeply as he submerged, Rey let himself bob to the surface dead-man style, where he floated until the need to breathe forced him to stand on the soft bottom. Ignoring the silt he stirred up, Rey scooped up more water, drank his fill and a little more. Then bobbing, diving, splashing, and swimming, Rey thoroughly soaked himself. Only when something brushed his leg did he regain some common sense and wade to shore.

Rey stripped off his wet clothes, laying them on rocks to dry. Then he sat in a clump of soft grass with his back to a rock and ate jerky.

"That felt good, Ollie," Rey said, forgetfully.

Suddenly remembering his friend, Rey retrieved the water skin, squatted by the pool, and submersed it, letting it fill. As the air bubbled from the skin, an animal waddled down the path behind him. Shaped like a frying pan, the animal was two feet high, with a long thin tail that ended in a knob. Armor covered it from its small triangular head to the weapon on its tail. Arching ridges protected even its eye bulbs. Rey doubted a bullet could penetrate that plating.

The little tank froze when it saw Rey, studying him carefully. Judging Rey to be harmless, the little tank waddled down to the pool, giving Rey a wide berth. When the water skin was full, Rey stood slowly, careful not to frighten the tank. The tank watched him carefully, but did not interrupt its drinking. Rey guessed tanks were hard to put on a dinner plate. Only a bone eater could cut through the armor.

Rey's buckskins were still damp, but he put them on anyway, slipped the strap of the water skin over his head, picked up his rifle and machete, and left.

Rey followed the path back, but now could not find where he had broken through the brush to the trail. When he was sure he had gone too far, he turned and retraced his steps. It took a third try before he spotted a broken branch and found the path he had hacked behind the bush. With a belly full of water and food, Rey felt rejuvenated and set a good pace. A light breeze blew south along the eastern edge of the Near Mountains, and with his damp clothes the walk was comfortable. It would be dark soon, so even when his clothes were dry the heat would be tolerable.

Rey had not slept for nearly two days, and with his hunger and thirst satisfied, his need for sleep asserted itself. Part of his mind tried to seduce him into stopping to rest.

Just forty winks, he said to himself. Just a quick nap.

When that did not work, his mind took another tack: You'll get back to Ollie quicker if you rest a little. You're too groggy to know what you're doing. You could get lost. Then what would happen to Ollie?

Rey was arguing with himself, and making sense. He needed sleep like he needed water a few hours ago. Only the memory of Ollie watching him walk away kept him going. In the growing gloom, his path was harder to follow, and he slowed, careful not to lose his way. Thunder rolled toward him from the plains, reverberating off the mountains Rey now called the Near Mountains. Rey hoped it was raining on Ollie, since it would buy Rey some time.

The gold crown trees were giving way to the ball trees, like the one where Rey had left Ollie. With the sun well below the Near Mountains, following the trail was difficult. Rey needed to reach the marked trees before it got much darker or he might have to wait until morning to find his way back. Ollie's body was not any better at water management than Rey's, and Rey had barely made it to water. Ollie would have gone two days without water before Rey could get back.

In the gloom, Rey managed to find his pack where he had left it. He put it on now, unwilling to leave it to the varmints for another day. Now there were no hacked off limbs to show Rey the way, and he began looking for the tree markers. The ball trees stood out easily in the sparse flora, and Rey could see one of his slashes. Rey started out again, noticing the light was better. Puzzled he walked to open ground, and looked ahead. The horizon was glowing red—prairie fire.

Now Rey ran, but in the dark he stumbled before he got thirty yards. Falling flat, he got up and ran again and soon tripped. Getting control of himself, he slowed to a walk, eyes alternating between the horizon and the trunks of trees, looking for his marks. When he had gone half of a mile without finding a mark, he started spiraling, spreading out his circles until he found a mark.

By now, the horizon was bright. Rey tested the wind. It was blowing southwest, but only gently. He did not know if it would drive the fire far enough south before it reached Ollie.

The smoke reached him about the time he found the last tree he had systematically marked. He could clearly see flames licking the horizon and he knew he had lost the race. The northern edge of the fire was still to his left and coming fast. Rey had no choice but to retreat.

"I'm sorry, Ollie! I can't get to you. I tried, I really tried!"

Then Rey turned, retracing his steps, hoping to outrace the flames.

39

FIRE

Rey weathered the fire by climbing up a pile of rocks and hiding in a crevice. The heat was intense, but the worst of the fire stayed south of him. Wetting his spare shirt, he covered his mouth, filtering the smoke. Nevertheless, he coughed through the night. The next morning the air was still gritty, spot fires burning here and there. Rey walked through smoke, checking ball trees, looking for his mark.

Rey examined another scorched tree. The flames burned the bark, but only charred it. Where the flames had touched, the bark had swollen, and sloughed off chunks. The flame-resistant bark had saved the tree, but Rey's marks were obliterated. Rey despaired, looking through the clearing smoke. He could barely make out another ball tree in the distance. One voice told him to give up and remember his mission, while another voice reminded Rey of Ollie's loyalty—the only one who had ever stood by him. Rey walked to the next tree.

Finding no mark, Rey walked deeper into the prairie. The smoke had dissipated enough to see the closest mountain, which he had used as a goal. It was too big and too far away to be an accurate guide, but he turned his back to it and walked back the way he had come.

The prairie fire had burned away all the grasses, and the parasitic bushes under the gold crown trees were nothing but blackened sticks. The golden leaves of most of the gold crown trees were gone, but on some trees only the bottom third of the leaves had been burned away. That gave Rey some hope.

Without the ground cover, walking was easier. Unfortunately, each step kicked up soot, covering Rey and filtering into his lungs, despite the wet shirt masking his mouth. Hurrying as best he could, Rey checked tree after tree, looking for marks he knew had been obliterated. Rey knew Ollie's tree was the first he had come across, so he only glanced at the limbs if there was another tree in sight. When the ball trees became scarce, he thoroughly checked the bottom limbs and then moved on.

Finally, he found himself standing in a sea of blackness with no more ball trees in sight. Knowing there could not be any more between where he stood and the east coast, Rey turned back. The alignment of the mountains seemed right to Rey and he walked toward it again. Eventually he spotted a ball tree slightly to his left and angled to it. He knew he had checked it before, but the trees were so few and far between this far into the prairie that it had to be Ollie's tree.

The ball tree's few leaves had been burned off the tangle at the top and the bark was gone. Standing under the tree, looking up at the lowest limb, Rey was sure it was Ollie's tree, but his only friend was not hanging under the limb. Rey checked the bottoms of other limbs that fed the mass at the top—no Ollie. Now he checked the ground, hoping not to find a burned carcass. He circled the tree, spiraling outward, finding no body and no signs.

Now Rey came back to the tree and examined the limb one more time, as if he could miss something as large as Ollie—no Ollie. Long ago, Rey had learned to control his emotions—he would not give his father the satisfaction of seeing him cry. That control was eroding. For the first time in twenty years, Rey had not been lonely. The wrenching change from total aloneness to companionship taught him a lesson that could not be learned when you bumped into people at every turn.

Briefly, Rey wished he did believe in God, since he had an urge to say a prayer for Ollie. Then anger welled up in him, both at the God he did not believe in, and at the Fellowship. He would not be hurting now if it were not for what they'd done to him. The Fellowship and their God had burned Ollie alive. Rey had more than enough reason to kill them, but now he promised Ollie that he would kill one especially for him.

"You were a good friend, Ollie," Rey said, slapping the tree. "I'll miss you."

Readjusting his pack, Rey stepped toward the mountain. Just as he did, a tentacle slapped his shoulder. Rey spun around, looking up. The tentacle dangled out of the tangle of wood at the top. Looking close, Rey could see Ollie's eyes.

"Come on down," Rey said, nearly giggling with excitement.

Ollie did not move. Quickly, Rey opened the water skin, holding it up so Ollie could get a drink. Rey guided the tentacle in, letting Ollie curl it back up. Soon Ollie's tentacle returned, repeatedly dipping. Rey let him drink his fill and then waited a few minutes while Ollie gathered his strength. Then Rey took out a piece of jerky. Slowly, Ollie emerged from his hiding place. On one side, Ollie's brown fur was burned nearly to the skin in a pattern suggesting the ball of limbs had partially protected him. Ollie lowered himself with difficulty, trying to clamp onto the soot-covered trunk. He slipped—something Rey had never seen. Rey caught Ollie, cradling him like a baby. Ollie did not like to lie on his back, exposing his nearly bare underside, but he lay there now, looking up at Rey.

"Miss me?" Rey asked.

Ollie snaked his tentacles around Rey's neck. Rey smiled.

"I missed you too," Rey said.

Rey fed Ollie piece after piece of jerky. When his eating slowed down, Rey watered him again, and then helped Ollie onto his shoulders.

"Let's go find some decent trees," Rey said.

Ollie hummed approval.

With the sound of Ollie's chewing in his ear, Rey turned toward the Near Mountains. His relief at finding Ollie alive morphed into anger over what his friend had gone through. Now Rey found himself talking to a God he did not believe in.

"You can't stop me!" Rey said. "You left me to die alone in the wilderness and I survived! You sent creatures big and small to kill me and I beat them all! You tried to burn me alive and then you went after my friend! But I beat you—we beat you! You call yourself a God? I'll show you how killing is done! Go ahead, warn them! Tell them I'm coming and tell them hell is coming with me!"

Rey picked up the pace, a small cloud of soot marking his path to the west.

40

HONEYMOON RUN

Master Rice's Farm
First Continent
AUTUMN, PLANET AMERICA

Cook offered to help Summer abort the baby. Horrified by the suggestion, Summer shouted "no" in Cook's face. Summer would not punish the baby for the sins of the father. Patiently, Cook explained that abortion was so common back on Earth, that no one gave it a second thought. She also said that with some women it was almost a rite of passage, like a first kiss, first alcoholic drink, or getting a driver's license. Summer declined, happy that she did not live on Earth.

Without Kerry, now only her baby kept Summer from running. She desperately wanted to go, to live out the dream of freedom for her and Kerry, but her slowly swelling belly was a daily reminder that it wasn't just her life she would be risking.

A few weeks before the Gathering, Summer stumbled

across something that made her wonder if God was giving her a sign. The mistress was off visiting friends, and Master Rice invited neighbors over for a hunt. Overseer Nkosi ordered temporary kennels constructed for the neighbors' dogs and everyone except Winnie and Summer squeezed together to make room for the slaves brought by the other masters. No one minded, since slaves from other farms brought news and gossip. Summer knew that after the hunt, she and Kerry would be the talk of every slave on every farm, west and east of New Jerusalem.

The hunters left early the next morning, and Summer was called to help clean the big house. The house looked like a pack of dogs had chased a weasel from room to room. Summer decided to start with the master's office. There were bookshelves there, and rows of books that no one ever read. With both the master and the mistress away, she might risk looking at a book or two. In the office she found photos spread across the master's desk. The hunters had used them to plot the route to the hunting ground. As Summer gathered them, she looked through the photos. She had heard of these photos, but never seen them. Left behind by the Fellowship when they abandoned the planet, they had been taken from orbit and mapped the continent Grandma's people lived on. Features on some of the photos were labeled—New Jerusalem, Squeaky's Lake, Feminist Falls, Snow Camp, Potter's Peak, Lumber Camp—Summer guessed that's where Lucy's boy, Leo, lived. Near the bottom was a photo marked "Honeymoon Valley."

Summer put the photos down and then hurried to the door, making sure no one was around. The master and the oldest boys were out hunting, the mistress away visiting. The younger children would be up soon, but they were too young to have much meanness yet. Closing the door, Summer studied the photo. Cook had told her if she ever ran away she would go to Honeymoon Valley. Summer thought she understood why. There was a cabin in the valley, a copse of trees, and a small lake—shelter, fuel, and water. Where there was a forest, there was game, where there was a lake, there were fish or fowl. Turning the photos over, she found them marked. Figuring out the system, she laid the photos out in a mosaic. Now she could see the route to Honeymoon Valley. She also found it was a long distance into the wilderness—many days by foot.

The baby had changed all her plans, so she put Honeymoon Valley out of her mind. Quickly gathering up the photos, she stacked them neatly on the desk, opened the door, and continued cleaning. Sweeping the floor, tears ran down her cheeks as she thought of Kerry and what could have been.

Excited about Summer's baby, Winnie became attentive and motherly. She scolded Summer if she didn't eat enough, encouraged her to work fewer hours, and picked up most of the household chores; Summer's life was easier than it had ever been. Yet, she was unhappier than ever. The simplest act took all her willpower. She felt half asleep during the day, and half awake all night long. Cook said she was "clinically depressed," but Summer didn't know what that meant. What kept her going was knowing there was life growing inside her, and her commitment to raise the baby to be everything its father was not.

Morning sickness persisted through the end of summer, so when it was time for the puff tree harvest and Gathering, Summer was left out of the harvest crew. It would be the first Gathering she missed since she was ten. She packed her trade goods in with her mother's. She and Winnie had a short list of items for the cabin they would like to trade for. Summer made a list of her needs that included baby things that could not be handed down from Hope, and gifts for her mother, Lucy, Patrick, Rocky, Lucy's children, and others. Nothing on the list was for Summer. Her mother noticed, but did not mention it.

Bad feelings swept the farm when Master Rice packed up the small wooden boxes that Kerry had crafted during slave time. They would bring a good price at the Gathering, since no one had seen anything like them, and no more would be made. When slaves died, goods were traditionally given to relatives. If the slaves had no relatives on the farm, most masters distributed the slave's goods to other slaves. Master Rice was one of the masters who took what he wanted and left the rest to be picked over. Usually, Master Rice's slaves left nothing much worth having, but Kerry's boxes were a small treasure trove. Slaves grumbled, but said nothing because nothing could be done.

Summer hugged her mother, Hope, Rocky, Lucy, and Winnie, and then stood with the rest of the skeleton crew being left behind. Wash rode by and winked at Summer. Quickly, Summer turned away, heading to her loom. On the way she passed Owen Conklin, who had been selected by the master to stay behind and watch the slaves. Conklin was a landless master who had lost his family in addition to his land. Conklin wore a short beard he obsessively trimmed. The barrel-chested man was disagreeable when sober, and mean when drunk, and only his fear of Master Rice kept him sober during the day. With the master gone, Owen already had a jug in his hand and was headed for the overseer's house, where he was staying. He smiled at Summer, looking her over from head to toe. Summer hurried to the old barn.

Night came early now, and Summer worked late, since there was nothing else to do. It was dark when she left the barn. Without Winnie, the tiny cabin felt huge, but also lonely. Summer lit several candles, feeling extravagant with the Gathering at hand and still having a large supply of candles. The light helped drive away the blues, but not the shadows of what could have been. Without Winnie's constant chatter to distract her, she thought of Kerry, a spring kiss, and of plans for a future that could never happen now.

Starting a fire in the stove, Summer fetched fresh water, putting it on to boil. When it bubbled, she stirred the fire with a poker to cool it a bit, and then added carrots, flour, a small amount of meat, corn, salt, and a ground leaf that Cook called "spice." Summer was filling a small bowl with soup when the door burst open.

"Surprise!" Wash said, standing in the doorway.

Summer dropped the bowl, soup splashing, broken pottery

scattering. She could smell the liquor on Wash's breath from across the room.

"Aren't you glad to see me?"

In a small cabin with only one door, there was nowhere to run.

"When the master finds out you ran off, he'll use his belt on you," Summer said.

"I'll be back before he knows I'm gone," Wash said.

"He'll use his belt," Summer repeated, feeling trapped and helpless.

"I'd like him to try," Wash said with false bravado.

Wash slammed the door.

"No one knows I'm here, and no one's going to know. You understand?"

Summer said nothing.

"What's for supper?" Wash said suddenly, taking off his coat, and throwing it on the bed.

"Nothing. You made me spill it."

"That's okay, you can cook me up something later. I'd rather start with dessert."

In three quick steps, Wash had her in his arms, trying to kiss her. Summer turned her head, pushing him away, the smell of liquor overpowering. Wash was strong, paying no attention as Summer pounded his back. Finally, giving up, Wash released her, and stepped back, admiring her.

"No sense fighting, Summer. There's no one coming to your rescue this time. Old Jesse's a day's ride away. So's your mother. Blind boy's in his grave. No slave will lay a hand on me after what happened to the chair maker. So who's left, Summer?"

"There's me!" Summer said, as she scooped up the poker, and struck Wash on the side of his head.

Wash dropped as if dead, now lying in front of the door. Summer raised the poker, ready to bash Wash's head in, just like he had Kerry's. She could not do it. She could not kill someone who had not accepted Christ as his personal savior. If she killed him, she was condemning him to hell. Only God should make that judgment.

Dropping the poker, she found rope and tied Wash hand and foot. Then she examined his wound. The blow tore through part of Wash's ear, and cut into his scalp. With his hair closely cropped on the sides, Summer could see the wound was not deep. It did not look as bad as Kerry's wound. The ear was doing most of the bleeding.

Summer sat on the bed she shared with Winnie, knowing her life was over. She was safe for now, but the only way to keep Wash from killing her and her baby was to kill him. She would not do that. If he died from his wound, she would be publicly whipped and then hanged in the town square—Grandma's Rule. Grandma Jones might keep her alive until the baby was born, but Master Rice would kill her before Grandma Jones could intervene. The only chance for her baby was to hide out until it was born.

Summer checked Wash's breathing—regular and strong. Then she gagged him, checked the knots again, and pulled him away from the door. His horse was outside. Stealing horses was a hanging offense, even for free people. She decided to take it. They could only hang her once. Wash's rifle was tied to the back of the saddle. Touching a rifle was another hanging offense for a slave. Summer decided to take it too. Hurrying to the old barn, she retrieved her pack and traveling clothes from her hiding place, and changed into trousers and wool shirt. Because of her bulging stomach, she had to leave the trousers partially unbuttoned, securing them with a length of cord. Then she loaded bags with seed, small tools, utensils, sewing supplies, thread and yarn, candles, a lantern, blankets, spare fuel, salt, and food. With a horse she could take more than she had planned. As she was carrying her supplies toward her cabin, a slave came out of the outhouse, waved at Summer, and then went into his bunkhouse.

Back in the cabin, Wash was still unconscious. Summer went through the cabin, taking personal items, but leaving most of her meager belongings. Summer took one luxury, the box Kerry had built for her. Bundling her belongings in sheets, blankets, and a quilt, Summer loaded them on Wash's horse. Summer kept Wash's saddlebags, knowing they would contain useful items. She left the rifle where it was—afraid to take it and afraid not to. She also kept Wash's canteens and bedroll, and then added her own. As she was finishing, she thought of another need. Going to the big house, she paused, looking around. No one was watching. By now, Owen Conklin would be drunk and the slaves relaxing. Whenever the master was away, everyone did as little as possible.

Summer entered through the kitchen, going to the master's office. His whip hung on the wall behind his desk. She averted her eyes, remembering what it had done to Kerry. Summer found the photos in a bottom drawer. She was about to take the one with Honeymoon Valley, but realized it would point an arrow to where she had gone. Instead, she took the whole set. As she reached the door, she stopped, realizing she was leaving a treasure behind.

Turning, she hurried to the bookshelves and ran her hand along, looking at titles. She spotted a Bible, taking it and noticing a thick layer of dust on top. Then she pulled eight more books, regretting she could not take more. Even with a horse, there were limits.

Back in her cabin, Wash was still unconscious. Worried that Wash might die, Summer checked his breathing again. It seemed fine. Then she checked his bonds and looked around the cabin one more time. When she saw Wash's nice fur lined coat on the bed, she took it. It was warmer than anything she owned and the nights were cold. Then she closed the door. Now she led Wash's horse to her mother's cabin and selected baby supplies and clothes that Hope had outgrown. Leaving that cabin was the hardest thing she did that night. She had been born in the cabin, learned to read by the stove, watched her brother be born, played with him, drank tea with Lucy and her mother, and played games with Patrick and Kerry. Except for Saturday nights, most of her best memories were tucked away in the nooks and crannies of that cabin. She closed the door on her life, and led the horse into the woods.

41

WASH

Master Rice's Farm
First Continent
AUTUMN, PLANET AMERICA

Wash woke in near perfect dark. Confused, head hurting, he tried to move but could not. He was tied hand and foot. Even his mouth was covered. Suddenly, he remembered—Summer had clubbed him. He listened hard—nothing. Twisting, he looked around the dark cabin as best he could. Sure Summer wasn't there, ready to club him again, he struggled with the ropes that held him. He couldn't loosen them and no amount of twisting and bending brought the knots within reach of his teeth.

Hurting, humiliated, and helpless, Wash struggled long and hard before he called for help. Calling was no use. The rag tied around his mouth effectively muffled his cries. His complete humiliation kindled the fire of anger. Ready to pay the price of embarrassment, he wriggled to the door, twisted around, and banged on it with both feet. Kicking it over and over, he waited for help to come. He waited all night.

Light filtered through the curtains when the door he had kicked all night opened a crack, a white face tentatively peering in. Seeing Wash tied, blood in his hair, the old slave's eyes went wide in shock.

"Master Washington, what happened?"

Because of the rag tied across his mouth, Wash could not curse the slave's stupidity. With a slave's slowness, the old man came in, knelt, and then examined the ropes binding Wash's wrists. Picking at the knots, the slave acted as if the ropes were more valuable than Wash. Wash shouted a muffled command. The slow-witted slave stared dumbly. Now Wash rubbed his face on the floor, showing the slave what he wanted. Finally, the slave understood and switched to untying the gag. After an eternity, he had the knots loose and pulled the gag off.

"Get a knife, you fool. Cut these ropes."

Now the slave painstakingly searched the cabin.

"There's a knife in my saddlebag," Wash shouted.

"Where's your saddlebag, Master Wash?" the old slave asked.

"On my horse!" Wash snarled.

Eyes averted, afraid to anger Wash further, the slave spoke softly.

"Where's your horse, young master?"

"Outside, you fool!" Wash shouted.

The slave did not move. Wash understood and now cursed Summer. A flicker of a smile touched the corner of the slave's mouth.

"Should I go find a knife?" the slave asked.

"Go! Run! Do it now!"

The slave left. Vainly, Wash struggled with his bonds, finally exhausting himself. Now he took stock of his situation. He had left the family without his father's permission, ridden back to take what his father had forbidden him, been overpowered by a pregnant girl, had his horse stolen—and his rifle, he now realized—and let one of his father's favorite slaves run away. Terrified of his father, Wash knew he had to fix this. He had to get Summer back and since he would have to pay for what he had done, he was going to make sure she paid first.

The slave shuffled back in, a kitchen knife in his hand. Wash held his breath as the slave knelt next to him and then exhaled as the slave worked on the ropes. Finally, the first rope parted. Jerking his hands free, Wash grabbed the knife and shoved the old man away. Wash attacked the rope holding his feet, the knife cutting through easily.

"You were stalling for her, weren't you?" Wash accused, pointing the knife at the slave, whose pale face was whiter than normal.

"No, master. I was afraid of cutting you."

"I'll deal with you later," Wash said, getting to his feet.

Legs and arms numb, Wash limped to the door. His horse was gone and all his gear. By Grandma's Rule, stealing a horse was a hanging offense for anyone, slave or free. Hanging was also the penalty for a slave who even touched a rifle, let alone stole one. Summer had done both. He could kill Summer under Grandma's Rules, and get away with it. He would still have to answer to his father, but it would go better for him if Summer wasn't around to tell her version of the story.

Still limping, Wash went to the big house and to the study. Guns, ammunition, and reloading equipment were stored there. Powder and bullets were kept in a stone hut far away from the other buildings. Knowing it was futile, Wash looked at the lock on the gun safe. It would take an hour to cut through it and another to cut through the one securing the ammunition. Worse, locks were rare and precious on America. Destroying two locks because he let a pregnant girl subdue him would add to his humiliation. Wash decided he didn't need a gun to recapture Summer. Instead, he took his father's whip from the wall. Feeling the weight in his hand, Wash pictured Summer tied to a tree, begging for mercy, as he tore the flesh from her back. Now energized, Wash hurried to the barn. Summer's head start was twelve or thirteen hours, but she did not know horses.

The only healthy horse left behind belonged to Wash's mother. Princess was all show and no go, but he had no choice. The only decent saddle left was his mother's, and too small for Wash. He took it anyway. He saddled the horse, and then gathered supplies. He would be lucky to catch her before dark. Frustrated with the delay, Wash put together a bedroll, food, and other survival gear. When he realized his coat was gone, he found an old one, and took his broad rimmed leather hat. Once the mare was loaded, he mounted and then stopped—which way? Returning to Summer's cabin, he dismounted, studying the tracks. The compound was hard packed and much trampled, but he could pick out his horse's tracks and the soft imprint of a woman's feet next to it. Walking slowly, eyes on the ground, he followed the trail to the edge of the compound. Once in the forest, the track showed clearly in the humus. Mounting, he looked back and saw a half dozen slaves watching. The old slave was there, trying to hide the smile on his pale face. Wash knew they were rooting for Summer. Once Wash was gone, the tale of what she did to Wash would be told over and over. Somehow, word would reach the Gathering and every slave on the planet would be laughing behind his back. Now Wash forced a smile, imagining what their faces would look like when he came back, dragging Summer's body. Then he turned into the woods.

42

SUMMER'S RUN

Western Wilderness
First Continent
AUTUMN, PLANET AMERICA

Her belly swollen with the extra weight of the baby, Summer considered the horse a gift from God. None of the plans she and Kerry concocted included stealing a horse, since that was a hanging offense. However, their plans did not include her being pregnant either. Following the route they had planned, Summer stopped at each of their hiding places, adding to her supplies. She did not bother to try and hide the tracks since the horse cut deep and erasing them would take hours.

When she got to the stump that hid the skis, she debated over whether to leave them or not. The horse gave her the mobility she needed, but there was high country ahead and she might not always have the horse. She ended up taking both pairs, afraid that someone tracking her might use them to chase her.

The horse was heavily laden, but Buck was as big as Wash's ego. Tired and sore from the long walk, Summer decided it was time to ride. Leading Buck to a rock, Summer gingerly climbed onto Buck's saddle, afraid he would live up to his name. Buck trembled, but took her weight. Knowing Wash, Summer guessed the bucking had been beaten out of the big horse. Clumsily, she guided Buck with the reins. The load of supplies clattered, creaked, rattled, and slapped Buck's sides, so Summer let Buck set his own pace. With that compromise, Buck was cooperative.

Traveling obliquely, Summer kept Buck moving until well after dark. When they came to a stream, she dismounted, unloaded some of the supplies, and then tied a rope around Buck's neck and removed his bridle. Buck began to graze. Summer settled under a tree, examined the rifle until she was sure she could use it, and then ate bread and cheese. She fell asleep leaning against the tree.

Rain woke her. She thought it was dawn, but the thick cloud cover made day almost indistinguishable from night. Buck was motionless, head hanging, chocolate colored mane drooping. Summer found Wash's oilskin overcoat in a saddlebag. She put it on, pulling the hood up. She repacked Buck, but when she tried to put the bridle back on he kept twisting his head. She gave up, using the rope to lead him. She walked until she found a fallen tree and then created a loop she could slip over Buck's snout, giving her a way to pull his head left and right. Then, steadying herself against Buck, she climbed up the log and onto Buck's back.

The rain turned to drizzle, but never let up. The overcoat kept the rain out, but she was damp underneath and soon shivering. After another mile, she came to a stream. Jerking on Buck's neck, she managed to turn the horse into the stream and used Kerry's trick of wading in the water to hide her tracks. The drizzle turned to rain, the rain to a downpour. Buck struggled for footing in the stream, but she jerked him back every time he tried to climb up the bank. The stream was a risk she was willing to take. When the rain became drizzle again, she turned Buck up the far bank.

The rain continued through the morning but the sky lightened. Around noon, the overcast was thin and the rain let up. Summer took a break, sliding off the horse and letting him graze. Summer was exhausted, but knew she could not stop. Checking the photos, she studied the topography. She was still angling away from Honeymoon Valley, but she had to be careful not to cut herself off from the only way into the valley. The problem was determining where she was. There were some obvious physical features—rivers, lakes, mountains, and meadows—but none could be seen from the floor of a soggy forest. With no clear options, Summer continued, letting Buck pick his way through the forest. She felt lost and alone, unsure of God's plan for her life. Then she felt a fluttering in her womb, reminding her that she was not alone. She had her baby and she had her Savior. A deep contentment filled her, and she rode on, determined to live for both.

43

HUNTER

Western Wilderness
First Continent
AUTUMN, PLANET AMERICA

When the rain started, Wash found another reason to curse Summer—she had his overcoat. Buttoning his fleece lined jacket to the neck, and pulling his broad brimmed hat tight, he kept the rain from running down his neck. It did not matter. In minutes, his coat soaked through. Wash's hope of catching Summer quickly fell through when darkness hid her trail. He dismounted and walked for an hour, straining to see the ground, and then gave up and camped for the night. A break in the rain gave him a few hours of sleep, but it was more rain that woke him the next morning. When the drizzle turned to a downpour, he panicked, kicking the mare into a near trot. Drop by drop, the rain nibbled away Summer's trail.

Humiliated, furious, and miserable, Wash rode through the storm. As the trail became faint, he had to bend over to see it. When he did, cold drops pelted the back of his neck. When he sat up, water dribbled down his spine. Only fantasies about what he would do to Summer kept Wash in the saddle.

Late in the day, Wash came to a stream. There was a break in the rain, but the western horizon promised more misery. Worse, he had been climbing steadily and the temperature was dropping. The mare dropped her head, drinking. With a jerk of the reins, and a vicious kick, Wash drove the mare across and up the far bank. Summer's track wasn't there. Wash pulled up, and then circled. Still, no trail. Wash went back to the stream and then stopped, first staring upstream and then downstream. Kicking the mare, he turned into the stream, following it downstream, since it was closest to the general direction Summer had been taking. From the back of the horse, it was difficult to see the banks. Worried he would miss the track, he dismounted, walking in the shallows. Now his boots were soaked. Then it started to rain.

Two hours later he was back where he started, sitting under a tree, drying his boots and clothes over a smoky fire. Wash shivered, pulling the blanket tight around his shoulders. He wanted to go home, get Cook to make him a hot meal, and curl up under the down quilt on his feather bed. But he couldn't go home, not without Summer, or Summer's body.

The rain gave him a break the next morning, and he used it to search upstream, again walking in the stream. He alternated sides, working up and back along the banks. An hour later he found torn ground cover. He walked into the woods where the canopy had protected the forest floor from the worst of the rain. Buck's tracks were there.

"Now, we're back in business," Wash said to himself, swinging into the saddle.

Picking up the pace, Wash broke out of the trees into a clearing. The sun burned through at the same time, the warmth as welcome as the down quilt he missed so much. With the trail clearly marked in the soft meadow, Wash kicked the mare into a gallop. Things were finally going his way.

44

CAUGHT

Western Wilderness
First Continent
AUTUMN, PLANET AMERICA

After another damp night, the weather cleared, the sun driving the chill from her bones. Summer packed the oilskin away, opening her coat so the baby could feel the sun. Buck continued at a languid pace, the load rattling, and Summer hoped the noise would keep the predators away. She had no confidence in her ability to shoot straight.

The sun made her complacent, and she napped at lunch, letting Buck graze. When she finally roused, she walked for a way, passing by a couple of rocks she could have used to remount. The forest was thinning, the trees spindly. Now Summer saw her first cabbage tree up close. From the master's farm, on a clear day, you could see dots of purple on the distant hills. Those that had seen them up close called them cabbage trees. Summer assumed this was because of the purple color, but now she saw there was another reason. The trees did not have foliage like any she had seen. Instead of needles or leaves, the intertwining limbs of cabbage trees were lined with ribbons of growth, purple on the top, but green underneath. The ribbon-covered limbs were so dense that virtually no light filtered through, leaving a black shadow underneath. Bright eyes peeking from the cabbage tree shadows encouraged Summer to give the tree a wide berth.

Mounting Buck, she passed the cabbage tree, climbing steadily and eventually breaking into a clearing. Charred stumps and blackened logs told the story of how the meadow came to be. As she entered, a herd of small brown animals disappeared into the forest. She did not recognize the animals, but they looked like something leapers would hunt. She stopped Buck, letting him graze and giving the herd time to get well away. Summer stretched, looking around. There was a good view from the meadow. She could see across the valley she had just crossed. She wondered briefly if she could see Master Rice's farm, then worried they could see her. Realizing it was silly, she was about to move on when she froze. About a mile behind her was another meadow and in the middle of it a man sat on a white horse— it was Wash and he had seen her.

Pulling Buck's head around, Summer kicked him. Used to Wash's kick, Buck barely felt Summer's prod. The horse began walking, but even after several kicks was barely walking faster than Summer could on foot. By the time Buck reached the edge of the meadow, she knew it was pointless to run. Wash would catch her in a few minutes. Her only advantage was Wash's complete disrespect for slaves.

Once into the trees, Summer slid off, tied Buck to a tree, and then pulled out the rifle. She worked a cartridge into the chamber, as she had practiced, and then paused, ashamed of herself. Wash was a despicable human being, but with Master Rice as his father, what chance did he have? Summer dug into the pack and found her sling. She would give Wash a chance; something he would not do for her.

Wash entered the meadow at a trot, and then slowed, leaning over, looking for her trail. The mare was blowing hard, her hot breaths steaming. The meadow was much steeper than Summer realized, and she was looking downhill at Wash—that was good luck. Wash straightened, and then viciously kicked the exhausted mare into a run. Confident that Summer was no threat, Wash charged recklessly toward Summer's hiding spot. Just as he reached her range, she stood, placed a rock in the pouch, and twirled her sling. Wash saw her but did not hesitate. When he scrunched down in the saddle, she knew he had seen the sling. Still, he did not slow. He intended to run her down.

Summer stood still, slowly twirling the sling. Wash was betting she could not hit a man on a running horse; at least not anywhere lethal. He was right, but Summer was not aiming at Wash.

Putting some muscle into it, Summer whipped the sling around and released one strap. The pouch opened, the rock flying true, striking the mare between the eyes. Summer expected the mare to pull up, and maybe rear and buck. Instead, the mare ducked her head low, as if she had clipped an overhanging limb and was trying to go under it. When her head went down, Wash was jerked forward and over the mare's right shoulder. Then the mare stumbled, and fell, throwing Wash, who hit hard, head and shoulder first. The mare crashed at the edge of the meadow, nearly rolling over. Kicking clods into the air, the mare scrambled back onto her feet, then walked a few steps, shuddered, and sighed deeply. In shock, the mare stood there, breathing deep and hard.

Switching to the rifle, Summer stepped into the meadow. Wash was still, lying on his side, his back to her. She was afraid she had killed him. Her earliest memories were of Wash's petty tortures, and part of her hated him, but God asked his people to love their enemies. If she could take pity on Wash, maybe she could do the same for Master Rice too. Now Wash rolled to his back, moaning. Sitting up, he reached across his chest, grabbing his left arm. With a grimace, Wash looked for the mare, and then cursed it long and loud. Then he noticed Summer, and his eyes fixed on the rifle.

"You'll hang for this, Summer. I'm going to personally kick the stool out and watch you swing."

Wash's left side was muddy, and a clump of grass was wedged over his ear. His left shoulder hung low, and he winced when he tried to get to his feet. Summer fired a shot into the ground next to him. Surprised, Wash froze. Trying to look competent, Summer worked another round into the chamber.

"Don't move," Summer said.

Shocked that a slave would shoot at him, Wash settled back down.

"You killed Kerry, and for that you should die," Summer said.

Alarmed, Wash could only see the rifle.

"He killed himself," Wash said.

"No, it was you. You and your brothers. You blinded him and then you teased him, and tortured him, and did every hateful thing that came into your head. Deny it all you want, Wash, but you killed him and you'll answer for it."

As she was talking, Summer had walked to only a few feet away, rifle pointed at Wash's chest.

"You'll answer to God for what you did."

Now Wash sighed, and then forced a smile.

"I'll take my chances with God," Wash said. "Kerry was a slave, just like you, and I had the right to punish him. It says so in the Bible. Slaves are supposed to obey their masters. Well, I was his master, and I'm yours too, so put that gun down and maybe I'll have mercy on you."

Now Wash tried to get to his feet again, wincing as he did. There was something wrong with his left arm, and it hung limp. Summer shot again. Startled, Wash dropped back down.

"Stay down," Summer ordered. "Now turn around."

Furious, Wash estimated his chances, tried moving his left arm, and then gave in and turned his back to Summer.

"If you turn around again I'll shoot you," Summer warned.

Summer did not want to kill Wash, but there were only so

many times a person could turn the other cheek. Backing away so she could watch Wash, she moved to the mare, which was now grazing. She nearly tripped over Wash's hat, which he had lost in the fall. She picked up the hat and shoved it under a saddlebag strap. The master's whip was tied to the saddle. The sight of the whip strengthened her resolve. Now Summer thought about taking Wash's boots, but decided against it. He needed a fair chance of getting home. Taking the reins, she led the horse to the trees.

"Don't try to follow me, Wash," Summer warned, "or judgment day will be sooner than you think."

Then Summer led the mare into the woods, stowed the rifle on Buck, untied him, and led both horses away as quickly as she could. A short distance later she turned, seeing Wash on his feet, trying to follow her. He was limping, his left arm still dangling. Confident now, Summer led the horses deeper into the forest. Wash would never catch her. Now she really was free, but free to do what? To live where? Free to raise a baby by herself in the wilderness?

Reminding herself to thank God for saving her from Wash, she resolved to trust God to take care of her and her baby. Today she would continue to lead any trackers away, and then tomorrow she would head to Honeymoon Valley. What happened next was in God's hands.

45

CHAIN MEADOWS

Western Wilderness
First Continent
AUTUMN, PLANET AMERICA

The draw ended in another unclimbable slope—the second dead-end today. Rey cursed his luck. God may not be able to stop him, but He was doing a good job of slowing him down. Crossing the center of the continent meant months of walking, suffering the heat, constant thirst, and boredom of an unrelenting drab landscape, but the journey had been quick. Now in the mountains, Rey found himself frustrated by the maze of valleys, draws, and canyons. This day he had made almost no westward progress. Yesterday had been little better.

With Ollie hanging above him, Rey sat against a tree, studying the photo again. The photos of this region were more detailed, but they showed no relief, making it almost impossible to tell a five hundred foot hill from a five thousand foot mountain. Valleys could be so shallow as to be indistinguishable or so deep Rey could not manage them. Worse, Rey could only guess about where he was. There were only a few clearly distinguishable features, like Big Eye Lake, or Omega Falls. He had yet to find one he could use to orient himself on the map.

Ollie dropped a tentacle holding a mass of a moss he was stripping off the tree. Rey refused it. Ollie's fur had grown back and thickened, as he prepared himself for winter. With cool days, and cold nights, autumn was getting ready to surrender to winter. Common sense told Rey to stop his search, build a cabin, and ride out another winter. However, wintering in an unknown forest was risky too. There was no guarantee he would survive until spring. He was not afraid of dying, but he was afraid of dying without keeping Jephthah's promise.

Giving up on the photo, Rey retraced his steps, choosing a new route. Steep hills on either side funneled Rey through a lightly forested stretch, speckled with small meadows. Looming on either side, the hills drew closer, until Rey was sure it was another dead-end. The hills never met, however, leaving a narrow gap. Once through, Rey found another meadow, and beyond that, the hills receded, leaving a heavily wooded valley. Rey was through one barrier; however, he still had no clear idea of where he was.

Travel was relatively easy now, the lightly watered land supporting a spindly forest, and little undergrowth. Creeks were frequent enough, and twice Rey took fawn size animals that were good eating. Now two shaggy skins hung from the pack, as Rey prepared for winter.

Two days later, Rey paused at the edge of a meadow. A dozen animals grazed in the open. The animals were built like rhinoceroses, complete with armor plating, but closer in size to an elephant. They had expansive flat antlers, sprouting from heads nearly as wide as their bodies. Their wide mouths cut swathes in the grasses like a lawnmower. Rey watched them graze, judging the danger. One drew near a small tree that had sprouted in the meadow. With sudden ferocity, the animal tore the seedling out by its roots, tossed it aside, and then settled back into its grazing routine. A few minutes later, another of the animals used its antlers to plow up a larger sapling on the far edge of the meadow.

"Something tells me that your species and his wouldn't get along too well," Rey said to Ollie.

Ollie dropped a tentacle onto Rey's shoulder, pulling him back. Ollie hated crossing open spaces and feared Rey was going to do that now.

"It's a long way around, Ollie," Rey said, standing.

Ollie pulled tighter.

"They look friendly enough. We can cut across that side."

Ollie did not climb down.

"Fine, follow along in the trees."

Rey stepped into the meadow. As soon as he did, three of the nearest tree haters charged, bellowing as they came. The ground rumbled under the tons of rampaging flesh. Rey fled into the trees, but the tree haters skidded to a stop at the tree line. With their massive bodies and wide racks, negotiating the trees would have been impossible. Rey felt safe.

When the tree haters were sure they had driven Rey off, they grazed their way around the perimeter, tearing out saplings as they went.

"I've changed my mind, Ollie," Rey said, catching his breath. "Let's walk around the meadow."

The tree haters were content in their meadow, as long as Rey did not put a foot in their territory. Their meadow connected via a narrow tree-free strip to another similar meadow. There were no tree haters in this meadow, but Rey kept to the edge anyway. They were nearly to the other side of the meadow when Rey had a thought. Dropping his pack, Rey dug inside, finding the roll of photos. The one he had been following was on top. He scanned it, finding nothing familiar. Putting it aside, he spread the photos on the short-cropped meadow grass. Now he examined each photo in turn. The third photo had what he was looking for. There in the photo was a dumbbell shape.

"This is it, Ollie," Rey said. "I know where we are."

Rey was exaggerating, but as he looked from photograph to photograph, he realized he was further north and west than he had estimated. The Near Mountains were nearer the coast than he had thought, and did not cut as deeply into the prairie as he estimated. With the photographs laid out on the edge of the meadow he traced his path from the cabin where they had marooned him to Omega Falls, then Mud Pot Valley, Big Eye Lake, and then across the prairie to the Near Mountains. He guessed where the Tank Pool was—where he had found the water that saved Ollie. From that pool, his convoluted path was virtually untraceable, but he could easily find the barbell shaped meadows that began Chain Meadows, part of an intricately connected string of meadows that spread nearly all the way to site #1. Excited now, he traced a path through the meadows.

"We can make it before winter, Ollie. We're so close now I can hear their hearts pounding with fear."

Now Rey thought of his promise to God—his offering. Had God really helped him to get here? No more superstitious than the next man, Rey decided it was best to give God credit where credit was due. As he had promised, he would kill the first person he met as a sacrifice for God. The rest he would kill for himself.

Ollie smacked Rey on the head.

"Ow! Cut that out."

Ollie hit him again, and then tried to twist his head around. Finally, Rey let Ollie turn him. A tree hater was charging down the path connecting the meadows. Quickly, Rey gathered his photos, grabbed his pack, and fled into the forest.

"Someone needs to learn to share," Rey shouted over his shoulder as he ran.

46

HONEYMOON VALLEY

Western Wilderness
First Continent
AUTUMN, PLANET AMERICA

Princess was easier to mount than Buck, so Summer rode her instead. If Wash was still trying to follow he was soon far behind. Summer found a stream the next day and waded up the creek until noon. Summer let the horses move slowly, picking their footing carefully. Now that she had a good lead, speed was not as important as caution. With everyone at the puff tree harvest, and the Gathering, it was unlikely a search party could have been organized by now.

After leaving the creek, Summer angled back toward Honeymoon Valley. Using the stream trick twice more, she slowly worked her way toward her real destination. Rain returned late the next day, helping to erase her trail.

Climbing steadily, the temperatures dropped, but with Wash's coat, oilskin, and his wide-brimmed hat, Summer was comfortable, even in the steady cold drizzle. Two days later, the valley Summer was traversing opened up and directly ahead was a flat-topped mountain. Summer stopped, letting the horses graze, and then pulled out her photos. Concerned, she studied the route she had followed from Master Rice's farm. Because of the need to confuse trackers, she had meandered here and there, but religiously kept track of the landmarks as she passed. Honeymoon Valley should be directly ahead. Instead, she found her path blocked by a mountain.

Summer studied the photo, looking more closely at the formations around Honeymoon Valley. She had assumed they were rock formations, but now she understood the significance of its oval shape—Honeymoon Valley was inside a crater. Joyfully, she remounted Princess and rode on. Despite how close the flat-topped mountain appeared, it took her until midafternoon to reach the base. The sides were steep and covered with loose rock. She rode the perimeter as best she could, deviating around broken ground and impassable thickets, and finally came to a stream on the far side that seemed to flow out of the base of the mountain. She camped by the stream that night, and then finished circumnavigating the mountain the next day. When she was back where she started, she did not know what to do.

Eating the last of her bread, Summer looked at the photo again. She could search for some other place to live, except she knew of no place else with a cabin. With a baby coming, she could not keep moving all winter. Already, her changing body made it uncomfortable to ride, and soon she would not be able to mount Princess. If Kerry were with her, they might have managed to spend the winter in a cave, but alone she needed a roof over her head. Deciding that it was best to stay, that left her with the problem of how to get into the valley?

Summer spent the day exploring, climbing the mountain at different points, mapping a way to the top—there seemed to be none. Late in the day she spotted a crack in the wall where a segment had fallen away. When she reached it, she found that the jagged tear in the mountain wall provided many footholds.

She spent the night at the base, building a big fire and then feeding it wood off and on all night long. Before wrapping herself in two blankets, Summer threw Master Rice's whip in the fire, feeling no satisfaction as the tongues of flame reduced it to ash.

Protecting her supplies occupied most of the next day. She spent it hanging them from trees, or burying them under rocks. Early the next morning she tied the horses on long leads and then took food, water, and rope, and started up. She rested often, reminding herself that she was risking two lives. Once in the crack, climbing was easier, but she had to backtrack frequently, finding many dead-ends, so when she reached the top it felt as if she had climbed the mountain twice.

The valley was everything she had hoped. There was a small stand of trees, a stream, a pond, and most importantly, a cabin. Excited, she wanted to run but cautioned herself to be careful. It was a long climb down.

Summer hadn't used the rope on the way up, but now it was essential. She picked her way among the rocks, wherever there was good footing. Going down was easier than climbing up, but it also used new muscles that soon complained. When she had gone as far as she dared without rope, she tied a rope to a rock, and then used it to slow her descent. She had two lengths and the second got her to better footing. Now she could not help herself, and she hurried, jumping off the last rock, her stomach extending with the impact. She cradled her abdomen in both hands to support it. Now, on the valley floor she was in the western shadow, the winter sun already below the rim. From the floor, the valley was an oval bowl, the sides sloping up more gradually than on the outside. Walking through knee-high grasses, Summer headed straight for the cabin.

The cabin was built of logs, with a shingle roof. There were windows in one side, and the glass was unbroken. There was a small, screened porch with an overhanging roof. The screen was torn in several places. The screen door was closed with a hook latch. Inside she found a swing hung from the rafters. The seat was padded with a cushion so dirty Summer could not tell what color it used to be. A wooden bar set into steel brackets secured the door to the cabin. The bar was wedged tight. Summer used a rock to beat the bar out of the brackets. Unlatching the door, she found the cabin was everything she hoped it would be.

A large bed dominated the room with a chest of drawers to one side. A mirror hung over the chest. A tarp covered the mattress, and stacked on the end of the bed were quilts and blankets. There was a small table with two chairs, the table covered by a tablecloth. Dragging her finger across the tablecloth, Summer discovered it was blue under the dust. There were matching curtains on the window. There was a sink, with a pump, and a stove. In the cabinets, Summer found a few dishes, pots and pans, dishcloths, dishtowels, ancient soap, sponges, candles, lanterns, and a few jars of canned goods—probably fruits and vegetables. On a table by the bed was a radio and electric lights hung from the ceiling, the bare bulbs covered with wicker shades. Summer flicked a switch on the wall. The lights stayed dim.

"That's okay, God. You've been more than generous. I wouldn't be so greedy as to ask for electric lights too."

Now Summer walked around the cabin, finding a machine sitting under a lean-to in back of the cabin. She guessed it was supposed to make the electricity. There was an outhouse, and she used it—another luxury she had no right to expect. Then she walked to the stream. The water was so clear it was invisible. Kneeling, she dipped her hands to scrub off some of the grime—the water was surprisingly warm. Now she walked along the stream. Almost immediately she came to a small pool lined with rocks. Larger rocks sat in the bottom. The water was steaming. She dipped her hand—hot.

Impulsively, Summer took off her trousers and sat on the bank. Slowly, she dipped her feet in the water, letting them get used to the temperature. It felt wonderful. Stripping off the rest of her clothes, she sank into the warm water, shivering involuntarily as she adjusted to the heat. She let herself sink down to one of the large rocks in the bottom. It was smooth, and comfortable to sit on. Summer hadn't felt this good since, as a child, she had cuddled up next to her mother under their down quilt. Summer stayed in the pool until she was so groggy she was afraid of falling asleep. Climbing out, she now paid for the luxury since she didn't have a towel. Using her blouse to dry herself, she picked up her clothes and hurried back to the cabin and inside. There was no wood by the stove, and the woodpile outside had been reduced to sawdust. Summer hung her blouse from the rafters, then put on the rest of her clothes and hurried to the copse of trees. On the edge of the small wood were three large apple trees. Rotten apples covered the ground. Several small volunteer apple trees had sprouted among their parents.

Gathering as much wood as she could, Summer hurried back and got a fire going in the stove. When she was warm again, she gathered a supply of wood, and then took the bed linens to the stream and washed them. She hung these to dry from the rafters of the cabin, keeping a good fire going. It was too late in the day to get back to the horses, so she prayed they would be safe from leapers and other predators.

She made a soup for supper, read her Bible by candlelight, and prayed a long thank-you prayer, and then another for the protection of everyone she knew. She missed her mother, Rocky, Hope, Lucy, Patrick, and the other slaves. She cried when she thought of Kerry and how perfect this place would have been with him. He was in a better place, however, and she envied him that. Then curling up on the bed, covered with two blankets, she slept safe and secure in her own home.

The next morning she climbed back out of the valley and down to the horses. Now that she knew the route, it took half the time. The horses were alive, and she thanked God for that mercy. Even so, there was no way to get the horses into Honeymoon Valley. That left her with two choices. Her needs told her to butcher the horses, since they were a good source of meat. They were too beautiful for that, however, and she had enough supplies to survive the winter. Instead, she took off their bridles and leads, and released them. Neither ran off, not realizing they were free. Instead, they grazed as if they had been turned into a fenced pasture.

Summer carried as much as she could back with her and then made a second trip two days later when the weather was good again. The horses were gone. She made a third trip the next day, now quite good at climbing in and out of the valley. She left the saddles and the skis under a hollow log, sealing them in with a large mound of stones. She doubted she would ever have use for them.

By the end of the first week in her cabin, Summer had cleaned the linen, scrubbed the knotty pine floor, washed the dishes, sewn up the gaps in the screens, and found that four of the jars in the cabinet contained fuel for the lanterns. She had beaten the dirt out of the braided rug, and then washed it. Much of the fabric was too rotten to salvage, but she took it apart, used what she could, and rebraided it into something smaller. All the fabrics were blue, and now when the sun shone through the windows, the cabin was as bright and cheery as the one she had shared with Winnie. However, this cabin did not have the dark memories of Master Rice's visits.

Summer set snares in the wood and along the stream, catching small brown rodents with thick fur. They had bushy tails and long whiskers that made their faces look like cats. They had little meat on them, but enough to supplement her diet. She picked through the apples, finding some fresh enough to keep, storing them in a wooden box she found built into one side of the cabin. The books she had stolen from Master Rice were lined up on the dresser, two smooth stones fished from the warm stream serving as bookends.

Her stomach continued to swell, and she watched her belly button slowly disappear on her daily visits to the pool. She would have been perfectly content, except for the fact that she had a baby coming and she was alone. She kept extra towels, a baby blanket, water, food, string, and the scissors next to the bed, just in case her time came unexpectedly.

It snowed off and on now, the valley floor covered in a light coating of snow. Despite the cold, every evening she sat on the porch, wrapped in a blanket, staring into the meadow, worrying, dreaming, and planning a life as a single mother. Tonight, she stood in the doorway, looking up at the stars. Picking out familiar constellations, she imagined what it must have been like for those who left their planet to come to America. The constellations were different there, she knew, and she could not imagine how it would feel to look up at an unfamiliar sky. A falling star streaked across the sky and she briefly wondered if the streak was the Fellowship returning. It would not be them, of course. At Grandma's insistence, the Fellowship had agreed to leave Grandma's people alone, so they were free to develop their own society. What would the Fellowship think if they could see what America had become?

The baby kicked, Summer pressing on the spot. It kicked again. She liked it when the baby kicked, since it meant it was alive and strong. She had been having mild contractions off and on for a couple of days, so she knew her baby would come soon.

"Time for bed, little one," she said.

Turning to go in, she felt a sharp pain. She gasped, took two steps, and then her water broke. Knowing it would happen did not prepare Summer for the real thing. Now the contractions came strong and hard and with crippling pain. Panting, tears in her eyes, she managed to get to the bed, pulled the quilt off, and then lay down. Pain like she had never felt racked her body, as her body began pushing the baby toward the world. Looking right and left she made sure she had her cloths, scissors, and other needs. The pains were coming close and fast and she could not catch her breath. There was something wrong. This was not like the pregnancies she had witnessed. Those deliveries had taken hours. Her baby was coming fast. Then the pain reached a new level as if she were being torn in half. Summer gasped as the contraction passed. Panting, knowing the pain would return, Summer had no one to comfort her, no hand to hold, no midwife to assure her everything was normal. Alone in her cabin, Summer felt her uterus begin to tighten again and she ground her teeth, preparing.

47

THE CABIN

Western Wilderness
First Continent
AUTUMN, PLANET AMERICA

Following the chain of meadows turned out to be harder than expected, since the tree haters were unrelentingly aggressive. Even a single step into a meadow was enough to invite a charge, and charge they did, day after day. Walking through the trees along the border was little better than cutting across country, but when there were no tree haters in sight, Rey risked walking in the meadows and made good time.

Twice the snow had been so bad he had built a shelter to wait out the storm, fearful that he would have to wait out the winter this close to his goal. On both occasions, thaws allowed him to move on.

When Rey found the chain of meadows, it was near its low point, and every step since had been uphill. Looking at how far he had to go, and how much he had climbed, Rey estimated the last meadow would be alpine.

Ollie was happier and fatter than ever, although if you parted his fur you could see scars from his burns. Ollie was an expert provider now, hanging from limbs and snatching small animals right off their feet. He would snap their necks, but never ate them, delivering his prizes to Rey for cleaning, skinning, and cooking. Ollie would eat meat raw, but like Rey, preferred it cooked. So efficient was Ollie, that Rey did not bother to hunt. If they had to spend the winter, Rey would have to bring down some big game, but Rey was betting he would reach site #1 before winter trapped him.

Occasionally, Rey spotted other animals in the meadows, but like Rey, they grazed the margin, never venturing far from safety. Most were gazelle-like, and looked fast enough to leap to safety. Studying his photos, Rey could not see anything else like the chain of meadows, suggesting that the tree haters were limited to the long valley he was traversing.

Tree haters were scarce by the time Rey reached the last meadow in the long chain. It was indeed high, yet there were still hills ahead, and then mountains north and south, although he could only speculate on elevation. Unfortunately, Rey estimated he still had two hundred miles to travel. Even if the weather remained mild, it would be midwinter before he found the Fellowship settlement. As if on cue, it began to snow.

"Ollie, I hate to disappoint you, but we may not make it this year," Rey said.

Ollie lowered himself to look in Rey's face and hummed consolingly.

"Don't talk like that, Ollie, I'm not giving up."

Ollie slipped his free tentacle into Rey's pocket. Rey pulled it out.

"Okay, we'll stop soon, but let's get beyond this meadow first. There should be a small one on the other side of this hill."

Ollie went for the pocket again.

"You go catch supper. I'll meet you up ahead."

Ollie pulled himself up a couple of feet, and then flipped out his tentacle to grab a branch on the next tree and swung away. Entering the forest, Rey took his rifle in hand. The remains of gazelles told Rey something was hunting these woods.

The canopy kept the light snow from reaching Rey. The undergrowth was sparse, and the climb steady and gradual. Ollie was out of sight, hunting. Rey did not worry. Ollie was a big boy now and could fend for himself. When Rey reached the top of the hill, he found a small open area where he could see ahead. The view puzzled him. Afraid he was lost, Rey took out the photo of the region and traced his way along the chain of meadows to where he had left the end. According to the photo, there should be a round meadow just ahead of him, but instead he was looking at a small flat-topped mountain. Slowly, Rey realized the mountain had once been a small volcano. At some point in the distant past, the peak of the volcano had collapsed. An overhead photo did not reveal elevation so what looked like a small round meadow turned out to be the center of a volcano.

Rey studied his options, deciding he could bypass Flat Top Mountain by keeping south where there was a wooded valley. Rey was about to start down when he suddenly froze, transfixed by the volcano. Rising above its rim was a wisp of smoke. Fearful it was steam, or a wildfire, Rey watched it closely, but it did not build like a wildfire, and it did not dissipate like steam. Instead, the breeze smeared the smoke across the sky.

Rey had to fight the urge to charge into the valley and up the slope of the volcano. Instead, he found a spot to set up camp and had a fire going when Ollie dropped a fat rodent in his lap. Ollie sensed his excitement and hummed happily as Rey fixed supper.

"It's starting, Ollie," Rey said, quartering the rodent and then spearing the pieces and leaning them over the fire. "You don't know how long I've waited for a little payback.

Now it's going to happen. I'm going to keep Jephthah's promise."

Ollie hummed happy agreement, but his eyes were on the roasting meat.

Rey was up with first light, annoying Ollie by rushing breakfast. Then he pushed hard down the hill and into the valley. That morning, a thin layer of snow covered open ground. Rey tromped through anything and everything in his path, reaching the end of the valley before midday, but it was another few hours before he started his climb. It took him that long to find a route to the top.

When he started his climb, Ollie hung back, reluctant to leave the trees to go cavorting among rocks. To Ollie, the forest had everything anyone could possibly want; food to eat, trees to swing from, and shelter. Bonded to Rey, Ollie went where Rey went, but he was unhappy, and let Rey know by smacking him with a tentacle.

"Careful, Ollie, this is slippery."

Ollie had six appendages to work with and managed the rocks better than Rey, who slipped back one step for every two he managed forward. Light snow continued, keeping the climb dangerous.

The higher Rey climbed, the steeper the climb got. Now Rey paused frequently, sharing water with Ollie, studying possible routes. There were no good ones. If this were Earth, Rey would be using ropes and pitons.

It was getting dark when Rey found a section of the wall that was easy to climb. Knowing he should quit for the day, nevertheless he climbed. He reached the top, nestling into a small crevice where he could look down into the crater. Ollie snuggled in next to him, leaning over and looking down, all four legs and both tentacles hanging on.

The volcano had indeed collapsed, leaving a small valley inside. Even in the dim light, Rey could see the valley floor. A small copse of trees filled one end of the valley, and the other held a small pond. A stream ran along the far edge of the valley, terminating in the pond. The stream was steaming like the mud in Mud Pot Valley. A powerful déjà vu feeling hit Rey. Sitting in the middle of the valley was a cabin: the cabin of his dream, smoke drifting from its chimney, the windows bright with light. There had been no snow in his dream, but there was no doubt this was the cabin. Sitting here, looking at the cabin from his dream, he felt trapped by his promise. He had bargained with God and promised Him that if God helped him find his enemies, and kill the first one he saw, that he would give faith a chance. Now he was here, and there was the cabin. It had been a game before, a way to keep himself going, but now his heart pounded with the thought that God might actually exist. Rey despised Proctor, who had tricked him, and Rey refused to be a hypocrite. He would keep his promise to God.

Rey worked his way lower, eventually coming to a rock with a rope tied to it. He was about to use it to get the rest of the way down when the cabin door opened. The little bit of light was bright, and he shrank back, bringing his rifle up.

"Time to keep my promise," Rey said, lining up the sights on the cabin door.

A woman appeared, leaning against the doorframe. She was pregnant—very pregnant. He hesitated since he would be killing two people. He shrugged the thought off. God had made the selection, not Rey. Even at this distance it would be an easy shot. She was leaning against the doorframe, looking at the sky, silhouetted in the light. Lining the sights up on her chest, Rey slowly squeezed the trigger.

48

BIRTH

Honeymoon Valley
First Continent
AUTUMN, PLANET AMERICA

Summer's baby was coming, coming faster than any baby she had seen delivered. There should have been hours of labor, but the contractions were hard and close together. Breathing so rapidly she could not catch her breath, Summer barely had time to rest between contractions and no time to recover from the pain. Alone in an isolated cabin, there was no one to check her, to see her progress, but God had designed a woman's body to deliver babies and she trusted it would do its work.

Panting, Summer reached for her water, but a contraction struck just as she lifted the glass and she dropped it, spilling it. Her mouth dry, her body wet with sweat, Summer could only let the contractions run their course.

It was full dark now, a lantern providing minimal light. Another wrenching pain, and she felt movement. The baby was passing down the birth canal. Excited and terrified, she now felt hope. Another contraction, and more movement. It was happening—she was having her baby. Another contraction, but this time a new sharp pain—the baby had not moved. Another contraction and more pain; unbearable pain. Summer screamed away the pain but was terrified. The delivery had stopped.

Now Summer felt her abdomen as if to diagnose the problem. Another fruitless contraction wrung another scream from her body. Afraid for herself, but terrified for her baby, Summer did not know what to do. She was helpless and at God's mercy.

"God, help me!" she shouted, before more pain choked off her words. "Save my baby," Summer prayed. "Please, God, save my baby."

Then the door burst open. In the flickering candlelight, Summer saw a horrific beast—or man. With shaggy, dirty hair on its face and head, it was dressed in skins and carried a rifle. There was a hairy hump on its back. The beast-man said something, and then through tear-blurred vision she saw the hump detach from its shoulders, extend ropes, and pull itself into the rafters. Then the man-thing stepped to the basin, and began to scrub its hands.

Convulsed by another contraction, Summer clamped her eyes closed. When she opened them the man-thing was at the bed, touching her.

"The baby's arm is wedged with the head," it said. "I'll try and free it. This will hurt."

Summer nodded, thinking she could not hurt any more than she already was. Then he was pushing and twisting and it did hurt more, but the body can only feel so much pain. Then another contraction came, and there was relief. The baby moved. Collapsing back, Summer let her body do its work, the man-thing taking the baby. Then the man-thing reached for the string and scissors, tied off the cord, and cut it. Holding the baby's head down, he rubbed its stomach, the baby spitting out fluid and then sucking in air. Then there was a loud cry.

"My baby," Summer whispered.

The man-thing held the baby a little longer; his thumb pressed to the chest, and then examined the fingers and toes. Then he took the small blanket and wrapped the baby, handing it to Summer, who cradled it.

"It's a girl," he said gruffly.

A couple of minutes later, Summer delivered the placenta and the man-thing studied it, and then set it aside. Then he cleaned Summer, replaced the sheet under her with a blanket, and then picked up her fallen cup and filled it with water, helping her drink.

As she drank, she looked through the mat of hair and saw two fierce, bronze eyes staring at her.

"Thank you," Summer said.

He said nothing.

Collapsing back, she saw the furry lump in the rafters. Two round eyes shone from amidst the fur, studying her.

"What is that?" she asked, her voice hoarse.

He looked over his shoulder and then back at her.

"That's Ollie," he said.

The thing in the rafters slowly extended ropes, dropping them toward the now quiet baby in Summer's arms. The man grabbed one of the ropes, tugging on it.

"Not food," he said, pointing at the baby.

Summer covered her baby girl with a protective arm.

"I better get rid of the afterbirth, or he'll want to eat that too," the man said.

Picking it up, he started for the door, the lump called Ollie watching him.

"Wait," Summer called, stopping him halfway out the door.

He turned back. In the dim light, she could not make out his face.

"You're coming back, aren't you?" she asked.

"Yes," he said after a few seconds. "I guess I am."

Comforted, Summer relaxed, letting her exhausted body rest. Closing her eyes, she listened to the soft smacking sounds of her baby. Opening her eyes again, she saw Ollie hanging just above her, studying the baby.

"Get back up there!" she said sharply.

The creature immediately pulled itself up, attaching to the underside of a rafter and pulling its head in. Summer could see the whites of its eyes as it studied her.

"And stay up there," she said firmly.

Then Summer rolled onto her side, pulled her little girl close, and fell asleep, even knowing a wild man was loose in her valley, and a lump named Ollie was hanging from her rafters. She could sleep, because she knew the two of them, strange though they were, were an answer to prayer.

49

STRANGERS

Honeymoon Valley
First Continent
WINTER, PLANET AMERICA

The hairy man was there in the morning, starting a fire in the stove. The Ollie lump still hung from a rafter, no head visible. In the daylight, the man looked cleaner. His hair was wet and some of the dirt was brushed from his clothes. She guessed he had been to the pool for a bath. He saw her watching him. Now he stood, reached up and patted Ollie. A head appeared, eyes wide, blinking away sleep.

"Go get breakfast," the man said, opening the door.

The lump stretched out ropes, wrapped them around the rafter nearest the door, swung to the wall, and then walked down the wall and out the door. Without asking, the man brought Summer water.

"Thank you," she said.

"You should try nursing," he said.

She hesitated, looking at him.

"I'll be busy in the kitchen," he said.

He kept his back to her while she opened her dress and lifted the baby to her breast.

"What's her name?" he asked.

"Faith. Her aunt's name is Hope. That's why I thought of it."

He had flour and lard and was mixing it together, using a little water.

"She's not feeding," Summer said.

"Sometimes they don't at first," he said. "You can try again after breakfast."

"What's your name?" she asked.

"Reymond Mann," he said. "Call me Rey."

Summer closed up her dress, and then wrapped Faith up again.

"I'm done," she said, embarrassed.

He kept working.

"Do you live around here? This isn't your cabin, is it?"

Now he chuckled. It was a soft, hoarse laugh.

"No, not around here."

With all the hair, Summer could not judge his age. He was older than her, and maybe as old as her mother.

Summer knew that when the Fellowship left, there were white people who had remained behind. They were hermits, mostly, but also a few families who lived away from the communities. Most of these were rounded up after the enslavement, but there were rumors of a few who still lived alone, closer to being animal than human. Summer guessed he was one of those. That worried Summer, since all the hermits were said to be crazy. The door rattled and Rey opened it, the animal named Ollie crawling up the wall, carrying a fish.

"Just one?" Rey said, taking the fish. "There are three of us now."

"Four," Summer said.

Looking over his shoulder, Rey held the fish up by its tail. It had a double row of suckers along its bottom.

"Are these edible?" he asked. "I've never seen one."

"Yes," she said, puzzled. It was a common fish.

Pulling a knife from his belt, Rey expertly filleted the fish.

"Did you stay behind when the Fellowship left?" Summer asked.

He stopped work, his head hanging.

"I was left behind."

"Were you a slave?"

He turned around.

"A slave? No."

He seemed as puzzled by Summer as she was of him. He turned back, putting the fish in a frying pan, and then putting his biscuits in the oven. While the fish sizzled and the biscuits baked, he offered to help Summer to the outhouse. Embarrassed again, she agreed, letting him half carry her. At first, she was uncomfortable being close to him, but by the return trip, his strong arms reassured her.

She was brimming with questions, but he was a quiet man, reticent, and uncomfortable in her presence. He brought her a plate with biscuits and fish, and then stood by the sink, eating, handing Ollie pieces of cooked fish and biscuits.

"You can sit at the table," she offered.

Staring blankly, he looked at her as if he had never heard anything so preposterous. Then he took his plate to the table, pulled out one of the chairs, and sat, awkward in the chair, as if he had never done it before. She wanted to suggest he use a fork, but did not want to insult him. Desperately curious, she held back, afraid of scaring him away. Instead, she asked about Ollie.

"What is that animal? I've never seen one."

"Ollie? He's a tree octopus. That's what I call them, anyway. Don't you have them around here?"

"No," she said, again wondering where he had come from.

"Ollie adopted me after I killed his mother. We've been together ever since."

Summer didn't ask about Ollie's mother.

"Just you and Ollie?"

With his long hair and shaggy beard, there was little skin showing. That little bit of skin flushed. He was angry.

"No one else!"

Feeding the rest of his food to Ollie, he stood and started cleaning up. Rey was angry, but she did not know why. When she had finished, he fed Ollie her scraps, and then cleaned and put away the dishes and pans. He and Ollie left then, but she was sure he would come back. Soon, she fell asleep.

She dozed off and on, and when she woke, she let him take her to the outhouse again. He prepared soup for lunch and more biscuits. After cleaning up, he left again, although she could hear him out on the porch, doing something. Faith began nursing that afternoon. She managed to walk to the outhouse in the afternoon, and discovered he had rigged a hammock on the porch—he was going to stay for a while. She was glad.

That night at dinner he had questions. They were sitting at the small table, avoiding each other's eyes.

"Are you part of the Fellowship?" he asked, glancing at her, and then looking at his food—something Ollie had caught.

"You don't know what happened?"

Genuinely puzzled, he shrugged.

"The Fellowship left America a long time ago," Summer explained. "They were afraid that the soldiers from Earth would find them. They haven't been back since."

He was skeptical.

"But you're here."

"Not everyone wanted to leave. There was a group that wasn't part of the Fellowship—they were all black people. A woman named Grandma Jones leads them. She talked the leader of the Fellowship into bringing them to America and when the Fellowship decided to leave, Grandma Jones refused to go. She and her people wanted to have America all to themselves."

"Summer, aren't you white—at least mostly?"

"I think my father was a master. My mother was one of the soldiers who came from Earth. The Fellowship destroyed their spaceships and Grandma Jones captured the soldiers who landed. Grandma Jones made them all slaves."

Now he looked away, shook his head, his face flushed. He was angry again and she did not understand why. Then their eyes met, and this time he held her gaze.

"Tell me why you are here," he said. "Why are you all alone?"

Then Summer opened her heart, and told him everything, and not just details but her feelings too, including the dreams that she and Kerry had shared. He cleaned while she talked, asking questions now and then, the stories flowing out of her. They moved to the porch swing after he finished cleaning, With Summer wrapped in a blanket, the two of them swung gently, Faith in her arms. Faith got fussy and she nursed her, now only slightly embarrassed by Rey's presence. She talked about her mother, her friends, life on Master Rice's farm, Grandma Jones, the Gathering, the puff tree harvest, and even weaving. When she talked about Master Rice, Wash, and the many cruelties of life as a slave, he asked her a lot of questions. She left some things out, not yet ready to talk about Saturday nights, and her life with Winnie. He never asked who Faith's father was. When she described her escape, he tensed. When he heard about the horses, he sighed.

"I guess you had to let them go."

"There was no way to get them into the valley."

It started to snow, but Summer and Faith were snug in the blanket, and enjoyed the gentle storm. Rey covered himself with a tanned hide, keeping space between himself and Summer, even on the small swing. Ollie hung from the roof, head tucked in. Late in the evening, Rey went in and fixed them both a cup of tea, also bringing a sliced apple. He gave her all the apple pieces. When she offered him a slice, he refused.

"You need the vitamins," he said.

"There are more apples in a bin outside," she said.

He hesitated, and then took two slices, feeding one to Ollie, who woke long enough to eat. The snow came hard now, but there was no wind and little drifting. They sat in the dark, but the bright snowy surface reflected the moon and starlight and they could see through the screens.

She talked until late, and only stopped when she yawned midsentence. He smiled at that, and then insisted she go to bed. The snow was deep by now, so he designated one of their pans a chamber pot and left it with her. As she snuggled under the quilt with Faith, Summer found she was happy. She was living with a stranger, yet she had never felt this secure.

When she woke the next morning, the front door was cracked open, and she looked out to find Rey on the porch, cleaning and oiling a rifle. Wash's rifle was there too, broken down, and freshly oiled. Rey had gone through Wash's saddlebags. Seeing the shaggy man with two rifles made her uncomfortable. He had not seen her yet, and he pulled a small pouch from his pocket, took something out, and put it in his mouth, chewing.

"There's some clothes in there too," Summer said. "If they don't fit I can alter them."

Startled, he quickly stuffed the pouch into his pocket and then mumbled, "I'll fix breakfast."

"I'll do it," Summer said, leaving him to work on the rifle.

She made corn cakes, mixing in a diced apple so there would be no argument about eating the apple. After breakfast, he left again, coming back to the porch with wood and limbs he had trimmed from trees. Then he spent the rest of the day working on something. Summer left him alone after asking him to fetch hot water from the spring. He did it without complaint, and she used it to wash Faith's soiled diapers. Faith was eating and eliminating regularly now.

He came in for lunch, but then went back to the porch to work. Summer spent the afternoon reading one of the books she had taken from Master Rice's library; a luxury she could only dream of as a slave.

Late in the afternoon the door opened and Ollie crawled in, up the wall, and to the rafters. He was carrying a fat bird that was larger than a chicken.

"Where did you get this?" Summer exclaimed, taking the bird as Ollie lowered it by tentacle. "Good work."

The animal hummed, surprising Summer. She hummed back, and then started plucking the bird. The feathers were white and speckled with brown along its bottom. The bird's neck was broken, but there were no other marks. The tree octopus was a good hunter.

She seasoned the bird with a little salt and spice, and then roasted it. She cooked up grits, and made biscuits. Ollie hung from the ceiling, watching every step in the process, dropping a tentacle now and then to beg a morsel. Deciding it was best to have the creature as a friend, she fed him off and on, trying to buy loyalty. When she called Rey in for dinner, he carried a cradle in with him, putting it in the middle of the table. Thick, bowed branches made up the rockers, with the body made of woven twigs and bark. Touched by his kindness, she hugged him. His hands hung limp, not knowing where to place them. When she released him, he looked away, his face flushed.

She placed the cradle by her bed, and used a folded blanket for a cushion. Faith was sleeping in the middle of the bed and she transferred her to the cradle, tucking her in. Faith stirred, so Summer rocked her back to sleep.

"It's perfect," she said.

He said nothing. Ollie crawled over, watching Summer rock the baby. When she stopped, he dropped a tentacle. Summer tensed, but Ollie merely took hold of the cradle and moved it up and down just as Summer had. His curiosity satisfied, he crawled back to his spot near the stove.

Ollie's bird was as meaty as a turkey, and just as tasty, and they all ate their fill. There were leftovers that would keep for a couple of days, thanks to the cold weather. The snow had accumulated all day and now was two feet thick. After supper, Rey went out and cleared snow from the roof. The cabin had managed to stand for decades, but Summer appreciated the caution. When Rey came back, he had a deck of cards.

"I found these in the saddlebags," Rey said. "Would you like to play?"

They played until late, breaking only to feed and change Faith. Having played since she was little, Summer won most of the games, frustrating Rey.

"You're cheating," he said finally, after losing another hand.

She laughed.

"Being better isn't cheating," Summer said.

"I never lost this much before," Rey said gruffly.

"Who did you play? Ollie?" Summer asked.

"Yes, we played four-handed bridge. Ollie played three hands."

Summer laughed.

"At least he didn't gloat when he won."

"I'll let you in on a secret," Summer said. "You stroke your beard when you're bluffing."

"No, I don't," Rey started to say, then found his hand pulling on his beard.

She laughed again, and he chuckled. Then he called to Ollie, who was asleep above them.

"Crawl over behind her, Ollie. Let me know what she's holding."

Bright eyes opened briefly from the folds that hid Ollie's head, and then the lids closed.

They played until Faith needed feeding, and then Summer went to bed reluctantly. She nursed Faith in the middle of the night, and then woke to the smell of frying meat. Summer gasped when she saw a stranger in the kitchen. The shaggy man was gone, replaced by a clean-shaven stranger, with brown hair cut to just below his ears. He wore a wool shirt and cotton pants—Wash's clothes.

"Rey?" she asked tentatively.

He turned, smiling shyly.

"There was a razor in the saddlebags," Rey said.

Rey's face was deeply tanned around the eyes, and across his forehead. His lower face was white, making a sharp contrast. Small scabs marked several nicks. His face was rectangular and symmetrical, with bronze-colored eyes, thick eyebrows, and now a mane of brown hair, so dark it could be confused with black. He was good looking, and Summer blushed when she realized she was staring.

"The sleeves are too short," she said quickly.

"The pants too," he said. "It's all a little tight but it still feels good. I haven't worn anything but buckskins for a long time."

They ate, talking about the snow, and how to make the cabin more weather-tight. The roof leaked, the caulking around the stovepipe needed to be replaced, and the wind whistled through gaps in the log walls. He asked about supplies, and they inventoried what they had. Getting meat would be harder with the snow. From the hot springs to the crater wall, the stream would not freeze, but the pond was upstream. Summer had brought enough food for herself, and a little more, but without Kerry she hadn't planned on food for two.

"I can climb out if we run short," he offered.

With the crater walls covered with snow and ice, Summer knew it would be dangerous, if not impossible, but she felt he meant it. This stranger would risk his life to save her and Faith.

"There will be enough," Summer said, and then she smiled, realizing they were making long-range plans.

After breakfast, she changed and fed Faith, and then examined Rey's new clothes, planning the alterations. Then she had him take them off. He brought them back, dressed in his buckskins again.

"I'm going for firewood," he said.

Threading a needle, she took her scissors and began clipping the threads along the cuff. Turning the pants over, she felt a lump in the pocket. She pulled it out. It was the small pouch she had seen in Rey's hand. Small, gray seeds filled the bottom. Summer took out a few, looking at them. Master Rice had a taste for sunflower seeds, and they grew some on his farm, but these were much smaller. She tossed them in her mouth, chewing them. The taste was slightly bitter. Tying the pouch, she set it on the table.

Summer worked expertly, lengthening the legs, and then working on the waist. Most clothes were made with extra at the seams so they could be altered, and Wash's pants had just enough to make them comfortable for Rey. Despite the cold day, and the meager fire, Summer was hot. Taking off her shawl, she continued to work, but found herself thinking about the apples and about how much Rey seemed to like them. She decided to make him a pie.

She left the sewing and searched the kitchen, finding flour, lard, salt, water, and sugar. There wasn't much of any of them, but plenty for a pie. She started mixing the dough, but then realized she had not peeled the apples. There were only a couple left in the fruit basket, so she had to go to the bin. She thought about a coat, but was so hot, she decided the cold air would feel good. Wearing her nightgown, and no shoes, she left the cabin, the screen door slamming behind her. Still in her cradle, Faith began to wail. Focused on getting apples, Summer disregarded her baby's cries.

The fruit bin was buried under a foot of snow. Digging with her hands, she threw snow right and left. When she finally found the lid, it was frozen shut. Scraping at the ice, she broke three fingernails before her heart threatened to pound through her chest. Angry, she struck the lid. Suddenly, she knew what to do and went looking for Rey—he had an axe. Wading through the snow toward the copse of trees, she found the going hard, even as strong as she felt. Then she remembered the skis—she could glide over the snow.

Snow came again as she turned toward the rim wall. The snow was fresh and cold, so that it compacted well, and the footing was good. However, when she got to the loose rocks near the rim, she realized she was not wearing shoes. She tried the rocks anyway, and was pleased to find they did not hurt her feet. She started up, having difficulty getting firm footing. She fell, got up, fell again, and hit her cheek. Tasting blood, she hesitated, but Summer really wanted her skis. She started up again, making it to the top of a large boulder. She paused. She felt strong, but her heart was pounding as if she had run a mile. Her breaths were as rapid as her heart now, but still she scrambled up the slope further, and then stumbled, and fell backward.

Strong arms caught her, lifting her. Her heart thundering, Summer pressed her hands to her chest to keep it from bursting through. Lying back, she let herself be carried. Snowflakes fluttered down from a black sky. She could see the intricacies of each flake. Lost in their crystalline beauty, time became meaningless. Suddenly she was plunged into hot water. Enveloped by the warmth, she sighed with pleasure. But then her fingers and toes tingled, and then stung. Bee stings spread along her arms and legs, and she brushed and slapped at the insects, crying out in pain. Now strong arms pinned her arms to her side so she could not strike herself.

"It hurts," she cried, but still she was held in the water.

"It's too hot. I'm burning up," she said, begging to get out of the pool.

The man held her tight. Heat sapped her strength, and she relaxed, exhausted. Discovering the snowflakes again, she contemplated their beauty, barely aware of the fire raging in her body. Then she was being carried, the cold air barely rousing her. Somewhere between the pool and the cabin, she lost consciousness.

50

COMPANIONS

Honeymoon Valley
First Continent
WINTER, PLANET AMERICA

An aching head woke Summer, the pain radiating from above her eyes clear to the base of her spine. The mucus in her mouth was pasty, her limbs trembled when she tried to move, and she was nauseous. Forcing her eyes open, she winced from the bright light streaming through the window. Closing her eyes, Summer searched her memory. She did not remember getting sick. What she remembered was feeling good—too good. Now she remembered jumping from activity to activity, and the insane attempt to climb out of the crater in midwinter.

A calloused hand lifted her head, and she sat up, opening her eyes again. The movement sent waves of pain through her head and down her spine.

"Drink this," Rey said.

She sipped the water.

"All of it," Rey said.

Summer managed to drink half. He let her collapse back into her pillow.

"Can you nurse Faith?" he asked.

"Yes," she said with effort, not sure that she could.

He helped her sit up, and then gave her the baby. She discovered she was not wearing any clothes. Instead, she was covered with every blanket she owned and one of Rey's hides. Rey sat in the kitchen, giving her as much privacy as a tiny cabin could afford. Faith sucked greedily.

"What happened?" she asked.

He avoided looking at her.

"I left some seeds in my pocket. I think you ate some."

She thought hard and remembered the pouch and the little gray seeds.

"Yes. I saw you eating them and tried a few."

"A few?" he said, shaking his head. "They're an amphetamine," Rey explained.

Summer did not know what that was and frowned.

"It's a drug that gives you more energy, but if you take too much it can make you do crazy things."

"Like try to climb a mountain in winter," she said, remembering.

"I'm sorry, Summer, I never meant you to find those. I would have warned you if I knew."

Summer shifted Faith to the other side, the baby crying in protest.

"I don't think I've seen her this hungry," Summer said. "How long did I sleep? It must be noon."

"You ate them two days ago," Rey said.

Summer was shocked.

"Faith hasn't eaten for two days?"

"I fed her as best I could, with a mix of water and cornmeal."

"You should have woken me."

"You couldn't nurse her with the amphetamines in your body. They could pass to her in your milk."

Summer understood. She finished nursing Faith, then burped her, and wrapped her again. Once wrapped, Rey put Faith in her cradle. Then he brought her the sack of seeds and held it out.

"No thanks," she said, surprised he would offer her more.

"I want you to hide these," Rey said.

"Throw them away," Summer said.

"If it wasn't for these, I wouldn't have made it this far," Rey said.

Again, Summer wondered about his past.

"They're medicine if they are used right," Rey said.

Summer understood. Patrick collected anything found to have medicinal value, and had a large collection of bark, berries, roots, bulbs, petals, leaves, and seeds.

"Why do I have to hide them?"

"Because I can't stop eating them," Rey said candidly.

Summer had seen what alcohol had done to her master's wife, and many other men and women. She often wondered why they did not just decide not to drink anymore. However, even now, with an aching head and upset stomach, Summer kept remembering how good she felt the night before. Summer took the pouch, tucking it under her pillow. The next day, she made a tiny bag out of scrap cloth, and poured the seeds into it. Then she tucked the little bag into the secret drawer in the box Kerry had made.

For the next couple of weeks, Rey was irritable, keeping to himself, refusing offers to play cards, or talk. Weather permitting, Rey worked outside, caulking the gaps between the logs, patching holes in the roof, and chopping wood. Twice, when coming back from the outhouse or the bathing pool, Summer found her things disturbed and knew Rey had been searching for the seeds. He never found them.

Ollie did most of the hunting and fishing, never coming home empty-handed. The warm creek attracted winter birds, and small mammals, and they had no experience with a predator like Ollie. The pond never iced, suggesting the volcanic activity spread at least that far, and Ollie managed to pull out a bewildering variety of fish and amphibians. The fish were all good, but the amphibians were not edible—except by Ollie.

After Rey's revelation about his addiction, Summer and Rey were more intimate. Once Rey had shared one weakness, he shared other bits and pieces of his life. When the worst of his physical longing passed, he could sit with her again, and they spent evenings at the kitchen table, playing cards or reading to each other, or on the porch huddled under blankets watching the night. She learned Rey had been in the military, enlisting after high school. He did not like to talk about his service, but she learned he had been cross-trained as a medic.

Rey used the feathers of Ollie's speckled chicken to stuff a small mattress for Faith's cradle, and then tanned the skins from other animals Ollie caught, making gloves and slippers for Summer, and a hat and sleeping bag for Faith. The hat was made from the skin of a striped animal that reminded Rey of a skunk. Summer knew of animals called "skunks" near Master Rice's farm, but they were not striped. She loved Faith's fur-lined bag, the little girl fitting snugly inside, the bag tied closed with rawhide strips. Rey also fashioned a sling so that Summer could carry Faith on her back, or slung across her chest.

Summer finished altering Wash's clothes for Rey, and they soon lost all association with Wash. The tan on Rey's face evened out, and he let Summer trim his hair above his ears, tapering it up the sides and back.

"A haircut this nice would cost thirty bucks where I came from," Rey said, admiring her work in the mirror.

Summer was sure that was a compliment. Rey was not like Kerry, who never lost his smile, had the gift of gab, and was a bit boastful. Everyone liked Kerry instantly; they were comfortable with him, and not intimidated. Rey's countenance was the opposite. When relaxed his face was stern, his stare piercing, and his lips tight as if he was angry twenty-five hours a day. Yet, Summer came to know that was not the only Rey. His bronze eyes twinkled when he played cards, he lied audaciously when caught cheating, and he doted on Faith as if he were her father. Then again, she could not deny he had a dark side, so she was shocked one night when he asked if they could read the Bible.

"Of course," she said quickly.

She retrieved her Bible from the side of her bed and returned to the table where he fiddled nervously with the deck of cards.

"Would you like to hear about Jesus' birth? Or maybe I could read you some of the Psalms. They're poetry, you know?"

"I've read all those many times," Rey said.

Her skepticism showed.

"A Bible was the only book I had," he said, holding up a well-thumbed and dirty Bible.

After many weeks together, Summer still did not know how he had come to America, and how he had avoided slavery.

"Start in Genesis. I want to know how it all got started."

Puzzled, she opened the Bible she had stolen to the first chapter of Genesis and then paused.

"Why haven't you read Genesis?" she asked.

"My Bible doesn't have it," Rey said, handing her his Bible.

She found most of Genesis missing.

"I used the pages to start fires," Rey said. "I didn't know it was the only book I would read for twenty years."

He rolled his eyes when he said it, and she could not help but laugh.

"It's not funny," he said, trying to look angry.

"You're right, it's not funny," she said. "It's hilarious!"

"Are you going to read it or not?" he asked.

Summer could not stop laughing.

"Give it to me," he said, reaching for the Bible.

She held it out of reach, and controlled herself.

"All right, I'll read it," she said, opening the Bible on the table in front of her. "In the beginning, God created the world and everything in it and everything in the heavens, and then God had it all written down in His book. And God said, 'Let no man tear pages out of my book lest he look foolish and have to beg a woman to read to him.' "

Rey jumped up, circling the table.

"Give me that," he said.

Summer stood, holding the Bible behind her, and backed around the table.

"That's what is says," Summer said. "Don't you trust me?"

"Give it to me or I'll take it," Rey said.

"The next part says, 'No man who burns his only book shall harm a woman.' "

"Give it to me," Rey said again, advancing.

"Come and get it," Summer dared him.

Rey lunged for it, and Summer ran, but there was no place to run in a one-room cabin, so the chase was short. Rey caught her and wrapped his arms around her, reaching for the Bible. Summer wriggled, kicked, and pushed with her free arm, but only managed to trip them both and they fell onto the bed, Summer giggling, Rey laughing. Finally, Rey wrenched the Bible free and then, lying next to her on the bed, opened it to Genesis.

"Liar," Rey said. "You violated one of the Ten Commandments."

"At least you didn't tear that part out," she said, lying next to him, laughing.

They laughed some more, until they realized they were on the bed together. Sobering, Rey got up and leaned against the doorframe, studying her. Summer sat up, strangely uncomfortable, confused about her feelings for Rey. There was a long silence.

"Rey, I know almost nothing about you. Where did you come from? How did you come to America? You're too old to have been born here, so why didn't you leave with the Fellowship? Why don't you know much about the animals around here? How did you find Honeymoon Valley? Tell me something. Anything."

Rey studied the floor. Finally, he spun one of the table chairs around and sat, leaning on the back.

"I was brought here as a prisoner," Rey said. "Back on Earth, I tried to shoot down one of the Fellowship's spheres, and got caught by a man named George Proctor—ever hear of him?"

Summer had not.

"Proctor and I had one thing in common: we didn't care much for the law. Instead of turning me over to the police, he locked me up in his own private prison. Then one day he came to me and offered me a deal. He would set me free if I told him who hired me. I made him swear on a Bible to keep his agreement, because I thought his religion meant something to him. The next thing I knew the building where they held me was under attack and I was hustled out through a tunnel. Then I was locked in another cage and put into one of their spaceships. Eventually, they marooned me on the opposite end of this continent. Proctor, who claimed to be a Christian, lied to me."

"You were set free," Summer said carefully.

"I was given life in solitary confinement," Rey said. "That's not freedom."

For most of her life, Summer had longed for the kind of freedom that Rey had, but now she saw the other side of it.

"You said you were on the opposite end of the continent?" Summer asked, unsure of how far away that was.

"Yes. Here, I'll show you."

Rey went to the porch, rummaged through his stuff, and came back with a roll of papers. When he unrolled them, Summer saw they were photos, like the ones she had stolen from Master Rice.

"Wait, I have some too," Summer said.

Puzzled, Rey watched as Summer retrieved her photos from a saddlebag. She could feel Rey's excitement as he saw her photos. The table was too small, so they spread the photos on the bed, creating a mosaic of the continent.

"Where's this?" Rey asked, excited, holding up a picture that included a city.

"That's New Jerusalem. It's the biggest city on America."

"Do a lot of people live there?" Rey asked.

"Yes. Sure. As I said, it's the biggest city. Just about the only city."

Rey looked thoughtful, and then picked up another photo.

"That's near where we live," Summer said, thinking about Master Rice's farm.

Now Summer began to point out farms, Lumber Camp, the Puff Tree Forest, and the meadow where they held the Gathering. She talked about life as a slave. She had told him much of this, but now she added detail—unpleasant details. She told Rey of Saturday nights when she would have to go to Lucy's, and the black eyes and split lips her mother would have the next day. She told him about Winnie, and at last found the courage to tell him how she had taken her mother's place in Master Rice's rotation. He tensed when he heard that part of the story, and she rushed on. Finally, she told him about Kerry and how Master Rice had whipped him. When she told him what Wash and his brothers had done to Kerry, and how Kerry had killed himself, Rey interrupted.

"Someday I'd like to meet the Rice family," Rey said.

Rey's eyes had the fierceness she had seen on the night he had burst into her cabin.

"All that's behind me," Summer said quickly.

"Don't you want justice?"

"Not if the price is too high," Summer said. "Besides, Jesus teaches that we should turn the other cheek."

Now she looked at him mischievously.

"Or was that torn out of your Bible?"

Rey stifled a smile, and then turned solemn.

"You're a better person than I am," Rey said.

Summer did not ask him to explain. She could sense a part of him that frightened her.

"Your turn," Summer insisted. "Where did you come from?"

Reluctantly, Rey shuffled his photos, holding one up.

"I started near the east coast," he began. Once the telling started, Rey's story poured out with fascinating detail. Summer learned about his life in a lonely cabin, his many attempts to find a pet, and the meal he made of the last "King." She learned he had built a canoe, paddled and walked for hundreds of miles, and eventually found Ollie. As he told the story he pointed to features on the photos—Omega Falls, Big Eye Lake, Bone Eater Plains, and Mud Pot Valley. He told her about the skin worms and the healer birds. He told her about catching Fawn, teaching her to carry Ollie, and their long walk across the plain and how they found rivers and streams hidden under river vines. She learned how Fawn died, and how Ollie almost burned to death. When Rey told her about Chain Meadows and the tree haters, she looked at the photo he pointed to long and hard—this was close to home. Then he told of seeing the smoke from her chimney and climbing into Honeymoon Valley.

It was an amazing story, and she asked many questions. Even then, she knew he had left out many details—how could someone tell about a two-year journey in a few minutes?

When it was over, she asked him to take off his shirt. Puzzled, he complied.

Summer examined the scars across his back.

"I thought you were making it up," Summer said honestly.

"It's hard for me to believe too," Rey said. "I thought I would die on the way, but I couldn't live one more day like I was."

"I couldn't either," Summer said.

Now Summer stood, building up the fire in the stove, putting a pot of water on for tea.

"I'd like to see those places you talked about," Summer said.

"I'd love to show you," Rey said, smiling.

"Then show me, Rey," Summer said impulsively. "It's not safe for Faith and me to stay here. They'll come looking for me when the snow melts. Eventually they will find this valley. Take me and Faith somewhere safe, Rey. Somewhere they can never find us."

Summer regretted asking as soon as the words were out of her mouth. Rey avoided her eyes, shifting in his chair.

"Summer, you don't know what you're asking for. If you knew who I was back on Earth—"

"Earth means nothing to me, Rey. I've never been there, and I'll never go. I don't need to know any more about you than I do now. I'm judging you by your deeds, not your history. God will forgive you for your sins on Earth, and I don't care about who you were, only who you are. Leave your Earth problems on Earth."

"It's not that easy, Summer. I didn't choose to come to this planet; I was kidnapped and brought here against my will. My problems came with me."

"But the Fellowship is gone," Summer said.

"No, your Grandma Jones was in league with the Fellowship."

"But what can you do? What is it you want from them?"

Now Rey did not answer, and she was glad. She was afraid of what he would say.

Rey withdrew for the next few days, talking only to answer questions. He found ways to avoid her, even in a small cabin in a small valley. Then one night he asked her to read the Bible again. She made no jokes this time, and he listened patiently until it was late. After that, they read for an hour or two a night, taking turns, working their way chapter by chapter, through the entire Bible. When they finished, Rey started asking questions about the nature of God, Jesus, and the Holy Spirit. They discussed grace, baptism, forgiveness, faith, and natural revelation. They argued, they laughed, they wondered together. Summer had never been happier. Then one night, after a long discussion of Romans 14:13, Rey asked Summer how she became a Christian.

"I asked God to forgive me for my sins," she said. "I knew He would, because it says so in the Bible, and then I asked Jesus into my heart."

Summer remembered how scared she was at that moment. She was opening herself to God, and turning her life over to Him. She did not tell Rey about her fear. Her voice softened to a hush.

"And then I felt the Holy Spirit fill me and I was shivering and sweating at the same time. I've never felt anything like that before. I think God gives us a little taste of heaven, just to keep us going."

"Is it like that for everyone?" Rey asked.

Summer hesitated. Rey was reaching toward God, and she wanted to encourage him, but the truth was that being a Christian was not all joy all the time.

"People come to know God in different ways," Summer said. "My way was right for me. It might be right for you."

Rey either did not understand her offer, or ignored it.

"How old were you?"

"I was seven," Summer said.

"Seven? Did you even know what you were doing?"

"I knew," Summer said. "And every day since has confirmed my decision."

"Even Saturday nights?"

Summer was not offended.

"Especially Saturday nights," Summer said. "I could not have survived those without God."

Rey asked nothing more. She let him think, closing her eyes and praying he would give in to the Holy Spirit.

The next morning, Rey was gone. Summer found Ollie hanging from a porch rafter, but no sign of Rey. At Summer's request, Ollie fetched a fish for breakfast. Rey missed lunch and dinner too and was gone all the next day. On the third day, he returned at suppertime, opening the door timidly. Ollie caressed Rey with both tentacles, while Rey avoided Summer's eyes.

"I'll get you a plate," Summer offered.

"Summer, I did what you said. I asked God to forgive me and for the Holy Spirit to enter my heart."

Embarrassed, Rey avoided her eyes, talking softly.

"Nothing happened. Not like with you."

"It's different for everyone, Rey. God wants you no matter how you come to Him."

"But shouldn't there be some kind of sign?"

"The Israelites were shown sign after sign, and could not keep the faith," Summer pointed out. "Faith has to come from within, or it won't last."

Rey thought about that.

"All right, I'll give it a try, but I need something to seal the deal."

"Something . . ." Summer said, confused.

"I need to be baptized," Rey said.

"But there's no pastor," Summer said.

"Then you'll have to do it."

Summer was uncomfortable, but soon realized Rey was right. There was no one else.

"When?" Summer asked.

"Now," Rey said. "And it's got to be immersion. Sprinkling may be okay for some, but I need a good soaking."

Summer began putting her coat on.

"Let's go to the bathing pool, then."

"No. To the pond."

"But it's so cold," Summer said.

"It would feel like cheating to soak in that hot water. I know I'm not supposed to have to pay for my sins, but I'll feel better if I pay a little price for my soul."

"What about me? I've got to get in that pond too."

"So, you'll save souls only at room temperature? Is that what they call a lukewarm Christian?"

Summer punched him in the arm.

"I'm going to enjoy dunking you," Summer said. "How long can you hold your breath?"

Checking to make sure that Faith was still sound asleep, they walked toward the pond, arm in arm. There had been many barriers between Rey and Summer, and one by one, they were falling. Rey's agnosticism had been the biggest barrier, and that had just fallen. Holding his arm to steady herself, as they trudged through the snow, Summer let herself enjoy being near him.

51

LOVERS

A month after Rey's baptism, Summer asked him to marry her. After the baptism, each day brought them closer, and Summer gave up hiding her feelings. Rey was more reserved, and she guessed the difference in their ages bothered him. During the day they shared chores, took turns caring for Faith, and found creative ways to stretch their meager supplies. At night, they played games, read books and the Bible, and argued over the meaning of stories and passages. In every way, they were man and wife, except one. With the limited food, Summer's body had quickly returned to what it had been before her pregnancy, and often Summer caught Rey looking at her in the way that said he wanted her. Something was holding him back.

One evening, Rey had the Bible open, looking for a story he wanted Summer to explain. Summer put her hand on the Bible, covering the pages. He looked at her playfully.

"Rey, would you marry me?" Summer asked.

Rey looked like he had been punched. Shocked, he rocked back in his chair, putting distance between himself and Summer. He said nothing. Summer decided to risk it all.

"I love you, Rey. I don't know how it happened, or when, but I know you and I were meant for each other. I know you feel something for me too, and maybe it isn't love, but whatever it is, it's good enough for me."

Keeping his distance, Rey spoke carefully, as if afraid he would offend her.

"Summer, it's not like you have a choice of men," Rey said, indicating the cabin.

"I've known a lot of men, and most of them wanted me," Summer said. "I thought Kerry and I would be together, but Wash took that away from me and then Master Rice took me. You're the first man I'm offering myself to."

Rey rocked forward and took her hand.

"There's still one secret you need to know," Rey said.

Rey took the Bible, turning to the Old Testament. Then he turned the Bible around for Summer to read, pointing at a passage. Summer saw it was the story of Jephthah.

"I know this story," Summer said. "Jephthah was an outcast who became a great warrior and leader of men. He fought for Israel and won, but he paid a terrible price. He promised God that if He gave him victory, that he would sacrifice the first person who came out of his own house and it turned out to be his daughter, but he kept his promise to God. He killed his own daughter."

Rey looked solemn.

"Why is this story important to you, Rey?"

"I made Jephthah's promise," Rey said. "I promised God that if He helped me cross the country, I would kill the first person I saw as a sacrifice to Him."

Summer understood.

"I was that first person?"

"Yes," Rey said.

Suddenly, Summer was afraid of Rey, as she had been the night he burst into her cabin. She wanted to argue him out of killing her, but for a month she had been drilling into him the importance of following the Scriptures. Thinking back on their many conversations, Summer now understood why Rey had wondered whether the New Testament superseded the Old Testament.

"But Jesus made the only sacrifice necessary for salvation," Summer argued.

"This wasn't about salvation, it was a covenant. God kept His part of the bargain, and he brought me here safely."

"So, now you need to keep your end of the bargain," Summer said.

"Summer, you don't understand. That first day, I saw you in the cabin door and I took my rifle and I lined up the sights on you. I'm a good shot, Summer, and at that range I could not miss. Looking down the sights, I could see you were pregnant, but I took aim anyway. I knew I would be killing two, not just one. Then I squeezed the trigger."

Agitated, Rey paced the cabin, avoiding Summer's eyes. Summer had never seen Rey like this. She was also shocked to know how close he had come to killing her and Faith. Now Rey settled into a chair, face in his hands.

"But you didn't shoot us, Rey."

Summer put her hands on his shoulders, looking down at him. Rey looked up, making eye contact.

"But I did, Summer. I pulled the trigger. I tried to kill you, but it was a misfire. The only reason you and Faith are here is because my ammunition is twenty years old."

Shocked, Summer stepped back, frightened by something that never happened. Overcoming her emotional reaction, Summer pulled the other chair around, and sat next to Rey, arm across his shoulder.

"Rey, I'm glad there was a misfire," Summer said, trying to sound light-hearted.

"But I tried to kill you and your baby!"

Summer leaned against Rey.

"Rey, remember the story of Abraham and his son, Isaac?"

Rey did not seem to hear.

"God asked Abraham to sacrifice his son, Isaac, but at the last moment stopped him from going through with it. God found out what He needed to know without the death of Isaac. Because Abraham was willing to go through with the sacrifice, the sacrifice was not necessary."

Rey looked up.

"Do you think God was testing me?"

"Rey, I honestly don't know, but you meant to kill me. You

kept your promise to God. If God wanted me dead, it would have been easy enough to fix a cartridge."

Rey accepted her reasoning.

"You're right. It wasn't my fault there was a dud in the chamber. I couldn't know that before I pulled the trigger."

Summer felt uneasy, hearing how close she and Faith had come to death. Rey, however, was becoming his old self.

"It all makes sense to me now," Rey said. "Why couldn't I see it?"

"Well, you are the kind of man who uses his only book for kindling."

Rey faked a frown.

"That's why they say God works in mysterious ways," Summer said.

Rey's mood changed quickly, now. He smiled, and then hugged Summer.

"Summer, I have to be honest with you. I came here looking for vengeance, but I found you instead. I thought God helped me to cross a continent, because of a deal I made with Him. Now I see that God had His own plans. He brought me here to meet you."

Summer smiled, but inwardly squirmed. She couldn't imagine she was part of some large plan of God's.

"Yes, Summer, I will marry you," Rey said.

As awkward as teenagers on their first date, Rey and Summer leaned toward each other and kissed.

"How do we do this?" Rey asked. "We can't go to New Jerusalem to find a preacher, not to mention we don't have a marriage license."

"Slaves can't marry anyway," Summer pointed out. "And Master Rice would never give me permission. We did the baptism ourselves and we can do this too."

It took Summer three days to fashion a dress. On their wedding day, Rey went hunting with Ollie and the two of them came back with a large turkey bird, which he cleaned and stuffed, and then put in the oven to slow roast. Summer wanted to be married under the stars, so they waited until dark, and then dressed in their wedding clothes. Summer wove blue strips of cloth in her hair, to match her dress. When Rey knocked on the door to see if she was ready, he smiled wide and long when he saw her.

"I don't deserve you," Rey said.

"And don't you forget it," Summer said, smiling.

The snow was deep, but Rey had cleared a path so they could get away from the cabin lights. America's night skies were thick with stars, the tiny moon not bright enough to wash them away, and with no light pollution from cities, every star twinkled bright. As Ollie watched from the roof of the cabin, and with Faith snug in a pack on Summer's back, they stood facing each other, holding hands. Then they took turns pledging themselves to each other, promising to be faithful companions in every way. Then they asked God to bless their marriage, promising to live their lives together according to God's plan for men and women. Then they pronounced themselves man and wife and kissed. By then they were shivering with cold, and held each other close as they walked back to their cabin.

"Does this mean I don't have to sleep on the porch anymore?" Rey asked as they came to the cabin.

"It means we get to find out why they named this place Honeymoon Valley," Summer said.

As they closed the door behind them, Summer said, "But Ollie sleeps on the porch."

52

NEW LIVES

Honeymoon Valley
First Continent
WINTER, PLANET AMERICA

Rey finally thought he understood what the Bible meant by
being "born again." He felt like a new man, a different man
from the one who had come to Honeymoon Valley, and not
even the man he had been on Earth. He was different, and he
was willing to acknowledge that God had some role in it, but
he gave most of the credit to Summer. She was unlike anyone
he had ever met. She was kind, generous, courageous, re-
sourceful, and the most spiritual person he had ever met. Rey
had known lots of men and women who claimed to be Christians, Muslims, Buddhists, Wiccans, and Scientologists, but
you could not distinguish them from their atheist brothers
and sisters without their label. Summer was different, and it
was the way Summer lived, not talked, that led Rey to Christ.

Rey knew he would never have a relationship with God
like Summer's. He didn't feel the Holy Spirit, like she did,
but Rey finally understood that God had uses for all kinds of
people, and could relate to them in all kinds of ways. Rey
also could not deny that God had used a dream to lead him
to Summer. That may have been the unique way that God re-
lated to Rey.

Life in Honeymoon Valley was nearly perfect. True, they
were running low on food, with even the game getting
scarcer, but there was enough to keep them alive until
spring. However, no matter how much they loved life in the
valley, they could not stay. As the days grew longer, Summer
worried that her former owners would come for her.

"I won't let them take you," Rey assured her repeatedly.

"There are too many," Summer would say. "And I don't want anyone hurt because of me. Especially you."

"I have skills they don't," Rey said.

"No, Rey, let them be."

So, they made plans to leave. They would cross the continent together and live in Rey's old cabin. Between the seeds that Summer had stolen, and those Rey had buried before he left, they would have a full range of crops. Summer had also collected apple seeds, and had a few peach pits to start an orchard. The cabin provided other supplies such as bedding, tools, lanterns, cutlery, crockery, pots and pans, and of course the few precious books. The more they talked and planned, the longer their lists of needs and wants became.

"Summer, we can't take all of this," Rey said one evening, while they rocked on the porch.

Outside, there was the steady drip, drip, drip of melting snow.

"Not without the horses," Rey added.

They had argued about the horses before.

"If this thaw keeps up, I can climb out of the valley in a few days. If I can't find the horses in a week or so, I'll come back and we'll just take what we can carry."

Under their blanket, Summer took Rey's hand.

"Let's just take what we can carry and go," Summer said.

"With Faith getting as big as she is, she'll be about all you can carry," Rey said. "We'll have to leave behind most everything else except food and water. Ollie and I lived off the land, eating what we could, when we could, but that's harder to do with four. We almost died of thirst once, and came close a couple of other times."

"I'm not afraid," Summer said. "As long as we're together, we can take care of each other."

A tentacle dropped from the ceiling, touching Summer's face. Summer looked up. Ollie hummed his worry from a rafter. The tree octopus was sensitive to people's mood and bothered by Summer's distress.

"Ollie will take care of us," Summer said cheerfully.

Satisfied by her new tone, Ollie retracted the tentacle, and tucked his head back in.

"As long as you're nursing Faith, you have to eat right, Summer, or it will affect her. Once she's weaned we'll have to feed her too."

Summer was going to protest again, but he cut her off.

"I'm not just thinking about crossing the continent, I'm thinking about our life once we get there. Faith will have only what we bring with us. We need to make sure it's the best quality life that we can give her."

"But you don't know where the horses are," Summer said. "They probably wandered back to Master Rice's by now."

"Maybe, but let me show you something."

Rey went into the cabin and got a lantern and one of the photos. Settling back under the blanket, he put the photo in her lap.

"Here's where you released the horses," Rey said pointing. "If they went home, they're gone for good. If they went southeast, they might have reached Chain Meadows, but the tree haters would keep them from grazing."

"Those meadows are probably covered in snow," Summer pointed out.

"Right, although these down here are much lower than where we are. But look, to the northeast," Rey said pointing. "There are meadows along the creek the hot spring empties into. If the creek is warm enough, there might be grass along its banks all winter. If the horses followed that, they might have found these meadows."

"Rey, you don't know where the horses are. They were probably killed by a leaper, anyway."

"Just a week, Summer. It could make the difference between scraping by and a good life."

She gave in reluctantly.

"Promise me you will come back."

"I have no life without you, Summer. I'll come back. I promise."

The thaw continued, and Rey left two days later. He wanted to leave Ollie with Summer, but there was a practical reason for taking Ollie. The horses would be half wild by now, and Ollie could help catch them.

When Rey and Ollie reached the rim, Rey looked back into the valley. Summer stood in front of the cabin with Faith on her hip, hand shading her eyes. He waved goodbye. Summer waved back and then moved Faith's hand in a waving motion, pointing Rey out on the rim. Racked by doubt, Rey started down the mountain. He did not like leaving his family alone and vowed he would not leave her alone a second longer than absolutely necessary.

Using Summer's directions, Rey found where she had stashed the saddles and bridles. He took the bridles. Then, using one of the photographs, Rey followed the curve of the mountain, working through the forest to the northeast, following the creek that ran from under Flat Top. The stream was warm, and the banks were lush. Working his way down, he found the thaw had progressed faster at the lower elevations, and soon there were green patches with new growth.

He reached the first meadow by nightfall, but found no horses, or any other grazing animals. He checked for droppings, but the only ones he found were not horse. He camped that night on the edge of the clearing, Ollie hanging from a nearby limb.

Up at dawn, Rey worked his way toward the next meadow, finding it by noon. It too was empty, but most of the snow was gone from this one. The snow persisted under the canopy of the forest, but the sun was clearing the meadows. The terrain forced Rey away from the creek, and Rey began to think the horses would have found an easier route. He reached the largest meadow in the photo by midmorning the following day. A dozen of the small pronghorns grazed along the edge—no horses. Rey systematically searched the meadow, finding a surprising variety of dung. Near the middle he spotted horse droppings—he thought. Now he studied the ground, and could see the marks of a horseshoe. Unfortunately, the meadow had so many visitors, following the track was beyond his skills.

Rey walked the perimeter, but could not pick up a trail.

Instead, he consulted his photo, and then headed for the next meadow. He passed through two small clearings, and by nightfall, reached the second largest meadow in his photo. The horses were not there, but he found droppings and tracks. Rey camped, planning to get another early start. Ollie would not like it, but tomorrow would be his fourth day, and traveling back would be uphill. If he found the horses, he could keep his "one week" promise, but if he did not, Summer would have to worry a day or two before he could get back.

At dawn, Rey crawled out from under the hide he used for a tent, and began packing. Out of the corner of his eye, Rey saw movement in the meadow—the horses. Buck and Princess were alive, and grazing happily.

Suppressing his excitement, Rey reached up and patted Ollie. The tree octopus squeaked annoyance, then hummed in irritation. Rey pointed toward the horses, and Ollie instantly quieted. Signaling Ollie to follow, Rey led him through the trees. The creek Rey had been following bordered one side of the meadow, and two animal trails led out of it. Rey posted Ollie along one of the trails and then returned to his gear, took a rope, and then worked his way through the trees to the other trail. Forming a noose, Rey walked slowly into the meadow. A small herd of pronghorns grazed to his left, and shied away as he entered. Both Princess and Buck raised their heads, watching. They knew humans, but they had not seen one in months, and had never seen Rey.

Princess dropped her head to graze again, but Buck remained on watch. Rey came on slowly, taking a step, pausing, and then another step. Princess took her cue from Buck, letting him decide whether Rey was a threat or not. When Rey was ten yards away, Buck walked away, Princess following. Rey paused, letting them get comfortable again. Then he took a few steps forward. Buck walked away again, with Princess right behind.

Now Rey called their names, talking to them.

"Easy Buck. Easy Princess. Easy, easy."

The horses still kept their distance. Rey tried over and over, but the horses would not let him get close. However, he had slowly worked them toward the second animal trail. Now he opened a big loop in the rope, and then boldly walked forward. Rey's assertive air brought out their training, and both horses stood still, as if waiting for the bridle. Then Buck turned and trotted away, Princess right behind. Rey ran to keep up. Buck headed down the animal trail, but suddenly a tentacle shot out, snagging an ankle. Princess pulled up as Buck fell to his knees, and then struggled to regain his feet. A second tentacle snagged another leg, and now Buck was hobbled.

Princess darted around Buck, and fled down the trail. Quickly, Rey tossed the rope over Buck's head, and then tied the free end to a tree.

"Let him go, Ollie," Rey shouted.

Ollie hesitated, expecting Rey to put an arrow into the horse, or to cut its throat. Rey shouted again, and the tentacles released. Buck clambered to his feet, neighing, and struggling with the rope. It held.

Ollie climbed the tree he had been anchored to, and then worked his way to a spot over Rey. Then he dropped a tentacle, slipped it under Rey's chin, and tilted his head up, humming expectantly.

"Not food," Rey said.

Ollie looked at the horse, and then pulled Rey's chin up again, glaring at him.

"Ollie, this is not food," Rey said. "This is like Fawn. We ride these."

Ollie did not understand, so Rey gave him a piece of jerky, and then sat down to wait. Slowly, Buck calmed down. Rey shortened the rope, making Buck skittish again. This time Buck settled down quickly, and Rey walked up to him, putting a hand on his shoulder. Buck shuddered, but did not move away. Then Rey walked around the animal, inspecting him. He was in good condition, although thin after a winter of scrounging for food.

Keeping a hand on him, Rey felt Buck calm down. Finally, Rey pulled one of their last remaining apples from a pocket, and sliced it, feeding it a slice at a time to Buck—except for the two slices Ollie insisted on. When the apple was gone, Rey found he could lead Buck back to his camp. Rey hobbled Buck, but kept the rope around his neck. Buck grazed along the edge of the meadow, and Rey settled in to wait. Ollie found a good limb to hang from, and took a nap. Watching Buck graze, Rey knew he was halfway to making a better future for his new family. He also thought about having more children. They had an entire continent to fill, so the more children the better, but bearing babies was dangerous, especially without a doctor to assist.

His hopes for the future were a roller coaster of emotions, because for every good dream he had, there was an accompanying risk. Still, they would make the move. There was nowhere else to go.

Princess showed up an hour later, coming hesitantly, and then grazing near Buck. Rey took another rope and approached Princess, who shied away briefly but then saw that Buck was not afraid. Taking his time, Rey was able to walk up to Princess and slip the rope over her head.

With the horses under his control, Rey decided he could take an extra day to gentle them, and get them used to a rider again. The first time Rey swung up on Buck's back, Buck reminded the world of how he got his name. It took Rey three tries before Buck would take his weight. After that, Buck quickly responded to the reins, with Rey guiding him around the meadow. Princess bucked him off only once, and then was a steady mount, and perfect for Summer and Faith.

Rey left the next morning, letting Ollie swing through the trees, following along, sometimes out of sight and sound. Ollie was in his element and as happy as Rey was, living with Summer in Honeymoon Valley. The horses cut Rey's travel time in half, and so they spent only one more night in the open. They would be home by nightfall, and Rey could not wait to see the look on Summer's face when she learned of the horses.

53

ALONE

Even with Faith to care for, Summer felt alone. Since the night Rey burst through her front door, she had not felt this way, and hated the feeling. As a slave, she had fantasized about running off and living free, but she had found something better. She had given up her freedom for love.

Gurgling, cooing, and babbling, Faith was a joy, helping to pass the days without Rey. With the warming weather, Summer took Faith to the bathing pool every day, her baby girl in her arms, splashing and laughing until their fingers and toes wrinkled. Sometimes, Summer put Faith in the backpack Rey had fashioned, and walked Faith around the meadow, her little fingers tugging on Summer's hair. Summer pointed out sucker fish, turkey birds, and the squirrels that Ollie loved to bring home for supper.

After five days of good weather, the apple tree buds were swelling, making Summer wish she could stay to harvest the apples. It was not possible, however, so apple pie would have to wait a few years. Early sprouts pushed through the sod, and Summer recognized one type, digging out the edible bulbs. Boiling a couple of the bulbs, she then mashed them, feeding them to Faith, who was taking solid food now. She saved the rest to serve at Rey's welcome home dinner.

For the first four days, Summer prayed every night for Rey's safe return. On day five, she began watching the rim for Rey, and prayed for his safety three times. On day six she began to worry and prayed for Rey's safety every hour. She knew it was silly, but she worried anyway. Worry and praying were all she could do. On the morning of the seventh day, she hurried to the porch, studying the rim, but came away disappointed. After feeding and changing Faith, Summer took a load of diapers to the creek to wash, and then laid them out in the meadow to dry, all the time watching the rim. She collected the diapers at noon and thought she saw movement in the rocks. Shielding her eyes, she studied the rim and the route in and out—nothing. Disappointed, she finished with the diapers and took Faith inside.

After feeding Faith, she put her down for a nap, and then fixed herself lunch. She was just sitting down to eat when she heard the porch door open. Excited, she wiped her hands, took off her apron, and hurried to the door.

"Faith, Rey's home," she said, not caring if she woke the baby.

Happier than she had ever been, Summer opened the cabin door. She had time for only a vague impression of men crowded in the porch, Wash's grinning face, and then his fist struck her between the eyes. She was unconscious before she hit the floor.

54

HOMECOMING

Honeymoon Valley
First Continent
SPRING, PLANET AMERICA

After all the trouble, and luck, of finding the horses, Rey hated to leave them while he climbed back into Honeymoon Valley. Tying them with long ropes so that they could maneuver and defend themselves, Rey gave them a fighting chance. Rey planned to climb into the valley, tell Summer the good news, and then climb back out to spend the night protecting the horses.

Starting up the mountain, Ollie nearly climbed over Rey, as anxious to get home as Rey. Pausing at the rim, Rey called out, letting Summer know he was back. Without waiting for a reply, Rey hurried down, eventually reaching the rope that allowed him to slide to the bottom. While he was gone, most of the rest of the snow had evaporated, leaving only patches in permanent shadows. Reaching the floor, Rey ran, leaving Ollie waddling behind. Strangely, the porch door was open, but Summer was nowhere in sight.

Calling frantically now, foreboding filled him. Barely slowing, Rey rushed through the door. The table and a chair were tipped over, their belongings were scattered, and shards of pottery littered the floor. Blood stained the braided rug. Fearfully, Rey looked into Faith's cradle—empty, a smear of blood on the feather pad.

Fighting back tears, Rey forced himself to study the scene. Now, he saw the spilled food, and the unfamiliar boot tracks. Rey knew part of what had happened and he fought back panic. Ollie climbed through the open door, taking his usual spot on the ceiling. Ollie hummed a worried hum, missing Summer and Faith, and sensing Rey's mood.

Rey had become a new man since meeting Summer and accepting Christ; a better man. But now the old Rey surfaced, and a cold calm filled him. If Summer and Faith were alive, he would get them back. If they were dead, he would spill enough blood to fill Honeymoon Valley. Quickly searching the cabin, Rey found the spare ammunition was gone, as were knives, books, and the photomaps—both sets. Rey would have to find Summer's kidnappers from memory. Summer's clothes were still there, but the saddlebags and men's clothes that Summer brought were gone. Summer's fancy box was gone too. Everything of value had been taken.

Turning to leave, Rey froze. A man was coming in the door, rifle leveled at Rey's chest. Carelessly, Rey had left his rifle leaning against the wall by the door. The man behind the rifle was black, bearded, and about Rey's age. With a thick chest, but spindly legs, he looked top heavy. If Rey could put a shoulder into him, Rey was sure he would go down easily, but he would not get two steps before the man got a shot off.

"We thought she must have had help," the man said, advancing slowly into the cabin. "No girl could hide from us that long by herself."

Rey stepped back, letting him inch in further.

"Just who are you, slave?" the bearded man asked.

Rey did not answer.

"You talk to me, slave, or I'll kill you here and now. No one's gonna know what happens way out here, except you and me, and you won't be doing the telling."

"I'm not a slave," Rey said, taking another half step back.

"You're white, so you're either a slave, a runaway, or a hermit. It doesn't matter much to me which you are," he said, smiling broadly. "I'm just trying to decide whether to kill you here or take you back to the farm to die."

"Funny, I'm trying to decide the same thing," Rey said.

Now the bearded man lost his grin.

"Come to think of it," the bearded man said, his finger tightening on the trigger, "I just made up my mind."

"Me too," Rey said, looking to the ceiling and nodding.

The bearded man looked up just as Ollie slapped a tentacle around his neck. Rey dove onto the bed as the rifle went off, the bullet creasing his side. Ollie strained, lifting the bearded man by the neck as he struggled to reload. Quickly, Rey rolled off the bed and wrenched the rifle from his hands. Ollie continued to lift, the bearded man now dancing on his toes, hands clawing at the tentacle around his neck. When he reached for the knife in his belt, Rey pulled it first, and then patted him down for other weapons.

Now the strangling man's toes left the ground. Rey's fury was such that he wanted him to die, but he had always been good at reasoning under pressure. He needed information more than revenge—at least for now.

"Drop him, Ollie," Rey said.

Reluctantly, Ollie let go and the man fell to the floor, gasping and coughing. Rey gave him a minute to catch his breath. Finally, the man rolled over, getting to his knees, looking up at Rey. The rifle lay on the bed behind Rey. Rey saw him glance at the gun. Without a word, Rey kicked him in the solar plexus.

"That's for what you were thinking," Rey said.

The man was back on the ground, gasping for breath again.

Rey felt so good, he kicked him again, and then a third time.

"Those were just to get you in the right frame of mind," Rey said.

When the bearded man could breathe again, he looked at Rey fearfully, but spoke defiantly.

"Master Rice will whip you to death, slave," he muttered, still struggling to breathe.

Rey remembered Summer's stories.

"You're from the Rice Farm?" Rey asked, pleased with the discovery.

"Who are you?" the bearded man asked. "I don't know you. You must have run away from the lumber camp, or the mines."

The bearded man was regaining his composure, confidence returning.

"Give yourself up now and I'll speak for you. Maybe you'll just get whipped. Maybe Master Rice won't hang you."

Rey had none of the conditioned deference of slaves, but the bearded man had grown accustomed to a world where slaves cowered in his presence.

"Ollie," Rey said.

A tentacle circled the bearded man's neck. Again, he clawed futilely at Ollie's tough tentacle. Ollie slowly pulled the man to his feet, and then to his toes.

"When he releases you, I'm going to ask you some questions. I would answer them if I were you."

Rey waited until the man was almost unconscious before

telling Ollie to release him. Clearly annoyed, Ollie let him go abruptly, humming defiantly.

Collapsing to his knees, the bearded man massaged his neck, gasping.

"Now, where are my wife and daughter?"

55

CAPTIVES

Master Rice's Farm
First Continent
SPRING, PLANET AMERICA

Summer returned home, dragged behind Wash's horse. With a broken nose, one cheek bruised purple, and an eye nearly swollen closed, Summer stumbled along, eyes on the ground, watching her footing. Her clothes were dirty, bloody, and torn from being dragged whenever she fell. Wash showed her no mercy, and she expected none—not from Wash, and not from Master Rice. Summer had humiliated Wash, but betrayed the master. As much as she hated the life he forced her into, he saw it as a kindness.

Half blind, she heard her mother's voice, calling to her. Slaves gathered as her name was shouted across the farm. Dropping tools, hands ran in from the fields. Her mother was close, following, but when her mother tried to get to her, men on horseback pushed forward, blocking her way. Nkosi managed to work his way next to Summer, catching her when she stumbled, keeping her on her feet.

"Be strong, girl," Nkosi whispered.

"Get away from her," Wash snapped. "Don't you coddle her, not after what she done."

Defying Wash, Nkosi stayed close, steadying her whenever

she stumbled. Forced to walk all the way back from Honeymoon Valley, Summer was half sick, half starved, and exhausted. Her only breaks came when Faith's crying forced Wash to stop so Summer could nurse her. However, with little water to drink, Summer's milk was drying up.

After her capture, she had hoped that Rey would rescue her, but with each passing day, hope faded. Although she denied that anyone shared the cabin with her, Wash was suspicious, and ordered Conklin to stay behind, just to be sure. When Rey returned he had walked into a trap. After three days on the trail, she gave up hope and grieved for Rey. Wash had taken two loves from her. Only Faith gave her a reason to live. Thinking of Faith, she looked for her mother.

She found her, walking parallel, kept at a distance by mounted men. Lucy was there too, and behind them Nicole and Winnie.

"Take my baby," Summer begged. "Her name is Faith."

Her mother heard and understood, running forward to Wash, touching his leg, pleading.

"Let me take the baby," she begged.

Wash kicked her away, cursing her.

"Do whatever you want with it," he said, digging his heels into his horse, and jerking Summer into a staggering run.

Montiel was carrying Faith, and now he split off from the others, riding to where Casey stood. Leaning over, he gently placed Faith in her grandmother's arms. Lucy and Winnie crowded around, checking the baby.

With Faith safe, Summer had no more reason to live, and prayed to God to take her home.

When Wash pulled up at the big house, Summer collapsed to her knees, head hanging nearly to her lap. She had no strength, no will, and no purpose.

"Pa, come see what I brought," Wash called, stomping up the porch steps.

Only his sisters came out to see, staring wide eyed at the ragged pile in the courtyard. Cook came out too, and was shocked at Summer's appearance.

"Master Rice was called to council," Nkosi said. "The mistress went with him."

Disappointed at first that he could not show off his prize, Wash quickly recovered his swagger.

"That makes me the master," Wash said, sounding more confident than he was.

Malcolm and Will came up from the direction of the barn.

"She stole my horse, so I set the punishment," Wash said.

"You have no right," Montiel said, dismounting, and looking at Summer sympathetically. "You're not the master unless the council names you."

"Pa doesn't care what the council says, and neither do I," Wash said. "They let that old woman run them."

"She's the founder," Montiel said.

"She's an old woman who should have been dead long ago," Wash said. "That's what Pa says."

"That's right, Wash," Malcolm said, stepping close. "Summer took your horse, so you have the right to punish her."

Summer kept still, but she could hear Satan tempting Wash through Malcolm's words.

"That's right," Wash said.

"Hanging's the punishment," Malcolm said. "She took your rifle, didn't she? You can hang her for that too."

Wash nodded agreement, not realizing Malcolm was playing him.

"She hit you too, didn't she, Wash? And tied you up? And stole your coat? And your hat?"

Wash's brothers and sisters were grinning; some were covering their mouths to keep from laughing out loud. Realizing he was the butt of Malcolm's clever tongue, Wash's lips tightened, and he glared at Malcolm.

"You could hang her three or four times for what she did to you, Wash," Malcolm continued, "but what fun would that be? Let's whip her first."

Now Wash relaxed, warming to the idea.

"You don't have the right," Montiel argued.

"A whipping ain't a hanging," Malcolm said. "Besides,

Pa's new whip hasn't been tested yet. Now, what happened to his old whip? Oh yeah, she stole that too."

Wash looked at the faces of the hired men who had helped track Summer, making sure they knew their place. None of them challenged him. Beyond them were the slaves, listening, but avoiding his eyes, shuffling their feet as slaves do.

"She's got it coming," Malcolm said, pushing Wash in the direction he wanted to go.

Wash glanced at Cook, who stared back defiantly. No woman had been whipped at the Rice farm since Cook. Slaves were cowards, but they did not like their women whipped and tended to become restless. Hesitating, Wash looked down at Summer, her hands tied, kneeling at his feet. Remembering the humiliation of being discovered bound on her cabin floor, and the sting of his father's slaps when he came walking back without Buck, Princess, or his rifle, Wash made up his mind. Summer had to pay.

"Tie her to the post," Wash said.

Malcolm and Will cheered. Only Montiel gave Summer a pitying look, and then retreated into the house. The men hired from neighboring farms mounted and left for home, wanting no part in what was going to happen. No one moved to take Summer.

"Nkosi, I said tie her to the whipping post," Wash said, nearly screaming.

Reluctantly, almost tenderly, Nkosi helped Summer to her feet, untying her hands.

"I'm sorry, little one," Nkosi whispered.

"I forgive you," Summer said. "It's not your fault."

With his arm around her shoulder, Nkosi half lifted her, half hugged her, helping her across the yard.

"I'll get the whip," Malcolm offered, and then raced for the house.

With the slaves trailing behind, murmuring worries, Summer was paraded to the whipping post. Reluctantly, Nkosi stretched out her arms, tying them by her wrists. Already bruised from being beaten and dragged, weak from hunger and thirst, and exhausted from walking long days down a mountain and across country, Summer knew the whipping would send her to be with Jesus. Afraid of the coming pain, she nevertheless rejoiced in the certain knowledge of her salvation and life everlasting. Behind her, Summer heard Malcolm return with the whip.

"Fifty lashes," Wash declared.

The slaves gasped and muttered.

"I'll give half myself," Wash said.

"Let me do a couple," Malcolm begged.

"Maybe," Wash said. "Nkosi, you do the first twenty-five."

Wash held out the coiled whip. Nkosi made no move to take it.

"Whip her, Nkosi," Wash ordered again.

"You're not the master," Nkosi said.

"I will be," Wash said, the threat clear.

"But you aren't now, and I won't do it," Nkosi said.

"Nkosi, do what you have to do," Summer whispered. "Don't sacrifice yourself for me."

"It's not for you," Nkosi said in a voice Wash could hear. "It's what's right."

"Coward," Wash declared inexplicably. "I'll do it myself. Hold my rifle, Malcolm."

Summer heard the crunch of his boots behind her, and then felt his knife cut through the collar of her shirt. Grasping the top edges, he then tore the shirt down to her waist. Now his heavy steps moved away. When she heard the sound of the whip shaken out, she trembled. Ashamed of her fear, she prayed for strength.

"Do it, Wash, do it," Malcolm said excitedly.

Summer heard the whistling of the whip, then felt the burning slap across her back and shoulder. Nothing in her life had prepared her for this, and the pain was unimaginable. Summer screamed, and then sagged, sobbing, praying to die.

"That was a good one," Malcolm said.

The whip struck again, crossing the track of the first, and when Wash jerked the whip away, she felt it tear through her flesh.

"Better'n the first," Malcolm said, excited.

Then through her pain and tears, she heard people talking, gasping. Summer turned her head enough to see the slaves parting, and through the gap came a bearded man—Owen Conklin—and behind him was Rey, his rifle on his hip. Even at this distance, Summer could see the fierceness in his eyes. This was the old Rey, the Rey who crossed a continent for revenge. Now Summer prayed for the Rice family.

Summer read the pain in Rey's face when he saw Summer hanging on the whipping post. Then Summer saw the gun come off Rey's hip.

"No, Rey," she managed hoarsely.

Then Rey fired.

56

CASCADE

Master Rice's Farm
First Continent
SPRING, PLANET AMERICA

Owen Conklin was particularly fond of breathing, so he became very cooperative very quickly. With the day almost gone, Rey only had enough time before dark to get out of the valley, and then to find Conklin's horse. At first light, he found the saddles Summer had hidden, and saddled Buck and Princess. Buck, who was still half wild, resisted, but when Rey lost his temper he sensed it, quickly becoming cooperative.

Using the blindfold trick he'd learned with Fawn, Rey got Ollie up on Princess, and then mounted Buck. With their day and a half lead, Rey would have to hurry to catch the men who kidnapped his wife and daughter. Despite the constant threat of asphyxiation, Conklin's arrogance returned. Knowing Rey needed his help to find the kidnappers, combined with his conditioned disrespect for slaves, Conklin became passive, not volunteering information, slowing them down.

"Which way?" Rey asked, at one point.

They had just crossed a creek, Conklin behind, a lead tied between his horse and Buck's saddle horn. Princess and Ollie trailed on another lead.

"It's as clear as the nose on your face," Conklin sneered, and then spat in the creek.

"Which way?" Rey repeated, turning Buck around and riding back so now he was parallel with Conklin.

Nervous now, Conklin tried to keep his haughty tone.

"That way, of course," Conklin said, making only the slightest movement of his head.

Rey punched Conklin in the chest, knocking him off his horse and into the creek. Conklin, his hands tied, had to roll onto his face to push himself up and to his feet. Soaked, he scrambled out of the cold mountain water. The day had been dry, but the sky was overcast, the air cool.

"You can't treat me like that," Conklin said, water dripping from his hair and beard. "It's not right."

"Conklin, you don't need all ten fingers to point the way." Rey pulled Conklin's own knife, then started to dismount.

"It's that way," Conklin said, pointing with bound hands in exaggerated motions.

"Let's go," Rey said.

"I could catch my death," Conklin said. "I need to get into dry clothes."

"You should have thought of that before you decided to go swimming," Rey said.

Conklin was not a bright man, and required several lessons before he led Rey to cultivated land. That sight sent a thrill through him. His pathetic little garden on the east coast was the only cultivated land he had seen in more than two decades. Here, before him, were the fruits of civilization: wide sections of cleared land, with long straight furrows. At the far edge of the field, Rey saw two men running toward a house in the distance. Rey stopped, still in the tree line, worried he had been spotted. Conklin rode up next to him, saw the receding men and called out. Rey's fist knocked him out of the saddle.

Quickly, Rey dismounted and tied up Conklin. Conklin moaned when Rey forced a strip of rawhide into his mouth—Rey might have cracked his jaw.

"Ollie, watch him," Rey said.

Ollie shot out a tentacle, swung from the back of Princess to the trunk of a tree, and then crawled to a limb over Conklin.

Taking his rifle, Rey hurried through the trees, now cursing the open ground between him and the buildings. There was a knot of people gathered in front of a house, some men mounted and many on foot. Most were slaves, he realized, seeing their white skins. He did not think they would interfere, but there were half a dozen black men in the crowd, at least some armed.

Rey circled around the buildings and then crept along the side of the house, until he could hear them talk. Now as close as he dared, he heard Summer's name.

"That's right, Wash," a young voice said. "Summer took your horse, so you have the right to punish her."

"That's right," a deeper voice echoed.

"Hanging's the punishment," the younger voice continued. "She took your rifle didn't she? You can hang her for that too."

Rey's grip on the rifle tightened.

"She hit you too, didn't she, Wash? And tied you up? And stole your coat? And your hat?"

Rey knew who Wash was now.

"You could hang her three or four times for what she did to you, Wash," the young voice said, "but what fun would that be? Let's whip her first."

"You don't have the right," someone argued.

"A whipping ain't a hanging," the younger one said. "She's got it coming."

There was a long pause.

"Tie her to the post," Rey heard Wash say.

Fighting the urge to rush around the corner, Rey's mind kicked into military mode. He would be outnumbered, so he had to take what advantage he could. Creeping back along the wall, he hurried to his horses. As he did, he saw some of the armed men riding away—good news—better odds. Reaching Conklin, he cut the rawhide holding his legs, and then jerked him to his feet. Jamming the gun in his back, Rey urged Conklin forward.

"Watch the horses, Ollie," Rey said.

With Conklin as his hostage and shield, Rey headed back toward the sound of muttering voices. The knot of people had moved away from the house, nearer the barn. Slaves blocked his view of what was happening, but suddenly he heard Summer scream. With a vicious jab in Conklin's spine, he forced the man to hurry. Then he heard the crack of a whip. Fighting the urge to run to Summer, Rey and his hostage reached the back of the crowd of slaves. When the first slave saw Conklin and then Rey, he gasped, stepping back. Then one by one, they touched slaves in front, who would turn and gape. Quickly, a gap opened. Rey walked through, assessing the threat—none from the slaves, all of whom were falling back as if Rey carried the plague.

Ahead he saw three armed men, a boy holding a rifle, one unarmed black man, and a tall, muscular young man holding a whip. To his left, Summer hung from a cross-shaped post, blood trickling down her bare back. Keeping his hand on Conklin's collar, Rey came on, slowly, bringing his rifle down. The shocking sight of an armed slave gave Rey an advantage. Then, one of the armed men brought his rifle to his shoulder. With his rifle pressed against his hip, Rey fired. Dropping his rifle, the man staggered two steps back, then sat, heavily, both hands pressed to his left side.

"Drop your guns!" Rey ordered, reloading.

Seconds passed, the men looking at each other and then at the fallen man.

"I said drop those guns," Rey repeated.

The boy dropped his rifle, putting his hands in the air. One by one, the others did the same. Wash continued to hold the whip.

"It's against Grandma's Rule for a slave to touch a rifle," Wash said, foolishly.

"All of you, line up," Rey said, motioning the men to clump together with Wash.

No slaves moved to help him, so Rey pointed his gun at one.

"Cut my wife down," Rey said.

At the word "wife," murmurs spread through the crowd. Now the man and two women rushed to Summer, untying her hands, and lowering her gently to the ground. Another man came through and began examining her wounds, dabbing at her back.

"You," Rey said, picking out another slave. "Pick up those rifles."

Eyes wide, the man Rey selected hesitated. Suddenly a plump woman pushed through the crowd.

"I'll do it."

Quickly, she picked up the rifles, distributing them to reluctant slaves, ordering them to point them at their owners. Trusting the plump woman's take-charge attitude, Rey walked close to the man examining Summer. Summer's eyes were closed, her head hung low. Her back had two long bleeding cuts. Blood caked her nostrils and she was filthy. The man nursing Summer did so with confidence and some medical expertise.

"How bad is it?" Rey asked.

"I'll have to stitch part of this," he said, pointing. "It cut deep." Then he glanced at her face. "I haven't had a chance to look at her nose."

Rey did his own assessment. Summer would live, but with scars. Relief at finding Summer alive was replaced by rising anger.

"Jack, Alex, and some of you others, go round up the rest of them," the plump woman was saying. "We can't have them running for help. Make sure the girls stay in the big house."

"You'll hang, Cook," Wash said to the plump woman.

"You tell them, Wash," the younger boy said.

The slaves stopped when Wash spoke, all looking to Cook now.

"Get on with it," she ordered.

Confident the situation was under control, Rey let his anger direct him.

"Drop the whip," Rey said, his rifle on Wash.

His nostrils flared, but Wash dropped the whip. Walking directly toward Wash, Rey watched his eyes, seeing the fear. At the last second, Rey deviated and grabbed the brash younger brother by the collar of his shirt, dragging him toward the whipping post.

"Let go of me, slave," the boy said, his arrogance wilting like a cut flower.

Rey shoved him against the post and then checked to be sure no one had moved. "Hold this," Rey said, handing his rifle to another slave, who held it awkwardly, but then suddenly snapped it to his shoulder like the soldier he once was.

They were helping Summer away, now, a woman holding a folded cloth to the deepest wound on her back.

"You just wait till my pa gets hold of you," the boy said.

"So you like to whip women," Rey said, stretching out one of the boy's arms.

The boy resisted. Rey punched him in a kidney. The boy gasped, and then relaxed his arm, whimpering softly. Rey tied his arm and then stretched out the other and tied it.

"You leave my brother alone," Wash threatened half-heartedly.

Rey ignored him. Then Rey cut off the boy's shirt.

Now Rey walked back to where the whip lay, eyes on Wash. Only Summer's receding groans could be heard. The slaves cowered, frightened by what was happening. Eyes on Wash, Rey stooped for the whip, and then walked back to the boy.

"Do unto others as you would have others do unto you," Rey said.

"My pa will kill you," the boy said, fighting to keep from crying.

Rey marched back toward Wash, and then spun, laying the whip across the boy's back. The boy gave a satisfying scream, which quickly dissolved into crying. Unmoved, Rey slowly pulled the whip back. This was the boy who seduced Wash into whipping Summer, and then begged to deliver some of the lashes himself. Rey struck again; another satisfying scream. Rey wanted to give the boy Summer's full fifty, but for Summer's sake, he stopped. Leaving the boy hanging and crying, he turned to Wash, who stepped back involuntarily, eyes darting from side to side.

"I'm not going to whip you, Wash," Rey said, throwing the whip aside.

Eyes on the whip, Wash did not believe him. Taking off his coat, Rey waved Wash forward.

"I know you like to beat up women and blind boys," Rey said. "Want to try it with me?"

Humiliated and furious, Wash stood frozen, unsure of what to do. When he realized the slaves were watching, he had no choice.

"And when I beat you, they'll shoot me," Wash said, looking for a way out.

"No one hurts him!" Rey said. "No one but me. If he wins, he walks away."

"You heard him," Cook said. "Anyone who doesn't like it can take it up with me!"

Even Wash accepted the cook's word as law. With no choice left, Wash came forward, quickly getting cocky.

"Come and get some, old man," Wash said, dancing around Rey.

Letting Wash advance, Rey watched him move. Rey could see his strength and quickness, and there was no doubt Wash would match Rey's ruthlessness. What Wash lacked was discipline.

Wash rushed Rey. Tucking his head, Rey took Wash's blow on his shoulder, and then drove his fist toward Wash's solar plexus. Rey's fist struck high, but the loud smack and accompanying gasp was gratifying. Bear-hugging Rey, Wash kept close, recovering from Rey's blow. Suddenly Wash pushed off, swinging wildly. Tucking his head again, Rey took the beating. When Wash danced back a couple of steps to rest, Rey straightened, looking like nothing had happened. Wash's face fell. Quickly recovering his composure, he came again.

This time Rey got the solar plexus, and now Wash bent over, gasping. Rey circled, working Wash's kidneys. Surprisingly tough, Wash winced with each punch, but kept his feet, turning, bringing his hands up to protect his face. Spotting an opening, Rey struck just under Wash's ear. Stunned, Wash's guard dropped. Rey broke his nose and knocked out a tooth in quick succession. Blinded with pain, Wash sagged, confused and half conscious. He was going down, but Rey was not finished. As Wash slumped forward, Rey moved behind him, stepped back, and then kicked him in the groin, nearly lifting Wash from the ground.

With Wash moaning in a heap, Rey's awareness expanded, sensing the crowd. The boy continued to weep, hanging from the whipping post. Slaves were grim, the hired hands terrified they would be next. With effort, Rey took pity on Wash and left him alive. Taking back his rifle, Rey went looking for Summer. Even Rey did not like the man who had beaten Wash.

"Lock them up," Cook ordered as Rey walked away. "Put them in Conklin's cabin. Search it first and seal those windows! Make sure Tyrell doesn't bleed to death. Patrick will look in on him later."

Some slaves responded to Cook's orders, while the meekest simply melted away, making room for Rey to pass.

"Where's my wife?" Rey asked, and a slave pointed toward a cabin.

Rey found Summer in a small cabin, surrounded by a knot of people. A woman stood next to her, holding Faith. Catching his eye, Summer smiled, and opened her arms. Rey bent, letting her hug him. Then, kissing her on the cheek, he stood again.

"Are you all right?" Rey asked. "I was almost too late."

"I'll be fine," Summer said.

Now Summer looked worried.

"What about Wash?"

"I didn't kill him," Rey said.

"Anyone?" Summer asked, sensing an evasion.

"No one," Rey said, not mentioning that one man was alive only because of Rey's poor aim.

Summer smiled with relief. Now Summer made introductions, Rey meeting her mother Casey, Lucy, Patrick, Rocky, Winnie, baby Hope, and others. Having lived twenty years alone, Rey found so much human contact unnerving. Forcing himself to be sociable, Rey met relatives he never expected to see in his lifetime. They were important to Summer, so they were important to Rey.

Hugged and congratulated like a hero, Rey endured it, smiling until his cheeks hurt. Inside, Rey felt nothing heroic. He had whipped a boy and beaten a man simply for revenge. Ashamed, he was also impatient. He and Summer were fugitives and needed to be on the move. More people crowded through the open door. Long shadows made Rey restless. Suddenly there was a scream and the crowd outside pushed back from the cabin door. Then, a furry lump with dangling tentacles crawled through the door, paused, and then up the wall and along the ceiling. Summer's friends and family shrank back.

"It's just Ollie," Summer said.

"What is it?" Casey asked, coming forward to get a closer look.

"It's supposed to be a horse guard," Rey said, scowling.

"It's a tree octopus," Summer said.

Slowly, family and friends closed in as Summer told stories about Ollie. Patrick came close, speaking to Rey.

"You have horses?" Patrick asked.

Rey told him where he had tied them, and Patrick sent a boy and girl off to collect them. Restless, Rey nevertheless enjoyed seeing Summer happy. Rey's family life drove him to join the army, where the drill instructors were less brutal than his own father. Summer's family had actually missed her.

People began feeding Ollie, Lucy squealing at the first touch of a tentacle. Then children crowded in, taking turns. Ollie took every morsel, liking everything they fed him. Rey lost himself in the fun, a happy spectator. Finally, with dark coming he had to break in.

"Summer, can you travel?" Rey asked.

Pulled away from the fun, Summer looked puzzled.

"Yes, I'll be fine," Summer said.

"Then we need to go. There's still enough light to get a few miles away."

Now the crowd quieted, Casey putting her hand on Summer's shoulder, Faith bouncing in Summer's lap.

"Rey, I have some good news," Summer said.

All eyes were on Rey, reminding him he was an outsider.

"They're all coming with us!"

57

PREPARATIONS

Master Rice's Farm
First Continent
SPRING, PLANET AMERICA

Events were cascading out of control. Rey expected to snatch Summer and run, following through on their dream of returning to the east coast to start a new life. Now he sat at a crowded feast, with strangers chattering about running away. A few silent, saner adults sprinkled the circled tables, but as the celebration continued enthusiasm for the trip grew.

Cook, as everyone called her, had organized the feast. Raiding the farm's food stores, she distributed hams and roasts for cooking in every oven on the farm, and then ordered others to find tables, chairs, tablecloths, and cutlery.

Somehow, potatoes and yams were peeled, vegetables cut, dough kneaded, and butter churned. After two hours of hive-like activity, Rey sat at the head table, with Summer and her family and friends, in a courtyard lit with lanterns and torches. When it was all ready, everyone remained standing, looking toward the head table at Rey. Seeing his confusion, Summer rescued Rey, offering a prayer of thanksgiving for their liberation and thanking God for the food. Having been thanked by nearly every adult slave on the farm, the prayer added to Rey's discomfort since everyone deferred to him as if he were heaven-sent. Although Rey now conceded God had given him a vision, sending him to Honeymoon Valley and Summer, there had been no vision of the Rice farm crowded with slaves.

Despite the unwanted attention, Rey enjoyed the feast. Rey gorged himself on three kinds of meats, a half dozen vegetables, three kinds of bread, and canned fruit he had not tasted in decades. Then, when he could eat no more, a shy young girl proudly brought him the first plate of shortcake. The shortbread was smothered with a berry sauce, and topped with a generous mound of whipped cream. The entire community paused, watching, as Rey picked up his spoon, tasting the unfamiliar concoction—it was excellent. He smiled and waved. The shy girl beamed, others clapped, and all went back to eating, talking, and planning what Rey knew to be impossible.

Others were still eating when Rey got up to walk off a few of the thousands of calories he had consumed. Trying to look casual, he strolled by the cabin where the prisoners were held. Two armed slaves guarded the men. Caught eating shortcake, they quickly put it down and jumped to their feet, their heads bent, eyes avoiding Rey. Rey hurried on. Walking the farm, he saw what a community could be, with horses, cows, tools, gardens, cultivated fields, orchards, lumber, and neighbors. In the big house, Rey found comfortable furniture, a polished dining room table with wicker-back chairs, a hutch, fine china, a study with a large desk and shelves filled with books—all from Earth. Rey was examining the titles when he heard a stern voice and then saw two little black girls skip by and then run up the stairs, followed by the pretty red-headed girl named Winnie. Then he saw Cook, who called after them.

"Winnie, you make sure they brush their teeth right, and not just the front ones."

Rey recognized Amber and Jewel as the only members of the Rice family ruling class who had attended the feast, where they sat at a small table with slave children, oblivious about what had happened.

Cook spotted Rey and came in. Cook was a big boned woman, and would have been heavy even if she did not carry forty extra pounds. Gray hair tied back, the wrinkles, creases, and bags on her face showed every year of her hard life. Underneath that visible record was the strength and determination of a woman who had never given up. She motioned for Rey to follow her. In the kitchen, she indicated a chair, and then filled two mugs with a hot brown liquid, handing one to Rey. Cook sat down opposite Rey, arms resting on the table, and studied him. Uncomfortable, Rey sniffed the drink.

"Coffee?" Rey asked, surprised and delighted.

"No," Cook said, "but it's as close as you can get on this planet. We ran out of coffee fifteen years ago. You can't grow it around here and we have no way to get to the tropical regions. There's a rumor that the Fellowship had a plantation on a peninsula at the southern tip of the First Continent and that coffee bushes have spread for miles. People say that coffee beans are everywhere, and you can scoop them up by the handful. Around here, a single sack of coffee beans would be more valuable than gold. So, many young masters have dreamed of sailing along the coast and making their fortune."

"If no one can get there, how do they know all this?" Rey asked.

"It's folklore," Cook said. "Don't expect it to make sense."

"This is good, whatever it is," Rey said.

"Roasted coffee nuts," Cook said. "We're not very original

at naming things. The nuts come from trees that grow west of New Jerusalem, nearer the coast. Master Flagg has a monopoly on the nuts. They're so expensive that slaves rarely get a taste."

"But you drink it," Rey suggested.

"I grind the beans. I brew the drink. I serve the drink. I clean the pot. And I get the first and last taste."

Cook smiled briefly, an expression unfamiliar to her face. Rey sipped the drink, listening to the sounds of celebration filtering through the walls. Somewhere a fiddle was playing. There would be dancing. Unconsciously, Rey shook his head.

"Feeling overwhelmed?" Cook asked.

"It won't work," Rey said. "This many people can't escape. Half will be caught in two days. Most of the rest within a week. Any of them that make it through the mountains will die on the plain."

"You crossed it," Cook said.

"I had help," Rey said.

"That octopus thing?" Cook asked doubtfully.

Rey hesitated to speak his mind to a stranger.

"God wanted me to cross the plain," Rey said.

Cook stared, thin lips tight, eyes expressionless.

"For the sake of argument, let's say that's true—God favors you. Why would God's help end?"

"I don't know why God helped me cross the continent, and I won't presume to speak for God now. I just know that it's not possible to get this many people through the mountains, and across the plains without getting caught. I think I can get Summer and Faith safely across, and maybe a few of her family and friends, but that's it, and that's not certain by any means."

"Did you enjoy the feast?" Cook asked, seemingly at random.

"Sure, yes. It was very good. I haven't eaten like that for more than twenty years."

"Do you know who put that together?"

"You?"

"Yes, me! I knew we needed to celebrate our freedom, and that it had to be special. That meant a lot of cooking and baking with very little time to make it happen. The first thing I did was make a list of what needed to be done. Then I put the tasks in the sequence that would get them done at the right time. The roasting and baking had to start first; the tables, chairs, and place settings could come later. Along the way I encountered problems—there weren't enough ovens, there wasn't enough firewood, one of the oven vents was plugged, there weren't enough tablecloths, there wasn't enough time to bake apple pie for dessert—so I problem-solved. We doubled up on the larger ovens, baking meats and breads together. I ordered a boy up to the cabin roof to unplug the oven vent—it was a bird's nest. We used bed sheets for tablecloths, and we switched to shortcake, because we could use canned jam for topping."

"You did a good job—"

"I'm not finished," Cook said, cutting Rey off. "I organized workers into groups. There were bread bakers, potato peelers, vegetable cookers, a dessert crew, lighting crew, and a furniture crew. Children were given simple tasks like fetching kindling, older children carried firewood and peeled potatoes, and specialists milked cows and goats, and baked and stewed. The strong carried tables and fetched water, the weak set out the cutlery. Three hours ago that courtyard was empty, and now there is the remains of a feast for a hundred people."

Cook was not a subtle woman, and Rey got the point.

"No one was trying to stop your feast," Rey pointed out. "You had no enemies."

"You don't think Wash would stop us? The hired hands? Those who would stop it were locked up and guarded. Time was my enemy too, and I beat it."

"A party isn't the same as a mass escape, not to mention crossing a continent."

"It is the same thing," Cook argued. "It's a complex problem that needs to be broken down into manageable pieces. Now, what's your biggest concern?"

Rey knew she was dangling bait, but took it anyway.

"There's not enough time to get away before the word gets out about what happened here and a gang of armed men shows up."

"Let me tell you a few things about life around here. Each farm is almost entirely self-sufficient. It's not uncommon to have no contact with another farm for a week or more. This being Master Rice's farm, we have another advantage, since most masters take slaves to church with them. Master Rice skips more Sundays than any other master. We could go weeks before someone suspects something."

"But don't visitors come here?"

"Sometimes, but they often stay overnight, and sometimes for days. If we leave a couple of people here, we become flypaper. Anyone who shows up gets stuck and does not leave. Between assuming whoever it is decided to stay overnight, and how far they traveled to get here, that buys us a minimum of four days."

"What about Master Rice himself? When is he coming back?"

"Unknown," Cook said. "Councils sometimes take a week, but if he does come back, then flypaper."

Cook was bright, articulate, and smart. Frustrated, Rey tried another tack.

"Do you know how much food it would take to feed these people? What about water? Just for the sake of argument, let's say that we managed to do it, and get across the plains clear to the east coast. There's only a small cabin waiting. We would have to start from scratch. Where would they live?"

"That's three problems. First, we must escape and not be recaptured. Second, we must be able to carry sufficient supplies to maintain us on the journey—food and water. Third, we have to plan for arrival and setting up a new self-sustaining community. The second and third problems overlap since there will be a risk of eating our seed stock before we arrive."

"I did leave a small supply of seed . . ."

Rey silently cursed himself for letting her suck him in.

"That's good to know."

The redhead peeked in the door, waiting to be acknowledged.

"What?" Cook said impatiently.

"Jewel's asleep, but I told Amber she could read for a little while. I left a lantern burning."

"That's fine," Cook said, and then had another thought. "Winnie, go tell Patrick and Lucy to get over here right now."

"Yes, ma'am," Winnie said, and with a quick admiring look at Rey, hurried on.

"Look, this won't work," Rey tried again. "We would need wagons to carry enough for this many people, and we can't get them over the mountains."

"Why not?"

"There aren't any roads," Rey said.

"The wagons are built for rough terrain and the draft horses are incredibly strong. Master Rice has the finest on the planet. Master Rice also has two of the last working chain saws on America."

"There are some animal trails that are pretty wide," Rey mused. "If we could get the wagons to Chain Meadows . . ."

Patrick and Lucy came in, Cook telling them to help themselves to coffee.

"What's up?" Lucy asked.

"Planning," Cook said. "Patrick, you're in charge of organizing transportation. I'll organize supplies for the journey. Lucy, you will plan for setting up a community on the other end."

Immediately, they began brainstorming, selecting other slaves to work with them on their tasks.

"What about me?" Rey asked, giving in to their impossible dream.

"You are in charge of escape and defense," Cook said. "Nothing we do matters if you fail."

The new Rey despaired, but inside the old Rey rejoiced. Defense often meant killing, and that was something Rey had once excelled at.

58

DIVERSION

Master Rice's Farm
First Continent
SPRING, PLANET AMERICA

Careful not to touch Summer's back, Rey hugged and then kissed her. The crowd "oohed" when he did. With a quick peck on Faith's cheek, Rey mounted Buck and kicked the horse into a walk. Six mounted men and one woman followed. It could be weeks before Rey and Summer saw each other again. It was hard for Rey to leave Summer and Faith behind; he also had to leave Ollie, who now squealed with displeasure from the top of the cabin.

Two nights before, the planning and dreaming of the slaves turned into a quicksand that sucked Rey in. Despite his better judgment, he couldn't help but assist, detailing for Lucy's committee the limited facilities and seeds he had stored in the east. He also told them about native plants they might make use of, and the kinds of animal life in the region. Cook insisted on learning everything Rey had hunted and eaten on the way west, although half of it consisted of nameless rodents snagged by Ollie. Garret's group tackled wagons and carriages, cutting them down, reducing width, reinforcing suspensions, raising them for clearance, and most importantly, reducing weight.

Rey spent an uncomfortable day participating in planning and preparation when he knew they should be running. That day ended with an open-air worship service, where he noticed some slaves did not participate. Cook joined worship, although by the exaggerated greeting she received, he knew it was her first—as it was his. Rey's parents got married in

a park, and never cared to take him or his sister to Sunday
school or worship. Baptism would never have occurred to
them. As a soldier, Rey had been in many bombed-out
churches, but no active ones. Rey enjoyed worship, the collective singing, and especially Winnie's soprano solo. He com-
mented on it only once, however, after Summer responded
with an intense glare.

Preparations had continued all night, the sounds of ham-
mering a steady background rhythm that set the pace. Only
the youngest slept. Then it was time to go. Now, as Rey rode
away, he kept praying over and over for Summer's safety.
The last two years had taught him to trust God, but he did
not trust a plan cooked up overnight at a kitchen table.

New Jerusalem was a full day's ride on horseback from
the Rice farm; closer to two by wagon. On the way they
passed through a village that was really just a few houses and
a church that doubled as a school. Skirting the village, they
rode hard and long, reaching the Pax River just after nightfall. A stranger in a strange land, Rey depended on his companions.

Sheila Yoshino led the way. Only Sheila was comfortable
on horseback. Since at the Rice farm, slaves either walked
or rode in the back of a wagon. Sheila, who was of Asian an-
cestry, had grown up in New Mexico, herding cattle. She
was thrilled to be back in the saddle. A petite woman with
short black hair, dark oval eyes, and tanned skin, she had an
exotic quality men liked. Sheila handled the horse like the
rodeo queen she once had been, while Rey and the others sat
stiffly in the saddle, feeling every jolting step.

After a few hours of sleep, they forded the Pax River, and
then spent another long day, stopping only to rest and water
the horses. Avoiding the road the coffee wagons used, they
traded speed for security. Toward dusk they began a slow descent into a valley. As the horses picked their way down
steep trails, the humidity increased, and the air warmed.
Twice they rode past cave openings from which warm air
flowed out. As they descended, the vegetation changed, becoming lush, with vines wrapping tree trunks, and large tree

ferns growing ten feet high. Seeing the thick, intertwining canopy, Rey thought of Ollie and how much he would love this valley. Animal noises increased, and once Rey spotted long-armed creatures traveling in groups high in the tree-tops.

Master Flagg's farm was just ahead, the last bit of civilization between New Jerusalem and the coast. As they leveled out on the valley floor, they came to cultivated land. Dismounting, they rested, eating and waiting. At midnight, Sheila and a skinny teenager named Jimmy Zinn crept through the woods and across the vegetable fields toward the slave cabins. Leaving one man with the horses, Rey and two others crept in closer to provide cover fire if needed.

Sonny Flagg's farm was similar to the Rice farm, with a large house for the master and his family, and small slave cabins. The Flagg slave cabins were lined up in an orderly fashion, unlike the Rice farm, where the cabins were sprinkled around the compound. Rey hated leaving the close work to Sheila and Jimmy, but he was a stranger to the Flagg slaves, and busting into their cabins in the middle of the night would terrify them as much as being visited by Master Flagg.

Occasionally, Rey heard sounds in the distance, and sometimes loud voices. An hour later, Rey heard the thud of horses' hooves. Twenty mounted slaves appeared in the gloom, children riding double with parents. Sheila rode behind an Asian man, who had a rifle slung over his shoulder. Sheila slid off, facing Rey.

"This is my husband, Dai," Sheila said.

Rey nodded greeting. Dai responded, reserved but friendly.

A small man with a shaved head, Dai had the lean, wiry look of field slaves.

"Do they all know what they are getting into?" Rey asked.

"We know," Dai said.

Rey looked at the others, who all nodded, eyes on him.

"Then we ride west," Rey said. "Strap those children to your bodies, we're riding all night."

They fell into line behind Sheila and Dai, who led them west, through the coffee nut orchard. Rey rested his rifle across his saddle. The chance of encountering masters increased with each step, and Rey had no intention of ever being a slave.

59

COUNCIL

New Jerusalem
First Continent
SPRING, PLANET AMERICA

The last of the masters entered the old church, greeting each other but most studiously avoiding Jesse and Grandma. Jesse sought out his allies, forcing a handshake on them, slapping backs, reassuring the weak. Grandma sat in her chair at the front, nodding a greeting to the few who acknowledged her. Behind Grandma was the empty chair where Theresa normally sat and whispered advice. The timing of Theresa's death could not have been better, Jesse thought, as if he'd planned it himself.

Surreptitiously, Jesse counted those who greeted Grandma and those who avoided her eye. As the last of the masters arrived, Jesse knew he would carry the night.

Jesse had arranged the meeting, and now he called for order. The masters settled down quickly, finding seats in the pews, anxious to get the evening over with. Grandma rocked gently, showing no worry, letting Jesse get things started. Jesse stood between the first pew and Grandma Jones, his back to the community matriarch.

"Thank you for coming tonight," Jesse said. "You know me, and you know I've never exercised my right to call a meeting of the Council of Masters before. So you knew before you walked through that door that we are facing a crisis. All of you know what that crisis is."

Jesse paused, scanning faces, measuring support.

"Grandma Jones is planning to free the slaves!" Jesse said.

Everyone knew that, yet every man acted shocked.

"Let me be clear about one thing right up front," Jesse said with as much sincerity as he could muster. "I support freeing the slaves when the time is right. There isn't a man here who can't trace his family history back to Earth's plantations in the Old South. Grandma Jones can do the same thing, so we know when she made the decision to enslave the invaders that she had a powerful reason for doing so."

Jesse paused, seeing heads nodding.

"The reason she did it was so that we could stand on our own two feet and not have to carry the burden of racism and prejudice. Grandma wanted nothing to stand between us and our destiny on this planet. Many of us doubted the wisdom of that decision, but time proved she was right. Look at all we've accomplished."

Now there were voices of approval.

"Every man in this room, and every person on this planet, knows that slavery is a dead-end. I'm not here to argue for it to continue forever. I'm just here to say that this isn't the time to set the slaves free. Think about your farms. Who's going to plow your fields? Plant the crops? Harvest them? What about the puff tree harvest? Who's going to bring in the fiber, comb it, bleach and dye it? Who's going to boil the lye for the soap? What about the mines and the lumber mills? Are you going to do it? Your children?

"When food production falls off, what are you going to tell your children when their bellies rumble? And what about those of you who live in town? Without surplus food, the farmers won't be trading for your goods."

The expressions in the room told Jesse they were considering life without the slaves, who did most of the work.

"Why, without my slaves, I would be lucky to farm a

quarter of my acreage. So it's not practical, but there is another reason not to do this now. Grandma Jones herself spoke about what this community needs—roads, medicines, dams, and all the other things that would make life better. Just when we're getting to the point that we can reach for these things, she proposes to take away the foundation we are standing on. Freeing the slaves will knock us back a decade, not move us forward. We can't be building a dam when we have to plow our own fields."

Every eye was on Jesse now, and he could read widespread agreement. It was time to lock in the first decision, by putting the second on the floor.

"Grandma's plan makes no sense, but there's no crime in having a bad idea. Everyone does, now and then—I know I do. That's why the council always talked through ideas before Grandma made a new rule. It's because Grandma was willing to talk with us before she decided anything that we didn't make any changes in leadership when we landed here. Grandma earned the right to be the first leader because she got us here in the first place. She ruled only because we supported her. I supported her even though she is my mother-in-law."

His joke elicited weak laughter and also suggested the logical line of succession.

"But now she has repeatedly violated the process she herself set up. Where was the discussion when she decided to give the slaves time off? Anyone remember it? Was I sick that day? What about slaves getting money? I must have missed that meeting too. Then there's this nonsense about freeing the slaves. Grandma says this community needs to change, but I say it has changed; it has changed at the top! Grandma Jones has turned her back on a process that has served us well for more than two decades. Do you know what you call a leader who makes decisions without input from the people? A dictator. That's the change that's taken place in this community. I propose, here and now, that we go back to the system that has been key to our success. I propose that we thank Grandma Jones for her service, and then elect a new leader, someone who will listen to the people."

Cheers and gasps spread through the room. Change would be hard for some, but he had softened the conservatives up with the fear of starvation and doing their own work. He only needed half of those in the room to claim a right to make a change.

Most of the conversations Jesse overheard were supportive. No one was speaking in outright opposition. Then Grandma Jones pushed herself up, out of her rocker. To Jesse's irritation, every master settled down immediately. Jesse took a seat in the front row, pleased with himself. Grandma looked every man in the face before she spoke.

"My son-in-law paints an ugly picture and if half of it were true I would step down and you wouldn't need a vote. Let's see now, Jesse said I planned to free the slaves. But if you remember, what I really said was that I would let them earn their freedom. Jesse said I was making decisions without discussion, but the slaves aren't free and here we are talking about it. I won't go through every claim Jesse made, but if he was wrong about those two, you might just consider how right he was about the rest."

"We never discussed letting the slaves have time off," Jesse said, feeling the bank being undercut beneath him.

"You had your chance to speak, and now I get mine," Grandma said. "Or is that another change you want to make?"

Furious, Jesse bit off his rejoinder.

"Now let's look at that nonsense about widespread starvation if the slaves were to be free. Slaves have to eat. Slaves have children. Are they going to let their children starve? Where will they get their food? You own all the farmable land and all of the farm tools. Do you know any slave that owns a plow? A horse? If they want to eat, they have to help plant and harvest. They'll still work for you. The important difference is that now you are responsible for feeding the slaves, and if they were free they would have to feed themselves."

"That's right," a master said. "Let's see how lazy they are when food isn't handed to them."

Jesse turned, trying to see who spoke, just as others murmured agreement.

"So Jesse was wrong again, and that should make you pause and think a little more for yourselves."

"Think about this," Jesse said, jumping to his feet. "Grandma says that freed slaves will work for you to get food. Why? Why would they work for the people who kept them as slaves when there is another way to get food."

Jesse paused dramatically, letting the interest build.

"They could take it," Jesse said. "Most of you know that the slaves won't work without an overseer standing over them with a whip. Take away the whip and you have a lazy, hungry man. Grandma claims the slaves will stay on the farms, willingly working for their old masters. Does that ring true to anyone? Or maybe you see it like I do, with gangs of dirty slaves raiding farms, murdering the masters, raping the wives and children, and stealing everything in sight."

"They have no weapons," Grandma said.

"Until they steal one," Jesse said.

The room erupted in heated discussion, masters on both sides of the argument. Jesse smiled at Grandma, feeling the argument shifting in his direction. Surprisingly, Grandma smiled back.

"Jesse was right about one thing," Grandma said in a strong voice.

This time it took a minute for order to be restored.

"What did she say?" the last audible voice asked.

Grandma spoke slowly and clearly. "I said, Jesse was right about one thing. It's time for a change in leadership."

Everyone was shocked. Jesse could feel victory and with it, power.

"I was the one who started this community, and with God's help, and Mark Shepherd and the Fellowship, I brought my people to this planet. I did it for my children, and grandchildren. This community was my baby, and I gave birth to it, and like a parent I made the rules and expected my children to follow them. But you're all grown up now. You don't need your mama anymore, you need to set your own rules, and then follow them or not."

Now only the creak of the wooden pews could be heard. Jesse fought back the triumphant shout he wanted to give.

"So I agree with Jesse, that it's time for you to elect a leader. You'll need to think about things like length of term, whether they can serve more than one term, and who can vote."

"All that can come later," Jesse said, seeing Grandma trying to limit his rule.

"Wrong again, Jesse. All of that needs to be talked through now and written down so no one can dispute it in the future."

"That's right," Jackson said.

"Let's get it written up now," Flagg agreed.

"There's one other thing you have to watch for," Grandma said.

Grandma had bought credibility with her offer to resign, although Jesse could see she was putting that day off for years by making the masters work on a constitution.

"The worst thing that could happen to this community is to develop a class system. We're halfway there already."

The masters shifted uncomfortably in their seats.

"The ruler needs to have the confidence of all the people, and not rule just because they are rich, or come from the right family. We need to nip that in the bud right now before it blossoms. For that reason, I propose that no one from my family be considered for leadership for a generation or two."

"That's not fair," Jesse said, jumping to his feet.

Jesse's outburst revealed his ambitions, and every eye was on him. Now Jesse knew that even if he managed to block a formal ban of his family, he would never get elected. Defeated, Jesse turned murderous eyes on Grandma. Before he could speak, the door burst open, and the overseer from the Flagg farm stood there, townspeople crowding in behind him.

"Most of the slaves are gone," the overseer said to Master Flagg. "They took horses and guns."

Jesse sensed victory.

"I told you what the slaves would do if given the chance, but you chose to listen to her. Now you've got an armed band running loose in the countryside. What are you going to do about it?"

"Catch them!"

"Stop them!"

"Hang them!"

"That's right," Jesse said, calming them down. "They need to be caught and taught a lesson. Who's the best man for that job?"

"You are," Carl White said, as if rehearsed. "You're the man to take charge."

"I will go get them," Jesse said. "Because when there's a crisis you don't need a leader who sits around and tries to talk a problem away, you need someone who does something about it."

Then Jesse walked down the center aisle, and pushed his way through the gathering crowd. He smiled to himself; he had just snatched victory from defeat.

60

POSSE

New Jerusalem
First Continent
SPRING, PLANET AMERICA

News of the escaping slaves spread among the masters and their families, arousing fear and uncertainty. Jesse jumped on the opportunity, exercising authority he didn't have. No one questioned him.

With the masters gathered in New Jerusalem for the council meeting, most wives and some children had come along to socialize, but most of the younger men, hands, and overseers were back on the farms. The younger men usually tracked down escaping slaves. Jesse sent word to the closest farms, but most of the posse would have to be men from town and masters still fit enough to ride hard. They would have some hounds, but the best dogs were on farms a day's ride from New Jerusalem, including his own. He sent a rider to his farm, with orders for Wash and Nkosi to bring the best hounds. It would be at least two days before they could get back, however, so they could not wait. The escaped slaves already had a head start.

According to the Flagg overseer, twenty adults and their children had revolted, the other slaves hiding in their cabins, not running away but not helping the overseer either. Only after the slaves had ridden off had one of the remaining slaves released the overseer and the hired hands. That's when they discovered the missing guns and ammunition. The slaves also took the best mounts, leaving the overseer to ride a plow horse to New Jerusalem.

Jesse dragged Kent Thorpe from his shed and put him to work, organizing. The ugly, misshapen slave had collapsed from fear when Jesse kicked open his door and dragged him out of bed. After he'd recovered his wits, Kent began advising Jesse on what he would need. Lists of supplies were generated, locations where they could be found, and which slaves should be sent to gather them. When Jesse complained that it would take too much time to gather that much equipment, Kent immediately adapted. Jesse would leave almost immediately with a smaller armed group, while others followed, using the Flagg farm as a forward base. As pursuit continued, more advanced camps would be set up, and supplies relayed forward. Jesse liked the plan. If Jesse could not catch the slaves quickly, he would run them out of food. Jesse issued orders based on Kent's plan, and the other masters nodding approvingly.

Horses, guns, and supplies were commandeered. No one dared object, and few would. The fear of armed, marauding slaves spread like an infectious disease. At dawn, Jesse led fifty armed men out of New Jerusalem. Jesse paraded his posse down the only paved street on the planet, eyes straight ahead, sitting tall in the saddle. Townspeople shouted support or applauded. "Bring them back for hanging, Jesse," someone shouted. "Hang them on the spot," another said. "God bless you, Jesse," a woman called. As they turned onto the road west, Jesse saw Grandma Jones on her porch, rocking. He tipped his hat at the old woman, and then kicked his horse into a trot. "If only we'd had flags," Jesse thought as he savored his triumph.

The posse soon slowed to a walk. It was a hard ride to Flagg's Valley, and no fresh horses were waiting there. With few breaks, they reached Flagg's Valley with a couple hours of daylight left. Four hired hands met them; the remaining slaves had been confined to their cabins. The hands were apologetic to Flagg, who assured them it was not their fault. Jesse would not have been that generous.

Jesse heard the story of the escape again, with few new details. The first thing the overseer knew about the revolt was when the slaves entered his cabin, tying him up. The other hands told a similar story. The one new detail was that a hand overheard the slaves talking about someone they called "the stranger" who instigated the escape. The stranger was not one of Flagg's slaves.

They released kitchen slaves and forced them to feed the posse from Flagg's stores. After dinner, Flagg described the terrain. The slaves had run toward the ocean—western slaves usually did. There was a lightly traveled route to the coast. Salt traders used it, as well as hunters and occasional fishing parties. There were coastal shellfish that were popular in season. Getting them back fresh was the challenge. If you could, they had high trade value.

They left at first light the next morning. The path out of Flagg's Valley connected to the coastal trail. It was little more than an animal trail that paralleled the Pax River to the Western Ocean. Jesse ordered two men to range ahead, Flagg picking two of his own men familiar with the terrain.

"If you find them, make no contact. One of you stays to trail them, and one of you gets back here as fast as he can. Understand? No shooting."

There was little chance of contact for a couple of days, since the slaves had that much of a head start. Still, slaves were a stupid lot, and prone to mistakes. The meager supplies they had rounded up would not last long. In a few days he half expected some of them to come dragging back with their tails between their legs, begging for forgiveness. Taking the guns had been their biggest mistake. That would violate Grandma's Rule, and Jesse planned to enforce it before she did. Grandma was done getting credit for the work of others.

61

ON THE RUN

West Coast
First Continent
SPRING, PLANET AMERICA

Rey stared across the Western Ocean with an unexpected feeling of satisfaction. He was probably the only man on the planet who had seen both oceans that bracketed the continent they lived on. Rey had never been an explorer and it was ironic that he had seen more of planet America than anyone, since he was the only one on the planet who never wanted to come to America. Still, he wished Summer and Faith were there to share it. They would never have a chance to see this ocean. Once they ran east, there was no coming back.

The others were spread out, riding their mounts in the waves, skipping stones, or just staring. None of them had expected to see an ocean in their lifetime. Older slaves remembered Earth's oceans, and several were near tears from warm memories. The salt air, the sound of the waves, and the fishy smells called up so many memories from Rey's childhood that his mind jumped from one to another in rapid succession. A few of those memories included his mother, a motel room near the beach, and splashing with her in the waves. He remembered two or three years of summer beach trips, sand castles, collecting seashells, and eating corndogs and salt water taffy, but mixed into those good memories were shouting matches, hours left alone with the television while his parents went out, and cuffs and slaps for being too slow, or just in the way. His father was the abuser, although the few memories of his mother never included her rushing to his defense. Still, he did not blame her.

There were other memories too, including a weekend with his service buddies in Mexico that included local girls and a party on the beach. That memory ended in a fuzzy blur of vomiting and a fistfight. Shaking off the memories, Rey called the others in.

Only fifteen riders remained. The rest had peeled off a day after leaving Flagg's Valley. The best horses, and best riders, remained. The difficulty of travel virtually guaranteed Rey's band a two-day head start. Unlike other escaped slaves, they were mounted and could travel as fast as their pursuers. If they wanted, they could head south, searching for the fabled coffee plantation. Summer and Faith, however, were headed east and that's where his heart was.

"Now's the time you have to decide what path you will take," Rey said. "I know some of you have talked of riding south, and maybe finding an abandoned Fellowship village to live in. You might even want to search for the coffee plantation. If I didn't have a family, I might go that way myself. But my family . . ."

Rey teared up as he spoke of "family" and had to pause.

"Well, you know where my family is. Each of you has to make his or her own decision, but as for me, I'm turning back."

"I'm with you," Sheila said, riding to his side with Dai.

Others kicked their horses a few feet toward Rey. Rey wondered briefly about Dai and Sheila. The couple could run for it, and without children to slow them down they might get away and make a good life for themselves. Rey remembered his loneliness on the east coast, and how he longed for just one other person to share his life with. Now, however, he wondered if one would be enough? Overwhelmed by community after two decades of solitude, Rey found he enjoyed diverse company. The joking, arguing, bantering, and laughing nurtured the human part of him, keeping the animal at bay. Somehow, even silence was more satisfying in the company of others.

"Okay then," Rey said, wrestling with his emotions. "Sheila, show us the way out of here."

With Sheila in the lead, they rode along the shore, well away from the water, tearing up the groundcover. The beach ran a mile in either direction, and they rode south, as escaping slaves should. As the beach ended, they rode up a rocky outcropping, their tracks barely distinguishable. After another mile they came to a rocky shore, and they rode onto this. The pebble covered beach curved away into the distance, ending at a steep bluff. Now they rode straight into the forest. Sheila and Jimmy Zinn dismounted, brushing away their tracks. Moving slowly, they worked their way back around the rocks, and then straight down into the water, Sheila and Jimmy still erasing their tracks. Then they all mounted, splashing south in the water. With a tiny moon, America's tides were inconsequential, and could not be counted on to wash away their tracks.

Normally, their ruse would not fool a competent tracker, but the men pursuing them did not respect slaves, believing they were stupid and predictable. When their band reached the end of the beach, they rode back into the forest, erasing their tracks one more time. Soon they were riding hard.

62

EXODUS

Even with Cook's organizational abilities, you could not make a wagon train move quickly through an untamed land. Scouts ranged far ahead, marking trail, followed by men who cut and cleared, creating a hint of a road. Even over the din of people, horses and equipment on the move, the roar of the chainsaw could be heard as much as a mile distant. Everyone insisted that Summer ride, although she was recovering quickly. She relented, as long as they let her walk during difficult uphill stretches. She rode on one of Master Rice's wagons. The wagon's springs had been raised, the wheel span narrowed, and a canvas cover installed. At Summer's suggestion, a small platform was built just behind and above the driver's seat. Ollie rode there, out of the reach of dogs.

Master Rice's dogs were all hunting hounds, and although they had never seen anything like Ollie, they were sure he was game. Ollie had complete disdain for the dogs, keeping out of reach, punishing them with whip-like cracks of a tentacle that made even the toughest dogs yelp and cringe. As the preparations continued, and Ollie kept out of reach, détente developed with the hounds. The dogs kept an eye on Ollie, but stopped the constant barking, and Ollie stopped torturing the dogs in return. Nevertheless, the dogs kept near Ollie's wagon, regularly sniffing the air to be sure he was still on the platform.

The escaping slaves traveled twenty hours the first day; a long day of hard work that purchased only a dozen miles.

When they finally stopped, exhausted, they posted guards, and then tended the animals. Only then did they eat. Cook had them organized into groups, like a ship's mess, where small groups of sailors fixed their own meals. Summer, her mother Casey, Cook, Lucy, Patrick, and the children shared a mess. While food was plentiful now, Summer knew they would need the preserved food later. So, she climbed up on the wagon seat and talked to Ollie.

"Ollie, would you go get dinner?"

Ollie perked up, stood on his four short legs and whipped a tentacle down the side of the wagon, pulling up a whining dog.

"No, Ollie, something else."

Ollie hummed in frustration and dropped the dog, which landed with a yelp. Now Ollie snagged another dog and lifted it for Summer to see.

"No, Ollie," Summer said.

Ollie dropped the dog and snatched a third; this one a different color.

"Ollie, we don't eat the dogs. Not food! Understand?"

Ollie dropped the dog, hummed a burst of noises that sounded like the low range of a harmonica, and then pulled himself into a tree and swung away. Thirty minutes later Ollie was back with a thick, meaty fish. Landing on his perch, Ollie lowered it to Summer, who handed it to Cook with some difficulty.

"It must weigh thirty pounds. Have you ever seen a fish like that?" Summer asked.

Shaped like a torpedo, the fish had three gills symmetrically spaced around its tapered head. It looked built for speed. Cook shook her head.

"Only a few miles from the farm and we never even knew these existed," Cook said. "Makes me wonder what else is out there?"

"God made us curious," Summer said. "And then He filled the universe with wonders for us to explore."

Cook gave her a half smile.

"It all makes sense to you, doesn't it?"

"Doesn't it to you?"

"Let's just say that some parts make more sense than others."

Cook filleted the fish, cutting it into thick steaks. There was enough for everyone, including Ollie. They cooked over open fires, since if the plan was working, no one would be on their trail yet. If it was not working, there was no hiding their trail. After dinner, everyone settled in to sleep, the only activity the exchange of guards. Cook roused them at dawn, and they ate a cold breakfast as they walked.

With each hour, they became more efficient, specializing in work—scouting, cutting, hauling, driving teams, herding animals, winching wagons across streams. The sun had just cleared the trees when they reached a meadow, giving the train a burst of speed and a bit of rest. At noon, they found another meadow, and again there was a spurt of speed. For the horses' sake, they stopped at noon, eating another cold meal. As they prepared to leave, a rider approached, waving his hat excitedly.

"Master White's people are coming," Les Neely shouted.

Les was the son of Eudora Neely, and a member of one of the few white families that had refused to leave when the Fellowship evacuated America. Les was age fifteen when they were left behind, and was now thirty-five and a skilled blacksmith. Les pulled up by Summer's wagon, looking to Cook and then to Summer, unsure of who was in charge.

"I crossed paths with one of their scouts. They locked up their masters and overseer, and packed it up just like we did. They are on their way to join up."

"That's wonderful," Summer said. "How many are coming?"

"All of them, I think," Neely said.

Summer was excited by what she saw as a miracle. Cook was sober, worrying over the number. White's operation was smaller than Rice's, but his slaves must number fifty men, women, and children.

"I hope they had the sense to bring supplies," Cook grumbled.

"If they didn't, then God will provide for them," Summer said.

"Summer, when you say God will provide, what I hear is 'Cook' will provide," Cook said.

"That's right," Summer said cheerfully. "God works through us."

"Well, next time you talk to Him, tell Him to try working next to us."

Cook smiled when she said it, and Summer hugged her. This was not the Cook Summer had known most of her life, and although Cook would deny it, day by day, she was responding to the call of the Holy Spirit.

"Get down, Les," Cook said, "and get something to eat out of the back of the wagon."

By late afternoon Master White's slaves had caught up, using the trail cleared by the Rice farm slaves. Despite Cook's gruff orders, they lost nearly an hour of daylight as friends and family reunited, rejoiced, and shared stories. At Cook's request, Summer, Casey, Lucy, and Patrick broke up the reunion and got the train moving again. Summer tried to encourage Cook, assuring her that everything would be all right.

"They didn't bring much with them," Cook said. "Too many horses and not enough livestock and seed. Not to mention they'll run out of food before we reach the plains."

"We can share and we'll live off the land," Summer said, ever optimistic.

Two long and hard days later, Lonnie Zagjewski came hurrying up from behind. Summer had not spoken to him since she had found Lonnie and Kerry hiding in a sourberry patch.

"Summer, Cook," Lonnie said excitedly, bouncing in his saddle from inexperience. "More are coming."

"What are you talking about?" Cook demanded impatiently.

"I was riding with the rear guard and we spotted Wilson Nabors following our trail."

Wilson Nabors was a slave on the Jackson farm, one of the smallest farms on America.

"He said all of the slaves know about what we're doing and they're coming to join us."

"All of Master Jackson's slaves?" Summer asked.

"No," Lonnie said, "every slave east of New Jerusalem has revolted and is coming after us."

Lonnie was excited, but now Summer felt some of Cook's anxiety. What had started out as the escape of a few slaves had grown into a mass exodus.

"The masters will be coming now," Cook said, shaking her head. "If word has spread from farm to farm, it's sure to get to the masters."

63

WITHOUT A TRACE

West Coast
First Continent
SPRING, PLANET AMERICA

Each day that the escaped slaves eluded him, Jesse became more unpredictable, and more dangerous. Famous for his weasel-quick temper, Jesse lashed out at every slight, mistake, failure, or even just bad news. And there was nothing but bad news. Not only had they failed to catch up to the slaves, they had now lost their trail.

Jesse rode at the lead, the rest of the posse spread out, threading through heavy forest. The slaves had foolishly left signs in the ground cover, and they followed it into the forest. As expected, the trail led south. What angered Jesse was that the trail had slowly evaporated. Now they had wasted a day trying to pick up the trail. Even the dogs were useless, often tempted into running down game instead of slaves.

Dusk came, but still the men searched, casting furtive glances Jesse's way, dead tired, but too afraid to suggest they break for the day. Finally, Jesse called out for them to camp. The men kept far from Jesse, giving him no opportunity to vent. They had a fire going, and a pot of coffee on when a new rider came through the woods, pulling two packhorses. It was Rollie White. Rollie was set to inherit the White farm and took after his father with a barrel chest, large head, and square jaw. Rollie lacked his father's bulging stomach, but he was young yet. Rollie dismounted and nodded to his father but spoke to Jesse.

"I was sent to tell you that supplies and fresh riders are now at the Flagg farm. I brought food for your posse."

The men took charge of the packhorses, digging for fresh food.

"That slave Kent wants to know whether to set up a forward camp at the beach or not."

"I haven't decided yet," Jesse snarled.

Rollie read his mood and kept silent, helping himself to a cup of coffee. Finally, Rollie said, "Oh, I'm supposed to ask you to send back some of the slaves to help with the cooking and farm chores. We've been cooking and cleaning for ourselves."

"What slaves? Does it look like we've got slaves here?" Jesse snapped.

"You don't have any slaves?" Rollie asked, looking confused and peering around the camp.

"No, I wouldn't trust a slave in a posse."

"Not all of my slaves were ungrateful runaways," Flagg said, holding his tin coffee cup in two hands. "There's enough left to keep things going until I get back."

Scratching his head, Rollie cocked his head sideways as if a different angle would help everything make sense.

"No, sir," Rollie said. "There's not a slave left at your place. We thought you took them all with you."

"None left?" Flagg said, puzzled.

Then it dawned on Jesse—he had been suckered.

"Mount up, we're riding back."

"Now?" Master White asked.

"I said now!" Jesse barked, and everyone jumped to get their gear stowed.

64

REVOLT

New Jerusalem
First Continent
SPRING, PLANET AMERICA

Kent understood the extent of the revolt long before most of the masters. As he coordinated supplies for the posses hunting down the escaped slaves, he was in position to hear odd reports and had the intelligence to notice what they did not. For example, the runner that Jesse Rice sent to his farm to bring his tracking dogs never returned. Other runners were overdue too, all from eastern farms. Then a report came from the Flagg farm that the slaves who had not escaped with the others were now gone. When a handful of slaves from town disappeared, along with a half-dozen horses, the masters finally caught on.

Of all the slaves, only Kent understood what a catastrophe the mass escape was—for Kent. While the other slaves whispered about how much they would like to join the runaways, Kent knew they would be caught, and many of them hanged. Any who did escape would die in the wilderness. Worse, from Kent's perspective, the right to purchase freedom would never be offered to the slaves; at least, not in Kent's lifetime. The money Kent had hidden in the wall of his shack was now as valuable as the kindling next to his stove. Concerned only with his own life, Kent's mind was busy, struggling for a way to salvage something from the disaster.

Strangely, Grandma Jones sat apart, rocking on her porch, letting events flow around her. When the first of the town slaves escaped, the rest were rounded up and kept in warehouses. However, when the masters discovered they would have to do their own work, slaves were released under guard. So when Jesse Rice pounded into town at the head of an exhausted posse, the masters had a fair idea of the extent of the revolt.

"We've lost contact with every farm east of New Jerusalem," Jim Wish said to Jesse, as Jesse turned over his reins to a slave.

Jim Wish was president of the co-op, and Kent worked with him. Wish was a tall, thin man with a chocolate skin tone. With long, skinny limbs, and large hands and feet, he moved like a post-pubescent teenager who had not grown accustomed to his new size. With a beard, but no mustache, he resembled a black Abraham Lincoln. Kent hovered in the background, listening, analyzing.

"I was about to ride out with a few men to check the farms myself," Wish said.

"Good thing you didn't," Jesse said. "You would have gotten yourself killed. Just leave the slave hunting to me."

The townspeople gathered around the posse, the masters spreading out, quizzing townspeople, farm overseers, and slaves, and reporting back to Jesse. Soon Jesse pieced together an ugly picture. The revolt had started on Jesse's own farm, and spread to Master White's, and then from farm to farm. There was also talk of a stranger who had come to liberate the slaves—a stranger from the east. Locked up in cabins and barns, overseers and hired hands had only heard snatches of conversation, but agreed the stranger was big, strong, and accompanied by a vicious animal that obeyed his commands.

"One of them called it a demon," one said. "A demon with eight legs."

"Nonsense," Jesse said. "That's ignorant slave talk."

"No one lives in the east," Master White said. "It's all nonsense," he added, echoing Jesse.

"It's a myth," Jesse said. "Some slave made it up to convince the others to run away with them."

"There's something else," one of the hired hands said, looking to the others for support. "I heard them say—we heard them say," the man continued, indicating two or three others who nodded reluctant agreement. "They said that this stranger whipped one of your boys and beat Wash nearly to death."

Jesse stiffened. The myth had struck home.

"You sure about that?" Jesse demanded.

"That's what I heard."

"What about my children?" Fancy called, trying to push through the crowd.

Jesse ignored his wife, thinking. The crowd was silent now, watching Jesse. After a long moment, Jesse spoke, calmly but firmly.

"We outnumber them ten to one," he said. "We'll take back the farms one by one, starting with mine. We'll run down every slave and bring them back, dead or alive. And I will cripple any slave that laid a hand on my boys, or anyone else's children."

Then, looking directly at Fancy, he said, "They will pay for what they did."

No one argued. No one dared. No one offered a different plan or even a suggestion. Every man and woman was frightened by the thought of the slaves they had abused and exploited, running free with weapons. Grandma's people desperately wanted the comfort of their old life, and they would listen to anyone who promised to take them back there, no matter how irrational those promises were.

"Round up fresh horses. I'll take fifty men with me tonight. Carl White will bring the rest in the morning."

"We've got a problem," Jim Wish said gingerly, keeping out of Jesse's reach.

Jesse turned on him, grinding his teeth.

"They've stolen a lot of the good horses and scattered most of the rest. We're rounding them up as fast as we can, but it will take a couple of days to mount all of the men."

Jesse wanted to scream with frustration. He was surrounded by incompetence.

"Then get some wagons and load up men. When the wagons are full the rest can walk. I want five hundred men armed and provisioned by dawn."

"Jesse, it . . . I . . ." Wish stammered.

"Spit it out," Jesse snapped.

"I can't do that by tomorrow. I've got to have more time."

"Kent!" Jesse roared.

Keeping his eyes down, Kent pushed through the crowd.

"You run when I call for you, you twisted jackass," Jesse snarled as Kent excused himself through the last layer of people.

"Yes, sir," Kent said, hiding his fury.

"You help Jim Wish organize. If there aren't five hundred men on the road in the morning, you'll lose your hide."

"Yes, sir," Kent said, his mind reeling with the scope of the problem.

"Well, get to work."

Kent hurried away, glad to be out of Jesse's reach. As Kent began thinking through the tasks ahead, he couldn't help wonder about who would be foolish enough to whip one of Jesse's sons, and strong enough to take on Wash Rice? Whoever it was, Kent was sure he'd never see him alive.

65

TRAIL

Western Wilderness
First Continent
SPRING, PLANET AMERICA

Rey and his band skirted the Rice farm, walking their horses through the trees. It was just past dawn and there was little activity. The men Rey had left to guard the farm were gone by now. They'd been told to stay a week, if possible, and it had been nearly two. Rey's diversion had bought them more time than he'd ever imagined.

Rey could see the post where Summer had been whipped and where he had taken his revenge on Malcolm Rice, and then Wash. If the Rice children were still on the farm, it would be too early for them to be up. With few animals left to tend, and no slaves to do it, the formerly active farm looked deserted. Rey resisted the temptation to ride in and resupply his group. Rey had no way of knowing whether word had reached New Jerusalem or other farms. If it had, there could be a hundred armed men hidden in the barn, waiting.

Once they were well clear of the house and cabins, they remounted and rode east. As they left the last of Master Rice's fields, Rey was horrified by what he found. He knew one hundred slaves with wagons and animals would leave a trail, but not the devastation he saw before him. Ground cover was virtually gone, and the soil churned to muck. Looking further, Rey saw fallen trees and limbs. A blind man could follow this trail.

"This doesn't look right," Patrick said, examining the ground.

"Some of these tracks are fresh," Dai said, kneeling. "The manure too."

"We might have outsmarted ourselves," Sheila said. "The masters may be ahead of us."

"Then our people will need help," Rey said.

They remounted and followed the trail, as easily as a super highway on Earth. Deep ruts marked where wagons had passed, and piles of manure dotted the ground. With each mile, Rey became more convinced that more than just the Rice slaves had passed this way. With their horses near exhaustion, they made slow but steady progress.

With spring advancing, the weather improved, daytime temperatures were comfortable, and nights were above freezing. The trail led them toward Honeymoon Valley, following the route they had mapped out on the kitchen table at Rice's farm. Three days past the Rice farm, Jimmy came up behind them, riding hard. He had been trailing the group, making sure they weren't overtaken.

"Riders coming," Jimmy called, breathlessly.

"How many?" Rey asked.

"I don't know. Several for sure."

"Into the trees," Rey said.

Galloping to cover, they dismounted, spreading out, all guns trained on the trail. A few minutes later, a group came out of the trees, careless, bunched together, with no scout. There were a dozen horses, most double mounted, some with three riders. All of the riders were white; a mix of men, women, and children.

Rey stood and walked out onto the trail. Startled, the newcomers nearly bolted before realizing that Rey was white. Wary of a stranger, they kept their distance until Sheila, Jimmy, and the others came out. Rey kept his distance as the two groups converged, hugging, shaking hands, and laughing.

One of the new women was large and mannish looking, with short dirty-blond hair. She was introduced as Cathy Lane. She had led the other town slaves out of New Jerusalem and down what they called "Freedom Trail." Having taken a circuitous route to throw off trackers, they were now trying to catch up with the others.

"How did you learn about the escape?" Rey asked.

"The overseer from the Jackson farm made it to town. There were others too."

"Jackson farm?" Rey probed.

"It's a small operation," Dai explained. "It's wedged between Master Rice and Master White's farms."

"They ran?" Jimmy exclaimed, delighted. "Good for them."

"If they knew, then White's slaves must too," Sheila said.

"Sure," Cathy said, puzzled. "Master White's slaves ran off too."

"How many slaves have run?" Rey asked, afraid of the answer.

"All of them, I think," Cathy said proudly.

Sheila, Jimmy, and the others were delighted, not understanding the implications. The more who ran, the slower travel would be, and the more desperate the masters would be to get them back.

"How many ran east?" Rey asked.

Now Cathy looked Rey over. She was as intimidating as Cook.

"Every one of them," Cathy said, pointing down the trail. "They're looking for a man who came from the east to liberate the slaves, and take them to a new life far away. They say he is eight feet tall, strong as a bear, smart as a fox, tough enough to beat Wash Rice to a pulp, and mean enough to whip a child. They also say he travels with an eight-legged demon that walks on the ceiling. Know anyone like that?"

"No," Rey said.

Jimmy slapped him on the back and Sheila hugged him.

"This is your man!" Sheila said.

"Where's your demon?" Cathy asked.

"Ollie?" Rey said. "He better be guarding my family!"

If the newcomers were disappointed in his ordinariness,

they kept it to themselves. After Rey ordered Zinn back as rearguard picket, the rest of them plodded on through the mud. Now Rey understood why the trail was so worn and the signs so fresh. He also understood that the masters would be coming soon, and they would be coming in force.

66

FATHER'S WRATH

Master Rice's Farm
First Continent
SPRING, PLANET AMERICA

Amber and Jewel squealed with delight when Jesse and his men came riding home. The delight was not for their father, but their mother, whom the girls thought was returning. When they discovered that only Jesse had returned, they scurried off to the side, keeping out of the way, enjoying the spectacle. Wash did not share their delight.

He watched his father approach, riding at the head of his troop, and calculated. How much humiliation was he willing to take from the old man? And if it came to a fight, could he beat him? Jesse rode straight to the big house, where Wash stood on the porch.

"I left you in charge of the farm," Jesse said, looking down from his big horse.

Montiel, Malcolm, and William came out on the porch, spreading out behind Wash.

"Now my property is stolen, my slaves are gone, and everyone knows this whole mess started right here on my own farm."

"I had everything under control," Wash said. "I tracked

Summer down just like I said I would and got her and her baby back. Then some white man showed up claiming to be her husband. He had a gun and shot Tyrell before anyone knew he was there. He got the drop on me before I could get to my gun. There was nothing I could do after that."

"Tyrell dead?"

"No, Patrick fixed him up before they ran."

"I heard you fought the stranger."

Wash squirmed at that memory.

"I fought him," Wash conceded.

"And you let a slave beat you in a fight?" Jesse asked, incredulous, shooting looks of disbelief at the men with him.

"Look at you," Jesse said. "Your nose is crooked and you're missing a tooth. He keep that as a souvenir?"

Remembering the pain, Wash rubbed his lip, feeling the gap underneath. Wash had coughed up blood the night after the fight and limped for a week. Only generous amounts of his father's hidden liquor had kept the pain manageable.

"He beat him bad, Pa, and he whipped me too," Malcolm said. "I've got scars."

Jesse looked down at Malcolm with more sympathy than Wash had ever received from his father.

"And you let a slave whip your own little brother," Jesse said, getting off his horse.

Montiel came forward to hold the reins.

"It's not Wash's fault," Montiel said.

Jesse ignored Montiel.

"He had a gun," Wash said. "There was nothing I could do."

Wash saw the blow coming but would not give the old man the satisfaction of flinching. Silently, he took the slap across his face.

"You're a coward, and I'm ashamed of you."

Pushing Wash out of the way, Jesse entered his house. Overseer Nkosi paused, as if to comfort Wash. Wash ignored him. When his father saw his decimated library, he cursed long and loud. Storming out of the house, his father visited the wounded hired hand. When he came back, he ignored Wash again as he went back inside. Wash stayed on the porch, giving his father time to calm down before he followed him in. Men filled every room of the house, with more outside. With no slaves, there was unfamiliar work to be done, including stripping off saddles, filling watering troughs, and feeding and grooming horses. Fires were being built around the compound, and the smell of burning food spread across the farm on a light westerly breeze.

"Send out six scouts tonight," Wash heard his father order.

Wash found his father and a group of masters leaning over the dining room table, studying a set of photomaps. Other masters had brought them, since the slaves had stolen his father's photomaps. Jesse looked up when Wash came in and then away, still ignoring him.

"Each of you captains is responsible for your men. Make sure each man is carrying his own food, bedding, and weapon. Every man should carry no less than one hundred rounds. If anyone is short, I've got . . ."

Jesse stopped and then looked at Wash.

"Do I have any ammunition left?" Jesse demanded.

"Fifty rounds they missed in the old barn," Wash admitted.

Jesse shook his head in disgust.

"Reinforcements and more supplies will be here by tomorrow night, but we'll be gone by then. I'll leave instructions for Jim Wish and my slave, Kent, to shuttle what we need out to us."

"Wilson's good with horses," White said. "I'll get him to check the mounts. We don't want any coming up lame."

"Yeah, do that," Jesse said as if it was his idea.

There were more details, more orders, and then the group broke up. Wash waited while the men filtered out. His father lingered, sitting at the head of the table, drumming his fingers.

"I want to go," Wash said bluntly.

"You don't have a horse," Jesse said. "Buck was stolen, remember? Stolen right out from under your nose!"

"And I aim to get Buck back," Wash said from the doorway.

"You lost one horse, but I lost nearly every horse I own," Jesse said. "Those horses would still be here if I had been home. No slave steals from me and lives to tell about it."

"He had a gun," Wash repeated. "He shot Tyrell."

"He didn't have a gun when you fought. I heard the story of how he beat you in front of the slaves, right after he whipped your brother."

"I had to hold back," Wash rationalized. "I was surrounded by armed slaves. If I beat him they would have killed me and my brothers too."

Jesse studied him, thinking.

"Who was this man? Why did he say he was married to Summer?"

"I don't know. I'd never seen him before and neither had anyone else on the farm. He must have been a hermit left over from the days of the Fellowship. I think he was living with Summer, though. When I tracked her to Honeymoon Valley, it looked like two people had been living there, but we just found Summer and her baby. I left Owen to ambush anyone who showed up. The fool let himself get captured. Owen said he would never have been captured except for that animal the stranger travels with. Owen said it lassoed his neck and pulled him off the ground and nearly strangled him."

"Conklin's a fool. You should have waited for the stranger yourself. But you couldn't keep your eyes off Summer, could you? You've always wanted what is mine, and she was mine—she is still mine, and I'll have her or no one will have her. The only reason you whipped her was to get revenge on me by marking her up."

"She stole my horse and gun, Pa. I had a right to whip her."

Jesse chuckled, shaking his head in disgust.

"She conked you on the head too," Jesse said. "Then her lover beat you stupid."

"All the more reason for me to go. I want another shot at that stranger. When we run him down, I want him all to my-self."

"All right, you can go," Jesse said, rocking back in his chair. "But that slave will answer to me. I'm going to make an example of him that the other slaves will never forget."

"What about Summer?"

"The stranger is going to watch her die."

67

CHAIN PROBLEM

Chain Meadows
First Continent
SPRING, PLANET AMERICA

Summer and Cook stepped into the meadow, eyes on the tree haters—four adults and three juveniles—grazing at the far edge. The tree haters kept their heads down—the humans had not been seen. Behind Summer and Cook, spread through the forest, were nearly two hundred slaves, waiting, hoping.

"Okay," Summer whispered to a group of riders behind her. "On the count of three."

Holding up three fingers, she let them fall one at a time. With the last digit, she shouted, "Go!"

A dozen mounted slaves raced across the clearing, directly at the grazing animals. Each man or woman fired over and over, wasting precious ammunition. The tree haters roused, heads up. Showing no fear, all four adults charged. The juveniles watched with mild interest, and then returned to their grazing. The horsemen veered in two directions to save their lives, racing for the trees. As the horsemen split up, the rhino-sized tree haters divided their force as well, chasing the riders out of the meadow, skidding to a stop at the meadow's edge, and then pawing and snorting, daring the riders to return.

"Well, that didn't work like we planned," Cook said,

turning to Summer. "We're going to have to shoot them. I'm sorry, but there is no other way. If we don't use the meadows, we'll never outrun the masters to the plains."

"I know," Summer said. Chain Meadows would take them through the rest of the mountains, and nearly to the plains. "But there has to be another way."

"Could we poison them?" Winnie said, coming up behind.

"With what?" Cook snapped, always impatient with Winnie. "I've only seen them eat grass."

"I was trying to help," Winnie said defensively.

Lucy came up behind, putting her arm around Winnie.

"It was a good idea," Lucy said. "I wonder if Patrick knows of something we could use to put them to sleep?"

"There's no time for this," Cook argued. "Look at the way they're all milling around," she added, indicating the slaves. "We're sitting ducks. We either need to shoot those beasts or start working our way through the forest."

The forest was thick here, and the last couple of miles to Chain Meadows had been the slowest of the trip. Rather than be caught while trying to negotiate the forest, it would make more sense to stop and build fortifications and then fight it out with the masters. Then Lucy squealed with delight.

As Lucy ran forward, spreading her arms wide, Summer saw Lucy's son, Leo, coming through the throng. A group of large young men followed. All of them were muscular, their heads shaved, their skin weathered and deeply tanned. Leo had been sold years ago by Master Rice, and sent to the lumber camp. No one ever came back from the lumber camp.

"Leo, what are you doing here?"

"I heard my mama was moving and I thought you might need some help with the heavy lifting. I brought some of my friends to help."

Summer enjoyed their reunion, realizing how far the news of their escape had spread. That realization renewed her sense of urgency. So far God had been with them, holding back the masters. She knew that could not last.

"Why aren't you moving? There's plenty of daylight left," Leo said. "What is this, a picnic?"

As Leo came forward he spotted Winnie, and then nearly ran into Cook when he couldn't take his eyes away. Winnie smiled, letting her eyes linger on Leo, and only then looked away.

"We're about to shoot some troublemakers," Cook said, indicating the meadow.

Summer had not seen Leo for years, but he had always been big for his age. The hard work of the lumber camp had put muscle on his six foot frame, his hands were calloused, and his face was the color of tanned leather. Numerous scars covered his arms, and the tip of his left index finger was gone. One of the men with Leo was missing a hand. Leo had large eyes, a round face, and a smile that could nearly swallow his ears. Brown stubble covered his shaved head and four days of growth covered his chin. His shaved head exaggerated the size of his ears, and his nose was crooked and scarred. His lips were thick, his eyebrows bushy. Leo was not a handsome man, but his good nature and huge smile made up for his deficiencies.

Leo looked into the meadow.

"Shovelers," Leo said. "We've got these near the lumber camp."

"We call them tree haters," Summer said.

Leo chuckled, his voice deep and loud.

"Tree haters! That fits. Mean suckers," Leo said. "What's the problem?"

"We need to use the meadow to get through the mountains, and they keep driving us out," Summer said.

"We need to shoot them," Cook said again.

"We tried decoying them, chasing them with horses, and scaring them off with gunfire," Lucy said.

"They're deaf," Leo said. "Can't hear a thing."

"Shoot them!" Cook said, exasperated.

"Any ideas?" Summer asked.

"Well," Leo said in his deep voice. "I know they aren't too fond of fire."

68

TOGETHER

Western Wilderness
First Continent
SPRING, PLANET AMERICA

By the time Rey spotted the smoke, he had collected thirty stragglers, all escaped slaves. When they learned that Rey was the "stranger from the east," they were so deferential that it embarrassed Rey. With the newcomers, Rey's band consisted of poorly equipped men and women with little food but an abundance of hope. The responsibility threatened to overwhelm Rey. Once in Honeymoon Valley, Rey remembered Summer telling him to "turn your troubles over to the Lord." Rey had been doing that for miles, and with each new arrival, Rey added him or her to his prayer list, letting God know of each new responsibility.

The smoke was a new worry; one Rey kept for himself. With the smoke strong in his nostrils, Rey flashed back to the fire that had nearly killed Ollie. This smoke originated from where Ollie and Rey's family should be. When they reached the first meadow in the chain, Rey saw that part of the meadow had been burned. Entering the meadow cautiously, he looked for tree haters, but saw none. Keeping on the meadow's fringe, he led his group through one meadow after another. In the third meadow, they found the first tree haters. The tree haters came through the smoke, staggering and disoriented. When one of the tree haters oriented in their direction, Rey led his band into the trees, giving the confused tree haters a wide berth.

A day later they caught up with the tail end of the slave train. A rider came out of the trees, whooping and hollering, greeting them. Forgetting his duty, the scout insisted on leading Rey and the others through the meadow to Cook and Summer. Rey posted two of his own people to take the scout's abandoned post.

Riding through smoldering meadows, they tied wet cloths over their mouths to ease their breathing. An hour later, they caught the trailing edge of the train. The size of the wagon train shocked Rey. It looked like hundreds of slaves, horses, livestock, and wagons. Men, women, and children were everywhere, walking, riding, carrying bundles, and herding sheep, cattle, and horses. The number of slaves had tripled while Rey had been away.

With Faith in the sling that Rey had fashioned, Summer walked in a group of women with Lucy, Cook, and her mother Casey. As men and women spotted Rey, they shouted his name and suddenly Summer turned. Even at a distance, Rey could see her smile and feel the warmth. Kicking his horse into a gallop, Rey closed the gap, pulled up, and then jumped off, running the rest of the distance. After a passionate kiss, Rey hugged his wife long and hard. When they finally broke, Rey found himself surrounded by relatives and friends. He met Lucy's son, Leo, who was a large man with a myriad of scars, a strong grip, and a wide smile. Rey trusted him instantly. Then a tentacle snaked around Rey's neck. At the same time a pack of dogs erupted in barks and howls. Rey was dragged toward a wagon where Ollie sat high on a platform. One tentacle pulled Rey closer as the other whipped at the dogs, sending them yelping away with tails between their legs.

When Rey was close, Ollie dropped from the wagon onto his shoulders, caressing Rey with one tentacle, and using the other to keep the remaining dogs at bay. Summer brought Faith and they all joined in a group hug. Rey was home.

Rey slept with Summer that night, covered with a light blanket. Faith's cradle sat nearby, draped with a cloth to keep her warm. Ollie hung from a nearby tree. Early the next morning Rey reluctantly wriggled out of Summer's arms, tucking the blanket tight around her against the morning chill. The sun was not yet up, and few were rising. Rey strolled the camp, with Ollie swinging from tree to tree, keeping close. Rey found few guards, and little activity. The wilderness gave way reluctantly, and exhausted slaves slept soundly. As Rey walked the camp, he counted, estimated, and assessed. Returning to his campsite, he found Cook sitting by a small fire, holding out a steaming cup.

"The plan worked like a charm," Cook said. "You kept them decoyed three times as long as we hoped."

Rey sipped the fake coffee.

"It's taking too long, Cook. If there were only ten slaves they would be well into the plains by now. Even thirty could have made it that far. Fifty would be close behind. But our three hundred are still two weeks away."

"That far?" Cook said, disappointed. "We've made much better time since we reached Chain Meadows."

"It doesn't matter. The masters will catch up to us in a few days; a week at most. When they do, people are going to die."

"You haven't learned a thing, have you?" Cook said, exasperated.

Rey sipped the fake coffee, trying to remember what the real thing tasted like, stalling. Cook's overconfidence annoyed him.

"I've learned to turn my problems over to God," Rey said. "He'll take care of everything."

Cook stared at him like he was the dumbest man on the planet.

"I'm new to this religion thing myself, Rey, but I seem to remember something about the Lord helping those who help themselves. The children of Israel weren't going anywhere until Moses showed up, and not a single slave had escaped alive until you came walking out of nowhere."

"The word 'escaped' is a bit premature."

"Rey, state the problem!" Cook said forcefully.

"The problem is that we're going to be caught in the open by a far superior force."

"Good statement. That's very clear. Now, how do we solve it?"

"That's only the tip of the iceberg, Cook. Not only are we

going to be caught out in the open, but we're also lightly armed, and most of the slaves haven't fired a gun in years. The masters are all experienced hunters. Unless we leave the animals and supplies, we can't run. If we do that we'll starve to death on the plains. Anyone who manages to make it across will arrive with nothing and starve to death there. If we choose to turn and fight, we'll be lucky to find a defensible position and even if we do, the best we can hope for is to slow the masters down. When they overwhelm us depends on how many casualties the masters are willing to take, but overwhelm us they will. If I were a master I would set up a siege and force us to consume our supplies. After a few weeks of watching our children starve, we'll beg them to slap the chains on."

"That's a pretty grim assessment," Cook said. "What's the good news you left out?"

Rey stalled again. Ollie dropped a tentacle, begging for a snack.

"Go get breakfast, Ollie," Rey said.

Ollie swung off through the forest.

"Well, most of the older slaves were soldiers once," Rey said reluctantly.

"Anything else?" Cook prodded when he hesitated again.

"When the masters get here, they will be at least as tired as we are," Rey added.

"They'll be overconfident too," Cook said.

"That doesn't seem possible," Rey grumbled.

Summer joined them by the small fire, shifting a fussing Faith around, and then nursing her. Summer's dress was rumpled and dirty, her hair tangled, her eyes puffy from sleep deprivation. Yet, all Rey could see was a beautiful woman holding their baby.

"Don't stop on my account," Summer said. "I heard what you were talking about."

"Let me get Patrick and Lucy. They were military. They might have some ideas," Cook offered.

"I know what has to be done," Rey said. "I just don't want to do it."

The camp was coming to life: people stirring, children crying, the *thwack* of axes cutting kindling. Sensing the coming work, horses whinnied and strained at leads. Summer and Cook waited, letting Rey select his words.

"We can buy more time if we send out skirmishers. A small group can ambush the masters along the trail. We can hit them hard and then run. We'll retreat along the trail and then ambush them over and over. If their losses are heavy enough, they will eventually give up."

"Rey, when you say 'losses,' you mean deaths, don't you?" Summer asked.

"I do, Summer."

The hurt on Summer's face was too much for Rey, and he avoided her eyes, watching the fire.

"Rey, they aren't all like Master Rice and Wash. Most of them are good people who love God. They are mothers and fathers, sons and daughters. God loves every one of them as much as he loves us."

Cook kept still. Like Rey, Cook was struggling to understand what the Christian faith expected of them. While both were older than Summer, she had a spiritual maturity that intimidated both of them.

"Summer, some of the slaves—"

"Former slaves," Summer cut in.

"Former slaves," Rey continued. "Some of them think I was sent by God to lead them to freedom."

"I believe that too," Summer said, shifting Faith to the other side.

"Summer, I'm just an ordinary guy."

"Not in my eyes," Summer said, smiling. "And not in God's eyes, either."

"All right, if I am the man they think I am, then you need to let me do the job I've been asked by God to do. The price of our freedom is going to be high and it will have to be paid in human lives."

"There must be another way, Rey. You're clever, you've gotten us this far and you can get us all the way to our new home with no more deaths."

"Summer, you ask too much," Rey said.

"With God's help you can do more than you ever imagined," Summer said.

Faith was finished, and Summer put her over her shoulder, patting her back.

"I'm happy to have God's help," Rey said. "Do you think He would mind if Sheila, Lucy, and Patrick helped too?"

"Of course not, we're all on the same side."

Ollie came back with a rodent almost his own size. Cook butchered it while they planned. Rey ordered the rest of the train to get moving, while he and the others huddled over the photomaps. Two dozen riders milled around, waiting for orders. The last of the wagons was long gone, and the sun high in the sky when they finally agreed on a plan. Breaking up to ride in different directions, Rey hid a guilty expression. He doubted the plan could work, but he had a backup plan, one that could drive a wedge between him and Summer. However, Rey now understood what love really meant, and if he had to give up Summer and Faith in order to save them, he would do it.

69

GRANDMA'S CHOICE

New Jerusalem
First Continent
SPRING, PLANET AMERICA

Simon set the tea down and then hurried away. Simon had served Grandma tea nearly every day for a decade, but lately their relationship had changed. The fact that Simon had murdered Grandma's best friend, however unintentionally, chilled her feelings for him. Grandma did not fear Simon.

She knew he was absolutely devoted to her. She was his protector and provider, and killing her would be to kill himself. However, the loss of Theresa was devastating. Others had come forward, trying to fill the void. Fancy, Grandma's oldest daughter, had tried, but her alcohol sodden brain left her incapable of anything but gossip. Grandma's grandchildren were some comfort, but were unaware of the intricate informal power networks that controlled their future. Grandma refused to introduce any of them to the ugly truth of power.

Fasting and praying, Grandma opened her heart and mind, asking God to give her guidance. Her plan to emancipate the slaves had blown up in her face. With the slaves in revolt, her people were terrified, and fear drove reason from the mind. And beyond the fear of armed slaves lay the specter of an ugly future where pampered men and women would have to do work they considered beneath them. Creating a leisure class was an unwelcome by-product of Grandma's decision to enslave the soldiers from Earth, a mistake she wanted to rectify.

Reflecting on her successes and failures, it was easy to see why things had gone wrong—people. People were God's most frustrating creation. Predictable, yet unpredictable, self-serving, yet generous and self-sacrificing, even to the point of giving up his or her own life for another's. Virtually all of her people were good-hearted, God-fearing, and sociable. Yet, like a flock of sheep, they let themselves be led by a few rams, and stampeded by dogs. It was leadership that shaped a community, and for good or bad, Grandma had been that leader. That was changing now, with Jesse undermining her, jockeying for power. Grandma had deftly blocked his rise to power until the slave revolt. Now Grandma was stuck on the sidelines, watching the game unfold without her. And there was a new player in the game—a stranger from the east.

Somewhere to the east Jesse was about to confront that stranger, and punish the slaves who had run away. It would be a massacre and she had no idea of how to stop it.

"God, where are you in all this?" Grandma prayed. "What am I to do?"

At the sound of her voice, Simon peeked out to see if he was needed.

"I was just praying, Simon," Grandma said.

Looking across the meadow at New Jerusalem, Grandma felt helpless. The future of her community was about to be decided, but miles from where she sat. At that thought, she understood what to do.

"Simon," she called. "Get my buggy and pack enough for a week. We're leaving in two hours."

Eyes wide, Simon nevertheless hurried to his tasks. Simon hated travel, but Grandma considered it part of his punishment for killing Theresa. Secretly, Grandma wished Simon had succeeded in killing his real target, Jesse. It was wrong to think such thoughts, but the truth was, Jesse's death might be the only way to stop the massacre.

70

UNWANTED ATTENTION

Master Rice's Farm
First Continent
SPRING, PLANET AMERICA

Kent rode in the back of the last wagon, eating the dust of the dozens of horses and wagons ahead of him in the train. He had walked much of the trail, but when he kept falling behind, Jim Wish let him climb into the back of a wagon. Kent kept quiet, covering his mouth to muffle his coughing. The masters were taking their frustration out on any remaining slaves. Being Jesse's slave helped protect Kent, since Jesse had always favored Kent. It was precious little protection, however, and Kent avoided eye contact, asked for nothing, and spoke only when spoken to.

When they reached Jesse's farm, Kent helped unload, although he was normally spared such work. The first chance he got, Kent begged food from the kitchen, and then scurried away to find shelter. The farm was flooded with masters, occupying the slave cabins and pitching tents. The barns were filled with masters, who scowled when Kent peeked inside. Finally, Kent found a woodshed and pulled out enough wood to create a space to lie down in. Filling the space with straw, Kent curled up under more straw, and fell asleep.

A kick in his back woke Kent. It was dark.

"Get up!" Jim Wish said. "You're leaving."

Scrambling out of his hole, Kent saw a faint glow on the horizon.

"Back to New Jerusalem?" Kent asked.

"After the runaways," Wish said. "Jesse sent orders for you to be brought along."

"There's more to do here—"

"Shut up, slave," Wish snapped.

Kent and Wish had often worked side by side, as close to equals as slave and master ever got, but that had changed. Wish, who was tall and thin, glowered down at Kent. As the scope of the disaster sank in, even the gentlest master was looking for a scapegoat. Having the only white face on the farm made Kent a target.

Kent hoped to ride in a wagon, but instead he was put on a horse. Masters climbing into wagons cursed Kent, some spitting on him.

"I should walk," Kent offered, trying to slide off.

"Stay in that saddle," Wish said, slapping him across the back with a rope.

"But Master Wish," Kent said. "There are masters walking."

"Jesse wants you at the front right now, so you ride."

They did not trust Kent with the reins, so a lead was tied to Wish's saddle. Kent held on to his saddle horn, worrying. He could not understand why Jesse would want him. The supplies were organized and flowing, the men he wanted on the way. Bouncing painfully on the back of the horse, Kent imagined all kinds of horrors ahead.

71

ATTACK

Jesse rode at the head of his troop, Carl White on his left, Wash on his right. His men were undisciplined and fanned out behind, an amorphous mass, constantly changing shape. Scouts ranged ahead, probing for the slave party, on alert for ambushes. The valley they were riding through smelled of smoke, and the skies were hazy.

"What do you make of the smoke, Jesse?" Carl White asked, riding at Jesse's side.

"Cooking fires," Jesse said. "They're too dumb to know how far smoke spreads."

No one said anything. Wash cleared his throat, but held his tongue.

"At the rate we're catching up, we might just surprise them at breakfast."

Behind Jesse someone picked up his comments, and word spread down the column: "We'll jump them in the morning."

A few minutes later they came to a clearing that had been burned.

"Cooking fires?" someone muttered. "That was one big breakfast."

Fuming, Jesse kept his eyes straight ahead, scrounging for another explanation.

"They might be trying to cover their tracks," Jesse said.

"Sure, that's what it is," Carl White said.

"Seems unlikely," Wash said. "You can see the smoke for miles."

"No one asked you!" Jesse snapped.

Pausing at the edge of the clearing, Jesse peered across the blackened meadow. The spring lushness had checked the fire before it completely scoured the meadow, and a narrow green strip edged the far side. Several large animals grazed the strip.

"Anyone know what those animals are?" Jesse asked.

None of the leaders did, and Jesse was too impatient to ask among his troops.

"Let's keep moving," Jesse said.

Rifle fire peppered the column. Jesse flinched, jerking his horse around, but found panicky men and horses blocking the way. Jumping from his saddle, Jesse pulled his rifle free and hid behind a tree just as another volley whistled overhead, or smacked into trunks. After a few seconds, Jesse risked a peek. Six mounted slaves were far down the meadow, aiming their rifles. Jesse jerked his head back just as another volley raked the trees overhead.

"They can't hit the broad side of a barn," Carl White called.

Wash chuckled from behind his own tree. Jesse peeked again and saw the slaves turn and run.

"Let's get after them," Jesse said.

Swinging into the saddle, Jesse kicked his horse into a gallop. Wash and White were close behind. A few at a time, other men broke out of the chaos, following Jesse. Jesse slowed, making sure men caught up with him. As he charged across the meadow, Jesse kept low, his head behind the horse's. Jesse saw the slaves disappear into the trees at the far end of the meadow. Then, out of his peripheral vision, Jesse saw movement—large animals were charging across the meadow. They were coming fast. Jesse would not make it to where the slaves had run. Peeling left, Jesse ran for the trees with an animal the size of small elephant right behind.

72

ASSIGNMENT

Western Wilderness
First Continent
SPRING, PLANET AMERICA

Bloody bruises covered Kent's bottom by the time they came to the first burned meadow. Carcasses of the largest animals Kent had seen on America littered the landscape. The blackened fields connected one to another through narrower passages. Patches of green mixed with smoldering sections. Nearly every meadow had carcasses, including two horses. They rested one night in a small camp serving as a hospital. Three men had arms in splints, and another his leg. Others were bandaged, their wounds more superficial. All had been attacked by dead beasts in the meadow. These men, in particular, despised Kent's white face. After begging some food, Kent found a space under a wagon, where he ate and slept.

Two excruciating days later, they caught up with Master Rice. Rice sat behind a small table, cutting pieces off a large hunk of charred meat. Kent stood before him, watching him eat, waiting. Wash was there, glowering, circling slowly, until he stopped behind Kent.

"You're right, Wash," Master Rice said, with his mouth full and ignoring Kent. "Those monsters are pretty good eating."

Kent looked past Master Rice into the meadow, where a carcass like those they had ridden past had been butchered.

"I'd have a steak fried up for you, Kent, but you don't have time."

"I could make time," Kent said, not understanding.

"You arguing with me, slave?" Master Rice snarled.

"No, sir. Forgive me. I guess I just don't understand. Why don't I have time?"

"You don't have time because you're running away."

"No, sir! I would never do that! I've never given you trouble, Master Kent. I've served you well."

"You've served yourself," Master Rice said. "Then you tried to kill me."

Kent swayed from shock—how could Rice know?

"I would never!"

"Show him, Wash," Master Rice said.

Wash stepped around Kent and poured a few crystals on the table next to Master Rice's plate. Kent recognized them as the same type of crystals he had gotten from Melissa at the pharmacy.

"You always were a sneaky little rat, Kent. That's what I liked about you. Of course, you did try to bite the hand that feeds you."

"Who told you all this? It's all lies."

"Shut up, Kent. I'm not going to kill you. You did me a favor by killing Theresa. In fact, I should have thought of it myself. No, Kent, you'll live a little longer. At least if you do what I tell you."

"Anything. I've always done everything you asked."

"Give it to him," Master Rice said.

Wash handed Kent a walkie-talkie. Kent had not seen one since the troops had been stripped of their equipment.

"Do you know how to use one?" Master Rice asked.

Kent choked back irritation. Kent had a Ph.D. in physical chemistry, yet they treated him like the average moron.

"I can operate it."

"Don't change the frequency. There's no risk of anyone listening in since I've got the last working walkie-talkies on the planet."

Holding even a simple bit of technology in his hand made Kent wistful for the complex technology he had once mastered. Once, back on Earth, with a lab filled with state-of-the-art technology, Kent had single-handedly rebuilt a Fellowship sphere. Now he lived in a shack the size of one of his lab's storage lockers. The Fellowship had burned that lab. It had been as emotionally devastating as losing a child.

"They have a fourteen mile range," Master Rice said. "You take this one and run off and join your slave friends. You check in with me every day. I want to know how they are armed, what their plan is, and anything else I can use."

"Sir, I am not popular with other slaves."

Master Rice and Wash laughed.

"I imagine not," Master Rice said. "But that's your problem. You don't have to get yourself elected king, just snoop around and feed me information."

"How far? Which way?"

"Any idiot can follow that trail, and take that horse. I'm not waiting for some lazy slave to shuffle a few miles."

Kent turned, and then stopped, facing Master Rice again.

"Those large animals . . ." Kent started to say.

"Stick to the edge of the meadows. Run like hell for the trees if one comes after you. They're meaner than I am."

Master Rice and Wash laughed again. Kent got two steps before Master Rice called his name.

"Kent, if you try to run, I'll make it my life's work to hunt you down. You'll never make it back to New Jerusalem, because when I find you, wherever I find you, I'll string you up and peel every inch of skin off your body."

Master Rice's face told Kent he would enjoy skinning a slave.

"Just to properly motivate you, I'll promise you something else. With my son as a witness, if you do this, I'll set you free and you can do whatever you like. Work for me, or the co-op, or run a book business."

Kent gulped. Master Rice knew everything.

"I'll even give you your pick of any female slave on the planet—except mine, of course."

Master Rice smiled broadly.

"That's very generous, sir," Kent said. "I'll do my best."

Kent hurried away, knowing half of Master Rice's promises were lies. The only promise that he could count on would be the one about skinning him alive.

73

NEWCOMER

Western Wilderness
First Continent
SPRING, PLANET AMERICA

They left Chain Meadows and raced for the plains, if ten miles a day could be called racing. Chain Meadows led through the mountains, and now the land was increasingly arid, the trees less dense, the underbrush shorter and sparse. The route was easier, sloping down, and they picked up speed. The ground became firmer, then rocky, and then strewn with boulders.

Somewhere to the rear, Rey and a band of freed slaves harassed the masters, slowing pursuit. Summer grieved over the near constant separation from her husband, longingly remembering the winter spent in Honeymoon Valley with Rey, Faith, and Ollie. Since then, they had spent only a few days together, with precious little privacy. It had been Summer's idea to invite the Rice farm slaves to run away with them, but now Rey was carrying most of the burden from that decision. If anything happened to Rey, Summer would never forgive herself.

Dai and Sheila came riding through the crowd, a horse and rider sandwiched between them. The white-faced rider was round shouldered and hung on to the reins for dear life, bouncing alarmingly in the saddle. Summer, Casey, and Cook walked together, and now they stopped, studying the newcomer. Winnie carried Faith in the pack that Rey had fashioned. Patrick and Lucy were driving a wagon, and pulled up, curious.

Rey was the unequivocal leader, but in his absence everyone turned to Summer. As they approached, Sheila leaned out and grabbed the bridle of the stranger's horse, pulling it to a stop.

"We found him following us," Dai said, angrily.

Summer studied the newcomer—it was Kent Thorpe. Now Summer understood Dai's emotion. Slaves considered Thorpe a collaborator because he curried favor with masters and exploited fellow slaves. Summer knew Thorpe traded in books, but she had never had the resources to rent one from him. Summer had last seen Kent at the Gathering, where he had stared at her lasciviously. In that way, he was like many men she knew.

"I'm so glad I found you," Kent said, with an expression Summer could not read—fear? "Let me get down, I can't sit in this saddle another second."

Summer nodded and Kent climbed awkwardly off the horse. Dai and Sheila dismounted, standing protectively near. Kent gingerly touched his bottom.

"I've been searching for you. I want to go with you. I want to be free, just like you."

"He's lying," Sheila said. "He's in bed with Master Rice. Bet on it."

Kent's dark eyes darted back and forth, his misshapen head stationary.

"I ran away, just like you. If you don't take me, I have nowhere to go. If I'm caught, they'll kill me just like they will you."

"Kent, you can barely ride. How did you get all the way out here without being caught?"

"Master Rice put me in charge of their supplies. I organized everything—food, water, animals, ammunition, feed, and even the masters themselves. Then Master Rice had me help bring it out to his farm. When they sent some of the supplies further east, I went along. I slipped away while they slept."

"You organized their supplies?" Cook asked.

"No one else could have," Kent said proudly.

"You helped them get the supplies east?" Sheila asked.

"It wasn't easy, we had to move three hundred men and most did not have horses."

Socially inept, Kent did not sense the gathering anger. Summer came to his rescue.

"We've all had to do things we regret," Summer said.

Kent looked confused, only now recognizing the anger of those surrounding him.

"I never would have helped them if I had had a choice," Kent said quickly. "I had to do it. You understand, don't you?"

Summer took the old man by the arm, pulling him away from the others. Summer's charity knew no bounds, and she would turn no slaves away, not even Kent Thorpe.

"Let me get you something to eat," Summer said.

A tentacle dropped on Summer's shoulder—Ollie fishing for treats.

"Is that the creature with eight arms?" Kent asked, looking up at the furry lump.

"That's Ollie," Summer said. "He won't hurt you."

Not quite believing it, Kent touched the tentacle with a dirty finger.

"Is the stranger around? You know, the one who owns this thing?"

"No," Summer said, careful not to add details.

Loving the unlovable was the real test of Christian love, and Summer was going to practice her tolerance on Kent. Deferential and eager to please, Kent was not a threat to their plans. As Summer dug bread and fruit from the back of the wagon, she did not see Kent's busy eyes, taking everything in.

74

RACE

Western Wilderness
First Continent
SPRING, PLANET AMERICA

The one bright spot in the whole debacle, Jesse thought, was that the slaves were terrible marksmen. Repeatedly attacked with hit-and-run tactics, only a few men had minor wounds. Three horses were hit, however, and two had to be put down. Even after tripling the pickets, the slaves managed to get within rifle range, firing from a ridge. The plan of the slaves was transparent. They wanted to slow pursuit so that the main body could get away. Until now, Jesse could do nothing about it. That was about to change.

Jesse had the photomaps spread out under a leafy tree. Masters crouched in a circle, listening. Wash squeezed his way in. A cloud of tiny green insects hovered over the map. A dozen waving hands kept the insects dispersed. When the hands stopped, the insects would settle on the map.

"This is where we are," Jesse said, pointing. "And this is where the slaves are going—this pass here that opens out onto the plains. Our spy tells me that once on the plains, they plan to cross the entire continent to where the stranger came from. None of that would matter if we could catch them, but that stranger is the smartest slave I've ever heard of. He's the reason the leaders of their little revolt aren't swinging from a tree limb. But he's over-confident. He thinks that if they can get onto the plains, they can get away. He's wrong about that, but he's not going to live long enough to find out. We're going to cut them off right here."

Jesse tapped the passage to the plains.

"How are we going to do that?" Carl White asked. "Every time we get to moving, they pepper us with rifle fire."

"Yeah," said another master, "and those meadow monsters aren't making it any easier."

"We're going to do it the old-fashioned way—we're going to cut them off at the pass," Jesse said dramatically, finishing with a smile. Only the older men laughed.

Now Jesse dragged his finger backward through Chain Meadows, which they had been passing through, and then traced another route north, linking small meadows through the mountains.

"The slaves can't drag their stolen wagons this way, but a small group traveling light can get through and get ahead of them. When the slaves get to the pass, they'll have a little surprise waiting for them."

Everyone laughed except Wash, who studied the photos intently. Jesse noticed his son's lack of enthusiasm.

"You got something to say, Wash?" Jesse asked.

Everyone tensed. Wash looked at his father, showing no fear.

"These meadows look passable, unless they have those meadow tanks, but there's no telling what's in the sections between. And look at these open patches here and here," Wash said, pointing. "What are these dots? And over here, this looks like a river. This is all unexplored territory. It isn't going to be easy, not by a long shot."

"No one's asking you to go, boy," Jesse said.

"I'm asking," Wash said, locking eyes with his father.

"Even with a river and some dots?" Jesse mocked.

"I tracked Summer all the way to Flat Top Mountain and got her back. I have the experience for doing this. Give me twenty-five men, and we'll hold that pass. They won't get past us."

Jesse studied his son, seeing him in a different light. He was becoming an equal.

"All right, Wash. Pick whoever you want. Travel light, and fast. You need to get ahead of that pack of slaves and we don't know exactly where they are. It's a race, boy, a race you can't afford to lose."

Wash stood to go.

"Say hello to Buck, if you see him," Jesse said.

The dig stung, but Wash walked away from the snickers, never looking back.

75

SPY

Western Wilderness
First Continent
SPRING, PLANET AMERICA

Kent, who was ostracized by the rest of the slaves, was reluctantly taken in by the leaders. Only Summer welcomed him with open arms; most of the others were suspicious of his motives, and emotionally distant. Summer's kind heart and trusting nature made her an easy mark for Kent, who ingratiated himself in any way he could. Kent collected firewood, washed dishes, and rinsed out diapers for two babies. He even allowed others to ride his horse, giving the blisters on his bottom time to heal. Walking kept him close to the leaders anyway. Every bit of the work was beneath Kent, but then the last two decades had been beneath him. Kent hated everyone, from the people who ordered him about to the other slaves who acted as if they were his equal. Back on Earth, Kent would have been at the top of the social hierarchy, not the bottom, and the half-educated and half-smart men and women he was forced to associate with here would have worked for him. Thanks to the foolishness of the slaves, Kent thought, he had a chance to improve his lot in life.

Once a day, Kent slipped away, reporting in to Master Rice. Leaving the safety of numbers terrified Kent, especially since he needed to get far enough away so that the hiss and screech of the radio could not be heard. The distinct sounds of an amplified voice would make anyone on America curious. Master Rice acted displeased with what Kent provided, but listened to every bit, and asked questions.

Kent was carrying water back to the leaders, during a dinner stop, when Summer's husband rode into camp. He was a big man, the size of a field hand, filthy with trail dust and wearing a big leather hat, stained with sweat. His clothes were ragged and filthy too. With a three-day growth of beard he was hardly the "savior" Kent had pictured. Kent brought the water, keeping in the background, listening, looking for tasks to keep him close.

After a long embrace and kiss, Summer hung on Rey's arm while he greeted the octopus thing, and then played with the baby. Rey then accepted a cup of coffee from Kent's hand, looking at him warily.

"This is Kent Thorpe," Summer said. "He was a town slave."

Rey nodded greeting, and then ignored Kent.

"Get Rey some of that lunch meat, Kent, and an apple," Cook said.

Kent did as he was told, moving quietly, listening.

"We've slowed them down, but the gap is closing. They're only a few miles behind now."

Cook retrieved photomaps from the wagon and they studied them. Lines and circles traced their route and resting points. Rey marked where he had most recently encountered their pursuers.

"This pass is the key," Rey said, tapping an eastward point on the map. "If we can get through it we can keep them from following. The west end of this valley, which leads to the pass, is open and funnel shaped. Nearer the pass it's rocky, with steep walls. I didn't take time to explore the area last year, but if we position our guns carefully we can easily pick them off."

"Or warn them off," Summer suggested.

"Warn first, then pick them off," Cook said.

Kent kept out of the circle, but within earshot. He listened to their worries, their hopes, and their plans. Despite their exhaustion—people and animals too—they were going to walk from dawn to dark. If the weather cooperated, and America's pitiful moon provided enough light, they would walk at night too. Kent reported all of this to Master Rice, the first chance he got.

76

UNKNOWN TERRITORY

Western Wilderness
First Continent
SPRING, PLANET AMERICA

Wash led his men, not as an equal, but as their commander. Still a teenager, he was now older than his years. Hardened by the abuse of his father, the humiliating beating he suffered in front of the slaves, and getting bested by a woman, the Wash who rode a borrowed horse through the high frontier was not the boy who had cornered Summer in a cabin. Wash vowed never to suffer abuse again. The next person who raised his hand against Wash would pay dearly. Wash's tongue played in and out of the gap in his teeth, a constant reminder of his pledge.

Setting a reckless pace, Wash traded caution for speed. He spared no men as scouts, gambling that the slaves were not guarding this path. Wash had decided to die rather than fail. The tracing his father had made of the map suggested the route was passable, but rugged, and like any unexplored territory full of surprises. After a leaper attack, the men now carried their rifles across their laps. After one man's horse strained a tendon by stepping in a hole, they now rode single file. When a flying mammal the size of a weasel sank fangs into the neck of another horse, the men began to watch the skies. When they approached a tree covered with the flying weasels, they gave it a wide berth.

At this altitude the stands of trees were thin, and Wash could see a good distance ahead. On approaching one of the open spaces sprinkled with dots in the photomap, Wash slowed, looking for danger. The open area was unusually bright, the sun reflecting off heaps of gray, glittering slag, and the photomap dots turned out to be huge cones rising from the shining mass. Now his horse shivered, and hesitated. Wash kicked the animal, urging it forward. Now closer, Wash could see dozens of shapes moving across the strange surface. Still inside the trees, Wash stopped short of the meadow. Cautiously, the others spread out, lining up.

"What are they?" Owen Conklin whispered. "They look like giant bugs."

The dark colored animals crawling across the meadow's surface were segmented, like ants, with four legs to each of three segments. The segments connected by way of black stalks. If they had hair, it was too short to be seen. The front segment had eyestalks, with marble-sized eyes at the tips. Pincers protruded just below the mouth. There was no tail. Occasionally, one would stop, the front segment lifting up, the front four legs used like hands.

"Look there," one of Wash's men said, pointing.

Wash saw one of the animals at the edge of a slag heap, regurgitating a milky substance while other animals spread the material, which hardened quickly.

"The whole meadow is made of puke!" Conklin said, disgusted.

"So's honey," Wash pointed out.

Wash dismounted, handing Conklin his reins. Rifle ready, Wash approached the edge of the nearest gray mass covering the meadow. The animals ignored him, keeping up their seemingly random behavior. Wash tapped the surface with his toe.

"Hard as rock," Wash said.

At the sound of his voice, every one of the creatures froze, eyestalks all twisting toward the sound. Standing perfectly still, Wash prepared to run. Then one of the horses snorted, and the foot-long creatures scurried toward the cones, racing up the sides and down into the hollow center. In a few seconds, the meadow was clear.

"Well, that did the trick," Conklin said.

Swinging back into the saddle, Wash looked for a better way around, but the steep terrain made bypassing the meadow difficult.

"Who's got shotguns?" Wash asked. "All right, two in front with me, two in the back. If anything pokes out of those cones, you splatter them."

Urging his reluctant horse forward, Wash tested the surface. It held their combined weight. The horse's hooves clattered as if on the main street of New Jerusalem. Mindful of his horse's footing, Wash hurried across as fast as he dared, his men following. The creatures remained in their cones. Soon the terrain improved, and sloped down. They passed several more cone meadows, scaring the animals into their dens each time. With each mile, Wash's confidence grew. Once he cut the slaves off from their freedom, he would take his revenge on Summer and her lover.

77

GUNFIRE

Western Wilderness
First Continent
SPRING, PLANET AMERICA

An exhausted company worked through the narrowing pass, as steep rocky walls grew on both sides. The promise of freedom had brought joy to the slaves, and a sense of adventure. But the drudgery of the trail had drained every drop of excitement from their aching bodies. Many were so spent that they now regretted their decision to run away. However, none would dare turn back, knowing the punishment waiting for them.

Summer, Casey, Lucy, Patrick, and Cook circulated, encouraging the slaves, cajoling, and leading by example. With her long red hair tied back in a ponytail, Winnie relieved Summer and Casey by carrying Faith and Hope in turn, doting on the babies. Despite the dust, sweat, and dirt of the trail, Winnie was still beautiful. When not skirmishing with the masters, Leo walked with Winnie, and the two were soon considered a couple. Leo discovered Winnie's singing voice, and sometimes they sang as they walked. Leo's bass contrasted perfectly with Winnie's soprano.

As the pass narrowed, the train slowed and lengthened, and the slaves were forced closer together. Summer was at the rear of the train with Winnie, feeding Faith, when gunfire erupted somewhere ahead. People were seen rushing back from the front of the train, and the slaves around Summer began to panic.

"Take cover!" Summer shouted, handing Faith to Winnie. "Stay calm. Take cover!"

Standing in the open, apparently unafraid, Summer quieted the crowd, preventing a stampede. People gathered children, taking cover behind wagons, trees, and rocks. With little natural cover, many slaves huddled in small groups. After making sure Faith and Winnie were safe, Summer crept toward the gunfire. It came sporadically now, some of it coming from the slaves. Finally, Summer found Patrick bandaging a wounded man, tightly wrapping his leg. Lucy bandaged a woman's arm. Kent held a pan of water.

"They got ahead of us, Summer," Lucy said as she worked. "There are two dead and two more wounded up further."

Summer sagged to her knees in confusion. They were so close to freedom. Would God bring them this far and then abandon them? She could not believe it.

"There must be a way around," Summer said.

"Not unless you're a mountain goat," Patrick said. "We'd send out scouts, but they'll be sitting ducks on those rocks."

Patrick finished with the bandage, and then sat, looking at Summer.

"We can wait until dark, and then try to sneak through the pass," Patrick said. "A few might get through."

"Only a few? There must be another way."

"We could attack," Lucy said, finishing her work. "We might overpower them, and work our way up the hillsides. Some of them would die, Summer. We would take casualties for sure. But if we could pry them out of those rocks, the survivors might get away."

Summer paled, thinking about the potential carnage. Now more gunfire could be heard, but this time from the rear—the masters were now attacking both ends of the caravan.

Keeping low, Summer hurried back toward the rear. Soon, she was pushing her way through terrified people running in the opposite direction. The train of wagons stretched nearly a mile, back through a wood and into another meadow. The gunfire was steady and ten times as intense as the fire coming from the front.

Darting from tree to tree, Summer approached cautiously. At the edge of a meadow, some of the trailing wagons had been tipped over, and used for cover. Other slaves spread through the trees in an arc, protecting their flanks. The slaves she passed tried to stop her, and begged her to turn back. Ignoring them, she crawled from the trees toward the wagons, where Rey crouched. He was not happy to see her.

"It's not safe, Summer. I don't know if we can hold them off."

"Then it's not safe anywhere," Summer said.

Then there was motion in the trees behind them, and Ollie swung out, dropping on top of the wagon. With bullets whining overhead, Rey stood, wrapped both arms around Ollie, and pulled him off the wagon. With tentacles wrapped around his waist, Rey dropped to the ground. Now Summer hugged them both, with Ollie sandwiched in the middle, humming a worried hum.

78

STANDOFF

Western Wilderness
First Continent
SPRING, PLANET AMERICA

Patrick, Leo, Dai, Sheila, and Lucy followed Rey, darting from the timberline to the rocks. They paused in the rocks, listening, straining to spot riflemen. The dark was an equal-opportunity protector.

Hearing nothing, Rey started up, careful with each step. Despite extraordinary care, occasional pebbles skittered down the slope. The others followed, spaced across the hillside, working from rock to rock, exposing themselves only a few seconds at a time. Rey was a third of the way up the slope when he was shot.

The bullet creased Rey's neck. He dropped behind a rock, bullets raining on his position and ten yards on either side. Blood dribbled down his shirt collar—Wash's shirt collar. Rey felt the wound, and wiped away blood. Using his knife, Rey cut a strip from his shirt and tied it around his throat. As he worked, the hail of bullets diminished. Rey adjusted the bandage, settling on a tension that helped stem the flow but allowed him to breathe. The rifle fire finally stopped. He waited another thirty minutes, dozing as he did. Then Rey crawled carefully back down the hill. The others were waiting inside the tree line.

"Let me see your neck," Patrick said.

"It would take a mortar to get them out of those rocks," Lucy said.

"We could use lantern fuel to make firebombs," Sheila suggested. "They won't give us the explosive power of a grenade, but if we get lucky we could get a few of them."

"The smoke would give us cover, too," Dai added.

"If we try it at night, the flames will light us up," Rey said, "and in the dark, we won't know where to throw them. We'll be guessing. Also, you can't see well enough to move fast in the dark. If we do it, we'll have to do it in the daylight."

Everyone knew how high the casualties would be in a day-time assault.

"I don't know about you," Patrick said as he cleaned Rey's wound, "but I can't throw a jar of alcohol even a quarter of the way up that hill."

"Pat's right," Lucy said. "Unless we climb that hill, we'll need a catapult or maybe slings, if we're even going to get close."

"We could climb as much as we could at night, and be in position at first light," Dai said.

Rey had heard enough. There was much to plan, and much to consider. He broke up the meeting. They weren't going anywhere anytime soon. Returning to camp, they dispersed for the night. Armed men and women had been waiting, ready to rush the pass and the hill if the assault succeeded. Now they all turned away, disappointed. Rey found Summer and Ollie awake, waiting. Summer fussed over his wound, and Ollie hummed a scolding tune. After Summer was satisfied Rey would not die, Rey gave Ollie a good head scratching, and Ollie pulled himself into a tree for the night. Then Rey snuggled under a blanket with Summer.

"Summer, I'm sorry, but I can't think of a way to do this without a lot of casualties."

Summer said nothing.

"They dropped more trees across the only route the wagons can take. Even without wagons, horses will have trouble navigating the pass. We'll be easy targets."

Still Summer said nothing.

"Sheila thinks we could make firebombs and try to burn them out. Unfortunately, the riflemen are high in the hills. Without some way to launch the bombs, we'll have to carry them close enough to throw. If we do that—"

"Stop, Rey," Summer said. "Don't talk about it anymore tonight."

"I just want you to know I tried."

"Rey, I know you're doing your best. No one could have done better than you, but tonight we need to turn this over to God."

"Summer, I've been trying—what does that mean? Turn it over to God?"

"Pray with me and we'll ask God for His guidance."

"And how will God answer, Summer?"

"I don't know, Rey, but we'll know God's answer when we see it. Trust God, Rey."

"Tonight, I'll trust you. Tomorrow, maybe I'll give God another chance."

Rey tried clearing his mind, and joining Summer in prayer, but his mind kept coming back to the problem of saving his family, and while Summer prayed, Rey designed a catapult in his mind.

79

UNEXPECTED ARRIVAL

Western Wilderness
First Continent
SPRING, PLANET AMERICA

Jesse treated himself and his boys to bacon and eggs. Montiel and Malcolm had arrived the night before; come to see their papa's triumph. Montiel continued to be a disappointment—weak like his mother—but Jesse still hoped something would snap the boy out of it. Malcolm, however, was a treat, and interested in every aspect of the siege.

"We've got them bottled up, Malcolm," Jesse said. "Wash

did something right for a change and got around them. He plugged the narrow end of this valley and I plugged the other end. I've sent reinforcements around to Wash so there's no way out."

Wash checked in each day by radio. The slaves had probed his position, but Wash reported he had driven them back each time.

"Are you gonna attack 'em, Pa?" Malcolm asked, sitting on the edge of his seat. "You should kill them for what they done. They stole everything, Pa, and they whipped me too."

"We're going to wait them out," Jesse said, his mouth full of egg. "Eventually they'll have to surrender or make their move. We'll be ready either way. Then I'll cut the man who whipped you out of the herd and teach him not to touch one of my boys!"

"Yeah, you'll show him, Pa," Malcolm said. "Let me help. Will you, Pa? Will you?"

"Maybe I'll leave you a little piece," Jesse said.

It promised to be the warmest day since leaving New Jerusalem. This side of the mountains was drier than the west side, and since coming down to the lower elevation, the threat of rain had diminished. With the slaves bottled up, and good weather, the masters were in a happy mood. Hunting parties brought back game, and cooking fires roasted meat morning, noon, and night. Jesse and his boys had just eaten the last of the fresh food brought from his farm.

"Can we go see the slaves, now?" Malcolm asked.

"Sure," Jesse said. "Montiel, you coming?"

"Might as well," Montiel said, getting up reluctantly.

"What's the matter, Montiel?" Jesse asked. "You got a soft spot for slaves?"

Before Montiel could answer, a commotion started. Jesse walked out from under the trees into the clearing. Men were parting, letting a horse and cart through. Simon drove the horse and sitting next to him was Grandma Jones.

Cursing under his breath, Jesse quickly composed himself, ready to face the old woman. The slave revolt had revived Jesse's ambitions, and once he dragged the surviving slaves into the New Jerusalem town square, he would be proclaimed the new leader. The era of Grandma's Rules was coming to a close.

Simon stopped the cart next to Jesse, but when Simon started to get out of the cart Grandma Jones stopped him.

"We're not staying," Grandma said, looking straight at Jesse.

"You came a long way for just a little sightseeing," Jesse said. "You might as well eat before you head back."

Jesse gave Simon a hard look, letting Simon know that Jesse knew his role in the poisoning. Pale and weak, Simon cringed.

"I'm not going back," Grandma said. "I'm going forward."

"To where?" Jesse asked, surprised.

"I'm going to speak to the slaves."

Men were gathering, listening, watching for Jesse's reaction. Masking his confusion, Jesse returned to bravado.

"Our rifles are doing the talking now, and they are speaking loud and clear!"

The growing crowd laughed and murmured agreement.

"Those dumb slaves walked into my trap. I've got them boxed and now we can take our time and let them sweat. When I decide to let them out, they'll come crawling out, begging for forgiveness."

More murmurs of agreement rippled through those listening. Everyone relished the idea of grinding the slaves under their heels.

"And how long is this siege of yours going to last?" Grandma asked.

"As long as it takes. The hungrier they get, the lower they'll crawl."

Men cheered Jesse, but the old woman shook her head, looking down from her perch on the wagon.

"The hungrier they get, the more desperate they'll become," Grandma said. "Have you forgotten who these slaves are? They came here as soldiers, and don't think for a second they forgot that training."

"I'm not afraid of a bunch of tired old soldiers," Jesse said. "Besides, we culled the worst of that bunch out of the herd."

Jesse smiled to the crowd, and they responded with guilty laughter.

"And while you're waiting them out, who's planting the crops?"

"That's slave work, and they'll be doing it soon enough," Jesse said.

"We're past the time for some plantings, now," Grandma said. "We can still get some crops in the ground, but if we wait much longer we'll be lucky to have enough growing season to get a harvest."

"That's what the stores are for," Jesse said.

"There isn't as much in storage as some think," Grandma said, searching the crowd for Jim Wish, and then turning back to Jesse.

Jesse swallowed hard, wondering what the old woman knew. A loud roar interrupted Jesse's response. It took a few seconds to recognize the machine sound.

"Sounds like they're using your chainsaw, Pa," Malcolm said.

Then there was the sound of falling trees. Everyone hurried to the barrier marking their forward position. Across the clearing from the masters, the slaves had stationed wagons for cover, and taken positions behind them. Now the wagons were being pulled inside the tree line, and trees dropped behind the wagons. Masters harassed the slaves with random rifle fire.

"They're building their own prison," Jesse shouted so all could hear. "They're saving us the work."

As if she were invulnerable, Grandma came riding up in her cart, looking over the barrier the masters had erected. Simon cowered next to her, starting at every shot fired by a master.

"Jesse, stop and think for a second. Why would they do this?"

"It doesn't matter," Jesse said. "They aren't leaving this valley unless they're wearing chains."

"You tell her, Pa!" Malcolm shouted.

Grandma silenced Malcolm with a withering glare. The boy shrank back, stepping behind his father.

"Hey, Jesse, maybe we better take a closer look," Carl White said, nodding toward the slave lines. "There's a lot of activity over there."

Jesse turned to the barrier and peeked over the top. Trees continued to be felled, but when the saw was silent, Jesse could hear axes at work. In the shadows of the forest, Jesse could see wagons moving away.

"Where they taking those wagons if there's no way out?" Carl asked.

His brow furrowed, Jesse wondered the same thing. All along the line, men were looking to him, waiting for an answer.

"Pull one of these trees aside, and I'll ride over and ask them," Grandma said.

Carl and the others looked to Jesse. Jesse said nothing, confused. The slaves were not acting trapped. They were preparing for something.

"Malcolm, you run back and get the photomaps," Jesse said.

"Carl, you make an opening, I'm going through," Grandma said.

"You're not going anywhere," Jesse snarled.

Men tensed at the insubordination. Grandma had been the planet's leader as long as they could remember. It was Grandma's Rules that were the constitution of their community. No one defied her.

"It's not safe," Jesse added quickly, reducing the tension. "When we know what's going on, then we'll see about letting you through."

Malcolm came running back, handing Jesse the photos. Spreading them out, Jesse, Carl, and some others squatted, studying them. Jesse saw no other way out of the valley.

Jesse sent men up the steep hillsides, trying to get a better view, but slave snipers kept them under cover. As the day wore on, the chainsaws stopped, and the axes rested. Now on the slave side of the clearing was a line of logs, resting just inside the tree line.

"Looks like they are expecting an attack," Carl said.

"Then why move the wagons?" Jesse asked. "They were good cover."

It was nearly time for Wash to check in, so Jesse walked back to camp. Wash called on schedule.

"Wash, what's going on in the slave camp? They pulled their wagons out of the meadow on this side."

The radio hissed while Jesse waited.

"We can't see anything," came the reply. "They're all under cover."

"Can you see the wagons?" Jesse radioed.

"No more than there were before," Wash called back.

"Well, keep on your toes, boy. The slaves are up to something."

Jesse spent the day studying the slave end of the meadow from every angle he could manage, discovering nothing new. Grandma walked from camp to camp, with Simon a step behind, talking to the men, reminding them that there were crops to be planted, animals to be tended, and families that would need to eat next winter. Grandma's seditious talk worried Jesse, but he could not shut the old woman up without killing her, and killing her would make her a martyr, and get Jesse hanged. Instead, he circulated too, negating her arguments, and assuring his men that the slaves would work twenty-hour days to make up for the lost work, just as soon as they got them back. What Jesse did not say was that he had no quick way to get the slaves out of the valley. The next morning, the slaves made their move.

Gunfire in the distance woke Jesse before dawn. The sun was just breaking above the eastern horizon; shadows filled the valley and the deep crevices along the hillsides. But far in the distance, high in the rocky hills where Wash and his men held the pass, there was the flicker of fire. Then, in the dim light, Jesse saw something flying through the air. A few seconds later, there was a burst of fire in the rocks. Jesse raced for his walkie-talkie. As if he expected the call, Wash answered immediately.

"They're bombing us," Wash said, the sharp crack of gunfire in the background.

"Bombing? With what?" Jesse demanded.

"Fire. It's all over both hills. Look out, look out!" Wash shouted.

The radio hissed. Jesse shouted into the radio, demanding a reply. In the distance, fire continued to bloom on the hillsides. Twenty minutes later, Wash radioed again.

"They've taken one side of the pass," Wash said. "And we're getting shot to pieces. Half the men are down."

"Dead?" Jesse shouted, shocked.

"Dead or wounded! Some are burned."

Shouts in the background, and then the radio hissed. Wash was back. "They're heading through the pass! We can see them. They're making a run for it."

"Stop them, Wash. Do something right for a change! Stop them!"

Now Jesse shouted commands.

"Mount up!" Jesse said. "The slaves are running."

Men scrambled to saddle horses. Chaos ensued, and Jesse found he had to chase down his own horse. By the time half the men were mounted, most of the hillside fires were more smoke than flames. Jesse shouted for logs to be pulled aside, so his men could charge through. As he waited on his fidgety horse, he saw Grandma Jones strolling inside the barrier, nervous Simon behind her. Jesse ignored her and loaded his rifle, waiting for the last remaining log to be pulled out of the way. Just as it was, a flaming object arced out of the forest where the slaves' rearguard hid. Jesse froze, seemingly mesmerized as the fireball soared closer. It looked like it was coming straight at him. Jesse suddenly jerked the reins and kicked his horse, colliding with Carl White, who clung to his saddle horn as his horse danced away from Jesse's aggressive move. With a flash, the object burst into flames on the meadow side of the opening. The horses panicked, and Jesse fought to keep his under control.

Another flash, and another bomb impacted the logs they had used to build the barrier.

With a third impact, the chaos became panicked flight. With flames flickering in the background, and men and horses running in all directions, Jesse saw Grandma Jones standing calmly with a smug "I told you so" look on her face.

Jesse gave up, letting his horse have its head, and let it carry him away from the flames.

80

FLIGHT

Western Wilderness
First Continent
SPRING, PLANET AMERICA

Back at the head of the caravan, the masters had been driven away from the cliffs and the slaves now held the high ground. Below them, families and friends streamed through the gap toward the plains. Although the masters seemed to be in full retreat, Rey ordered his people to fall back in waves. Rey, Leo, and his Lumber Camp friends took turns backing down the rocky slope, covering each other.

"Okay, hold this line, Leo," Rey said when they reached a good defensible position. From here, Leo and his friends could keep the masters at bay, their rifles powerless to stop the mass flight below.

"I don't want any of you taking chances," Rey said, preparing to leave. "If anything happened to you, Lucy will have my hide."

"Look who's talking about not taking chances," Leo said. "You're the married man. You ought to be with the others, not playing chicken with bullets."

"Just be careful, or it won't just be Summer I'll be answering to. There's a redhead back in camp who'll blame me too."

"You think?" Leo said, excited.

"I think," Rey said.

Rey worked his way down the hill cautiously, more afraid of being shot by a slave than by a master. He reached the bottom and found Summer tending the wounded. The plan had worked, and the butcher's bill had been low, with only two dead. Six were wounded, and one of those might die. Still, when the old Rey did the calculations, he judged the losses acceptable. Thanks to those losses, the bulk of the slaves were passing through the gap without the murderous fire from above.

Rey found Summer cleaning a master's wound; three masters lay at the base of the hill with the wounded slaves. A guard stood nearby.

Rey squeezed Summer's shoulder, and she gave him a smile.

"See what can happen when you let God handle things?" Summer said.

"Don't I get some credit?" Rey asked. "Cook, Patrick, Lucy, and I came up with the plan, and I designed the catapults and bombs. Where was God when wagons had to be disassembled? Where was God when we were cutting down the trees and making the bombs?"

"Get away from me, blasphemer," Summer teased. "I don't want the lightning bolt to hit me too."

Seeing Summer's good spirits, Rey decided not to tell her about those who had died. Leaving Summer to her nursing, he hurried against the stream of people and animals, and into the forest. Ollie swung through the trees, keeping pace. Rey slowed as they approached the clearing, and met up with the rear guard. Sheila and Dai were there, and he crouched next to them. On the masters' side of the clearing, trees were burning, the smoke flowing west, away from their position.

"If the breeze comes around, they could use the smoke to cover an attack," Sheila said.

"Summer says that God is on our side," Rey said. "So I guess that means the breeze will continue to blow in their faces."

"I wouldn't let Summer hear you talk like that," Sheila said, grinning.

"Neither would I," Rey said. "Are our surprises in place?"

"Yes," Dai said. "Everything is ready."

"Will this work?" Sheila asked.

"We'll buy as much time as we can," Rey said evasively. "It depends on how bad they want you back."

"They haven't done a bit of work in twenty years," Sheila said. "They want us back bad, real bad."

Rey knew this was not just about who would do the work—Rey suspected the masters did more work than the slaves would admit—it was about revenge, humiliation, and ego. With every ugly human emotion in play, they had little chance of getting away. While they could hold off pursuers for now, at some point the rear guard would also have to move through the pass. They could do it in waves, but once they abandoned the choke point they now held, the land flattened out and they could easily be flanked. Once out on the plains, the masters could run them down, and there would be little protection. Rey saw no hope, except in Summer's faith in God.

Through the smoke, Rey spotted a white flag on a long stick. Someone was slowly waving it back and forth. Then a small figure appeared, coming from the masters' side of the clearing. It was a woman wearing a long skirt, and a shawl over her shoulders. She had a mass of gray hair and walked slowly, occasionally using the stick with the flag like a cane, and then putting it back in the air. Dai lined up his sights.

"What are you doing?" Sheila asked. "That's Grandma Jones."

"I know," Dai said, his finger tightening on the trigger.

"No, Dai," Sheila said, resting a hand on the sights of his rifle.

"The Grandma Jones who runs the planet?" Rey asked, looking again at the old woman. He had pictured someone more formidable.

"That's her," Sheila said. "She's the one who made us slaves."

"Anyone there?" Grandma shouted. "I said, is anyone there?"

"What do you want?" Rey shouted back.

"To talk. Just to talk."

"Don't trust her," Dai said.

"I agree," Sheila said. "But she would make a good hostage."

"We're going to respect that white flag," Rey said.

"Why?" Dai asked.

"Because we may need to use one ourselves." Then Rey stood, shouting. "Over this way. Keep coming."

The old woman crossed the clearing, calling repeatedly for directions. While she came, Rey sent Dai and Sheila into hiding. When Grandma Jones arrived, Rey was alone. Grandma Jones inspected him from head to foot, and then concentrated on his face.

"I don't recognize you. You must be the stranger."

"And you're Grandma Jones," Rey said.

"There are so many things I want to ask you, but not enough time. We need to act now if we're going to stop it."

"Stop what?" Rey asked.

"The slaughter," Grandma said, "and I know just how to do it."

81

CHALLENGE

Western Wilderness
First Continent
SPRING, PLANET AMERICA

"I'm coming in," Grandma Jones shouted.

Jesse had her in his sights, and fought a desperate urge to pull the trigger. Only the presence of one hundred witnesses stopped him from killing her. Still carrying her white flag, she came to the barrier and stood, exposed, in the opening.

"Get behind something," Jesse snarled.

"You can all come out. It's safe. They've agreed to my proposal."

"Proposal? What proposal?" Jesse demanded. "You had no right to make a deal!"

"You don't speak for me either," Carl White said, jumping in on Jesse's side. Other masters gathered close, listening, still cowed in Grandma's presence.

"What kind of terms of surrender did you offer?" Jesse asked.

"They won't surrender, Jesse, I told you that. They would rather die than become slaves again."

"That can be arranged," Jesse said.

Several men echoed Jesse's feelings.

"Was it that bad for them?" Jim Wish asked. "We treated them fair. They had enough to eat, a warm place to sleep, and honest work. That's all God calls on us to do. It's in the Scriptures."

"Would you trade places with one of them? If the answer's no, then you just answered your own question."

"Have you forgotten who they are, and what they came to do?" Jesse said, angrily.

"What of their children? Your children?"

The men avoided her eyes.

"Why punish them for the sins of the fathers?"

"It's their lot," Jesse said, "and it makes no sense to talk about right and wrong. Is it wrong for a dog to serve its master? Is it wrong for a horse to pull a plow? Is it wrong for one man to be bigger and stronger than another? No. It's just what is, that's all. Just because some of us can remember when it started doesn't change a thing. In twenty years, there won't be a slave alive that wasn't born a slave. We'll get to that point a lot sooner if I have my way."

Carl White led the men in nervous laughter.

"We were doing pretty well until that stranger showed up," Jesse continued. "We didn't have trouble with the slaves. The harvests were good, our wives and children were plump and happy, and the slaves were content too. Remember the last Gathering? Remember how happy they were when we marched them down Main Street? Remember the way they partied after the feast? It can be that way again, if we can get rid of that stranger."

"Funny you should say that, Jesse," Grandma said. "That's part of the deal I negotiated."

"You had no right—" Jesse roared until Grandma cut him off.

"Listen to me, Jesse. All of you listen. I talked with the slaves and explained that they will never get away. I told them you would hunt them down no matter where they ran or how far they ran. They believed me. In return, they want you to know that they are willing to fight to the death to stay free. They promised to kill at least one of you for every one of them."

"Let them try," Jesse warned.

Grandma silenced him with a wave of her hand.

"Jesse, you just reminded me that some of them came here as soldiers. You should remember that yourself. Those slaves aren't making empty threats. Look how they broke out of your trap."

"If you would shut up we could go after them," Jesse said.

"They've stopped running," Grandma said. "Instead, they've agreed to my proposal. It's a way to stop the killing. I offered to put their fate in God's hands. They will send out a champion to fight for them. You will do the same. If their champion wins, we must let them go. If your champion wins, then they agree to return as slaves."

"It's a trick," Jesse argued. "I'll bet they're running right now."

"You can check that, Jesse," Jim Wish said. "You've got that radio."

With every eye on him, Jesse had no choice. He sent Malcolm for the radio.

"Wash, are you there?" Jesse repeated several times.

"I'm here, Pa," Wash finally returned.

"What's happening over there? Are the slaves still running away?"

"Not anymore," Wash radioed back. "They're just standing around now. I can kill them easy if I work in a little closer."

"Tell him to stay where he is," Grandma ordered.

Jesse hesitated, because obeying reinforced Grandma's authority.

"Hold your position for now," Jesse said. "I'm leaving the radio on. Call me if they start moving again."

"The slaves are keeping their part of the bargain," Grandma said. "Is your word as good as theirs?"

Jesse did not like the way this was going. His men were considering the idea.

"The sooner this is settled, the sooner you can get your planting done," Grandma said, trying to close the deal. "If you wait much longer you'll be eating your shingles by Christmas."

"It's a fool's bargain," Jesse said. "They're betting with our own money."

"They've selected their champion," Grandma said, ignoring Jesse and talking to the crowd. "They've picked the stranger to fight for them."

"That's the one who whipped me, Pa!" Malcolm said. "You can beat him, can't you, Pa? You be our champion."

Jesse's blood boiled, thinking about what the stranger had cost him.

"Is it a fight to the death?" Montiel asked.

"It is," Grandma said.

"Then don't do it, Pa," Montiel said.

"Don't listen to him, Pa," Malcolm said. "You can take him, I know you can."

"It's not your decision, Jesse," Jim Wish said nervously. "It affects all of us."

"Who would you rather have fight for us?" Carl White asked. "You? Me? I'll take Jesse over any man here."

Jesse listened to the debate about who should fight. The masters had accepted Grandma's proposal without question. Jesse ignored the argument, seeing Grandma staring at him. Then she nodded toward the gap behind her. Jesse looked through the smoke to see a man standing in the clearing—the stranger. Jesse stepped closer, and Grandma whispered in his ear.

"He wanted you to see him, to know he's no Goliath. He wants to fight you, Jesse."

"Why me?"

"Because of what you did to Summer."

"I didn't do nothing to Summer that wasn't my right."

"That's the way you see it, Jesse, but is it the way God sees it? This is your chance to prove it. If God is on your side, you will win back all the slaves, including Summer, Casey, and Winnie."

The stranger was big, but not as big as Jesse. Jesse had fought bigger men, and won, but not recently. Not even drunks had been foolish enough to challenge him for years. Jesse studied the man, and suddenly recognized the stranger's clothes. They belonged to Wash. As stupid as his boy was, he was Jesse's, and everything he had belonged to Jesse. Stealing from Wash was stealing from Jesse.

"What's the matter, Jesse?" Grandma asked. "Past your prime? Maybe it's best that you let someone else fight him and stick to beating up women."

Jesse whirled on Grandma, his face contorted with rage.

"Old woman, you just pushed me too far. First, I'm going to kill him, and when I'm the champion I'm taking over and if you get in my way, I'll kill you too."

Grandma did not flinch. Instead, she smiled.

"So, you'll fight him?"

Ignoring Grandma Jones, Jesse stomped back toward the others, who were still arguing.

"I'm fighting the stranger," Jesse shouted. "Anyone who wants to argue with me step forward now, and we'll settle it now."

"Pa, don't do it," Montiel said, touching his father on the shoulder.

Jesse's backhanded blow knocked his son to the ground. No one challenged Jesse.

"You fight tomorrow morning," Grandma said.

"Let's do it now," Jesse said, walking toward the meadow.

"No," Grandma said. "The slaves are going to spend the day in prayer and so will you. Pray that your champion will be victorious. Tomorrow at noon, you will find out whether God is on your side or not."

"And what will you pray for?" Jesse asked.

"I will pray that God's will be done."

82

RENDEZVOUS

Long evening shadows created hiding places for the unknown. Kent jumped at every sound, afraid of every noise and imagined movement. Only fear of Jesse Rice kept him going.

At every opening in the canopy, Kent searched for the jagged hilltop that had been described to him, keeping himself on track. As terrified as he was of meeting Jesse Rice in person, he was equally terrified of trying to find his way back in the dark.

"Over here, Kent," Master Rice said from a shadow.

Master Rice stepped into the light. Kent had forgotten how big Master Rice was. Rice towered over Kent. Master Rice wore a leather hat with a wide brim, a tightly woven puff fiber shirt, work pants, and finely tooled boots. Despite the lingering heat of the afternoon, Rice wore leather gloves.

"Why didn't you tell me about their attack plan?" Master Rice demanded.

"I couldn't. I woke up yesterday morning and they put me to work—everyone worked right up until they attacked. When I finished one job and tried to slip away, someone would grab me and give me another. I wanted to warn you, really, but I wasn't left alone for a second."

"One of my boys almost got killed because of you."

"Not me!" Kent said quickly. "I didn't have anything to do with it. It was that stranger. He was the one who built the catapults." Kent shook his head in unwilling admiration. "He used the leaf springs from the wagons."

"Kent, you disappoint me."

"I've done everything you asked."

"Tomorrow I'm taking matters into my own hands. I'm going to put things back the way they were before the stranger came. In the morning I'm going to kill him. What happens to you after that depends on you."

"I'm sorry I couldn't get away to warn you. I should have tried harder."

"I'm giving you one last chance, Kent."

Master Rice held out a small leather pouch. Inside were clear, shining crystals.

"I want you to put one of these—just one—in the stranger's food or drink."

"Poison?"

"It won't kill him. I'll do my own killing."

"But they don't trust me."

Master Rice chuckled.

"Who would? Just find a way and get it done."

"What if I can't?"

"Then you die," Master Rice said, matter-of-factly, and then disappeared into the shadows.

83

CHAMPIONS

Western Wilderness
First Continent
SPRING, PLANET AMERICA

Horrified by Grandma's solution, Summer begged Rey to call it off, then nagged him, and then tried to walk to the masters' camp to talk with Grandma Jones. Rey had Ollie lasso her, and hold her tight even as she beat and slapped at the animal. Sensing her distress, Ollie hummed sadly but took the abuse, not letting go. Then, as she calmed down, Summer returned to begging, and then crying. When she could not shake Rey's resolve, Summer began to pray, refusing food and water, and staying on her knees all night, breaking only to nurse Faith.

Rey hated the wait. The old Rey would have slept, since he had no conscience and no loyalties, but the new, "saved" Rey spent much of the night worrying about what would happen to Summer and Hope if he failed them. He also worried about the rest of the slaves, who had allowed him to fight their battle for them.

Rey had wandered through the gap, listening to the slaves talk around their campfires, and there were few dissenting voices. When the masters had caught up with them, their dream of getting free had turned to nightmare. Then the battle of the gap had given them a dose of reality. Many of them would never make it to the stranger's promised land. At many of those fires, Rey heard worried parents comforting terrified children, assuring them that after tomorrow they would not have to be afraid anymore. The slaves were trusting Grandma Jones's word, and Rey's strength.

Near dawn Rey tried to sleep. Within an hour he woke to a quiet camp, where no one spoke to him but tended to his every need. A steady stream of slaves wandered near, trying to get a glimpse of Rey, but not wanting to disturb him. He let them look. They had a right to see their champion.

Cook puttered around, fixing breakfast and snapping at Kent, who tried to make himself useful. They usually ate quickly and got on the move, but this morning the only one with anything to do was Rey. When Cook volunteered to make breakfast for him, Rey refused; but he did accept a cup of the fake coffee from Kent, sitting down with it on a nearby log.

"Rey," Summer began, sitting on the same log.

"I'm going to do this, Summer. If I win, then we'll all be free. If I lose, you and Faith will live."

"But you won't," Summer said, leaning against him. "And I'll be alone again."

"You'll have your family."

"What about Ollie? If you don't love me enough not to fight, what about Ollie? What happens to him if you die? Master Rice will kill Ollie."

"Ollie knows how to take care of himself," Rey said, sadly. "Besides, Summer, have some faith. I've fought men like him before."

"Did you always win?"

"I'm here, aren't I?"

A single gunshot sounded from the meadow.

"I've got to go, Summer," Rey said, standing.

Summer stood with him.

"I don't want you to see this," Rey said.

"I won't stay behind."

Rey did not bother arguing. Taking off his coat, Rey left it on the log. Grandma had set the rules, and they were to fight bare handed. Besides, a coat would only give Rice something to hang on to. The forest was full of slaves, all moving to the meadow's rim. They parted for Rey and his entourage, made up of friends and family. Winnie carried Faith, following a short way behind. Ollie swung from limb to limb, keeping close to Rey. Ollie's strident hum could be heard above the dozens of footsteps.

More slaves were already positioned along the edge of the clearing, and on the far side the masters were lined up. Rey stepped out from the trees, taking off his shirt and then squatting and rubbing dirt into his hands. When he stood, he swayed.

"Rey, are you all right?" Summer asked.

"I'm fine," Rey said, feeling his eyelids grow heavy even as he spoke.

Shaking his head, and forcing his eyes open, Rey tried to wake himself up. Now he regretted not getting more sleep. Instead of the adrenaline surge he normally felt before going into battle, Rey felt as though he had been awake for days.

"Rey, what is it?" Summer asked.

"It's nothing," Rey said.

Cheering on the other side of the meadow announced

Jesse, and the masters parted to let their champion through. Shirtless, Jesse's broad muscular chest gleamed in the morning light.

"He's oiled himself," Rey said, his speech slightly slurred. "I should have thought of that."

"I can get some," Summer offered.

"No, Summer. It won't matter. I'm not going to let this become a wrestling match."

Each of Rey's words had to be forced, as if his mouth had been numbed. Grandma stood in the middle of the field, a tall thin man with a beard next to her. She waved Rey forward, and then Jesse. When Rey stepped into the clearing, Ollie slapped him with a tentacle and pulled him back. Rey turned, looking up at his friend.

"You never did like open spaces, did you?" Rey said. "You stay with Summer, Ollie. Protect Summer."

Rey said it forcefully. He and Ollie had been separated many times in the last month, and Ollie never took it well. Still, the winter in Honeymoon Valley had built bonds between Summer and Ollie, and even with Faith.

Pulling Ollie's tentacle free, he set it on Summer's shoulder, emphasizing what he wanted Ollie to do. Then Rey stepped back into the meadow. The slaves cheered. Then the masters drowned them out with a combination of cheers and gunshots. Jesse took giant strides across the meadow, and looked powerful and confident. Two steps into the meadow, Rey stumbled. Now the masters laughed and jeered.

Catching himself, Rey took a few more steps, trying to shake off the lethargy. Instead, he felt his limbs going numb. His sluggish mind finally made sense of it all. Poison.

Rey turned back, silencing both sides of the meadow.

"There's one slave who knows what's good for him," Jesse shouted.

The masters erupted in laughter and cheers. Summer came a few steps into the meadow, meeting Rey, her face a mix of hope and concern.

"I've been drugged," Rey whispered.

"What? Then you can't fight. I'll get Patrick."

"No, Summer. If I don't fight, someone else will try. They can't beat Rice."

"But you can't fight like this."

"I need the seeds," Rey said.

Summer understood. With a lingering touch, she turned and ran for their wagon. Rey watched her melt into the puzzled crowd, and then turned, straightened his shoulders, and forced his body to obey. The slaves cheered again as Rey marched forward.

Grandma and the tall man met them. Grandma studied Rey intently, sensing that something was wrong.

"Are you ready for this?" Grandma asked.

"Yes," Rey lied.

Grandma continued to study Rey.

"Aren't you going to ask me if I'm ready?" Jesse sneered. "You're not playing favorites, are you, old woman?"

Grandma whirled on him.

"Are you ready, Jesse?"

"I've been waiting since yesterday for this. Let's get to it."

"If the champion for the slaves wins, the slaves go free. If the champion for the masters wins, the slaves return with the masters. Do you both still agree?"

Grandma looked from one champion to the other. Jesse and Rey both nodded.

"Then may God's will be done."

Grandma backed away from the two men. Rey crouched, widening his stance, expecting Rice to charge. Rice had a size advantage, and Rey guessed he would try to get in close, and use his bulk to overpower Rey. Instead, Rice stood still, watching Rey, an ugly smirk on his face.

"So you're the stranger," Rice said. "I thought you would be bigger."

"I'm more than you can handle."

"We'll see," Jesse said. "They tell me you and Summer pretend to be married."

"We are married," Rey said.

At the mention of Summer's name, Rey felt the first stir of an adrenaline fire in his belly. His weariness soon extinguished it.

"Slaves can't marry, not without the permission of a master. I never gave Summer permission."

"The slaves are done asking for permission," Rey said.

Now Jesse walked in a slow circle. Rey adjusted his position, knowing that each sluggish move made Rice more confident.

"Still, you and I have one thing in common," Rice said.

"We have nothing in common," Rey said, shaking his head again.

"We've both shared a bed with Summer."

Rage energized Rey and he attacked, lunging and swinging for Rice's jaw. Rice easily dodged, and countered with a fist to the side of Rey's head. Rey stumbled past Rice, and turned sluggishly. The drug given to Rey slowed him down, but also numbed the pain. He could barely feel the pain from the blow. Rey was dimly aware that the masters were cheering and that the slaves were silent. Rice smiled confidently.

"Yes, we've both shared her bed," Rice taunted, "but only I will share it again."

Rey lunged again. Deflecting Rey's blow, Rice struck him twice, the blow to his solar plexus knocking the wind out of Rey. Rey found himself on his knees, gasping for breath while the masters roared approval.

84

EYES

Wash and his men had worked their way along the steep hill-side until they could see the meadow where his father and the stranger were to fight. Six of his men were dead or missing, and three more were injured. One had a gunshot wound, the other two burns. Wash's triumphant moment, the blocking of the pass, had turned into a defeat, and a rout. The day before, Wash had been a hero for stopping the escape of the slaves, but in a matter of hours all his success was forgotten. His father had retaken center stage. Wash could see him now, arrogantly walking into the meadow, the stranger approaching from the other side. His men cheered for Jesse, but Wash watched glumly. Then something odd happened. The stranger turned back, and a figure came out to meet him—Summer. Even at this distance, Wash recognized the girl who had humiliated him.

Wash stood, leaning forward as if to hear their conversation. Then, abruptly, Summer ran from the meadow into the crowd. Wash could see movement, as people got out of her way. Summer was running back toward the gap, and Wash studied the slave camps there, looking for others. The children were deeper into the gap, cared for by older siblings and a few adults. The rest of the adults were at the meadow, watching the fight.

Seizing the opportunity, Wash hurried through the rocks. Behind him, intent on the fight, his men did not notice him leave.

85

SEEDS

Summer raced through the forest and into the clearing where they had camped. Smoldering fires still sprinkled the now empty space, creating a smoky fog. Hurrying to the wagon, she dropped the tailgate and then pulled their belongings out, dumping them on the ground. Failing to reach what she needed, she finally climbed in and dug through clothing, bags of grain, pieces of a loom, tools, and food. Finally, she found the canvas bag with her belongings. Pulling it from the wagon, she dumped the contents on the ground. There was the box Kerry had built for her. Wash had taken it from the cabin in Honeymoon Valley, and Summer had taken it back when they left Master Rice's farm.

When Summer picked up the box, someone struck her across the side of her head, crushing her right ear. Summer dropped the box, staggering sideways and hanging on to the wagon to keep from falling. Blinded by the pain, she did not see the second blow coming. Hit low in the back, she snapped back so hard it felt as if her spine would break. Now Summer fell to her knees.

"How do you like getting clubbed from behind?" Wash asked, coming around so she could see him.

Wash smiled, and she could see a gap in his teeth. His tongue slid in and out of the space.

"Wash, there's a truce. Everyone agreed."

"No one asked me," Wash said. "Besides, this is just between you and me."

Wash carried his rifle casually. He was not going to shoot her. He was going to beat her to death. Now Wash knelt slowly and picked up Summer's box.

"I remember this," Wash said. "That slave, Kerry, used to make these before his accident." Wash laughed sadistically. "You had this in Honeymoon Valley. What's so important that you had to run back and get this in the middle of the big fight?"

Cheers could be heard in the distance.

"Please, Wash. Let me go."

Summer grabbed the wagon and pulled herself up. Wash jabbed her in the ribs with the rifle butt. Summer collapsed, gasping.

"Stay on your knees," Wash said. "That's the way I like my women."

Through waves of pain, Summer saw Wash pull out the drawers, looking at the contents, dumping them on the ground.

"There's nothing here but ugly jewelry, fishhooks, and buttons." Wash held out the box. "What's so important about this box?"

"Nothing," Summer managed.

Wash dropped the box.

"Then you won't mind if I break it."

Wash stomped on the box, smashing it to pieces. When he stopped, he looked down and then squatted and brought out a small pouch.

"What do we have here?" Wash asked.

With a loud plop, the wagon vibrated, and then Summer saw Ollie's head peer over the side and down at her. He hummed a worried sound.

"What is that?" Wash said, frozen.

Dropping the pouch, Wash slowly brought his rifle up. Summer pointed at Wash and shouted "Food, Ollie! Food!" Summer lunged for the rifle, shoving the barrel toward the ground just as a tentacle wrapped around Wash's neck. Instinctively, Wash's hands clawed at his neck, as his windpipe was pinched closed. Summer threw the rifle aside as Ollie dragged Wash toward the wagon, where his body anchored. Then Ollie whipped his free tentacle onto a tree limb. Summer found the pouch and ran toward the meadow, just as Wash's kicking feet disappeared into the canopy. In the distance, Summer could hear the masters cheer.

86

KISS OF LIFE

Western Wilderness
First Continent
SPRING, PLANET AMERICA

Through his fogged mind, Rey understood it was no longer a fight. It was an execution. Rey would have been dead by now, except that Jesse had a greater purpose. Knowing he could end the fight at any time, Jesse was using Rey to impress the other masters. By slowly, methodically beating Rey to death, Jesse empowered the masters and terrified the slaves. When Rey finally died, the old social order would be restored. Rey staggered back, taking the next three blows on his arms.

"You're afraid of me," Rey said softly, his ribs aching if he took deep breaths.

Rice laughed.

"I think I must have scrambled your brains," Rice said. "Do I look like I'm afraid of you?"

"You poisoned me."

Rice smiled.

"Not me. You were betrayed by one of your own kind."

"That's not the first time," Rey said.

"I guess that's just the way it is with slaves," Rice said, and then feigned a blow. Rey cringed, and Rice laughed. "Any time you're ready to die, just start begging."

Jeering and shouting distracted them, and Rey turned to see Summer running into the clearing. As Rey turned, Rice struck him on the side of the head. Rey came to on the ground, with Summer kneeling over him. Blood dripped from a torn and swollen ear.

"What happened?" Rey asked, reaching toward his bleeding ear.

Pushing his hand away, Summer kissed Rey. As she did he felt her thrusting small objects into his mouth with her tongue. Rey accepted them. Suddenly, Rice dragged Summer off by her hair.

"That's right, kiss him goodbye, Summer," Rice said.

"Let her go!" Grandma shouted, coming across the meadow with Jim Wish behind her.

"She broke the rules," Rice said.

Rey crunched the seeds into tiny bits, and then swallowed them with a mix of saliva and blood.

"Summer, go back to the others," Grandma said. "We agreed to put this in God's hands. We all have to live with what happens."

"Or die with it," Rice said.

Reluctantly, Summer stood, and started to walk away.

"Tell Winnie your cabin is waiting for you," Rice said.

Summer hesitated, then kept walking. Rey rolled to his knees, and then got on his feet. He still felt half asleep, although there was little pain. The seeds were old and may have lost potency.

"Jesse, will you spare this man's life if he surrenders?" Grandma asked.

"If he gets down on his knees and begs me, I might take him on as a slave."

Rey jabbed Rice in the face. The punch was ineffectual and only managed to make Rice more confident.

"There's your answer, Grandma," Rice said. "Now get out of the way, you don't want to get blood on your dress."

87

ALIVE

Western Wilderness
First Continent
SPRING, PLANET AMERICA

Wash woke disoriented. His head ached, and his throat burned with each breath. Gradually, he realized he was hanging upside down. Twenty feet off the ground, Wash's legs were wedged in the fork of a tree branch, and jammed tight with broken limbs. He thought he could wiggle free, but if he did, he would fall. Lifting his dangling arms hurt, but he got them to his belt where he hooked his thumbs and raised his head, letting the circulation return to normal. Then he walked his hands up his pant legs, folding at his middle. Bending his knees, he lunged, grabbing the thick limb that he hung from. Now he wiggled his feet, working his legs loose. They dropped, and he almost lost his grip as his arms took his weight. Swinging, he threw a leg over the limb, and wriggled his way on top of it.

Wash lay there a few seconds, and then remembered the animal that had nearly strangled him. It was gone. Cheers in the distance reminded him of what was going on. Carefully, Wash inched back toward the trunk, and then climbed down, dropping the last six feet. Wash felt his neck. It stung like rope burn.

Wash's head ached worse than any hangover as he gingerly walked away from the trees. He came to the wagon and the pieces of the smashed box. The pouch was gone but his rifle lay a few feet away.

Retrieving his rifle, Wash walked toward the hill where his men watched the fight. Summer had humiliated him again, and this time he was lucky to get away with his life. When she told this story, his father would use it to make his life miserable. No one would respect him, and even slaves would snicker behind his back. Halfway to the hill, Wash changed direction and started jogging back. This was one story Summer would never tell.

88

DEATH MATCH

Western Wilderness
First Continent
SPRING, PLANET AMERICA

With a flurry of punches, Rey went down. Covering himself, Rey took the pounding as Rice knelt and beat him. The blows hurt now—a good sign.

"Let's make sure they get a good look," Rice said, dragging Rey to his feet by his hair.

With hair being torn from his head, Rey stumbled along, dragged by Rice closer to the slaves. Then Rice threw him to the ground. Rice towered over Rey, ignoring him.

"Here's your champion," Rice shouted to the slaves. "You put your future in this? Why? We cared for you, we fed you, we sheltered you, and yet you turned your backs on us and stole our property. We won't forget what you've done and how you repaid our generosity."

Summer stood a step in front of the others, looking at Rey, crying.

"You all know I was kind to Summer and her mother," Jesse shouted. "Out of that same kindness, I'll not drag this out any further."

Rice walked behind Rey and knelt, wrapping an arm

around Rey's neck and locking it with his other. Rey reached for the arm as it choked him, but Rice was too strong. Strangely, Rey was not afraid. His mind raced with possibilities, but he never considered dying. With his heart pounding, and warmth spreading through his limbs, Rey repeatedly jabbed with his thumbs, probing for Rice's eyes. Rice twisted, trying to avoid the thumbs, finally releasing one arm and grabbing at the probing thumbs. Rey twisted violently, raking Rice's face with his nails. Rice flinched, and Rey was free, rolling away, and getting to his feet.

A small trickle of blood dribbled down Rice's cheek. Rice wiped it away.

"That's the best you can do?" Rice asked, although some of his confidence was gone.

"It's a start," Rey said.

Now Rice charged. Rey danced aside, feeling like his old self—better than his old self. Rice swung out wildly as he stumbled past, and Rey took the blow on the shoulder, and then delivered his best punch yet, low and hard. Rice gasped, tangled his feet, and fell face first. The slaves exclaimed, and then roared approval. Now the masters were silent.

Rice's temper snapped and he came back, swinging recklessly. Rey stayed out of reach. Rice was stronger and Rey's body had taken a fearful pounding. Jabbing, punching, and moving, Rey made contact, but was doing little harm. Neither side of the clearing cheered now, unsure of who had the advantage.

Remembering that the seeds affected judgment, Rey fought overconfidence. He was feeling good now, energized and powerful. It was too good to be true, so he worked cautiously. Rice moved in again, taking a wide swing at Rey's head. Rey leaned in, and jabbed up with the heel of his hand, ducking under the blow. Rice's arm grazed the top of Rey's head just as Rey shattered the cartilage in Rice's nose. Rice's arm kept going, wrapping over Rey's shoulder and pulling him in. Rice had him in a bear hug now, and had taken the advantage. But Rice was nearly senseless and Rey managed to shove him away, knocking his arms wide. His nose broken and bleeding, and his eyes watery from the pain, Rice could barely see. He had enough sense to keep his arms up, protecting his face, but when blood dribbled across his lips, he reflexively moved to wipe it away. When he did, Rey lunged, striking his nose again. This time Rice went down, his ruined nose bleeding profusely.

The slaves cheered as Rice fell flat on his back. Rey thought he was unconscious, but then his head came up and he tried to push himself up. Rey walked behind him, and knelt, wrapping his arm around Rice's neck, just as Rice had done to Rey. With Rice's throat in the crook of his arm, Rey squeezed. Rice managed to make a few squeaking sounds with his last breaths. Like a gladiator, Rey slowly choked the life out of a man to the sounds of an excited crowd. Concentrating on Rice, the sounds faded, the meadow became still, and the only thing Rey could hear was a small voice inside of him.

"Is he so different than you once were?"

Confused, Rey thought Rice had spoken, but the man was dying, his eyes bulging, his mouth open in a vain attempt to suck in air.

"Can't you see yourself in him?" the voice repeated.

"No, I can't," Rey said. "I'm nothing like him."

"No, not anymore," the voice said. "But remember."

Rey's mind filled with memories. He was on Earth, fighting in a desert, burning a village, assassinating men and women. He derailed a passenger train, pushed a man in front of a subway train, and fired a missile at a Fellowship sphere. It was the most recent memory that was the most vivid: It was of Rey, aiming his rifle at a pregnant Summer and pulling the trigger.

Rice began to twitch, his legs and arms jerking uncontrollably. It was the last stage of hypoxia.

"You changed," the voice said.

"He never will," Rey said.

"As long as there is life, there is hope for redemption," the voice said.

Then Rey was repulsed by what he was doing. He was taking a man's last chance at finding the kind of happiness that he had. Rey released his grip just as Rice stopped twitching. Rey laid Rice's head gently on the ground and then wiped the blood from his lips. Putting one hand under his neck, Rey lifted. Rice's mouth gaped. Rey leaned down and blew into his lungs. Rey repeated the breath and then listened to Rice's chest. He heard nothing. Rey compressed Rice's chest twenty times in quick succession, and then blew into his mouth again. Rey repeated the heart massage, and then blew again. As he finished the last breath, Rice sucked in a lungful of air on his own, and then blew it out slowly.

Rey watched him breathe for a few seconds, and then slowly became aware of slaves and masters all around him. Grandma Jones and Summer stood inside the circle, studying him. Grandma was puzzled, but Summer beamed.

"He's alive," one of the masters said. "It was to be a fight to the death. This doesn't count."

"Jesse was dead," Grandma said forcefully. "Rey here just brought him back."

"It's not right," another master complained.

"You will live by your side of the bargain or I'll bring the wrath of God down on your head!" Grandma said, ending the grumbling.

Slowly the masters dissipated, wandering back toward their camp. Some slaves danced for joy, while others fell to their knees, thanking God. Parents hurried to the children's camp to tell them the good news. Others congratulated Rey, but kept their distance, letting him and Summer share the moment.

"Who were you talking to?" Summer asked.

"Wasn't that you?" Rey asked, confused. "Didn't you say that Rice was just like me?"

"Like you? No, Rey, Jesse Rice is nothing like you. I would never say that."

"Someone said it," Rey said.

"Do you know how I know you two are not alike? Because I love you, and I could never love Master Rice."

"He's not your master anymore," Grandma said, smiling broadly. "There are no masters anymore. No slaves either."

Summer hugged Rey, who touched her bleeding ear.

"What happened?" Rey asked.

"Later," Summer said, still holding him close.

"Now that you are free," Grandma said, "I don't suppose I could talk you into staying? Things will be different from now on. You can choose who you work for. You'll get wages for your work. Some of you might even get your own farms. There are still some abandoned Fellowship farms out there."

"No, we can't stay," Summer said. "Jesse and some of the others will resent us. They won't accept us as equals and our children will always be seen as inferior to yours. We need to live apart, somewhere where our children won't be reminded they were born slaves. They need to learn to think for themselves, and not expect to be told what to do."

Grandma smiled, and then squeezed Summer's arm.

"You're a special person, Summer," Grandma said. "Both of you are. Go ahead, take your people to your promised land. Maybe when our two communities meet again, we can face each other as equals."

Grandma directed a couple of men to pick up Rice, and then turned back toward the masters, while Summer and Rey walked arm and arm toward the tree line, where the former slaves continued to celebrate. Ollie was high in a tree, tentacles waving, confused by the day's events. Rey felt sorry for his friend, and promised himself to spend more time with Ollie. Just before they reached the trees a shot rang out, and Summer slapped her hand to her chest. Rey caught her, lowering her to the ground.

While Rey watched the blood spread across Summer's chest, slaves ran for cover and weapons, as the masters did the same. When no more shooting occurred, people soon came out from cover, confused. Slaves crowded around Rey and Summer. Grandma pushed her way through, bending over.

"Oh no, Rey. Is she alive?"

With his hand pressed to Summer's chest, Rey felt her last few heartbeats.

"No, she's with Jesus now."

Casey, Lucy, and Patrick pushed through, Casey collapsing in tears at her daughter's death. Men shouted for others to get their guns, and to hunt down and kill whoever had shot Summer.

"No!" Rey shouted, letting Casey embrace her daughter. Standing, Rey said, "Summer wouldn't want us taking revenge, and I'm sick to death of killing. Summer's dream was to be free, and she is now. You all are. God worked through Summer to make this miracle, and I won't let anyone dishonor God's gift, and Summer's sacrifice. I'm taking Summer's daughter—my daughter—and heading for the east coast, and I'm leaving the killing behind in this meadow. If you want to come with me, you have to do the same."

Tears flowing, Rey scooped up Summer's body, and then Rey and the slaves melted into the forest, leaving Grandma alone, watching them go.

89

CHAPEL

Western Wilderness
First Continent
SPRING, PLANET AMERICA

Rey and Leo dug Summer's grave on a small rise, east of the gap. From the top of the small hill, the valley opened up toward the plains. Rey wished he could take Summer all the way to the far coast as he had promised, but there was no way to preserve her body. Leo's friends from the lumber mill cut fresh planks for the coffin, and Patrick hammered it together.

Casey and Lucy lined it with fabric that Summer had woven, during hours spent in the old barn. It was an extravagant use of the precious cloth. No one complained; no one would. They marked the grave with a wooden cross, carved with "Summer Lund Mann, wife of Reynolds, mother of Faith. She Loved God, Obeyed God, Lives With God.

The funeral was simple, with the slaves circled around the coffin, singing Summer's favorite hymns. Winnie sang three songs and a duo with Leo. Rey cried, knowing how much Summer would have enjoyed the service.

"She loved church," Rey said.

"I know," Casey said. "Only now that it's too late am I beginning to understand why."

Cook organized a feast and the sadness over their loss of the woman who had planted the seeds of their freedom, turned to a celebration of her rebirth in heaven. Casey and Rey kept apart. Their grieving would be long and deep. Overhead, Ollie hovered protectively, confused, humming soft, unhappy sounds.

In the morning, they found Rey piling stones behind Summer's grave.

"I want something more permanent," Rey explained. "The wood in that cross will rot and then I'll never be able to find her grave again."

Everyone knew Rey would never return to the gap. Even so, they all began to gather stones.

"Let's do this right," Cook announced, taking charge.

Giving orders, she broke the workers into groups, sending the strong to bring larger stones, and others to work leveling the ground. Then she called the artisans together and they laid out a plan. Three days later, they put the finishing touches on a small chapel. Carved on one wall were instructions for any who chose to follow them to the east coast. On the other walls was a brief history of the escape of the slaves, and of Summer and Rey's roles. Embarrassed by the descriptions of his exploits, Rey insisted they make changes. No one listened to him.

Rey was the last to leave the chapel, most of the slaves

well out of sight now. Summer's family and friends waited for him. Kneeling inside, Rey thanked God for the months he had spent with Summer. Through Summer, he had come to know the Bible and Jesus, and eventually reconciled with God. He could never again be the wild man who had tried to kill Summer; he asked God to help him become the kind, giving, and forgiving person that Summer was. Filled with the Holy Spirit, Rey left the chapel, and closed and latched the door. Taking Faith from Winnie, he slipped her into her pack, and put it on. Faith tugged on his hair, gurgling behind him. With Ollie secured to his place on top of the wagon, and hunting dogs circling, they headed east, away from Summer's Gap.

90

LEADERSHIP

New Jerusalem
First Continent
SUMMER, PLANET AMERICA

One month later.

Grandma strolled the path that circled the meadow lake. Ahead of her, a small bundle of leaves moved slowly. Grandma poked at the creature hidden under the pile. It was a flounder-like animal that secreted a sticky substance. Leaves, needles, dirt, and even small animals, stuck to the surface. The camouflage protected them from birds, and the dogs did not like their taste, so there were many of them in the forest.

Two decades ago, the fleshy creatures had repulsed

Grandma. In fact, most of America's animals had elicited a similar reaction. Now it was as familiar as the animals on Earth. The children born on America found nothing strange in any of America's plants or animals.

Grandma's dream for her people had begun in a Chicago tenement, and taken them to another solar system. That dream had taken a dangerous detour when she made the mistake of introducing slavery, but now it looked like her people were on the right track again. Yes, they had grumbled at doing "slave" work, but the crops were planted, and their cattle and sheep were grazing in their meadows, now watched over by former masters. Men and women had blistered hands and feet, and children who had never done a chore in their lives now had morning and evening duties. Already there was talk about building machines to ease the workload, something the masters never considered when the slaves did the work. Jim Wish at the co-op had hatched a plan to build a dam to generate power, and they were scouring their stores, and abandoned Fellowship buildings, for all the wire they could find. Doing their own work rekindled the fires of creativity, and the community was on the move again.

Grandma rounded the lake, and as the sun neared the horizon she cut across the meadow to her cabin. Grandma used a cane all the time now, and picked her way carefully through the grass. Coming around the corner of her house, she saw she had a visitor. Jesse Rice rocked in Grandma's favorite chair.

"Good evening, Grandma," Jesse said, as she stepped onto the porch.

Jesse indicated the guest rocker, refusing to give up her preferred chair. On the table between the rocking chairs were two cups of tea. Grandma sat.

"Beautiful night," Grandma observed.

"Yes, it is," Jesse said. "Have some tea."

Grandma hesitated, searching Jesse's face.

"Do I have a choice?" Grandma asked.

"No," Jesse said.

Grandma took the cup, blowing on the tea. Now she looked in the cabin window.

"Simon has already had his cup of tea," Jesse said.

Locking eyes with Jesse, Grandma sipped her tea.

"The last of the slaves are gone," Jesse said. "They left the Browns without any help."

"They aren't slaves anymore, Jesse. They had a right to follow the others. Besides, the Browns can invite their daughter and son-in-law to live with them. It never made any sense to work two farms."

"It did when they had slaves."

"That era is over, Jesse. Can't you let go of it?"

"It suited me," Jesse said. "Although we're doing fine without slaves. Better, in fact."

"I knew we would," Grandma said, and sipped more of her tea.

"Of course, there's still Kent," Jesse said, snorting in disgust. "He came crawling back a week ago, half-starved, begging me to take him back. He said he had nowhere else to go. I put him to work on maintaining the rest of the Fellowship equipment. He's got some technical skills left."

"Did he shoot Summer?" Grandma asked.

"Kent? No, he wouldn't have the guts. No, not Kent. I think it was Wash, but he won't admit it. Something happened to Wash that he refuses to talk about. He has scars around his neck like he was hanged. Ugly things."

Grandma felt warm and drowsy, and content.

"You won't get elected governor," Grandma said, her words slightly slurred.

"I know. You fixed that," Jesse said. "But I'll be on the council. I've bought enough votes for that."

"It's a democracy now, Jesse. Everyone has a say about what the laws are."

"It's a democracy until the next crisis. Then they'll want strong leadership. When that happens, they'll turn to me, and not you, because you won't be here."

The cup slipped from Grandma's hand, spilling on her lap, and breaking into pieces as it hit the porch.

"No, I'll be gone, but God will be here."

Then Grandma Jones slumped in her chair, her breathing soft and shallow. A few minutes later she took her last breath of planet America's air.

*Books of the Holy Bible, Continuing Revelation**

OLD TESTAMENT

Genesis	2 Chronicles	Daniel
Exodus	Ezra	Hosea
Leviticus	Nehemiah	Joel
Numbers	Esther	Amos
Deuteronomy	Job	Obadiah
Joshua	Psalms	Jonah
Judges	Proverbs	Micah
Ruth	Ecclesiastes	Nahum
1 Samuel	Song of Solomon	Habakkuk
2 Samuel	Isaiah	Zephaniah
1 Kings	Jeremiah	Haggai
2 Kings	Lamentations	Zechariah
1 Chronicles	Ezekiel	Malachi

NEW TESTAMENT

Matthew	Ephesians	Hebrews
Mark	Philippians	James
Luke	Colossians	1 Peter
John	1 Thessalonians	2 Peter
Acts	2 Thessalonians	1 John
Romans	1 Timothy	2 John
1 Corinthians	2 Timothy	3 John
2 Corinthians	Titus	Jude
Galatians	Philemon	Revelation

CONTINUING TESTAMENT

The Fellowship	Breitling	The Book of Summer
Shepherd	2 Exodus	

---

* The Society for Biblical Preservation and Continuing Revelation is an interdenominational group committed to Biblical preservation and the ongoing documentation of God's interaction with humankind and therefore necessarily considers, and will consider until the second coming of Jesus Christ, the Bible to be an unfinished and ongoing inspired record.

Dramatis Personae

- **Simon Ash**—Grandma Jones's house slave, directed on Earth a foundation funded by Manuel Crow, and was dedicated to the destruction of Christian institutions.
- **Winifred (Winnie) Coleman**—Young, attractive slave with a beautiful singing voice who was purchased by Master Rice.
- **Sonny Flagg**—Master of a farm that specializes in growing coffee nuts located east of New Jerusalem.
- **Dai Hyoung**—Slave on the Flagg farm, secretly married to Sheila.
- **Carter Jackson**—Master of one of the smallest farms east of New Jerusalem.
- **Cathy Lane**—Slave in the New Jerusalem bakery.
- **Kerry Little**—Slave on the White farm and a runaway purchased by Master Rice.
- **Sean Lonnigan**—Dog handler on the Rice farm.
- **Cassandra (Casey) Lund**—Mother of Summer, a weaver owned by Master Rice.
- **Summer Lund**—Daughter of Casey Lund, owned by Master Rice.
- **Reynolds (Rey) Mann**—A mercenary who attacked the Fellowship on Earth and was marooned by the Fellowship on the east coast of the First Continent.
- **Melvin McNabb**—Boyfriend of Nicole, a slave on the Jackson farm.
- **Lucy Mills**—Mother of Leo (traded by Master Rice for a blue hound), Gill, Passion, and Dolby.
- **Leo Mills**—Son of Lucy Mills and now a slave at the lumber mill.
- **Eudora Neely**—One of the few members of the Fellowship who did not leave when they evacuated America.
- **Les Neely**—Son of Eudora Neely, a slave on the Rice farm.
- **Emeka Nkosi**—Overseer of the Rice farm.

- *Amber Rice*—Daughter of Master Rice.
- *Francine (Fancy) Rice*—Wife of Jesse Rice and daughter of Grandma Jones.
- *Jesse Rice*—Master of the largest farm on planet America.
- *Jewel Rice*—Daughter of Master Rice.
- *Malcolm Rice*—Son of Master Rice.
- *Montiel Rice*—Son of Master Rice.
- *Washington (Wash) Rice*—Master Rice's eldest son.
- *William (Will) Rice*—Youngest son of Master Rice.
- *Patrick Sampson*—Lucy's secret husband and father of two of her children.
- *Meaghan Slater (Cook)*—Cook and head of household for Master Rice, former director of the National Womyn's Congress on Earth.
- *Kent Thorpe*—One of Master Rice's slaves working for the co-op in New Jerusalem, attempted to recreate the Fellowship technology back on Earth.
- *Carl White*—Master of the farm adjacent to Master Rice's farm, owner of the second largest farm on America.
- *Rollie White*—Carl White's oldest son.
- *Sophia White*—Mistress of the White farm and the biggest gossip on America.
- *Teresa White*—Friend and neighbor of Grandma Jones while on Earth and on planet America.
- *Pastor Wills*—Pastor of New Jerusalem church.
- *Lionel Wilson*—Master of a large farm, influential member of the Council of Masters.
- *Jim Wish*—President of the farmer's co-op.
- *Sheila Yoshino*—Slave on the Rice farm, secretly married to Dai Hyoung (a slave on the Flagg farm).
- *Nicole Vale*—Slave on the Rice farm, girlfriend of Melvin.
- *Lonnie Zagjewski*—Slave on the White farm and a runaway.
- *Jimmy Zinn*—Teenage slave on the Rice farm.

A Guide to Planet America's Native Species and Geographical Features

PLANET AMERICA'S FLORA

- *ball trees*—Named for the tangle of limbs that tops the tree, forming a nearly perfect sphere. Virtually fireproof, the tree produces a natural fire retardant. This tree is common in semiarid regions of the First Continent.

- *bandage shrubs*—Medium-size shrub (up to two meters tall), with oval, absorbent leaves occasionally used to cover wounds or to absorb spilled liquids. Found primarily in the northeastern region of the First Continent.

- *box nuts*—A square nut varying in size up to twenty centimeters wide. While the interior is hollow, the lining of the nut is edible and used as a laxative.

- *cabbage trees*—Species of deciduous trees with unique foliage. Instead of needles or leaves, ribbons of purple and green flakes create a domelike canopy that from a distance resembles a giant cabbage. Found at higher elevations in the western region of the First Continent.

- *coffee nuts*—When roasted, these nuts resemble coffee in both flavor and aroma. Coffee nut trees grow west of the Pax River between New Jerusalem and the western coast.

- *gum trees*—A hardwood tree common in the eastern region of the First Continent. This tree is covered with a sticky, viscous fluid, which attracts and traps insects. No commercial value.

- *hat fruit*—A small, sweet fruit named for its shape. Hat fruit grow on climbing vines and ripen in the early spring.

- *midget trees*—Small trees (two meters tall) with wood so hard it makes cutting and milling impractical. The tree's few branches are covered with gray-green, clover-shaped leaves that attach with no stem. Native to the arid plains of the First Continent.

- ***pink tea***—A small bush with leaves that are green in spring and turn deep red in fall. The leaves dry to a light pink color and make a sweet tea. The tea is commonly used as a mild sedative.

- ***prickly fruit***—Shaped like a pear, this edible fruit has a crunchy texture and tastes similar to a plum. The core consists of a mass of tiny gray seeds. The seeds contain an addictive amphetamine. Common in the northeastern region of the First Continent.

- ***puff trees***—A softwood tree with a bark that swells in the fall and can be stripped to reveal fibers. These fibers can be bleached and dyed and are used for weaving cloths. Puff trees are covered with clumps of green leaves that turn gold in autumn. Native to the western region of the First Continent, puff trees are widely cultivated.

- ***river vines***—A vine that grows along the banks of streams and rivers in the Central Plain. The vines span water sources and interweave so densely that the water source may be virtually invisible from above.

- ***sourberries***—A common and popular berry found on low-growing bushes in the western region of the First Continent. The berries are protected by thorns until fall, when the thorns drop, allowing the berries to be harvested.

- ***tart trees***—Deciduous tree with mottled green, oval leaves that produces a small round fruit in the fall. When ripe, the yellow fruit is crunchy in texture and slightly tart in taste.

- ***tree cheese***—This yellowish tree fungus resembles curds. While edible, few people find it palatable. Found in cool, moist climates on the First Continent.

- ***whistle reeds***—Stiff, hollow reeds typically found bordering eastern forests. In a light breeze, the reeds will produce a whistling sound. Pitch and amplitude varies with reed diameter and wind velocity.

- ***yellow root***—A cultivated root native to America. This edible root sends up perennial, bell-shaped leaves, forming a small bush eighteen to twenty-four centimeters high. Roots can be harvested from late spring to late fall.

PLANET AMERICA'S FAUNA

• *bone eater*—Large, flightless, carnivorous bird that is the top predator of the Central Plains (aka Bone Eater Plains).

• *bullwinkles*—Sometimes called mini-moose, these compact herbivores are proportioned like a cow, but with large complex antlers and prehensile lips that are used for grazing. The lips are also used for the creation of complex vocalizations, with both males and females calling during the fall mating season. Coloration includes white, rust, brown, tan, and black, with contrasting stripes. Common in the eastern region of the First Continent.

• *buzzers*—Small flying insects that hive underground and swarm anything disturbing their nests. Buzzers are nonstinging and nonpoisonous; however, animals and people have died from aspirating large numbers of the insects.

• *deer*—No less than eleven species of animals are called deer by settlers of America. The features common to all "deer" are four legs, short tails, slim bodies, medium length necks, and tapering heads topped with antlers. Antlers vary in size and complexity. Coloration varies considerably and includes brown, white, green, and striped.

• *dingo*—A common predator found in the western and southern regions of the First Continent. Canine in appearance but with short, curly tails and shaggy manes (males and females). Dingoes are primarily scavengers but will bring down small game and have been known to attack in packs.

• *fox*—At least three distinct species are referred to as "foxes." The name is given to any small, furry predator that preys on domesticated fowl.

• *giant river snake*—Only the neck and head of this amphibian river dweller resembles a snake. This misnamed predator has a large body, with four fins, that remains submerged at all times. Giant river snakes are territorial and seldom migrate to new hunting grounds, preferring prey to come to them.

• *grass worms*—A species of tube worms commonly found near rivers and lakes. These worms extrude from a buried calcium cylinder that retracts when threatened. When extended, the sticky body of the worm collects insects and vegetable matter for absorption.

- *bealer birds*—Small parasite-eating birds that form a symbiotic relationship with larger mammals by removing parasites from the skin. Common to the eastern plains of the First Continent.

- *honey birds*—A popular game bird common in the western region of the First Continent. Like other "birds" on America, this bird's offspring are born live, and nursed. The largest honey birds are nearly fifty pounds. They are called "honey" birds because of the unusual sweet taste of their meat.

- *horse face*—Large herd animals of the Central Plains. These herbivores have prehensile lips, long front arms, and short back legs, giving them the gait of Earth's gorillas.

- *kings*—Small, caninelike quadrupeds, but with longer, thinner legs. With a flat face and snout, these omnivore scavengers resemble bulldogs.

- *leapers*—Feline carnivores with chameleonlike ability to blend into backgrounds. This territorial and aggressive species is known to hunt humans. Common to the western and southwestern regions of the First Continent.

- *mini-moose*—At about half the size of an Earth moose, these herbivores have a wide head and long, prehensile snout. Mini-moose antlers are thick and complex, with each pattern as distinct as fingerprints. Unusually large eyeballs give them nearly 360° vision. The same mini-moose herds will have animals that are white, rust, brown, tan, and black, and with contrasting stripes.

- *pinkies*—Large carnivorous swine, with long legs, long snouts, and protruding fangs. The name "pinky" comes from the color of its eyes. Also, occasionally referred to as "pigs." Aggressive pack hunters, pinkies are commonly found in the eastern and southern regions of the First Continent.

- *pronghorns*—A small, quadruped herd animal with two pointed horns. They are fast and maneuverable, with great leaping ability.

- *redbacks*—Ten-legged lizards with a triangle-shaped head and long tail. Named for the red stripe running from nose to the tip of the tail. Redbacks are poisonous, with a 20 percent death rate among animals and humans. There is no antivenom.

- *skin worm*—Larval stage of the gray fly. Each larva produces four to six adult flies.
- *spotted chickens*—Popular edible bird common to the western region of the First Continent.
- *sucker fish*—Edible fish common in the western region of the First Continent. This fish carries a double row of suckers on its belly used for respiration. It has no gill structure.
- *tanks*—Small armored herbivore with a bony knob on the end of its tail used for defense. Adults range from two to four feet in height and are wide and low to the ground and nearly impossible to turn over. These animals are so passive that children frequently ride on their backs.
- *tree-hater*—Large quadruped herbivore with a large broad horn used for defense, mating, combat, and establishing and maintaining meadows. Tree-haters have been observed uprooting trees and shrubs that encroach on grazing grounds. These animals are highly territorial and aggressive.
- *tree octopi*—Quadruped tree dweller with two retractable tentacles. Native to the east coast of the First Continent, these furry omnivores are nocturnal hunters who hang beneath branches and snag small-to-medium-size animals with their tentacles. Contrary to popular belief, tree octopi do not have eight legs.
- *turkey-birds*—Plump white birds common to the western region of the First Continent. The down of turkey-birds is popular stuffing for pillows, mattresses, and coat insulation.
- *walking mules*—Large bipedal mammal with long ears and the face of a horse.
- *weasles*—A small four-legged mammal coated with thick fur and a barely distinguishable head. With poor eyesight but powerful olfactory abilities, weasles rely on speed as their primary defense and have been clocked at forty kilometers per hour.
- *whoppers*—A fish found primarily in underwater caves and in lakes fed by underwater streams. Spawning takes place in darkness, where the eggs hatch, and hatchlings grow to adulthood before migrating to open waters.

- **wolves**—Quadruped carnivore with long legs, thin snout, and distinct fangs. This tailless predator hunts in mated pairs. Summer coloration varies with region, including brown, gray, and black. Beginning early fall, wolves develop a white outer coat that provides camouflage when the snows come. The winter coat is lost by early spring. Common to the northern region of the First Continent.
- **yellow tusk (aka tuskers)**—Large, yellow quadrupeds with long tusks and a camouflage pattern on their coats. Colorations include sage, yellow, and brown. Common to the northeastern First Continent.

PLANET AMERICA LOCATIONS

- **Big Eye Lake**—The second largest lake on the First Continent. Big Eye Lake has a large, oval island in the middle of the lake so that in orbital photos the lake resembles a large blue eye.
- **Bone-Eater Plains (aka Central Plains)**—The central, arid region of the First Continent. Named for the top predator of the plains.
- **Feminist Falls**—Waterfall located east of New Jerusalem. Easily reached by foot, the waterfall is popular with picnickers.
- **First Continent**—Refers to the continent first settled by the Fellowship when they arrived on planet America.
- **Flat Top Mountain**—A collapsed volcano in the western wilderness. The interior depression is known as Honeymoon Valley.
- **The Great Fault**—This feature is the meeting place of two continental plates, which splits the First Continent from north to south. The elevation difference between the two plates varies from twenty to five hundred meters.
- **Honeymoon Valley**—A small, fertile depression in the middle of a collapsed volcano (Flat Top Mountain). The Fellowship settlers used the isolated valley for honeymoon vacations.
- **Mount Whopper**—A hill bordering Whopper Lake.
- **Mud Pot Valley (aka Spa Valley)**—A region of volcanic activity that creates hot springs and mud pots. The warm waters and mud attract animals that use both to control skin infestations.

- *Near Mountains*—Northwestern mountain range between the central plains of the First Continent and the western valleys.
- *Omega Falls*—This waterfall, located in the eastern wilderness along The Great Fault, derives its name from its location in Omega Gorge.
- *Omega Gorge*—The omega-shaped gorge that contains Omega Falls.
- *Pax River*—A river flowing from the northeast, near New Jerusalem, to the west coast where it empties into the western ocean.
- *Squeaky's Lake*—A small lake in the western wilderness named for a Golden Retriever ("Squeaky") who died by the lake while protecting a visitor from a Leaper.
- *Summer's Gap*—A narrow pass through the Near Mountains of the First Continent. One of only three passes through the Inner Mountains and the first to be discovered.
- *Whopper Lake*—Near New Jerusalem, the lake is named for the fish caught in the lake.

TOR

Award-winning authors
Compelling stories